RETRIBUTION

BOOK FOUR OF THE HARVESTERS SERIES

LUKE MITCHELL

Dedication

As we draw to the conclusion of this, my first full series, my nebulous little writer's spirit has decreed that this one, finally, goes to my late father, David Mitchell.

(Side Note: He actually used to announce himself to me on the phone like that, full name and everything—I shit you not. But I digress...)

This one's for my father, David Mitchell, who sarcastically taught me the Three Sacred Elements of Good Story, and a whole hell of a lot about life.

I wonder what he would have thought of these books.

CHAPTER ONE

*O*ne month, she'd said.

Glass shattered, and a maddened scream split the air, only distantly recognizable as human.

Jarek hit the pavement in a half-crouch and pushed on without looking back, Fela's powerful legs pumping beneath him, pounding the ground as he fled the first of the horde with his cargo tightly clutched.

Three weeks ago, the sounds of the shrieks that spread through the streets behind him would've curdled his blood and given him a proper case of the heebie-jeebies.

Now, though...

Now that furor hordes seemed to be howling after them wherever they ran. Now that he'd seen more grown men and women tear each other to gory pieces more times than he wanted to count... All he could do was push on. It was all any of them could do right now.

That didn't stop the heebie-jeebies.

One month of this madness.

He could've taken them, of course. In small numbers, their fists and mindless rage weren't exactly fair matches for Jarek's armored exo.

In horde quantities, though?

Jarek had tried to avoid putting too much thought into it, but he was pretty sure Fela wouldn't render him invulnerable to them going Wookie on his ass and pulling him limb from limb if they managed to catch him and swarm him to the pavement.

So he kept moving.

"Talk to me, Mr. Robot. Good news only."

A deliberate moment's hesitation.

Then, "That's quite the lovely sunrise, sir."

On top of his crisp English accent, Al's tone was cautious, searching.

Jarek held his tongue, waiting for the digital construct to finish his sweep.

Everything else aside, his friend wasn't wrong. It was a lovely sunrise. The scrabbling feet and bloodthirsty calls of the horde just put a bit of a dimmer on things.

"No enemy ships detected nearby, sir," Al said after longer than usual, "though I'll remind you my eyes aren't as good as they once were."

Jarek grimaced and adjusted his cargo, shifting the enormous bag on his back and wrapping the straps of the second half-full duffle tighter around his left hand.

Between the Net inexplicably failing last week and the secondhand sensory array Pryce and Al had cobbled together on Fela's faceplate after a raknoth warlord had clubbed off the first one, Jarek imagined Al's senses felt about as unencumbered as he currently did trying to sprint with a giant sword and a couple of oversized duffles awkwardly strapped to his form.

That said, Al's words at least offered some mild assurance that the rakul themselves weren't about to drop down on his head. It was something.

Jarek cut left down a wide alleyway, thinking to shake some of his pursuers, and nearly ran headlong into one of the wild-eyed berserkers. The man bared his teeth and sprang forward.

Gently as he reasonably could, Jarek kicked the guy in the chest and sent him sprawling to the pavement ten feet back. As far as he could tell, the berserker's coughing and sputtering were probably more a matter of mechanical fact than pain or discomfort. Those would come later, when the furor passed and the poor bastard hopefully regained control of his mind.

For now, though, Jarek turned and leapt over a brown picket fence and into a heavily overgrown backyard.

From what he'd seen, Syracuse, like most northern cities, had been largely abandoned for some time now. Ever since the Catastrophe, people had had enough on their plates just to survive without willingly adding contending with the winter cold to their lists.

It was exactly what Jarek had been counting on when he'd ghosted into town at the crack of dawn. He'd even stuck to the outskirts as much as possible, just to be safe.

Canned food. Oil. Batteries. Solar chargers. Anything that might help them survive. He'd stuffed his bags as quickly as he could, determined to not spend a minute longer than necessary in the abandoned ghost town.

A harsh baying from the alleyway gave him an unneeded reminder that Syracuse was hardly abandoned now.

"What say we blow this party and get back to our merry men, buddy?"

Behind, the picket fence rattled with its first thudding blow.

"That seems most advisable, sir."

Aided by Fela's considerable strength, Jarek easily hopped the fence on the other side of the yard and took off once again, weaving through crumbling buildings at a hard northwest clip.

The sounds of his frenzied pursuit faded into the distance over the following minutes until the most prominent sounds were his labored breathing and the rhythmic pounding of his armored feet on the asphalt.

Pissed beyond all Earthly reason, they may have been. But, try as they did, the furor victims couldn't match his Fela-enhanced pace, even encumbered as he was. It was exactly why the group had agreed Jarek should make the run solo when they'd pulled up a few miles outside town in the first hints of the coming daylight. Not that anyone minded sitting out and letting Jarek do the heavy lifting.

No one but Mosen, at least.

That glinty-eyed bastard only saw Jarek's usefulness as a threat to his authority in the group. Why Mosen cared so damn much about that authority was still a bit perplexing to Jarek.

Maybe the guy had simply spent too much time immersed with the raknoth and their draconian pecking order. Or maybe it was just Mosen's way of trying to feel in control of the situation.

If it was the latter, then Mosen was even crazier than Jarek had already thought. Out of the many things they collectively were, *in control* was not on the list.

The rakul had seen to that. And then some.

The three-mile trek back to their temporary hideout fell quickly to Jarek's amped nerves and racing thoughts. Quickly enough, in fact, that he wondered if they shouldn't have holed up further out of town. At the very least, he probably should have taken off in a different direction and looped his way back around.

"No pursuit detected, sir," Al said in his ear, apparently sensing his hesitation as he finished tromping across a field of wild grass that might've once been a golf course.

"Thanks, buddy."

He pushed into the last little woodland divider separating them from the dilapidated apartment building they'd decided to bunk in for the day. A tiny weight tugged at the back of his mind, whispering frightening thoughts and forcing him to glance back over his shoulder, across the grassy expanse.

"Keep an ear out anyway?"

"Of course, sir."

Jarek closed his eyes, consciously let out a long breath, and forced himself to turn for the apartments. There wasn't anything left to do now but to load the new supplies, divide the food as best they could afford, and get some rest while they could.

They still didn't really understand whether there was some pattern to the furors, or exactly what goal the rakul were driving their puppets to pursue—outside of mindless violence. From what Jarek had observed, though, he doubted the horde would track him this far.

Plus, more likely than not, they'd be moving on from the apartments tonight anyway.

For all they knew, the rakul could be orbiting the planet, watching them night and day with technologies Jarek couldn't comprehend, but logic still dictated that traveling under the cover of night was probably the smart move. Especially for a band of squishy meat sacks like them trying to avoid the notice of the ridiculously powerful intergalactic conquerors that may or may not be currently tracking them like alien bloodhounds.

He ducked under a low-hanging branch, suppressing a shudder at the thought of bloodhounds and the memory it kicked up of the thing that had chased him and Michael out of HQ almost two weeks ago.

As if he'd needed more material for his never-ending vault of nightmare materials.

Along with the thought of their flight from HQ came the sudden and inevitable pang of aching worry, like a glob of churning ice water in his core. It was a sensation he was almost growing used to in a horrible kind of way. The same one he had every time any little thing reminded him of—

No. Not now.

He had hungry soldiers and a not-so-distant horde to worry about right now.

Later, when he could lay down to rest with some degree of certainty he wouldn't wake up to snarling teeth and wild eyes... then he could have his worry-streaked pitty party.

But until then...

One foot in front of the other.

And again.

And again.

THE SHIP WAS STILL THERE, right where Al had parked it that morning, under the partial cover of the encroaching tree line. Jarek considered stopping to leave what extra supplies they wouldn't immediately need inside but decided it wasn't worth the time or organizational effort right now.

Most of what he'd scavenged had been food anyway, and they weren't nearly so flush on food as to think today's haul would last longer than tonight. Turned out, keeping a platoon of hungry men and women fed wasn't a walk in the park when food was scarce to begin with and a pack of super-monsters had you on the run.

It wasn't like anyone had had time to pack rations for this lovely little adventure of theirs.

Whether or not the rakul knew it, if the hordes or the beasts themselves didn't catch and kill their group, the running—and the hunger it was driving them to—might.

A glance at each corner of the apartment building ahead showed that their lookouts were posted and watching him. He hefted the duffel in his left hand and shot a casual salute their way.

The Resistance woman, Chambers, returned a wave and a friendly, maybe even excited, smile.

In contrast, the reaction of the soldiers posted at the other two corners—Mosen's men—was like an icy slap to the giblets.

They stared at him and his cargo, looking like they'd rather eat him and take his suit than accept his handouts yet again.

So that was a no on the *thank yous*, then.

Suffice it to say, there was a reason Jarek hadn't stepped out of his armor in over a week—even after Al had upped the awkward ante and made it crystal clear, just in case any of their assembled forces should have any wild ideas, that Jarek was the *only* person on Earth the suit would be functioning for anytime soon.

It hadn't earned him or Al any points with Mosen or the other refugees from Camp Krogoth, but at least no one had tested Fela's durability with a knife while he slept. Yet.

Jarek stepped into the entryway, pulled the door shut behind him, and paused at the bottom of the rickety old stairs.

"Honey, I'm home," he called up.

Thanks to Fela's amplified auditory sensors, he didn't miss the irritated huff Mosen let out, and he could almost feel the a-hole rolling his eyes.

When Mosen leaned over the banister above, though, his practiced look of smug indifference was fully intact.

"Marvelous. You had me so worried." The red glint in Mosen's eyes as he scrutinized the duffels conveyed about as much worry as a hungry alligator closing on its prey. "What do you have for us, sweetheart?"

"Oh, you know"—Jarek slid his helmet faceplate open with a careful thought and started up the stairs—"this and that. Batteries. Bandages. Oil for Al's squeaky motors."

"I'm not the one who's weighing the ship down every day, sir," Al said out loud through Fela's speakers. "Or the one who beat it within an inch of scrap metal."

Jarek might have bantered back, but Mosen had paused from eyeing the duffel to shoot him an expectant, severe look. It kind of ruined the mood.

"And food," Jarek added, suppressing a sigh as he held the first duffel out.

He had yet to make up his mind on whether or not he, Michael, and the rest of the Resistance soldiers had made a mistake in partying up with Mosen and his faithful Mosenites when they'd unexpectedly crossed paths not far outside of what remained of New York City.

Joining forces had seemed like the smart move. They were all allies in this fight against the rakul, after all, and more soldiers meant more security, more lookouts, less sleepless nights. All objectively good things. But, then again, there were also more mouths to feed—and to listen to.

Mosen snatched the bag from Jarek's hand, his expression unreadable for a few seconds. Jarek expected him to tromp out, but Mosen hesitated for a second.

"Don't suppose there's been any news?" Jarek finally asked.

Mosen showed him a morbid grin. "What? Besides the entire world being fucked out of its mind?"

"Yeah, I don't particularly need a reminder on that one right now."

Mosen frowned. "You run into trouble out there?"

Jarek nodded grimly. "Another horde. Or maybe the same one. Shit, I can't tell."

Mosen hissed through his teeth. "Well fuck, maybe you could have started with that, Slater."

"Started with what?" came Michael's deep voice from the hallway beyond, followed a moment later by his dark, haggard face.

Christ, he wasn't looking hot.

Not that any of them were, having been on the road for nearly two weeks with little in the way of commodities most of that time.

"Started with the fact that those crazy bastards could've followed our Soldier of Charity straight back here," Mosen growled, shooting a disgusted look at Jarek before whirling for the doorway.

Michael held Mosen's eyes with a stern expression and took his time in stepping aside to let him pass.

"Mosen," Jarek said.

"I need to go tell my lookouts," Mosen said without stopping.

"Seth."

Mosen froze at Jarek's use of his first name, then rolled his shoulders and looked back to meet Jarek's eyes with frosty amusement.

"Yeah, Papa Slater?"

Jarek did his best to keep his expression peaceful as he nodded to the duffel in Mosen's hand. "See to it everyone gets their fair share?"

Mosen looked between Michael and Jarek, his amusement only growing. "I wonder what it is you two think passes for fair about any of this shit."

And with that, he left before either of them could say anything more.

Michael looked worriedly from the empty doorway back to Jarek but seemed to relax a bit when he took in the full bag still strapped to Jarek's back.

He didn't have to speak his mind. Jarek knew exactly what he was thinking.

It would be an interesting day, to say the least, if—or, more likely, *when*—they came up short on rations.

"I take it you ran into another furor out there?" Michael asked.

Jarek nodded. "Kinda feels a little too much like it's following us at this point. I could've sworn that town was deserted, and that was a pretty damn big horde that popped up."

Michael grimaced. "I hate that word."

Jarek didn't need to ask about that one either to know Michael was referring to the word, horde. They'd already had a few discussions about the mindless zombie connotations, and Jarek knew Michael could relate a little too much to the feeling of being made a telepathic puppet.

Speaking of which...

"You can go ahead and say it," Michael said, apparently picking up on the direction of his thoughts.

Jarek hesitated, opened his mouth, hesitated again, and shrugged. "Fine. Are you feeling okay"—he tapped the side of his head and dropped to a conspiratorial whisper—"you know, upstairs?"

Michael rolled his eyes and directed his gaze down the stairway as if the empty space suddenly required his subdued attention.

"You look like shit, Mikey," Jarek added, not hiding his concern now. "And I can only assume there's some angry telepathic juju floating around nearby if the..." He hooked a thumb toward town. "You know. I just, uh... Promise you'll talk to me if anything starts to..."

Michael watched him flounder with exactly what it was that *anything* might start to do then finally nodded. "I will."

Jarek was less than convinced. After everything he'd seen Michael go through, he didn't doubt the big guy was the *suffer in silence* type.

And if Michael *was* feeling the telepathic heat right now...

Suffice it to say, Jarek doubted walking around with the guy who was, as far as he understood it, basically a messenger satellite was doing any major favors to their efforts to lay low. But it wouldn't be the nail in their coffin—he had to believe that. As far as they understood it, Michael's condition was a one-way arrangement—receiving but not transmitting.

No. It wouldn't be the nail in their coffin. That blow would more likely fall if anyone decided to press the issue. Mosen had made it more than clear just how little he liked having Michael around, marked as he was. If Mosen or anyone else so much as caught a whiff that anything was awry with Michael… Jarek didn't want to think about how it would go for their happy little platoon if and when that happened.

So, instead, he unslung the duffel from his back and offered it to Michael. "Dandy. Wanna do the honors, then?"

If Michael thought his connection was putting the group at risk—and Jarek trusted the younger man would know better than him on that one—Michael wouldn't keep quiet about it. Probably.

It was good enough for now.

Michael took the bag with a slight frown. Ragged as he looked from their travels and, before that, from weeks of intermittent telepathic assaults, his burly frame still had no trouble supporting the hefty load as he slung it over one shoulder. "You're not coming?"

Jarek waved him on and pointed down the stairs. "Might just go, uh… For a minute."

Michael's expression softened, and he clapped a hand to Jarek's shoulder. "She's okay out there. Probably better off than we are. I have faith."

Jarek fought the urge to swallow against the sudden lump in his throat and managed to pull on a mask of mock sternness instead. "You know I don't approve of the F-word, young man."

A faint touch of amusement alighted over Michael's features. "My bad, Papa Slater."

Jarek shook his head, the title drawing Mosen back to the forefront of his thoughts. "That smug bastard."

Michael gave a knowing nod, looking thoughtful. "I'll say this much for him, though. Dude's loyal to his people."

That much was hard to argue. Much as he hated to admit it, and much as blind devotion never failed to scare the crap out of him, Jarek was actually pretty impressed by how hard Mosen had proven himself willing to fight for his men—and how faithfully those Mosenites followed him in return.

"Yeah…" Jarek waved at the duffel at Michael's shoulder. "Well, why don't you go make sure every hungry mouth in there knows we're loyal too? I'll be in soon."

Michael looked like he had something else he was thinking about saying—a few somethings, maybe—but he finally gave a nod and turned for the doorway.

"Hey, Mikey."

Michael turned, waiting, and Jarek found he couldn't quite decide what it was he wanted to ask—could only grasp at general directions, all of which suddenly seemed like topics for another time.

"Uh, make sure who's-a-what's-it on lookout gets a bite too."

Michael cocked his head. "Chambers?"

"Right. Like I said."

Michael's look was slightly quizzical, but he gave Jarek a thumbs up and left to go feed the troops without further question.

Jarek stood in silence for some time, his thoughts winding themselves in unpleasant knots. His stomach rumbled, reminding him he should've grabbed a can of something before he'd handed the bag over.

"You should eat, sir."

Al wasn't wrong. But the thought of stepping into a crowded space right now… Food could wait a little longer.

"Is that what that means, Mr. Robot?" Jarek asked, starting down the stairs. "It gets so confusing sometimes, being a real boy. The rumbles. The pulses. The massive erections. Who can keep track of it all?"

"Would that I could avoid it, sir. Particularly the latter."

Jarek smiled and stepped outside to take a seat on the building's front stoop.

"How are you doing, buddy? Still feeling like you're short a few limbs without the Net?"

"Short a few limbs and locked in a padded room, sir. And with you, no less. Can you imagine?"

Jarek shook his head. "The horror."

He wanted to say more, wanted to promise Al that they'd see this thing through. That they'd save the planet and eventually restore the Net and, along with it, all of the thousands of petabytes of information and media and other digital distractions his friend no longer had access to. He wanted to promise it to Al as much as he wanted to promise it to himself.

But they'd both know he was talking out of his ass, so, for a long while, he just sat there, trying to enjoy the companionable silence that he and his old friend had so often passed together.

One month, Rachel had said the last time he'd talked to her, just before the Net had cut out and their comms had ceased to function outside of close-range communication.

One month until Haldin and Elise would complete their... was merger the right word? No one seemed to know. Not even the raknoth.

One month until they finished doing whatever the hell it was those two were doing with Alton and Lietha, at least.

One month of surviving this relentless hounding, flying on some blind hope that the product of this apparently unprecedented raknoth-Enochian *merger* would somehow give them an edge against the rakul. Against the things that were so old and strong that even Drogan, Mr. *My-Warrior-Honor-is-Bigger-than-Yours* himself, had fled the scene like a frightened child when they'd first arrived in force.

After the run-in Jarek and Michael had had with that giant mutant-wolf-looking bastard back at HQ, though, Jarek couldn't say he blamed ol' Stumpy for being afraid of the things.

As for the Enochians...

Jarek didn't know what to believe.

Whatever happened, whatever shit hit in the end, the only thing Jarek knew for sure was that he wanted—needed—to face it with Rachel at his side.

But first, he had to find her.

CHAPTER TWO

Fifteen years earlier—or, hell, maybe even just a few months ago—it might have been a nice view that greeted Rachel as she skirted out from under the cover of the ruined apartment building and darted across the street to the overgrown lookout point. Now, though, she just felt naked out there, standing in the open in broad daylight.

She clutched her staff tighter, as if its tiny weight could somehow protect her.

If Johnny felt any similar consternation, he sure did hide it well.

"Hmm," the red-headed Enochian said, letting the tall grass slide back over the sign he'd been inspecting before looking back out over what crumbling skyline remained of Pittsburgh. "Wonder why they decided to call it Point of View Park."

Out of the corner of her eye, Rachel saw him turn an expectant grin her way.

"You know what I wonder?" she asked quietly, pointedly keeping her stare directed across the wide blue of the Ohio River and fixed on Heinz Field. "Why a freaking stadium?"

"Because you Earthlings love your football," Johnny said as if it were blatantly obvious. "I'll bet you five fortune cookies Nelken's dad used to bring him here. It's probably like his safe place or something."

She finally turned from the view to study the Enochian. "How the hell do you always know these things?"

"I mean, it's just a guess. Father and son bonding over the game and all tha—"

"Not the dad part. That part actually makes a surprising amount of sense. But how do you even know what football is?"

He shrugged. "I was stuck on a ship for a year with nothing to do but study Earth and get beat up by Hal."

The shadow fell across his face—the same one he always got now when he talked about Haldin.

He covered it up quickly enough, cocking his head in thought. "Well, beat up by Hal *and* Elise. And Alton. You get the point. And you'd be impressed how much you can pick up about a culture through their movies."

"If you two are finished," came Drogan's voice from behind, "perhaps we might consider taking productive action."

The raknoth drew up beside Rachel, his eyes warily sweeping the open sky before sliding down to their objective.

"Considering's the easy part," Johnny murmured. "It's the doing I'm less excited about."

"It'll be fine," Rachel said.

He grinned over at her. "Well now that you said so . . ."

Rachel turned to Drogan. "You're sure the others will be safe back there?"

They'd left the rest of Johnny's people—precious cargo included— back in the heavily wooded hills, on the other side of the giant urban butte they were currently looking down from.

She wasn't even sure why she bothered asking Drogan for the reassurance. They either would be okay, or they wouldn't. There was no true safety on this planet. Not anymore.

Still, it made her feel a touch better when Drogan gave her a confident nod. "As long as Franco and the others do nothing foolish to betray their position, our… maturing allies should be free to continue their change in peace."

Rachel sure as hell hoped so.

Haldin and Elise were two of the only hopes she'd had to cling to since the rakul had arrived and the Enochians had begun their respective melds with Drogan's raknoth kin, Alton Parker and Shieth'Lietha. The idea of raknoth establishing symbioses with their hosts rather than completely overriding them was a novel one. And, she was hoping, one that would produce something tremendously powerful, given how gifted Haldin and Elise had already been to begin with.

Drogan hadn't exactly kept it a tight secret that he was less than convinced Haldin and Elise would arise as the all-powerful weapons the rest of them were hoping for.

Rachel wasn't so sure what to think.

Johnny, unsurprisingly, had faith in his friends.

Rachel wanted to believe that faith was well-placed—not in small part because the alternative was that, if this gambit didn't pay off, they'd be stuck right back where they'd begun. Eleven preposterously strong Kul, a planet-full of potential furor fodder, and naught but her staff, Drogan's claws, and Johnny's guns to fight their way through the impossible odds.

Of course, there were other friendlies out there too. The scattered remnants of the Resistance, for one, and Zar'Krogoth's forces for another.

And then there were Jarek and Michael, who, last she knew, had somehow ended up on the road north with that savage bastard Mosen.

Her heart ached at the thought. She hoped to god they were still together watching each other's backs and that Michael hadn't fallen prey to—

No.

She couldn't think about that now.

With any luck, their mix-matched band of fighters would manage to rally here, just like they'd talked about before they'd lost the Net.

Nelken, Alaric, Krogoth—someone would have a plan. They'd pull together, make their stand.

No matter what happened, she was sure there wasn't a soul among them at this point who wouldn't go down swinging.

Maybe it would be enough.

But having a pair of Enochian-raknoth hybrid super soldiers in their corner sure as hell wouldn't hurt either.

In the meanwhile, Rachel would've gladly settled for the ability to reliably communicate with their brewing heroes.

Getting answers from the merging couples had been like herding cats—and cats who were tripping on ayahuasca, at that. As far as she and Drogan could tell, Haldin and Elise were floating back and forth between profoundly deep sleep and complete unconsciousness.

As for Alton and Lietha, that was a slightly stranger question.

At times, the raknoth seemed to be coupled in dreamlike states with their respective humans. Aside from the occasional brief stints where the raknoth would telepathically communicate mostly-coherent updates to Rachel or Drogan, Alton and Lietha spent the remainder of their time in their own kind of trance-like state that Drogan had referred to as "the builder's space."

Apparently, it was a thing—or at least a loose translation of one—with raknoth and their fresh host bodies during a standard body snatch and the subsequent remodeling.

Johnny had taken to calling it "the body shop"—a moniker that at some times amused him and at others seemed to depress him.

Rachel, upon first witnessing the crude "gastric inputs" Drogan had installed to allow them to give his kin the raw materials they required for said body-building, had decided she wasn't overly keen on delving into the details, as long as it worked.

At any rate, for now, it was just the three of them, and this rendezvous with Nelken and the Resistance wasn't about to happen on its own.

Pushing all thoughts of Jarek, the changing Enochians, and the future at large aside, Rachel gave Drogan a resolute nod.

"Let's see what there is to see, then."

The hike down to the nearest bridge wasn't far—no more than half a mile—but, between picking their way down the trail and Drogan stopping every hundred feet to perk his ears and sniff warily at the sky, it took them a good fifteen minutes.

The bridge itself was long and narrow, two lanes crossing the wide berth of the Ohio River, overarched with faded yellow steel. Harmless enough, as bridges went. But that didn't stop something about the heavy silence in the air whispering to her just how exposed they'd be out there in the middle of its paved span.

Drogan and Johnny seemed to be having similar thoughts, but, unless one of them happened to be hiding a boat in their pocket, the only real alternative was swimming, which carried all the same vulnerability and added the bonus of getting all their gear soaked.

So, by some unspoken agreement, they all started across the bridge at a light jog.

Much to Rachel's relief, no elaborate death traps sprang. No highwaymen popped out to collect their dues.

Nothing happened at all—until about three quarters across, when Drogan snared her arm in a steel grip.

"A ship," he hissed.

The intensity in his voice shot a tingling burst of panic through her chest.

"Where?"

She couldn't see anything but partially-cloudy skies all around.

"West," Drogan hissed, reaching for Johnny as well.

The westward sky seemed every bit as clear as the rest, but Drogan's senses were far sharper than hers. No reason not to trust him. Instead, she turned her attention to their next move.

Nowhere to run but forward or backward. Nothing but barren pavement and the faded yellow steel of the bridge's arch.

"Run?" Johnny asked.

"No time," Drogan grunted, shifting to wrap his arms around her and Johnny as if preparing to carry them along for a jump.

"No," Rachel heard herself say.

No time to run. Jumping would only leave them exposed in the water.

They needed to be invisible.

"Down," she growled, dropping her staff, grabbing fistfuls of both of their jackets, and falling to the road.

Maybe it was sheer surprise on both their parts, but Johnny and Drogan hit the pavement with her.

"Lie still," she whispered.

Drogan squirmed. "They may have already seen—"

"Shut up," she snapped.

She'd seen how fast raknoth ships could move. If it was one of the Kul out there, and if they'd already been spotted, it didn't matter now whether they ran or not.

So Rachel focused on what she could control, shaping her will into a single abstract thought, then she opened the channel and let the energy flow.

She'd never tried something like this before, but hell, if her mom had managed to enchant a virus that had brought the raknoth to their knees, why should invisibility be beyond Rachel's grasp?

The energy crackled through her body like an electric river, and the air immediately around them took on an odd, oily effect.

She tried her best not to focus on it.

Unlike most of the channeling she was used to, this feat was far more mentally strenuous than energy-intensive, bending and shifting light to present the facade of empty pavement where they lay—it was a lot to keep straight in her head as she channeled.

And, while the channeling demands were the secondary challenge, that's not to say they were negligible. Within seconds, she felt the beginnings of the channeling fatigue creeping into her bones.

Worst of all, she didn't even have any way to know whether it was working. But the lack of feedback hardly mattered now. They were out of time.

She could barely make it out as a faint blip in the distant sky, but something about the way it moved... That was definitely a ship out there—definitely not a human one.

And it was coming straight for them.

"We must take cover," Drogan whispered, though he didn't move a muscle.

"Let the lady work, Stumps," Johnny whispered. "Trust her."

"You do not call me that," came Drogan's hissed reply, followed by a murmured, "Flame Head."

Rachel closed her eyes and shut it all out—the visual input that was only distracting her, the tickling urge to break into manic laughter. All of it.

She sank deeper into her task, picturing nothing but empty pavement, willing the image to life, embracing the crackling stream of power flowing from the batteries on her belt, through her body, and into the air around them.

Time stretched.

Was that the soaring sound of a rakul ship cutting through the air, or just the rush of her own racing blood?

She couldn't stand another second of not looking, but she didn't trust herself to hold the illusion if she did.

That was definitely the rush of a ship soaring in.

"It's working, Rache," Johnny said quietly. "I think."

He thinks?

She resisted the urge to open her eyes and check for herself, making a mental note to give Johnny pointers on his pep talk skills at a later date. Once they didn't die here.

The sound drew closer, closer. It was north of their position, she was sure of it.

Maybe...

"It's passing," Johnny confirmed.

She let out a deep breath, careful not to release her illusion.

In testament to his words, the rushing was definitely fading eastward now.

"I think we might be..."

Screw it.

Rachel opened her eyes to see why Johnny had trailed off and saw with immense relief that the alien ship was indeed still rocketing off to the east, quickly fading into the distance.

"Yup," Johnny said, his face a shade too pale and his breathing a touch heavy. "I think we're good."

Rachel slumped to the pavement and released her hold on the illusion with a grateful sigh.

Johnny gave her leg an enthusiastic pat, earning himself a one-eyed glare.

"What'd I tell you, Drogan?" he said, not to be deterred. "Lady knows what she's doing."

Drogan just growled something under his breath about lucky fools and started pulling himself to his feet.

"So…" Johnny said, looking between the two of them. "Who's ready for some football?"

CHAPTER THREE

"You have no idea what you're talking about, Slater."

Mosen faced Jarek, wearing that punchable sneer and holding his arms crossed as Jarek was coming to find he so often did when making these territorial stands.

"We have no way of knowing your girlfriend or anyone else is still headed for Pittsburgh. We don't even know if any of them are still alive."

Jarek glanced around at the few Mosenites who'd looked up from further down the dilapidated hallway, no doubt hoping to see their fearless leader putting Jarek in his place.

He wondered what they'd do if he broke one of those sharp cheekbones of Mosen's right now—or, better yet, his neck.

With Fela, Jarek could've taken two Mosens, and it wasn't like a few guys with guns could stop him, either…

Jesus.

A couple weeks of trying times on the road, and there was Conner's black soul whispering its sweet nothings in his ear just as the man himself had tried to do when he'd been alive, "leading" his people.

Jarek let out a long breath and focused back on those cold

eyes. "You're right, Mosen. Bravo. You nailed it. We're flying blinder than old Aunt Sally here. And maybe we go and find out that no one made it to the rally point after all. But how is that any worse than what happens if we keep prancing around up here? Slim as it may be, Pittsburgh's the only hope we have of linking back up with any of our own."

The rhythmic tensing of Mosen's jaw and the furtive glance he shot down the hallway toward his men spoke volumes.

He was thinking. And if he was even a quarter as cunning as Jarek already knew damn well he was, there was no way it was anything other than petty irritation and jealousy that could be driving Mosen to argue at this point.

"We still don't even know Pittsburgh's the right location," Mosen finally said, speaking more quietly now.

That was technically true.

In the days leading up to the Net's untimely death, they'd collectively grown suspicious the rakul might be using the system to track them by their comms, or at least to listen in. Suspicious enough that no concrete details or location had been used during Jarek's last comm contact with Rachel and Nelken—the very call they'd been on when the Net had croaked.

In hindsight, that timing didn't exactly bode well in itself, but Mosen didn't need that extra bit of ammunition.

Point was, sure, maybe there was a little interpretation involved, but...

"He said 'the old pigskin field where men were forged in steel'."

Mosen shrugged, unimpressed. "Yeah. So he could be talking about the fucking colosseum for all we know. It's not exactly specific."

On second thought, maybe Jarek had given up on breaking the a-hole's neck a little too soon.

"You're right, Mosen. Nelken could be making some wild assumption we'd all realize he was talking about Rome—which, by the way, I have no idea how he would've gotten to in the first place. That's true. Or"—Jarek raised a finger—"and this is a real doozy... *or*, he could just be talking about his home town football stadium."

"That's still a stretch."

"Forged in steel, Mosen. They called their team the Steelers, for Christ's sake!"

"That doesn't mean—"

"Nelken grew up there! C'mon, man!"

Mosen pursed his lips, turning that chestnut over in his head, and Jarek decided to press the advantage.

"How about this," Jarek said, raising a hand as if in offering. "How about you remind me what great hint your mighty Zar left you. Where's our old pal Krogoth planning to meet his favorite human lieutenant?"

It was probably a mistake—the equivalent of poking a beehive for no good reason at all. Because, as far as he'd gathered, Krogoth had given Mosen little more than a cold *good luck* and a condescending reminder to die well if and when it came to that. And judging from Mosen's reaction, Jarek's intel must've been at least half accurate.

The man's expression went deadly flat in a way that made Jarek think of a viper preparing to strike, and he seemed to cycle through half a different starts and stops before he finally settled on his comeback.

"How about this, Slater? How about you go fuck yourself? Then do us all a favor and be on your way. We don't need you and your band of self-righteous idiots here. You go your way, we'll go our—"

"*Sir!*"

It took Jarek a second to realize the hissed whisper had come from Mosen's comm.

The two of them traded a wary look, their squabble dissipating at the tone of that single word.

Something was wrong.

"What is it?" Mosen asked quietly into his comm.

"It's—shit, there's a lot of 'em. It's a horde, sir. North of the course. You'd better come loo—"

"Quiet," Mosen said, his own voice dropping in volume but growing in intensity. "I'll be there. Don't move."

He tapped his comm and glared at Jarek.

"They've never followed me this far before," Jarek said, more to himself than to Mosen.

"Yeah? Go tell that to the fucking horde outside." Mosen shot a look toward the Resistance's half of the second floor. "If not you, it's probably the fucking human satellite dish."

Jarek clenched his jaw, wanting to argue with both accusations and not rightly sure he could deny either.

Could this be his fault? Or Michael's?

What else could it be?

"If they're north of the course," he said quietly, "we still have time to roll ou—"

"Just try something new and shut the fuck up, will you? And see to it your people do the same."

With that, Mosen rushed off to go check in with his lookout.

Jarek stood there dumbly for a moment, mind racing with questions

"Sir," Al said quietly in his ear, "if Michael is—"

"I got it," Jarek said, turning for the rooms most of the Resistance troops had bunked up in.

It was only a little past nine in the morning. Having been on the road all night and only fed properly a couple hours earlier, most of them would probably be asleep right now—with any luck, at least.

That would sure help with the whole *staying quiet* order Mosen had issued so indelicately. If they ended up needing to run, though...

One problem at a time.

Jarek padded toward the end of the hallway, peeking into each apartment as he went. They'd gotten into the habit of bunking like this pretty fast—doors all open, so everyone could hear you scream, and sleeping as many as each room could fit. Safety in numbers.

As he'd expected, the large majority of the Resistance troops were out cold, but some looked up as he passed. To those, he gestured with a finger to the lips and then pointed to the northern windows and mouthed, "Look out."

To their credit, once they'd peeked out and back to him with pale faces, they moved into silent action, quietly waking their comrades with enough confidence that Jarek had little worry they'd handle this thing admirably.

They were all stamped with cloaking glyphs, after all. And Mosen's men had their cloaking field generator—which he prayed to the Maker was tuned to an inconspicuous range, if there were such a thing.

Michael, on the other hand…

The room at the end of the hall was dim and quiet, but for a faint rustling. Everyone appeared to be asleep. As for that rustling, it seemed to be coming from—

Shit.

On the bright side, Michael's twitching form hadn't yet reached full on screaming seizure mode.

On the less-bright side, he looked like he was about ten seconds away from doing so.

Jarek crept into the room, cursing each creak of the old floor.

A few Resistance men stirred, but no one woke.

He needed to warn them, needed to get them on their feet. But first, he had to get Michael out of there—had to find some way to keep this quiet. But where? And how?

On the floor, Michael shuddered and let out a pained moan.

Shit, shit, shit.

Jarek bent down and shook Michael by the shoulder.

No good.

Michael's brow furrowed, and his eyes began racing behind closed lids.

Now or never, then.

Jarek scooped Michael's bulk from the floor as quietly as he could, blanket and all, and stalked for the door, stepping carefully over sleeping soldiers as he went.

By the time he reached the hallway, Michael's nonsensical muttering was coming steadily, and several soldiers were shifting in their sleep behind them.

Jarek looked down the hall, weighing his options.

Upstairs. Downstairs. The ship.

Not great options. And if Michael started howling—

A pair of sharp jerks from Michael informed Jarek he was out of time to think about it.

He hurried into the room across the hallway. It was on the southwest corner—the one furthest from the incoming horde.

It was also where Chambers was posted up for her lookout duties.

She spun at their entry, hand drifting toward her holstered sidearm, then froze, taking them in with wide eyes. "Slater? What the—"

"Shhh." Jarek touched a finger to his lips. Then, at a whisper, "Don't mind us." He hooked a thumb the way he'd come. "Do mind the horde."

"What?" she hissed.

"Company," Jarek whispered. "Coming from the north. Actually, if you could go quietly wake the boys and girls across the hall…"

Thanks to Fela's auditory sensors, Jarek could hear the horde drawing closer outside. He could almost see them in his mind's eye, some of them placidly plodding along, others mindlessly wailing on their helpless companions.

For an understandable moment, Chambers just stared at him, seemingly unable to decide what to make of any of what he'd just said. "I… Is he okay?"

"Who, Mikey?" Jarek yanked the blanket from Michael and tossed it at Chambers, who caught it without looking, her open-mouthed stare riveted to Michael. "He's great. Tripping on the R waves, we call it."

Chambers looked less than convinced, probably not least of which because Michael chose that moment to growl and violently thrash with his legs.

Jarek sank into the corner nearest the door, pulled Michael's back to his chest, and looped his legs around Michael's torso, hooking his feet into the back of Michael's thighs.

"I thought he wasn't…" Chambers said slowly, still fixed on Michael. "Anymore, I mean."

"I was sure hoping," Jarek said, wrapping an arm around Michael's chest. "Never a dull day here on Team Earth, though. Actually…" He paused from sliding his hand over Michael's mouth and instead held it out for the blanket he'd tossed.

Chambers shook off the remainder of her shock and came to hand it to him. "What do you need me to do?"

Jarek tilted his head toward the room he'd pulled Michael from. "Make sure everyone's ready to roll if this goes poorly. Quietly, if possible."

Chambers shuffled a few steps toward the door, not turning from them, pausing when Jarek placed the balled-up blanket lightly against Michael's mouth in preparation for any sounds that should try to escape.

Chambers glanced at the open window. She must've finally been picking up the sounds that were now disturbingly audible to Fela's sensors. Her eyes settled back on Michael, and she stood there by the door looking stuck, uncertain who to help and how.

He couldn't say he blamed her—especially not with a horde approaching and him sitting here looking like he was preparing to smother Michael in his sleep.

Softly as he could, he spoke. "It's Lisa, right?"

He'd only ever exchanged a few words with the woman, all of them in the past week, but he'd heard others call her by the name.

She finally pulled her eyes away from Michael to meet Jarek's gaze and give a small nod.

"Right, then. Lisa." He resisted the urge to lick his lips or otherwise fidget, holding her eyes steadily. "I need you to make sure the others are squared away, and I need you to keep this"—he nodded at Michael's writhing form—"quiet. We're all gonna get through this. I promise."

Lisa seemed to consider that for a long moment, then she set her face, nodded, and slipped out of the room.

Michael's struggles were growing positively insistent now. Even with Jarek's superior leverage, it wouldn't have been a fun ride without Fela. Then again, it wasn't exactly a fun ride as it was, either.

When the growls threatened to spill over into more vocal protest,

Jarek whispered his apologies on unhearing ears and pressed the balled up blanket more firmly to Michael's face.

That was a mistake. Michael's struggles intensified, and the first real sound that poured from his mouth instantly demonstrated just how ineffectual the blanket was going to be.

"Fuck," Jarek hissed, looking frantically around the room for some miraculous other option.

How in holy hell had he thought this was going to work?

Nothing. There was nothing.

Unless…

Shit.

With a sinking stomach, Jarek transferred the blanket to his other hand and slid his free fingers over Michael's throat, armored thumb and forefinger seeking out the carotid arteries on either side.

Gently, gently…

Michael's struggles and growls intensified for a second, then began to die, his head bobbing downward as if heavy sleep were trying to take him.

Jarek kept the pressure on, waiting to be sure.

"Sir," Al said quietly in his ear, "need I remind you that people tend to die when you do that to them?"

"Thank. You. Mr. Robot." Jarek said, whispering each word so quietly he could barely hear them himself.

The horde was passing outside now, not even a stone's throw away, save for the walls between them. Every shriek hit Jarek like a splash of ice water. Every thud of boots on dirt—or of limb on limb for those more given to friendly fire.

He held his breath, tense and waiting for each and every moment to be the one they were found out, the one the downstairs door would burst open and—

"That's enough sir," Al said.

With a jolt of panic, he realized he was still pinching Michael's throat. He released the pressure but kept his hand ready.

If this was the same horde he'd fled that morning—and he didn't see how it couldn't be—it was big enough that they'd probably be several minutes in passing. And contrary to every one of the considerable number of action movies he'd devoured in post-Catastrophe boredom, he knew Michael wouldn't stay out for more than a few seconds with his blood flow restored.

The first time Michael began to stir, Jarek waited against his better judgment to see if it'd be to understandable disorientation or to mad flails and growls, hoping that maybe Michael's slipping out of consciousness had served as some kind of reboot.

No such luck.

So began a slow, tense game.

Michael stirred. Jarek squeezed. Michael slumped.

Over and over.

And below, the horde continued its march all the while, so close he could almost feel their gnashing teeth on his armor.

Jarek lost track of time, too focused on the delicate balance of Michael's oxygen-deprived brain and the sounds of the hundreds of maddened civilians.

They were taking too long.

Had something caught their attention? One of the sounds that had escaped Michael earlier? Or maybe someone else in the building had lost their shit at waking up surrounded by a giant mob of violence-happy automatons. Jarek hadn't heard anything—nothing that stood out from the ruckus of the horde, at least—but...

Jarek had just applied what he was pretty sure was Michael's twelfth mini-strangulation when movement at the door nearly made Jarek jump out of his armor.

Chambers padded silently into the room, keeping low enough to stay out of the line of sight for any ground viewers who might happen to be looking up. She took in Michael's lax form and Jarek's ready fingers at his throat, looking like she wasn't quite sure whether to help Jarek or pry his hands off of Michael.

Jarek tilted his head questioningly in the direction she'd come from.

She swallowed, gave a shaky thumbs up, and crawled over to their corner.

"They're almost past," she mouthed, the tiny traces of the accompanying whisper only barely audible to Fela's sensors.

Jarek nodded, preparing to subdue a stirring Michael once again.

True to her word, the heart of the cacophony, while well within earshot, seemed to be drifting away southwest now. From the sound of it, though, there were plenty of stragglers still below.

Chambers watched the process of Michael's subduing with clear concern and took a careful peek out the closest window.

"I think maybe it's okay now," she whispered, glancing uncertainly down at Michael. "As long as he doesn't scream or anything."

Jarek wasn't about to hold his breath on those chances, having no actual understanding of how wide this furor net was spread right now or what was even happening beneath Michael's dark, curly locks. But, that said, he also wasn't eager to give Michael permanent brain damage from repeated strangulation—assuming he hadn't already.

So, cautiously, Jarek held off on the strangling and shifted Michael so he could see his face as the younger man began to stir again.

Jarek held his breath, waiting.

In the distance, the horde continued to recede.

"All clear below," Chambers whispered.

Michael's face scrunched in a kind of flinch as if he was having a nightmare.

Once. Twice.

Jarek raised a hand to Michael's throat.

Michael's dark eyes snapped open.

"Crap," Michael hissed. "Oh crap—I didn't..." He looked around, taking in their tense looks and, after the fact, Jarek's hand at his throat. "Uhh... Did I miss something?"

Jarek let out a relieved breath, patted Michael on the chest, and leaned back to relax against the wall. "Oh, you know. Bloodthirsty horde—sorry, *congregation*—rolling through. Tense struggles to keep certain parties quiet." He frowned in the direction of Mosen's half of the building. "Stubborn assholes who are probably already blaming all this on the two of us."

"You forgot half the grown men and women in this building shitting themselves in terror," Chambers said, still glancing out the window every few seconds, "but yeah."

Michael was opening his mouth to say something when approaching footsteps drew Jarek's attention to Fela's auditory sensors.

Halfway down the hallway already. Headed their way with cold anger Jarek could almost feel pulsing from each violent boot fall.

Three guesses who.

Jarek detached his legs from Michael and pulled them both to their feet, unruffling Michael's clothes and sliding the blanket into the corner behind them with one foot.

In response to Michael's baffled look, Jarek just held a finger to his own lips and turned to join Chambers at the window.

The hallway footsteps stopped at the threshold of their room, drawing Chambers' attention.

Jarek deliberately watched the fading horde for another second before turning himself to find Mosen watching them with hard accusation in his eyes.

"What are you two doing?"

Jarek didn't have to act too hard to come up with an irritated frown as he hooked a thumb at the window as if to say, *What the hell do you* think *we're doing?*

Mosen ignored him and stepped into the room like a hound on the prowl. He paused when he caught sight of Michael, who, admittedly, looked pretty ruffled, and not a little bit guilty.

Instead of grilling Michael, though, Mosen whirled on Chambers —who he must've figured was less likely to be in cahoots—and skewered her with a look that could've wilted a tree. "What's Carver doing here?"

Jarek's stomach sank at the thought of what came next when their story unraveled.

But Chambers only looked from Mosen to Michael and back again, her slight confusion either genuine or masterfully acted. "Is there someplace else he's supposed to be?"

Something about the look on Mosen's face flashed Jarek straight back to the first time he'd ever seen Rachel. The time when he'd found her on the floor of the Red Fortress' brig with Mosen's hands wrapped around her throat.

He tensed, the vivid memory begging him to attack right then and there.

But Mosen let out an aggravated huff and broke his tense glare before things escalated any further. "Whatever." He turned a cold stare on Jarek. "You still running off to Pittsburgh like a blind old lady?"

Jarek held his gaze, unflinching. "Why? You feeling spry?"

The glint of red that crept into Mosen's eyes, coupled with his cold, unreadable expression, was an unnecessary reminder of just how much time the man had spent under the thumb of his raknoth masters.

Finally, Mosen turned for the door and spoke without looking back.

"We should leave tonight."

Things could have turned out a lot worse, Jarek decided as Mosen left, considering that it'd been death by furor horde and possible civil war they'd been dealing with.

Lucky for them, Chambers had been ready and willing to hold her shit together under Mosen's creepy scrutiny.

Jarek shot her an exaggerated thumbs up as they listened to Mosen's stomping footsteps fade down the hallway.

For a moment, a small grin split her face. Soon enough, though, looking back and forth between him and Michael, the grin began to fade, replaced by a look that suggested she was wondering what the hell it was she'd just signed up for.

CHAPTER FOUR

Whether it was the lingering tension of having almost been spotted on the bridge or just par for the course, Rachel couldn't help but think the air along the riverside path was unnaturally crisp and still as they trekked quietly toward the stadium.

Probably just a healthy dose of the *too-damned-close call* nerves.

They'd jumped down to the narrow pedestrian underpass as soon as they'd reached the northern end of the bridge, not eager to spend a moment longer than necessary out in the open. Rachel had helped Johnny down with telekinesis. Drogan, unsurprisingly, had refused her aid—and gotten it anyway.

It wouldn't do to kick off their stealthy city prowl with a heavy raknoth thudding down to the ground.

Now that they were on their way, though, Rachel was having trouble giving much worry to whatever ears might be listening nearby. Her attention was far too focused on the eastern skyline, and the ship she was half-sure would come racing back at any moment, having only been feinting its failure to spot them on the bridge.

It was a silly fear, she kept reminding herself.

If the rakul had seen them, she highly doubted they'd feel the need for caution or trickery. They would have descended on them without hesitation. Right?

She shook her head at her own fretting and glanced over at the others.

Johnny, as she'd come to expect in these situations, had shed his nearly chronic grin for an expression of disciplined vigilance, the systematic scan of his gaze and the precise way he handled his odd rifle reminding her that he'd been a trained soldier back on his planet.

Drogan, on the other hand, seemed to be listening and smelling as much as he was watching, his skin tinged with the subtle flecks of green that told her he was still every bit as apprehensive about their near miss on the bridge as she was.

They passed alongside a huge white building whose outer curve matched the wavy way of the path and a small amphitheater that stretched from the path down the bank to the river's edge.

It was the exact kind of sight that never failed to make Rachel pause and try to grasp exactly what life had been like on this planet before the Catastrophe. Sure, growing up in Unity had been a much better approximation than what most kids—like Jarek—had experienced. And she had plenty of "normal" memories from childhood, too. But none of that could really hold the shiver of surrealism at bay.

Looking down at that old, abandoned amphitheater, it was impossible to deny that Earth had been violently robbed of its future.

But that didn't mean they couldn't take it back.

Rachel scanned the scene ahead and reached for her cloaking pendant as they cornered the large building and Heinz Field drew into view. On second thought, she dropped her hand from the pendant, opting to wait until they were closer before she started sweeping with her senses.

As far as she knew, all the men with Nelken would either be personally cloaked or hiding within the effect of one of her and Haldin's cloaking field generators anyway.

"That's a lot of cars," Johnny said quietly.

He wasn't wrong.

Whether or not you wanted to call it stealing, cars had largely become fair game to be taken for use or parts after the bombs had fallen. God knew most of their owners weren't coming back for them.

Even so, the two enormous lots between them and the stadium were still surprisingly full of vehicles, most of them looking exactly like they'd been sitting there for the past fifteen years.

Maybe it had been a game day when the bombs had fallen.

She pushed the thought aside and tilted her staff at the stadium. "Let's move while we can."

"Do we really think they're staying in there?" Johnny asked.

Drogan's sniffing was audible this time, and when she looked, his nose and mouth had begun to shift green and slightly elongate.

He noticed her looking and shook his head. "Not inside the stadium, I think. But close."

Johnny opened his mouth to say something, his usual grin returning.

Drogan silenced him with a raised hand, still staring at the stadium. "Save your pitiful jokes, Flame Head. Follow. Quietly."

With that, Drogan started across the closer of the parking lots, sniffing all the way.

Johnny watched him go with a long frown. "It wasn't even gonna be a joke." As he spoke, he held up one hand as if to shield his face from Drogan's turned back and shot Rachel an exaggerated pair of winks.

Rachel patted him on the back as she passed to follow Drogan. "Don't worry, Flame Head. They're not *all* pitiful.

"Sweet Alpha," he murmured, falling in beside her, "if this is gonna be a thing, can it at least be a cool nickname?"

"You want *Captain* Flame Head?"

Johnny thought about it and shrugged. "Moving in the right direction, at least."

They trod on quietly after Drogan, letting the raknoth have space to run point with his sharpened senses. The stadium loomed up as they drew closer, another bizarre reminder of the kind of things the world had chosen to place value in when day-to-day survival hadn't been on the table.

They were halfway past the expansive structure when Johnny snapped into a shooting stance. He moved so fast it took Rachel a moment to realize Drogan had likewise stiffened ahead, as if something had reached out and slapped him.

It took her another moment to realize the jolt of surprise shooting through her was not solely in response to their reactions. There was something else there, tickling at the edge of her awareness, right where her physical senses gave way to their extended counterparts.

Something she shouldn't be able to feel with her cloaking pendant dialed to short range unless…

Ahead, Drogan turned to face her, eyes glowing with soft red light, his hand drifting to the cloaking pendant at his neck as if by its own accord.

"Don't," she whispered. "It's them."

Drogan, hearing the whisper even twenty yards away, curled the hand into a fist and lowered it with deliberate effort as Rachel and Johnny hurried over to him.

He hadn't talked about it much aside from the occasional passing gripe, but it seemed like wearing the cloaking pendant was uncomfortable for Drogan—effectively cutting off one of his sensory modalities.

And given that it was rakul messengers whispering at the edges of their cloaks, she couldn't say she blamed him for wanting that particular sense back right now.

"How close?" Rachel whispered.

Drogan's cocked head and glare were all the response he gave, but she didn't need further explanation.

They wouldn't be able to tell. Not without flipping off their cloaks and lighting themselves up like lighthouses to any nearby rakul.

"Guys?" Johnny said, glancing between them. He wasn't a telepath, but he caught on quickly enough by the looks on their faces. "Shit. Messengers?"

Rachel nodded.

Johnny looked expectantly between them again. "Well, should we maybe move, then?"

Damn straight they should. The question was in which direction they should do it, and they all knew it.

"Bridge still looks clear back there," Johnny said. "If we back out and regroup we can—"

"We won't find them again," Rachel said. "Not without the Net. Not soon enough for it to matter." She swallowed, looking at Drogan and the stadium beyond. "Assuming they're actually here somewhere."

"I smell *someone*," Drogan said.

Johnny traded an uncertain look with Rachel. "What are the chances those someones are furor puppets?"

Drogan shook his head, fiddling with his cloaking pendant again. "I detect no signs of a horde. Yet."

Whatever they did, better sooner than later, and if Nelken and his people decided to blow town now…

They had to make the rally point—had to find out if Jarek and Michael had made it, or hold out until they did.

"I say we go," Rachel said before she could talk herself out of it.

Drogan turned back from the east to consider her. "I agree with Rachel Cross."

Together, they turned to face Johnny.

"Shiiit." Johnny shook his head and gestured to Drogan. "Lead the way then, Sniffs."

Their pace moving forward was decidedly more urgent as they attempted to cover ground as quickly and quietly as possible. Once they'd passed the stadium, they struck out across the next parking lot and down the next strip of buildings, following Drogan's busy nose. When Drogan perked up again, Rachel assumed it would either be good news or bad.

Instead, the raknoth waved them on. "Keep moving. I require better vantage."

Then he crouched and leapt fifty feet to the top of the building on their right.

"Aye, aye, then," Rachel grumbled.

She prowled down the street beside Johnny, dialing her cloaking pendant out to give her extended senses some room to explore.

With the additional sensory information at her disposal, it was only all the more startling when the pair of figures sprang out from the narrow alley on the left, rifles at the ready and aimed straight at Rachel's and Johnny's faces.

Johnny had his weapon trained before Rachel could even think about pointing her staff or reaching for energy to channel. She didn't quite get around to either before the face of one of their attackers registered in a swirl of surprised relief.

"Lea?" Johnny held up a *don't shoot* hand and slowly lowered his rifle. "Hey, fancy seeing you her—"

Lea lunged forward, wrapped Johnny in a hard but brief hug, and broke away. "We have to get off the streets. Now."

Her partner, who Rachel recognized as a Resistance fighter but not by name, was already backing toward the alleyway with an air that suggested they'd all better follow if they wanted to live.

"What's going on?" Rachel asked as Lea pulled her into an equally brief hug that segued into a pull toward the alley.

"We just lost our northeastern scout," Lea said. "Right after he told us—"

A crimson-eyed Drogan slammed down to the asphalt just ahead of them, eliciting startled jumps from all of them and a strangled growl of "Jesus Christ!" from Lea's partner.

"A horde approaches," Drogan said, ignoring their reactions. "Quite a large one, from the sound of it."

"Funny timing," Lea's partner mumbled with a dark look at Drogan.

"Adams..." Lea chided. Then, to them, "Did you guys see that ship?"

"Oh, we saw it," Johnny said. "Thought it had skipped right over this fair city, though."

"We need to get back to base," Adams said. "They're probably already starting evac."

A twinge of panic gripped Rachel. "Evac?" She grabbed Lea's arm. "Michael? Jarek?"

Lea licked her lips, the hesitance and sympathy in her expression all the answer Rachel needed.

Lea shook her head anyway.

She might as well have punched Rachel in the gut.

It wasn't that she'd been expecting anything else. The chances of Michael and Jarek beating them here had been slim at best.

Rachel just hadn't realized how desperately she'd been hoping they would pull it off anyway.

And if evacuation was on the table right now…

By some gentle combination of Johnny's pushing and Lea's pulling, they were all moving down the alleyway before Rachel could tell herself to pull it together.

Up on point, Adams and Drogan weren't bothering with any attempt at moving quietly now. The rest of them followed their example, and they all rounded out of the alleyway and set off across another large parking lot at a hard run.

Under an overpass. Across yet another lot.

Rachel ran, mind racing too fast for her thoughts to amount to anything more than white noise.

In the distance, the first horrible scream split the air.

Adams and Lea were angling toward the building on the right—an old hotel, from the looks of it.

Rachel caught sight of a few tense-looking shooters posted in the windows higher up. Then the doors were open, and they were all whisked into a hotel lobby that probably would've felt a lot larger if it weren't crammed full of men and women speaking in hushed voices and rushing about with packs and weapons.

There were dozens of them, many whose faces Rachel didn't recognize but plenty more she did, including one face she thought belonged to the non-scaly form of Al'Brandt, the raknoth from the temple in the Himalayas. He tipped a small nod her way a second before her extended senses confirmed her suspicion.

She nodded back and continued looking around until…

"Pryce!"

Rachel's exclamation earned her a few indignant looks—and a few more curious ones—from those nearby. But there was only one look she really cared about at that moment, and Jay Pryce's expression was far from indignant.

The frazzled old tinkerer pushed through the crowd and wrapped her in a surprisingly firm hug.

"Thank the Maker," he said softly.

He pulled back to inspect her company, his expression flickering from hopeful to wan as he confirmed Jarek's absence and looked back to her.

She swallowed against a growing ache in her throat, tilting her head toward the crowded room. "I was hoping…"

Pryce gave her an understanding nod and squeezed her shoulder. "As was I."

"Daniels," came a familiar stern voice from the left. "Report."

The crowd shifted to let through a limping Commander Nelken, still hobbled to the point of using a cane after he'd taken a collapsing section of the old HQ ceiling in the battle with Zar'Golga. It felt as if it had been years ago.

Nelken paused for a beat when he caught sight of Rachel, Johnny, and Drogan, then he continued forward, his expression recovering from surprise and relief back to disciplined order.

"All clear to the west, sir," Lea said. "Except these three."

Nelken shifted his gaze to Rachel. "The rest of your group?"

"Across the river," she said, the words demanding more effort than they should have. "Waiting for us to check that it's safe."

She half-expected Johnny to chime in with something, but Drogan beat him to it.

"You have heard nothing from Zar'Krogoth?"

Nelken shook his head, his expression grim. "Aside from the few we met on the road, you're the only ones to make it here. Once they took the Net down…" He just shook his head again, apparently lost for words.

"We can't leave here," Rachel said. "Not until the others make it. If we don't…"

Nelken was still shaking his head, looking like he was about to cut her off.

"You have cloaking generators running here," Rachel said quickly, dialing her cloak back in. "I can feel them. We can hide if the furor sweeps this way—get to the upper floors, keep quiet. If we leave now…"

She couldn't bring herself to say the words.

Leave now, and their chances of seeing Michael and Jarek again went from scary to hopeless.

But Nelken knew that. The tension in his jaw and the conflict in his eyes made that clear enough as he chewed over her words.

"Sir?" one of the men called from over by the lobby's front desk.

Nelken started to turn but paused to look back at Rachel. He opened his mouth to say something. Before he could, there was a wet ripping sound, and a few specks of dark red blood spattered his face.

That's when the screaming started.

CHAPTER FIVE

I f Jarek had to guess what the life of your average woodland rabbit felt like, he would've wagered their current travel conditions were a decent approximation—long stretches of benign existence, punctuated by the occasional moment of sheer, predator-induced terror.

The going of their convoy that night, as it had been since they'd gone on the run, had been tediously slow and maddeningly boring, save for those few moments when someone thought they saw something and the group proceeded to clench until Jarek could practically feel the vehicle trembling with the collective strain.

Without fail, though, the *somethings* in question had proven themselves nothing more than passing animals and ominous tricks of wind, branches, and shadow. Once, funnily enough, the culprit had even been a particularly large rabbit.

That was the problem with trying to fly under the radar when you weren't actually sure what manner of radar your enemy was even packing.

For starters, traveling at night and minimizing their light usage had seemed like no-brainers. For all they knew, the rakul could be watching from orbit, scarfing down space popcorn and waiting for them to show their sad little heads in the light of day.

Of course, by similar logic, one might posit that, if the rakul possessed such abilities, they might well be able to spot them in the dead of night all the same, lights or no lights. But there were only so many precautions they could take.

So Jarek had handed over the two pairs of night vision specs he'd had on the ship to two of their drivers. Jarek, having Fela's broad-range optical sensors, and Mosen, being a creepy raknoth spawn, took the wheels in the other two vehicles. Al, not really needing light to start with, hovered the ship along above them, packed full with the rest of their happy little platoon.

The fact that they were all still alive—and mostly unmolested—suggested the nighttime routine was serving its purpose, so they'd kept a healthy *if it ain't broke* mentality, despite the inherent inconveniences of their nocturnal activities.

Looking over at Michael in the passenger seat of their SUV, Jarek wondered whether he should apply that same logic to the younger man.

For probably the hundredth time that night, he resisted the urge to tell Michael to take a nap.

For one thing, he didn't really want anyone wondering too hard about just what had left Michael so damn exhausted. For another, after what had happened back at the apartments, he wasn't so sure it was the best idea to let Michael fall asleep with anyone else but Chambers around.

He knew next to nothing about the nuances of telepathic influence. Especially in Michael's case, which seemed to have perplexed even the experts. But he distinctly recalled Rachel having mentioned at some point that the telepathic range of a sleeping mind was considerably larger than that of its waking counterpart.

Whatever was going on with Michael, keeping him awake seemed like the safest play. At least until six of their Resistance allies weren't around to get a glimpse of what may or may not be the ticking time bomb named Michael.

"Okay," Jarek said. "Driver's getting tired. Who's ready for another round?"

"Not again," someone—Edwards, he thought—groaned in the far back.

"Hey, it's either that, or Mikey gets a bit handy up here to keep me up."

"Don't let us get in your way, lovebirds," Chambers said from the back seat. "Anything's better than another goddamn road game."

"Touché." Jarek looked over and gave Michael a shrug. "Looks like we're out of options, Mikey."

Michael just shook his head. "I have no idea why I keep agreeing to ride shotgun with you."

"Oh, I think I do," Chambers said.

Jarek wasn't quite sure what to make of the statement until he glanced back to see Chambers shoot him a wink only he could see in the dark.

She couldn't see his return smile, but the guffaws of the men around her made up for it.

Either Chambers happened to have a good working relationship with happy coincidence, or she was something of an evil genius. First, there'd been her stellar cover-up back at the apartments, and now there was this.

Maybe she was just joking around. But Jarek had a feeling it wasn't an accident she was helping kindle the idea of some kind of bromance between him and Michael right when they might be needing a good excuse to be spending some quality time alone—at least until they got to Pittsburgh.

"Don't listen to 'em buddy," Jarek said, making a point of reaching over to pat Michael's thigh, though the gesture might have been lost on the others in the dark. "They're just jealous."

It almost made Jarek want to laugh, even thinking about playing these silly little games when there were ten-thousand-plus-year-old super-beings hunting them like sad little vermin right now, but, somehow, this had become his reality.

Because, whatever happened, he wasn't planning on leaving anyone behind. Not even Mosen. And right now, the best bet at keeping everyone happy with the status quo was keeping Michael's episode quiet until they could quietly figure out whether it was going to become an issue again.

And speaking of which, he was going to need to act sooner than later.

The slow brightening of his faceplate display told him dawn was approaching even without checking the time. He cycled off the night vision and saw the sky was shifting from velvety black to the first dark shades of blue.

Decisions, decisions.

Bunking in the ship was probably the best bet. Jarek, Michael, and some of the other Resistance troops had already set a precedent of doing so at a few of their stops earlier on in this big happy team adventure.

The Mosenites probably wouldn't like it, and it might raise a few Resistance eyebrows as well, but screw it.

Jarek was getting too tired to worry about treading on toes at this point. And by the time real light was creeping out from the horizon and the convoy was starting to slow ahead, he didn't have any better master plans.

"Home sweet home, boys and girls," Jarek said, killing the SUV's power across the street from the pair of big white houses he assumed were Mosen's choice destination.

The Resistance crew wasted no time in piling out of the vehicle with a chorus of grateful sounds.

Jarek touched Michael's shoulder for pause when he started to follow his comrades.

"What say we crash in the ship tonight?" he asked quietly as the troops gingerly closed their doors behind them to avoid any loud noises.

Michael didn't say anything—just shot a worried glance at the rest of their unloading forces then nodded to Jarek, looking, of all things, embarrassed.

Jarek clapped his shoulder. "Good man. It'll be fun. We can make Al tell us ghost stories. Just let me do the talking out there."

With that, he hopped out of the driver's seat and went to help the others lug their dwindling supplies into their new day-homes.

Al, having heard the plan, informed Jarek he was tucking the ship down among a patch of trees behind the houses. Jarek strolled out back with Michael and Chambers to meet Al's debarking Resistance passengers and grab a few things from the ship.

That Michael and Jarek didn't exit the ship right along with everyone else shouldn't have been particularly suspicious, but…

"What are you two doing?"

Goddammit.

Jarek didn't have to look to identify the spiteful voice as Mosen's, approaching from the houses to stick his hateful little nose wherever he damn well pleased.

Was it just nosiness? An overbearing play for authority?

Or did Mosen suspect what they were up to?

Jarek decided he didn't really give a shit at this point.

He was just about to turn from his dresser to say as much when Al, bless his dignified circuits, powered on the filmscreen TV that hung over the dresser.

Jarek turned from the TV and the dresser to show Mosen his best *fuck-off* smile. "We wanna watch a movie, you a-hole. The day I can't do that in the comfort of my own ship is the day I'll crawl out of this suit and hand you the gun."

It was barely even a lie.

People were stopping to watch now, Resistance and Mosenites alike.

"I'd hardly need a gun," Mosen said, still eyeing them suspiciously. "What are you watching?"

Jarek waggled his eyebrows. "You don't wanna know, Mosen."

He needed to shut this down before it became a debate.

"And besides," he added, slapping the hatch release and shooting a wink at Chambers, who was watching this all unfold with a heavily furrowed brow, "it's no girls allowed."

That got a few chuckles from the Resistance boys.

Chambers shook her head and turned to walk away with what might've been a furtive grin.

Mosen, on the other hand, continued holding Jarek on the end of his glare until the boarding ramp clacked into place, sealing them away from one another.

"Super smooth," Michael said from the cot behind him.

"Discreet as always, sir," Al agreed quietly from the cabin speakers.

"Hey, it worked." Jarek shook his head, fishing in his dresser for a pair of sweats. "Everyone's a critic… Jesus."

Mosen, the rakul, and the rest of the universe be damned. Now that he was here, he was going to have himself a ship shower and enjoy the freedom of cotton for a night.

And hell, why not watch that movie?

Michael, unfortunately, had other plans.

"Why don't you stand up to him?" he asked. "Why are you letting him pretend like he owns this whole convoy?"

Jarek glanced over his shoulder and saw frustration building in Michael's expression—the same frustration Jarek had been sniffing lately from the rest of the Resistance ranks too, right on the back of every conversation Mosen butted his way into.

"I know he's got…" Michael continued. "Well, I know he's not just another human, but you could put him through the wall with Fela, couldn't you?"

He could. He absolutely could—and god, did he want to sometimes. But…

"Look, Mikey, I've seen what happens to guys who take the power because they think they know best." He pointed at the rear hatch. "Exhibit A—Seth 'asshat' Mosen."

Exhibit B—Conner.

Jarek suppressed a grimace and pushed down the unpleasant memories of his old outfit leader. "I don't need those people out there looking to me for direction. I just wanna get us all back to the others in one piece. Nelken and whoever else can take over from there. If that means letting Mosen parade around like a yappy little show dog for a couple more days, so be it."

Michael dropped Jarek's gaze and stared somberly through the wall. "And if they're not waiting for us in Pittsburgh?"

Panic made a hard grab for Jarek's throat, sudden and surprisingly intense. He swallowed, trying to fight it down.

The question was just that. A question. The same question he asked himself every day. It shouldn't affect him so strongly. But the closer they got to their hopeful rally point, hearing his own worries expressed through others' mouths... It all just gave tangible authority to the swirling murk of fear and doubt at his center.

"If that happens," he said, willing himself back to calm control, "we'll deal with it then."

Michael was quiet for a while. Then, finally, "He's not gonna stop until someone makes him." He met Jarek's eyes again. "If not you, who else?"

Jarek sighed. "You want me to put him in his place? What if I'm not so sure exactly where that place is? What if I get foggy on which lines should and shouldn't be crossed here? You really wanna deal with me going all dark-side dictator on your asses?"

"You wouldn't do that."

"You realize people said shit like that about every crazy evil bastard in the history of humanity, right? 'Oh no, not Adolf! He's just passionate—he'd never hurt anyone! Oh no, not Anakin! He's the chosen one—he'd never slaughter a room full of padawans!'"

Michael frowned. "Who's Anakin?"

"Dammit, Mikey! Not the point. The point—and side note, I know what movie we're watching now—but the point is that I'm not interested in knocking down assholes just to take their places. We'll get to Pittsburgh. It's enough for now, and—and why are you looking at me like that?"

Michael was studying him like Jarek was some odd creature, the likes of which he'd never seen before.

"You've just... changed," Michael said.

"Not out of this exo, I haven't, so if you'd kindly cease your babbling long enough for me to wash myself, maybe we can do something productive. Like educate your sadly lacking inner child."

Michael hardly seemed to have heard him. "I mean, what happened to the guy I watched cut down a church-full of marauders?"

The question took him by surprise.

"He—I…" Jarek studied Michael for a length of silence and finally rolled his eyes. "Christ, I'm gonna go take a shower. Fire up the movies, Mr. Robot." He started for the ship's tiny bathroom and turned back to jab a finger at Michael. "And no psycho-babble-bullshit when I get back."

Michael just smiled and gave him a crisp salute, and Jarek turned for the bathroom with a muttered curse.

CHAPTER SIX

For one horrible moment, Rachel's shocked brain couldn't comprehend where the blood on Nelken's face had come from. Was it his? The commander touched a few fingers to the crimson streak on his cheek, eyes wide with surprise, seemingly wondering that same question. Then there was a flicker of motion to the right, and they both got their answer.

The mangled body sailed across the room with frightening velocity and hit the front desk with a sickening crunch.

In the time it took Rachel to process the fact, another Resistance soldier slammed into the wall to her right, impaled a few feet up off the ground by... what?

There.

A flicker of shimmering motion, as if the room's daylight were bending around a section of thin air.

Drogan darted forward and drove a hard kick into that thin air.

Another flicker of motion, and then the wall seemed to implode as if a sizable projectile had slammed into it.

"Run!" Drogan bellowed.

No one seemed inclined to argue. Nelken included.

"Tunnel plan!" the commander barked. "Let's move, soldiers!"

Rachel was too busy reaching for her cloaking pendant and watching for more tenuous glimpses of movement to wonder what the hell the tunnel plan was. She dialed out her cloaking field, extending her senses.

She didn't have to search long.

To her eyes, there was nothing but the cracked wall of the lobby. Telepathically, though, the presence in the corner of the room was immense, dwarfing even those of the raknoth, at least on even footing with the power she'd felt in Kul'Gada, if not stronger.

That kind of presence could only be one of the Kul.

And it felt her prodding.

Her breath caught. A string of rapid pulses sounded off from Johnny's rifle beside her, and several small holes tore into the wall, accompanied by specks of an orangish fluid.

A grating shriek tore from the assaulted corner. Another flicker of motion, and two more Resistance soldiers fell dead almost before she knew it, one pierced by some unseen appendage, and the other cleanly decapitated.

Rachel cursed her own inaction and cast her mind around the thing like a net, drawing energy from the air around her to give strength to the mental construct.

Meanwhile, Drogan, Brandt, and the other two raknoth from Nelken's camp were shifting into battle mode and forming a semicircle to corral the thing from the soldiers frantically slinging bags over shoulders and heading for the exit behind Rachel.

The invisible Kul shifted to face them, the movement so quick and easy that she wondered if it even noticed the drag of her telekinetic restraints.

She sure as hell did.

Cold sweat was already beading on her forehead. She released the hold. It was futile to kill herself trying to telekinetically wrestle down something so tremendously strong. She had to think of a better way to help the raknoth with their enraged master.

Getting eyes on the thing would be a start.

She looked around the room for inspiration and found little.

Johnny was busy squeezing off more careful shots past their raknoth allies.

A hand grabbed her arm, and she spun to see Pryce, panting and gripping a fire extinguisher to his chest like a life vest on a sinking ship.

"Can you condense water from the air?" he asked in a shaky tone.

"I—what? Yeah, maybe, but—"

"When I say," Pryce said, his eyes wider and more frantic than she'd ever seen, "you soak that thing."

"What's that gonna—"

Ahead of them, the invisible Kul shrieked, and one of the raknoth hit the floor with his own pained cry, one leg missing from the knee down.

"Just do it!" Pryce snapped.

Then, taking the extinguisher's hose in his hand and tucking the cylinder beneath an arm, Pryce charged toward the fight he had no business being anywhere close to.

Rachel tried to cry out after him to wait, but—

"Now, Rachel!" Pryce cried.

Shit.

No choice but to trust the crazy old bastard.

She closed her eyes, focusing on the task. The moisture in the air was easy enough to feel. It was the large-scale action of accumulating it that was hard to wrap her head around.

If she'd had time, she could have thought of an efficient way to accomplish the feat. Pressed as she was, though, she simply held the moisture in her focus, opened her body to the energy, and channeled it all into a singular thought:

Soak the son of a bitch.

More energy buzzed through her than seemed reasonable for the job, and it felt about as efficient as pushing a car uphill with a rope, but it worked.

By the time she heard the turbulent whoosh of Pryce's extinguisher discharging, the invisible Kul was beading with a thin layer of water, and Rachel was beginning to grasp Pryce's plan.

She opened her eyes and watched as Pryce, reaching over Drogan's shoulder, emptied the canister of dry flame-smothering powder on the screeching Kul with a wordless cry of his own.

Moments later, they were looking at the stumbling, goop-caked outline of something large, spindly, and vaguely insectoid.

Pryce stood frozen, mouth agape, transfixed on the Kul as if he was only then realizing what he'd just done.

Drogan shoved Pryce back and stepped aside himself just in time to avoid the goop-coated appendage that came swooshing through the air for Pryce's head.

The Kul's spindly form flickered once more, then it dropped whatever it was doing to stay camouflaged, and Rachel saw that the insectoid descriptor was accurate, if maybe a little too benign.

The thing looked like the spawn of a demon and a giant praying mantis.

All attempts at stealth dropped, the six-legged monstrosity scuttled forward to engage the raknoth with another grating howl.

The three remaining raknoth fought bravely while Johnny dragged away their wounded brother and recruited Pryce to help him lug the one-legged raknoth to his remaining foot.

That done, Johnny turned back to the task of taking what shots he could without hitting any of their allies.

Rachel did much the same, though her attempts to telekinetically harass and unbalance proved largely ineffectual against the Kul's six spindly legs.

When the Kul caught one of the raknoth off guard with a lunging stab, Rachel telekinetically clamped down on the sharp appendage with everything she had.

The effort of matching that strength and the bulk behind it nearly took her to her knees, but the insectoid Kul drew up short in his attack.

His narrow head and oversized eyes twitched around in confusion.

The three raknoth took advantage of the moment and drove into him with a chorus of battle roars.

Rachel was surprised the wall didn't give out completely as the combatants all slammed into it, a writhing mess of growls and mismatched appendages.

Pound-for-pound, out in the open, it was clear the Kul was stronger than any of the raknoth. But they knew what they were doing. With one raknoth pinning each of the Kul's two sharp arms to the wall and Drogan wrangling its frontmost pair of legs, they had the thing tenuously trapped.

"Rachel Cross!" Drogan cried, struggling with a spindly leg in each hand. "Left leg!"

Assuming he meant an implied direction to hold said leg in place, she shook off the woozy tinge of channeling fatigue and prepared for another exertion.

She knew Drogan was strong, but the power it took to keep the Kul's left leg trapped in place made her marvel at how the hell he'd been wrestling down two of them.

As soon as she had control of the leg, Drogan dropped it and turned his full attention to the other.

"Now would be a good time to leave, guys" Johnny shouted over the growls.

Rachel risked a glance over her shoulder and saw most of the Resistance forces were clear of the lobby and hoofing it across the lot to a nearby parking structure. They were also, she realized with a sinking stomach, already dealing with the vanguard of the furor horde they'd heard approaching.

Good time to leave was putting it lightly.

"Drogan!" she called, her head starting to spin with the effort of keeping the Kul held in place.

There was a loud crack from the Kul's direction, and Drogan tore one of its front legs clean off.

"Go!" Drogan thundered to all of them.

The word was nearly lost to the head-splitting shriek that escaped the Kul. The creature tripled its efforts to escape, bucking in a wild frenzy and spewing a steady stream of god-awful noises.

Drogan managed to take the leg Rachel had immobilized with another sharp crack and a wet tear.

The Kul's struggles only grew more intense, finally bucking one of its arms free and knocking the raknoth who'd been holding it halfway across the room with a long gash in his chest.

Drogan narrowly ducked a swipe that would've taken his head and peddled furiously backward, still holding the Kul's second severed leg.

He cast the leg aside, hauled up the raknoth the Kul had batted over, and herded them all toward the exit.

"Come on!" Johnny shouted, pausing from firing at the Kul only long enough to nudge her toward the door. "Let's move!"

Seeing Drogan and the others doing just that and the now-four-legged Kul tripping over itself in its attempts to follow them, Rachel didn't argue.

Pryce was waiting for them just outside, hunkered down with a couple Resistance soldiers and the one-legged raknoth, who was busy swatting away any of the furor puppets who got too close.

As soon as they were all clear of the entryway, a van Rachel hadn't even realized was idling backed up and slammed into the lobby door, rear end first.

A grim-looking Lea crawled out through the opening where the windshield should've been, having apparently already thought that far ahead.

Rachel gave the younger woman an appreciative nod and a clap on the back as she caught up with them and they all set off across the lot after their allies.

The van probably wouldn't stop a Kul long—even an injured one— but it was something.

Raging berserkers pushed in at their group from both sides, numerous, but not enough so for Rachel to believe this was more than the leading edge of the horde. Though, from the sounds at their backs, the rest of the party wasn't so far behind.

And, on the tail end of a frustrated howl and a wrenching crash that sounded a little too much like a van being flipped, Rachel was pretty sure their mantis Kul wasn't either.

She could feel him well enough back there, pushing past the overturned van, but she couldn't help take a peek anyway. The poor wreck of the van quickly drew her eye, but the Kul was nowhere to be seen—until Rachel noticed the outline of extinguisher goop and the trail of orange blood it left in its wake.

"He's doing the invisible thing again!" she shouted.

More of those thrumming pulses filled the air, and more blood spattered the pavement.

Rachel turned back in the direction she was running to see Johnny moving at a rapid backpedal that kept him just steady enough to keep shooting. It was actually pretty impressive.

Just not as impressive as the car Brandt threw at the oncoming outline of the Kul.

Even missing its two front legs, the creature still somehow managed to scuttle clear of Brandt's car-missile.

And straight into Drogan's.

The Kul flashed back to visibility with a shriek, nearly tumbling over backward as it absorbed the momentum of the projectile with its rear legs.

Rachel didn't wait to see what it'd do next. She just kept running, keeping even with Johnny and Lea. It was only as they closed on the parking garage that Rachel remembered she had no idea what the plan was from there.

Now clearly wasn't the time to ask.

Their allies were waiting at the door, waving them in.

Drogan dropped back to swat a few berserkers off their flanks and watch their backs as they filed into the building and yanked the door shut behind them.

Rachel took a few seconds to fuse the door's lock to the frame, hoping it might at least slow down the Kul and his horde.

As soon as she turned to continue into the parking garage with the others, the meaning of *tunnel plan* became clear.

In addition to the concrete maze of ramps and tight spaces she'd been expecting, there was also an offshoot leading down to what looked to be some kind of underground rail station.

There was no tram or train to be found, but there also wasn't really any choice but to follow the Resistance crowd down the stationary escalator steps and trust there was more to the plan than trying to outrun a horde and a pissed off giant mantis in an underground tunnel on foot.

Then again, judging by the stream of soldiers disappearing down said tunnel on foot, maybe not.

Nelken was there, waving them on and waiting to see to it everyone made it in. Pryce was well ahead of them, ushered on by a pair of troops.

Rachel did a quick headcount to make sure they hadn't lost anyone in the dash, then she gritted her teeth and pushed into the dark tunnel, fumbling to switch on her comm light.

Nelken and his escorts fell in with them as they passed, and for a handful of moments, they all ran side-by-side, lost in the long echoes of their pounding boots and the storm of shaky comm lights and exhausted panting.

At least until a loud crash echoed down the tunnel from behind—the Kul busting in the door, Rachel could only assume.

"Blow it," Nelken said.

The woman on Nelken's left tapped at her comm, and a thick boom shook the tunnel, shortly followed by a sound like a thousand crumbling stones and a drastic decrease in ambient light.

Rachel didn't need to look back to know they'd just collapsed the entryway of the rail tunnel, but she did anyway and was rewarded with a sharp flare of claustrophobic anxiety.

She didn't notice she'd slowed until Johnny nudged into her, encouraging her to continue on down the tunnel. For a second, she couldn't seem to do it.

"C'mon," he said. "Better trapped in a tunnel than running free with a big angry insect, right?"

She pried her eyes away from the dark wall of debris she couldn't help but think of as their new tomb entrance.

"Yeah," she said, picking her pace back up. "Better. Sure..."

CHAPTER SEVEN

Once the dull pressure of the tunnel's darkness seemed to have alleviated the excitement for everyone—or for everyone *else*, Rachel thought with yet another claustrophobic shudder—it became abundantly clear Nelken's limp was their limiting factor. Of course, no one was eager to say it.

No one but the raknoth.

Before they could, though, Nelken spoke up himself.

"Al'Drogan."

He didn't have to say more. The grim frustration that showed on his face in the reflected light of their comms said it all.

Drogan didn't say a word—just scooped Nelken over one shoulder and turned to continue on. Brandt likewise took the moment to shift from merely supporting his one-legged raknoth kin to throwing him fully over one shoulder.

They probably hadn't made it more than a hundred yards when the first faint scrabbling sounds echoed their way to them from the direction of the collapsed tunnel entrance.

Great.

Even better, Rachel bit it while she was turning back around, and scraped her hand nice and good trying to catch her fall in the dark.

"How long do you think the debris'll hold him?" Nelken asked Drogan quietly while Johnny helped Rachel back to her feet.

"Not long," Drogan said. His breathing, like that of the other raknoth, was far more stable than theirs. "A minute. Perhaps two."

"Goddamn tunnels," Rachel wheezed out as they pressed on.

"If that part's bothering you," came Johnny's reply between breaths, "now's probably not the time to point out that I'm pretty sure we're under a river."

"Then why the hell would you do it?" she snapped, wincing inwardly as the crushing weight that was apparently already over them settled over her mind as well.

"Well…" More panting. "Doesn't everyone kinda wanna run faster now?"

In the darkness, someone blew out what was either a breathless laugh or a particularly heavy pant.

Rachel wasn't enough of a masochist to keep track of the time on her comm, but it felt like they'd been running for far too long.

Her lungs were on fire, and each step only increased her certainty she was going to die down there, either by the hands of the Kul or under the impossible weight of a tunnel collapse.

She was just finally convincing herself that the tunnel was indeed growing brighter ahead when the woman who'd blown the other entrance confirmed it.

"Almost there."

Thank Christ.

Rachel could see a few heads poking into the tunnel now from the platform ahead, waiting to make sure everyone made it. They nearly had when a furious shriek echoed down the tunnel to them from the way they'd come, clearly no longer cut off by a wall of debris.

Goddamn tunnels.

"Up the stairs!" Nelken shouted as they reached the tunnel's aperture. "Into the trucks!"

"With haste," Drogan added, setting Nelken down on the platform.

He didn't have to tell her twice.

Rachel clambered onto the platform beside Johnny and Lea and headed for the stairs behind Nelken's group, the raknoth bringing up the rear.

Up the stairs. Through the hall.

Outside, several trucks were already lined and loaded, idling as they waited for their commander.

"Go!" Nelken shouted. "70 West! Columbus if we're separated!"

The lead trucks pulled away while the last few waited to fill their remaining spaces.

Nelken's directions, coupled with the sight of the trucks departing put a pause in Rachel's step.

Jarek. Michael.

"Wait."

She had to leave something.

"Not the best time for waiting, Rache," Johnny said.

Another shriek echoed after them, emphasizing his point.

She ignored both, already busy at work sketching out a hurried pair of glyphs on one of the entryway columns using the blood from her own scraped palm.

One more damn thing she'd never tried before. But it had to work.

"Rachel Cross," Drogan said, quiet urgency in his voice.

"Move your ass, Cross!" Nelken added from his seat in the rearmost Humvee.

"Get to the trucks," Rachel snapped at the others still hovering around her.

Then she planted her hand to her blood glyphs and closed her eyes, focusing on the thought of Jarek as completely as she could. She bent close, opened herself to the energy, and began speaking.

It was only a few seconds—she didn't have time for more—but she still expected to find Johnny, Lea, and Drogan loaded and ready to roll when she turned.

Instead, they were waiting for her with grim determination on their faces.

"Let's go!" Rachel snapped. "Stubborn bastards..."

Any retort they might've made was killed in inception by the blood-thirsty howl from the station.

Not an echo. The Kul was coming.

The four of them scrambled into the back of Nelken's open-top Humvee. The soldier at the wheel gunned it. Tires squealed, and they rocketed forward just as the hellacious mantis came bursting through the station's glass-paneled doors hard enough to tear them from their hinges.

Johnny started to raise his rifle. Then, when it became apparent they were clear of the Kul's reach and his injured legs, Johnny settled for flipping the mantis his middle finger instead.

"Classy," Lea said between pants, shaking her head. "Real classy."

Rachel just slumped bonelessly into her awkward position in the Humvee bed, leaning against more than sitting on the seat between Lea and Drogan, too tired to do anything about it but groan.

"There, there…" Johnny patted her head. "We're all safe and sound for *at least* ten minutes."

Rachel was tempted to overcome her exhaustion just long enough to give the redhead a good staff jab where it counted.

Before she could, an ear-piercing squawk tore through the blissful quiet somewhere above, far too loud and vicious to have come from any earthly bird.

She snapped her eyes open and glared at Johnny. "You were saying?"

Johnny was scanning the sky with a troubled look on his face. "You think I woulda learned by now, right?"

Beside them, Drogan pointed back the way they'd come from. "Kul'Ahgo."

"That's what that thing was called?" Rachel asked, scrambling to sit up.

Drogan shook his head. "That was Kul'Shimo. *This* is Kul'Ahgo."

Lea's whisper of, "Oh my god…" didn't exactly inspire confidence. And when Rachel came upright on the seat and caught sight of the monstrosity soaring toward them, she kind of wished she'd just stayed down.

To say it was bird-like seemed too mild a descriptor for the viciously long talons and the obscenely thick musculature evident around its wings and neck, even at a distance. The gleaming razor edges at the front of its wings didn't help either, nor did the long, spear-like beak, or the crimson eyes burning just behind it.

"Can't catch a break," Johnny muttered. "Might as well catch a beak."

Rachel looked at him.

"What?" He gave a little shrug and moved into position to take aim with his rifle from the back of the Humvee. "Would you rather I shit myself every time this happens?"

He took his first shots, eliciting another squawk from Ahgo, who banked off to the left as their Humvee rumbled onto a bridge and under the partial cover of more yellow steel arches.

That cover, it turned out, was even more partial than Rachel thought.

"Do not let his wings touch us," Drogan said, standing to a ready combat stance beside her as Ahgo came out of his bank and veered around to approach the bridge side-on.

Rachel didn't have time to ask how the giant bird-thing would manage such a feat before Ahgo soared straight into the side of the bridge.

Steel beams gave way to razor-sharp wings with a chorus of sharp cracks. The Kul flew on, angled and ready to give their Humvee the same treatment.

Rachel pointed her staff and blasted the thing with as much telekinetic force as she could quickly muster.

Kul'Ahgo wavered, but it wasn't enough.

Then Drogan blurred past her and caught Ahgo in the throat with a flying kick.

The Kul jerked off course, the wing meant for them tearing a deep gouge in the bridge just behind their vehicle. Ahgo smashed into the opposite side of the bridge, warping the steel arch outward.

Drogan, having just kicked a sharp-winged wrecking ball, hit the pavement hard enough to crack it.

"Get him in!" Nelken barked up front.

Johnny leapt out of the slowing Humvee to rush to Drogan's aid.

Lea moved to join, but Drogan was already scrambling to his feet by the time Johnny reached him.

The two jumped back into the vehicle, and the driver hit the gas as Kul'Ahgo began to shake himself off and return to the task of getting them on the wing.

The Kul dove back through the gaps in the girders with an agility that was startling for a creature of his size. Stretched above the water, he threw his razor-tipped wings out and took flight, angling around to come after them as their Humvee cleared the end of the bridge.

"Get us in that tunnel, Williams!" Nelken shouted.

Judging from the engine's roar of protest, Williams was already coaxing every bit of speed he could out of the poor vehicle.

A quick glance back at the rapidly approaching Kul confirmed it was going to be a close one at best.

Johnny opened fire, but Ahgo wasn't so easily deterred.

Rachel pointed her staff, readying the energy for another strike, waiting until the last possible moment.

One more second, and—

Blue sky cut to dark concrete overhead, and Rachel began to release her hold on the gathered energy.

They'd made it.

She started to let out a relieved breath then jumped as Ahgo smashed into the tunnel entrance after them.

Hunks of concrete tore from the ceiling and walls and thundered to the ground. The Humvee engine roared. Ahgo gave a high shriek and bounded after them in a string of low, powerful leaps, partially gliding on his half-folded wings.

"You don't happen to have more charges planted up your sleeve, do ya?" Johnny yelled up to Nelken.

The apprehension in Nelken's expression as he looked past them to the charging Kul was all the answer any of them needed.

"Right," Johnny said, turning back to his shooting. "Looks like you're up then, Lady Zeu—Agh!"

Johnny rolled on top of Lea just in time to avoid taking Ahgo's lunging beak-thrust straight to the chest. The point of the Kul's beak punched through the empty seat like tissue paper beside him. Then Drogan grabbed Ahgo by the chitinous beak and punched the Kul square in the side of the head.

Ahgo staggered and, losing pace with the Humvee, swept his beak in a wide, last-ditch attack. Rachel reached out, too late to stop it.

Strong hands yanked her down, Ahgo's beak whistled by, missing her head by inches, and they all hit the floor in a tangled pile of limbs.

"Rache?"

She looked up from Drogan's chest, where she'd somehow landed, to find Johnny watching her from his pillow of Lea's hip.

"Not to be that guy, but I think we're all gonna die if you don't drop the roof on this fucker."

"You can do it, Rachel," Lea said.

"I believe in you, Rachel Cross," Drogan added.

Johnny and Rachel both glanced at him in surprise.

His crimson gaze shifted back and forth between them. "Is that not what humans say in hopeless situations?"

Johnny closed his eyes in a pained expression and shook his head.

Rachel just found a humorless grin tugging across her mouth as she took up her staff and stood to face the avian Kul who was quickly regaining his former pace.

Johnny propped himself on the back of the Humvee and resumed fire while Rachel dialed out her cloaking pendant and began to grasp the enormity of her task.

"Well I'm just learning all kinds of new lessons today," she muttered, climbing onto the rear-facing seats.

Standing tall with a steadying hand on the roll bar, she raised her staff overhead until it lightly grazed along the tunnel's flat ceiling, jumping and skipping roughly in her tight grip. She closed her eyes, refusing to think about how much power she was about to tap, about the risk of catching them in the fallout, or about anything other than burying Ahgo more thoroughly than even a Kul could hope to survive.

Instead, she sank into her extended senses, casting her will out through the tip of her staff, gathering more energy. And more. More than her body knew what to do with. She bade that body to shut up for a minute, and focused on holding her half-cocked plan so firmly in mind that she almost forgot where she was or why she was doing it.

She remembered all too well, though, when she opened her eyes a hundred yards later and saw the winged monstrosity rushing toward them beneath the long, gently glowing line her staff tip had trailed across the ceiling.

Energy screamed through her body, nearly blinding her, demanding to be released before it tore out of her on its own terms.

So Rachel cocked her staff back, thrust it into the ceiling, and let the energy loose with a scream of her own.

A blinding flash and an enormous cracking sound split the tunnel. Rachel hit the body-strewn floor of the Humvee.

No memory of having fallen. No hope of hanging on.

The unfathomable ocean of channeling fatigue crushed down on her, plunging her into darkness.

CHAPTER EIGHT

Jarek was running, but not fast enough. He never would be fast enough. Not to escape the dark shadow of claws and fangs hounding after him on all fours.

Not to reach Rachel.

She was surrounded up ahead. Close enough to see the fear and the grim defeat on her face and yet somehow too impossibly far away to reach, no matter how hard Jarek pushed his gelatinous legs to move. And, all around her, monsters—unspeakable horrors that corralled her onto a tiny island of stone, unperturbed by the lake of fiery lava they marched through to do so.

Jarek lowered his head and charged along the narrow walkway leading him to Rachel's island, doing his best to ignore the pool of red-hot molten rock awaiting him should he fall.

He ran, and he ran—squeezing every last ounce of power he could from his legs.

Hot, wreaking breath on his back confirmed it was not enough.

His heart threatened to evacuate his chest.

No time.

Any moment.

Something sharp and unforgiving caught his calf and yanked.

Ahead, Rachel screamed.

"Sir!" Al cried.

Jarek hit the ground hard, moving too fast and too far off balance to take the fall gracefully.

He couldn't breathe. Diaphragm paralyzed on impact.

The thing behind him yanked again, and then he was on his back, looking straight up into a long muzzle, dripping saliva over a set of vicious looking—

"SIR!"

Jarek snapped awake, adrenaline firing his senses from zero to a hundred as he looked around the ship, expecting to find fangs and crimson eyes coming for him.

There was nothing, save for the flicker of light from the still-playing display screen and the voice of Obi-Wan Kenobi screaming at Anakin Skywalker on low volume, "You were the chosen one! It was said that you woul—"

Jarek silenced the movie with a groggily raised hand.

No rakul. No berserkers.

Just…

"Mikey?"

Michael, ambling drunkenly toward the cockpit, made no sign he'd heard Jarek at all. Something about the way he moved made Jarek's stomach wriggle.

He sat up. "Hey, Mikey, what's up?"

Al spoke through the cabin speakers. "Sir, I don't think Michael's with us at the moment."

What was that supposed to—

Understanding hit Jarek's sleep-stained brain like an electric *Go* switch.

He sprang off the cot to grab Michael, but Al was faster, already stepping Fela into the cockpit doorway to cut Michael off.

Michael didn't even seem to notice at first—not until he bumped into Fela's extended hand.

He grunted and pressed forward again. Al held him gently at arm's length as he continued to seek entry to the cockpit, but there was something off about the whole scene.

"Hey." Jarek laid a hand on Michael's shoulder.

On edge as he already was, Jarek didn't have much trouble ducking the drunken backhand Michael spun around with, nor did he complain when Al stepped in to loop Fela's arms through Michael's pits from behind and catch him in a gentle headlock.

Michael squirmed against Al's hold, and Jarek got his first good look at the younger man's face.

He was completely expressionless, his struggles more that of a frustrated, disoriented drunkard than a rage-touched furor victim.

It was like he was sleepwalking.

Al held Michael fast as Jarek stepped closer.

He snapped his fingers and gave Michael's cheeks a pair of light smacks. "Mikey! Hey! C'mon, dude, snap out of it."

For a brief second, Michael almost seemed to see Jarek through the haze of whatever gripped him. Then it was back to the drunken struggling.

"Dammit. Any ideas what the hell this is, Mr. Robot?"

"A few hypotheses, sir," Al said, still holding Michael in place with Fela. "Most of which place this thoroughly outside our ability to control."

"Yeah. Was kinda worried you'd say that." He frowned at Michael's expressionless exertions. "You don't think I went too far with the whole strangling thing, do you?"

"I would argue that brain damage falls well within the category of things we cannot control, sir. But no, I don't think that's it."

"You're such a helpful robot sometimes."

"Would you prefer I go back to standby in the corner, sir?"

"Just..." Jarek looked around the room and back at Michael, who, while certainly not at ease, wasn't actually struggling all that hard. "Just hold on a second. I'll get the rope."

Five minutes later, Jarek sat on the cot, suited back up with Fela and watching Michael rock around in the recliner, protesting his new bindings with a string of quiet, discontented murmurs.

"Guess the ship was a good call, huh?"

"Your wisdom, as always, is awe-inspiring, sir. Though I will point out that this still could have ended badly had certain parties not been standing sentry."

Jarek bobbed his head in agreement, half-lost in thoughts of Rachel and rakul and lakes of lava. "Yeah... You did good Mr. Robot. Thank you."

"Happy to be of service, sir."

Jarek turned his attention back to Michael's waning struggles. "You think he was trying to broadcast our position or something?"

"That seems feasible enough, assuming this is indeed the doing of the rakul and not some coincidentally-timed parasomnia."

"Easy with the fancy words, buddy. You're gonna make me miss Pryce."

"I've already been missing him, sir. If I'm to be stuck without Net access, at least I could have a chance at titillating conversation. No offense intended, sir."

"Offense taken, dick-bot."

"Clearly I spoke too soon. Eloquence in motion, sir."

Jarek half-smiled, but it didn't last long as he watched Michael's blank expression.

He'd have been lying if he said he hadn't been missing Pryce too. And Drogan. And Lea. Nelken. The Enochians.

Rachel.

He closed his eyes, resisting the fear that tried to rise up from the darkness inside. The same darkness that had spawned his nightmare.

Yes. He missed them all—would have given a considerable amount to have his friends with him here to help decide how to handle all of this. But they weren't here.

This was on him, and if he couldn't figure out a solution to Michael's problem, their group cohesion out here, dismal as it already was, was going to get a lot worse.

After another ten minutes of weak, discontented struggling, Michael went still. Jarek watched silently for a few minutes, wondering if it was an indication that he might be able to wake the younger man now.

He was just about to get up and try when Michael's eyelids fluttered open.

For a couple seconds, Michael looked uncertainly around the cabin as if he was trying to establish where he was and what he was doing there. Then his eyes settled on his bindings and took in Jarek watching him.

Michael visibly swallowed. "Not just a dream, then?"

Jarek shook his head.

Michael nodded slowly, his eyes somewhere far away as he turned that information over.

"I can't stay with the group," he finally said.

"C'mon, Mikey. Don't go there. We don't even know what that was yet."

Michael gave him a patronized look. "I think we have a pretty good guess. That's two times in the past twenty-four hours I could have blown everything for us."

Jarek tried to keep his expression light as tense memories of the passing horde and his tactical strangling act flashed through his mind, whispering that Michael had a damn good point.

"Hey, Al and I have it under control." He gestured at Michael's bindings. "Nothing we can't handle with a bit of rope and some forethought. Unless... I almost don't wanna ask, but... you don't think they can tell where you are, do you?"

Michael gave a helpless shrug. "I have no idea. I don't think so, but... If Rachel was here..."

Hearing Michael say the words, the tightness in Jarek's chest took on a deep ache. Hopelessness crashed down on his brave façade, abrupt and nearly overwhelming. Michael didn't seem to notice the shift, too wrapped up in his own thoughts.

That was fine by him.

"She always made it sound like she thought the stuff I saw was all one-way," Michael continued. "Like I was a receiver but couldn't broadcast myself."

Jarek nodded. They'd been over this before, and he suddenly wanted little more than to settle this and move on. "Sounds like we're all good, then."

"You don't know that. And even if it were that simple,"—Michael held up his bound hands—"you think Mosen and the rest of them are going to sign off on traveling with a guy who needs to be tied up to keep himself from betraying everyone?"

That was a resounding *hell no*, but…

"Who said Mosen and the rest of them have to know?"

"Jarek, I don't think—"

"You wanna know what I think, Mikey? I think we've all lost too many people for ten lifetimes. I think I'll be damned if anyone else is getting left behind. It's only a couple more days. We'll crash in the ship, keep you secured during sleeping hours." Jarek leaned over and laid a hand on Michael's shoulder. "We're getting to that rally point together, and then we're gonna figure out how to fix this thing."

Michael let out an airy gush that could've been a sound of exasperation, strife, or even relief. Maybe all of the above.

They sat in silence for a while, lost in their own thoughts.

"There's something else," Michael finally said.

Jarek blew out his own huff of laughter. "There always is, isn't there?"

Michael didn't seem to share in his amusement. He kept his eyes fixed on the bulkhead, looking like he didn't really want to say whatever was on his mind. "That thing just now… I'm pretty sure that was Gada on the other end."

Jarek straightened at the name, resisting the urge to reach for the shoulder that still ached anytime he exerted himself too much. The shoulder Kul'Gada had torn almost clean through on the tail end of the blow that had sheered his old Whacker.

"What makes you say that?"

Michael thought about it and shook his head. "I can't really put it into words. Just something about the… I don't know, the feel of the presence or something. It's hard to explain. But something's telling me it was Gada out there, and that he was looking specifically for me." He swallowed. "And that he's really pissed."

That much, at least, made sense.

They'd nearly taken Gada down when he'd arrived on Earth ahead of his brethren. *Had* taken him down, actually. The vicious bastard had only gotten away because he'd run for it while they'd been busy ending his last-minute reinforcement, Kul'Armin.

Regardless of the extensive devastation that fighting had wreaked on Earth's combined human and raknoth forces, Jarek couldn't imagine the situation had earned Gada any points with his elder Kuls.

Plus, Gada had also realized his influence over Michael when they'd confronted him in the Himalayas.

The pieces all fit. The question was whether there was anything to be done about it.

"We beat him once, Mikey. We'll do it again."

They felt like empty words, and Michael didn't look overly convinced by them, but it was all he could think to say.

"We just need to find our people," he added. "Once we've regrouped…"

He wasn't exactly sure how to finish that statement without more empty words.

Michael didn't seem to expect him to.

"Just promise me something," Michael said after another lengthy silence.

Jarek met his eyes, listening.

"If something goes wrong," Michael said slowly. "If things get… out of hand. Promise me you'll stop me if it means saving the group. Promise I won't have to live with anyone's lives on my conscience."

Jarek hesitated, jaw tight.

Michael's eyes were imploring. "Jarek."

He wouldn't be able to keep that kind of promise if it came down to it. He was sure of it.

Saying the words, on the other hand…

"I promise, Mikey."

Michael searched his face, weighing his words, and finally nodded and settled back into the recliner.

Jarek stayed awake for a long while after Michael had fallen back asleep, in part because he wanted to make sure Michael wouldn't slip straight back into zombie sabotage mode, but also because sleep hardly seemed an option with all the questions and half-formed plans racing through his mind.

There was no getting around it, it wasn't going to be smooth sailing for the next few days. Maybe not after that, either. Still, Jarek had meant what he'd said to Michael about making this work.

Until the rakul themselves came crashing down on their heads, Jarek wasn't about to let anyone tell him he couldn't take it upon himself to keep Michael safe.

But what if this *wasn't* just a one-way issue for them to take precautions against?

He didn't want to think it, but there it was, staring him in the face as he sat against the bulkhead, wondering the worst.

What if it was only a matter of time before the rakul tracked Michael straight to them?

CHAPTER NINE

When Rachel woke, it was to light jostling and a sweeping wind that made the warmth of her pillow all the more alluring by contrast. She wrapped her arms tight around herself and nestled into the warmth, wanting nothing more than to enjoy it for a few moments longer.

Then she remembered.

Kul'Shimo. Kul'Ahgo.

The tunnel.

She snapped her eyes open, looking frantically around, half-expecting to find Kul'Ahgo soaring down on her.

All she found was Lea's concerned face hovering over hers. Her pillow, she realized, was Lea's leg.

Rachel tried to sit up and groaned. "What happened?"

"What happened," came Johnny's voice from the direction of her feet, "is that you kicked rakul-league ass back there."

Rachel looked around and saw they were still in the back of the Humvee, with her strewn across the back seat, head on Lea's lap, feet on Johnny's. Drogan, back in his sandy-haired human guise, sat on the floor against the tailgate.

Johnny gave her a grin and patted her leg. "I'm not even sure Hal could have pulled that shit off. Well played, lady."

"The tunnel—"

"Came down like a charm," Johnny said.

"And by 'like a charm,' he means 'almost killed us all,'" Lea said. Then, realizing what she'd just said, she quickly added, "Not that—I mean, it was amazing work, Rachel. You definitely saved our lives back there."

"She most certainly did," Nelken called from up front, leaning back long enough to give Rachel a somber nod. "It's good to have you back, Cross."

"Yeah, always a fun time," Rachel said, then she frowned and turned back to the others. "What about Kul'Ahgo?"

Johnny pursed his lips and looked expectantly at Drogan.

"I am hesitant to simply assume Kul'Ahgo perished in your collapse," Drogan said. "But," he added with the faintest traces of a satisfied smile, "if he did survive, he will likely require extensive excavation, at the very least."

Rachel blew out a breath and laid her head back on Lea's leg. "Well, that's something then." She shook her head. "I can't believe he followed us into that tunnel. All he had to do was wait for us on the other side. We would've been fucked."

Drogan tilted his head in acknowledgment. "Too long have the rakul lived in a position of utter dominance. They have forgotten what it is to fear death. It is perhaps our greatest advantage in this fight."

Huge advantage. Clearly.

She reached to scratch an itch on her nose and realized then that her scraped palm was miraculously cleaned and healed, just like new. Which was weird. Unless…

She looked at Drogan. "Did you feed on me?"

He shook his head. "I only tended to your wound."

"And then we skipped your turn and he fed on me," Johnny said. "Something about not wanting to weaken you," he added, with air quotes. Then, at a mumble, "We'll just weaken ol' Captain Flame Head instead."

"It was but a taste," Drogan grumbled.

Lea's hand came to rest on the top of Rachel's head, warm and gentle. "You should get some more rest for now, Rache. I can't imagine how much you need it after all that. We're safe for now."

Safe.

Rachel was pretty sure that was an ambitious choice of words. But Lea's invitation to rest called to her like siren song all the same. She felt hollow, her body little more than an aching husk after having played conduit to what she was certain had been more energy than she'd ever channeled before.

Just a little nap, maybe. Then she could figure out everything else. Where they were headed next. How they were going to find—

Panic trilled through her chest as she had a horrible realization. "The others. Hal. Elise."

"It's okay," Lea said. "The rest of the Enochians are all in the convoy ahead of us."

Rachel sat up, turning her confused look to Johnny. "Where's the ship?"

Johnny's expression had soured. "Well, we grabbed our stuff and turned off the cloak. And then Brandt took it to lead any would-be pursuit on a bit of a detour while we fled the scene."

If Johnny's expression was sour, Drogan's was pure lemons.

"I should have accompanied him, at the very least."

The tailgate, Rachel noticed, was dented where the raknoth gripped it.

"We've been over this," Lea said. "We need you here in case they find us anyway, and it didn't make sense to send more than one with the ship."

"Drogan volunteered to be our decoy rabbit first," Johnny said to Rachel. "And quite bravely, I might add. But Brandt pointed out that he's faster if it comes to running on foot and that..." Johnny's gaze dropped to the floor, suddenly somber. "And that he's already lost his clan anyways, and that Drogan should stay to protect his people while he still can."

Rachel looked to Drogan for any further thoughts, but the raknoth just stared sullenly at the wheel well opposite him.

"Right," Rachel said slowly, unsure whether it was wise to even try to reassure the clearly surly raknoth. "Wait, how long have I been out? Where are we?"

"About five hours," Lea said, consulting her comm.

"And about one hour west of that Columbus place," Johnny added.

"What?!" Rachel was halfway to her feet almost before she knew it. "Stop!" she called at the driver—Williams, was it? "Stop the car, Williams!"

Williams looked to Nelken, who spoke a command into his comm and nodded to the driver.

Rachel mantled the side of the Humvee and hit the grassy shoulder of the highway just as the vehicle crawled to a halt. Voices followed after her, surprised and concerned, but she barely registered what they said—could barely connect a single thought through the boiling pit of apprehension in her core.

Columbus.

That was all the further she'd made it with her instructions to Jarek. 70 West to Colombus.

Assuming he even managed to find her message. Or that the enchantment had even worked. Or that—

Someone laid a hand on her shoulder. Lea.

"What is it, Rache?"

Too much. That's what it was. Too much for her to even formulate into words right now, apparently.

"Michael?" Lea asked. "Jarek?"

Rachel nodded, cursing the growing ache in her throat.

Pittsburgh was supposed to have been the solution to their problems—the pivotal point where they were all going to rally and figure out how to make their stand together. And now…

They hadn't even made it to their allies' door before the rakul had blown that plan wide open. And now they were on the run with nowhere to go, no hope of finding their people.

No hope of finding Michael and Jarek.

"We have to go back," she said quietly.

Lea looked at her like she knew she had to tell Rachel no but couldn't quite bring herself to.

The soft thunk of a car door closing drew their attention to Nelken, shuffling over by cane—no doubt to do the job Lea couldn't.

"You're leaving them behind," Rachel said as he drew up to them.

Nelken's face was a mask of careful control. "We're in an impossible position here, Rachel."

"Which is bullshit for you're leaving them behind."

Nelken let out a sigh and tapped the earth with his cane, thinking before he spoke again. "What would happen if we tried to stay where they might find us back in Pittsburgh?" he finally asked.

Rachel clenched her fists and dropped his gaze, refusing to give him the answer they both knew was true.

The rakul would come for them in greater numbers than before, and they would all die.

"We could have gone looking for them," Rachel said.

Nelken nodded his agreement. "And we still can. But we've got a good hundred men and women here looking to us to survive. Roaming aimlessly around the countryside isn't the way to see that they do. If we want half a prayer of making it through this, they need walls to defend. We see to it that the people with us are secure, then we can see about finding the rest of them."

Rachel wanted to argue—wanted to tell him that this was Jarek and Michael (and god knew how many more) they were talking about and that neither hell, high water, or the goddamned rakul should keep them from roaming the streets, screaming their names.

But that was crazy talk, and she knew it no matter how badly her heart wanted to deny it. Still, she needed something more.

So she turned to Lea. "You're okay with this? With going to find a new hidey-hole when your mom could be walking into Pittsburgh looking for you?"

The hurt on Lea's face made Rachel immediately regret her words, but Lea set her jaw and nodded. "Wandering around trying to find our people is only going to get more of them killed. And finding them isn't going to do us any good anyway without a secure place to bring them. We just learned that lesson pretty clearly. This is the right move, no matter how badly you might want to think we're giving up on the people we love."

Rachel winced. "Lea, I didn't mean to—"

"It's fine," Lea said, though she refused to meet Rachel's eyes as she did so.

Dammit. This wasn't helping anything.

"Where are you going, then?" Rachel asked Nelken.

Nelken frowned back at the Humvee before answering. "Colorado, we're thinking."

Back in the Humvee, Johnny, who'd been surreptitiously hunkered down, perked up at Nelken's attention.

"Are you guys talking about Cheyenne?" he called.

He said something to Drogan, who nodded, and then he hopped out and hurried over to join them.

"So we're all in agreement then? Next stop Cheyenne Mountain?"

"We're thinking on it," Nelkin said, looking decidedly less excited about the fact than the Enochian did.

"What's at Cheyenne Mountain?" Rachel asked.

"Only the coolest mountain bunker on Earth." Johnny shook his head. "Sweet Alpha, I swear I learned more about your planet watching documentaries than you people learned living here."

"Cheyenne was Johnny's idea if you can't tell," Lea added, looking slightly less upset now, if not quite amused.

"Hey," Johnny said, "you tell me a better place on this continent to batten down the hatches and get our shit together while Hal and Elise sort their stuff out."

For a second, Rachel's mind flashed to her home village of Unity, and to her and Michael's dad, John. That had been a safe place in her mind, once upon a time. But she couldn't even think about going there now, for the same reasons she hadn't been able to when they'd first fled HQ.

The rakul would've rolled over Unity in the blink of an eye. She couldn't risk leading them there.

What they needed was a real fortress. A place like this Cheyenne, apparently.

The look on Nelken's face made it clear enough what he thought about hiding under a mountain waiting for a miracle, but Rachel swore she could see the moment the weight of his people's safety settled back on his shoulders, pushing his skepticism down to the realm of irrelevance.

"I might not call it a good plan," Nelken said, "but it's the best one we've got." He turned to Rachel. "Can you get behind that?"

She thought about Jarek and Michael out there fighting for survival—quite possibly fighting their way to Pittsburgh, expecting to find her. Pittsburgh, where, for all she knew, the rakul could be lying in wait.

The thought of walking away from that—of leaving them to wander aimlessly around at best or, at worst, to walk straight into a rakul trap...

She couldn't stand it.

But she'd made a promise to the Enochians as well. A promise to keep them safe, no matter what, until they were able to take care of themselves and, if the universe decided to be generous for once, to take care of their persistent rakul problem as well.

On top of that, Nelken and Lea weren't wrong about the wisdom of getting what people they could to safety before gallivanting off to scour untold amounts of countryside for a couple small groups that could be anywhere by now.

A couple days. Dammit all, it was a rough pill to swallow, but a couple days to get to Colorado, and then she could come back for Michael and Jarek when doing so would only mean her neck and not the entirety of the known surviving Resistance.

It would have to do. But she still couldn't just leave without a trace.

"I need to leave a message for them," she finally said.

Nelken traded a concerned look with Lea.

"We wanted to do the same thing, Rachel, but it's not safe. If one of the rakul found it..."

"I'm not talking about leaving a hand-written note, here," Rachel said. "I've got other methods. I already left one back at the station telling them to head west on I-70"—she winced—"for Colombus, which I apparently already missed."

Nelken's eyes had gone a bit wide. "You what?"

"It's okay," Rachel said quickly. "Only Jarek will be able to activate it." She frowned down at her feet. "I think."

It only then hit her that she was probably just as guilty as Nelken, if not more so, of leaving their allies high and dry. She'd only thought of Jarek and Michael. Should anyone else arrive in Pittsburgh looking to rendezvous, her glyphs would be of little to no use to them.

Part of her diligently reminded herself that it wasn't like she'd exactly had time to consider contingencies and plan accordingly with Kul'Shimo scuttling after them.

The rest just felt worse than it already had.

"I didn't really have time to think about it," she added. "I just..." She shifted uneasily, looking back to the east. "It's kind of crazy to even expect they'd ever manage to find it, but I just had to do something. I couldn't..."

"I understand," Nelken said. His gaze remained distant for a beat, his expression hesitant, then he seemed to come to some decision and focused on Rachel. "And if you're sure it's safe to leave another, I trust you."

Nelken gave Johnny and Lea a meaningful look and turned to start limping his way back to the Humvee.

"Convoy's back on the road in five minutes," he called without looking back.

Rachel watched him go, an odd mix of worry, guilt, and gratitude swirling in her stomach. Then she scooped a rock up from the thick grass and scanned her surroundings.

Trees. Fields of wild grass. A crumbling wooden house in the distance. Her mind turned with thoughts of hiding spots and signs and secret messages.

"Drogan?" she called, her gaze settling on the line of trees that partially obscured the adjacent field. "I think I could use a hand making some stumps."

CHAPTER TEN

It was by some combination of Jarek's theatrics, Michael's boy-scout-like innocence, Chambers' wily charms, and maybe just a sprinkle of good fortune that their dysfunctional little platoon managed to reach Pittsburgh after three incident-free days and nights. Unless Mosen's growing suspicion and the group's growing unease were to be counted as incidents, that was.

At least Michael hadn't fallen prey to the sleepwalk shuffle again, which kind of seemed like both a win and a slap in the face. A win because it added to the hope that the event in the ship the other night had been a fluke. A slap in the face because it made their non-negligible efforts to keep sleeping Michael separated from the group without arousing suspicion seem like a big, fat, and borderline risky waste of time.

Either way, Jarek counted his blessings that morning as the light of dawn arrived on the dilapidated outskirts of the Steel City. The warm and fuzzies tapered off quickly enough, though, when he reminded himself that, outside of a week-old and cut-off message about meeting near *the old pigskin field where men were forged in steel*, they had no real idea what to expect here.

At least they had a decent general area to start with.

Less encouraging was the fact that the first few bridges they passed were severely out of commission, to put it lightly. Luckily, it wasn't the wide blue waters of the Monongahela River they needed to cross, but those of the Allegheny, still ahead of them to the west.

Still, the downed bridges weren't a great sign.

"Kind of ironic for a place that's also called the City of Bridges, isn't it, sir?"

Al's quiet joke in his ear wasn't enough to cut through the apprehension that had been constricting steadily tighter around his lungs with each passing mile since dawn.

This was it.

She'd be here.

Or she wouldn't.

"Perhaps the subtleties of irony still elude me, sir," Al added.

They didn't, and they both knew it. Al was just trying to alleviate some of the tension he could read in the tightness of Jarek's body and the no-doubt-troubled swirling of his neural activity.

"I'm just a tad on edge here, buddy," Jarek whispered behind his faceplate anyway, quietly enough to keep the comment between the two of them in the packed SUV.

"Right, sir. Apologies."

Jarek said nothing, focusing on the road and on taming his rampant hopes.

The drive into the heart of the city, while plenty tense in their silent SUV, was mercifully uneventful. They passed a third downed bridge opposite a run-down campus that an equally run-down sign hailed as Duquesne University.

The sight of the next bridge intact marginally lightened the weight in Jarek's stomach, only for the one after that to ruin it.

The bridge that Al indicated on his helmet display map as Fort Pitt Bridge, while mostly intact, had clearly seen some kind of action. The pale yellow girders on the eastern side of the bridge bulged out at one point as if something large and unforgiving had slammed into them. Jarek zoomed the view on his helmet display and saw that several more girders on the western side had been sheared clean through.

He was thinking about calling for a convoy halt to go have a closer look when Mosen's voice crackled in his ear.

"Fort Duquesne Bridge is out up here. We're going to have to skirt up the Allegheny to the next one."

"Got it," he replied. Then, to himself once the short-range channel was closed, "And to think I used to like bridges…"

"Shall I cross over with the ship and have a closer look while you try the next bridge, sir?"

It was more of a loaded question than it should have been.

The group had already spent an impressive amount of the past twenty-four hours arguing as to exactly how Operation Find the Needle in the Monster-Strewn Haystack was going to play out—"the group," of course, largely coming down to Mosen and Jarek as it always seemed to in the end.

Unlike most of their past arguments, though, which had felt to Jarek more like Mosen's abstract dick-measuring contests than necessary conversations, this one had been tricky by merit of the fact that they were all genuinely uncertain as to the best course of action.

They couldn't help but think their going into the city at daylight felt like throwing caution to the wind and begging for a slap right in the giblets. Especially at the end of a long journey spent traveling cautiously at night. But if their allies were here—and most likely bunkered into a neat hidey-hole—what were the chances of finding them at night?

Similarly, entering the city with the entire convoy instead of sending in a small scouting force seemed like yet another bid for disaster. But after they'd all spent a few weeks on the road catastrophically failing to regroup with the allies they'd originally been driven away from, who could really feel like splitting up was the safe thing to do?

So they'd said cheers to getting caught with their pants down and decided to bite the bullet. And Jarek didn't see any strong reason, aside from Mosen's inevitable irritation, to depart from that mentality now that they were this far.

"Go for it, buddy. Just be careful."

"Rich, sir, coming from you," Al said as the ship gently accelerated into view overhead and glided quietly past the rest of the convoy and over the Allegheny River beside the thrice-cursed Fort Duquesne Bridge.

Jarek could almost see the cold rage frosting over Mosen's face three vehicles ahead as he caught sight of the rogue ship breaking free from the pack. The fact that he maintained radio silence felt ominous, but Jarek was certain he'd hear exactly what Mosen thought about the maneuver once they were face to face.

He couldn't bring himself to care much. The apprehension at what they might find ahead only grew in Jarek's chest with each passing mile, ratcheting tighter with each unusable bridge they passed.

Finally, they found what they were looking for.

Veterans Bridge, declared the sign at the mouth of the blessedly intact stretch of concrete and steel.

"There's another spot of irony for you, Mr. Robot," Jarek murmured.

He waited, expecting Al to point out that the congruence was more coincidence or quirky happenstance than actual irony, but his friend was uncharacteristically silent.

He was about to start worrying when Al finally spoke.

"Sir…"

His tone was like a lump of lead in Jarek's gut.

"What is it?"

"I think I found where they were hiding."

***

"WHAT THE HELL was your make-believe friend thinking, flying off like that?"

Despite the implied anger in his words, Mosen's tone wasn't nearly as venomous as usual as he stood beside Jarek, surveying the scene before them.

The old hotel lobby had been through hell.

Jarek could have said the same about the rest of the buildings in the city, of course. But not like this. This lobby, unless Jarek completely missed his mark, had been ravaged by a lot more than time and neglect.

The walls, smashed and riddled with bullet holes and smears of red and oddly orange blood in several sections, seemed to agree with him.

Rachel had been here.

He didn't know how he knew it. Maybe it was a lingering scent in the air or some complex alignment of his surroundings he hadn't even consciously registered.

Maybe it was just naïve, blind hope making a desperate push to convert desire into reality.

Whether or not he was deluding himself about Rachel, though, Jarek was at least pretty sure a furor horde had recently been through the area. That, or a fairly large and extremely pissed-off army.

Outside the lobby, past the van that had been violently overturned and likewise smeared with goopy orangish fluids, several bodies dotted the half-filled parking lot. The state of them—bloodied, emaciated, some only half-dressed—marked them fairly convincingly as fallen members of a passing horde. One that looked to have been marched long and hard.

It wasn't hard to follow where they'd been headed from the hotel. A gruesome path of smeared blood, torn clothes, smashed cars, and spent casings trailed across the parking lot to the adjacent building, clear as a giant neon sign that read *The Shit Went Down Right Here.*

After an unproductive minute of poking around the lobby that seemed to have been ground zero, Jarek and Michael set off for the building across the lot, trailed by a less-than-chipper Mosen.

"What are you thinking?" Michael asked quietly.

What Jarek was thinking was that he was about to lose his shit.

Each little bloody memento of the fight they'd missed chipped at the faint ember of hope in his chest, threatening to smother it completely.

What he was thinking was that, if he didn't find something to alleviate the cold panic clawing its way around his heart, he was going to either start flipping cars or hit the pavement dead with his first cardiac event.

But none of that seemed very Jarek-ly, so he just kept his mouth shut and tried to keep his stomach steady as they approached the door that had clearly fallen victim to either a speeding semi-truck or a Kul.

Visions of Rachel's trampled, bloody body pressed in at his mind's eye from all directions, thinning the air in his lungs.

"Sir?"

He hadn't meant to stop walking, but now that he had, he couldn't seem to start again.

Jarek had seen carnage—had seen the worst and the ugliest of what post-Catastrophe humanity had to offer to one another. He'd hewn more violent men to equally violent endings than he could count.

None of it had ever hit him like this.

"Sir?"

He couldn't breathe.

"Jarek?" Michael's voice, concerned, uncertain.

Couldn't breathe. Couldn't—

"Sir!"

Al's voice was like the crack of a starting pistol.

Jarek was running before he even knew it.

"Slater!" Mosen barked after him.

He kept running.

Through the demolished hole in the side of the building, following the path of orange ichor and gouged flooring. Two hops down an old escalator flight.

His heart leapt at the sight of the rail station and its partially collapsed tunnel. He couldn't say why, couldn't bother to think it through in that moment, could only give in to the desperate, frantic energy pushing his legs on.

"Slater!" Mosen's call echoed down the tunnel.

He kept running, Fela's optical sensors illuminating the way in the dark.

"Sir..." Al said. "Might I—"

"She came this way, Al," was all he said. "I can feel it."

Al didn't question it, didn't point out that neither one of them had any logical basis for that assumption. He just let Jarek run.

The tunnel might've been a mile long.

Jarek covered the distance in less than a minute.

Onto the platform. Up the stairs. Out the wrecked opening where the shattered glass doors had once stood. Onto the street.

Where?

Where next?

He spun around, scanning the surrounding area for something, anything, breathing with a heaviness that was only partly related to his frantic sprint.

"Oil marks, sir," Al said. "Recent, from the look and smell. Perhaps they had vehicles waiting."

Jarek followed the line of the road with his eyes until his gaze alighted on Fort Pitt Bridge in the distance, a clear shot from here with its oddly warped and severed girders.

Had they fled across that bridge?

Had the rakul followed them?

"Sir!" Al cried. "There, sir, the pillar at four o'clock."

Jarek spun, the frantic fire roaring back to full blaze in his chest.

There, drawn in what looked unsettlingly like blood.

A glyph?

No, he realized with a sinking feeling as he drew closer. Not like any other he'd ever seen Rachel make, at least.

But what then?

The design was simple enough—a circle circumscribed within a triangle. And, at its center, a single hurried, bloody letter.

J.

He reached slowly for the bloody mark, breath held, heart thundering.

His fingers touched smooth concrete, and the symbol came alive with sound and light that made Jarek's hand recoil out of surprise.

For a long second, he stared dumbly at the mark. The *glyph*, apparently.

Then he caught it. The faintest trace of a scent. Blood and fear and gunpowder, all swirling over the inexorable pull of something else—something a primal part of him recognized as belonging to Rachel.

Jarek plunged his palm against the glyph.

Noise erupted from the eerily glowing lines of blood, shouts and rumbling engines immersing him like surround sound. And the warmth…

He gasped, and for a second, he could have sworn it was not a concrete pillar that met his fingers, but Rachel's own hand.

"Jarek?" she whispered, so real and present he couldn't help but wonder if he wasn't hallucinating. "Jarek… If you're hearing this, go west on seventy. To Colombus. I'm with Nelken and Drogan and the Enochians and—"

A shriek split the air, shriveling Jarek's insides.

"Shit," she gasped. "I have to move. West, Jarek. Don't stop. Don't give up. Please."

The glyph dimmed, Rachel's warmth receding until nothing remained but cool concrete and the hollow silence of the abandoned street.

"No," Jarek heard himself whisper. "No, no…"

He pulled his hand away from the glyph and pressed it again, waiting, praying for her to come back to him. Again, and again.

Nothing.

Just a benign, bloody mark on the concrete.

"No…"

He squeezed the sides of the column until his armored fingers dug into the concrete. He fell to his knees, pleading with the unforgiving pillar in a series of incoherent, sputtering starts and stops.

She'd been here. Right here.

He'd felt her, breathed her in as surely as if she'd been here in his arms.

He clung to the pillar, eyes closed, desperately trying to hold on to every facet of the memory before it could fade.

West.

Seventy to Colombus.

Rachel. Warm and strong and telling him to keep going, to not stop.

He played it all back in his head, over and over again, until—

"Slater!" Mosen's unmistakable bark. "What the fuck was…"

It was only when Mosen paused that it really occurred to Jarek he was still on his knees, hugging a concrete column like it was his last tie to the world.

He probably looked bat-shit insane to the soldiers trickling out of the station after Mosen, like he was finally having himself the good ol' fashioned mental breakdown half of them probably already thought he was due for.

"What is it?" Mosen asked, closer now, his voice slightly less acidic, if not quite worried.

"Jarek?" Michael's voice this time from farther back, thick with concern.

Jarek was bracing himself to look up and meet them, to explain what had just happened—bracing himself to deal with Mosen's inevitable, scornful disbelief—when a horrible fear whispered insidiously in his ear.

"Al…" he said quietly.

"I heard her, sir," Al said softly. "Felt her, too. It was real."

It was all Jarek needed to hear.

He rose, composing himself.

Rachel was still out there, fighting alongside their friends. He was sure of it—wouldn't be swayed from the thought again.

And they were going to find her.

"What gives, Slater?" Mosen asked as he drew up to the column and leaned in to inspect the glyph. "You didn't finally crack on us, did you?"

Jarek opened his faceplate with a thought and turned to face him and the rest of the approaching soldiers with dire seriousness.

"We have to go west."

CHAPTER ELEVEN

After twenty-four hours of scattered napping, Johnny's emphatic assurances that this was "going to be awesome," and the steady roiling of guilty apprehension in Rachel's gut, Nelken announced they were drawing close to Cheyenne Mountain.

Rachel turned in time to see the faded road sign that corroborated his claim whiz by.

The drive hadn't been a thrilling one. A few short episodes with blown tires. One longer stop to scavenge a couple functioning solar trucks to replace their larger diesel that had finally run dry. All inevitable facts of traveling anywhere by ground vehicles these days.

They'd driven non-stop, or as close as they could, swapping drivers from their ample pool of anxious passengers to keep everyone as fresh as could be expected, all things considered.

For the past twenty-four hours, the entire convoy had seemed to radiate a kind of weary but desperate eagerness to reach the promised safety of this Cheyenne Mountain bunker. It was as if they'd all been holding a collective breath since Pittsburgh, one they'd agreed couldn't be let out until they were safely locked behind Johnny's so-called "ridiculously thick" bunker door.

Now, though, as they turned onto Norad Road and began the final shallow climb toward their hopeful new haven, a new apprehension—one that spoke of failing at the finish line—seemed to take hold of everyone.

Everyone except Johnny, at least, who looked kind of like a kid on his way to an amusement park.

Dense clusters of stubby green bushes scattered the gradual slope of the arid mountainside, pushing in on the road and partially obscuring their view of what looked to be abandoned housing developments off to the right.

"Honestly," Johnny broke the silence as if he'd been speaking all along, "I don't know why you guys didn't hole up here sooner. It's gonna be perf..."

He trailed off and turned as they rounded a sweeping corner and Nelken began to slow the vehicle.

"Looks like someone else had similar thoughts about this place," said Pryce, who'd come to join their vehicle during one of the convoy's stops.

Following their gaze, Rachel saw what he meant.

Crop fields stretched out ahead to the left side of the road, clearly abandoned, but maybe not for more than a few years by Rachel's admittedly inexperienced guess. They definitely hadn't been sitting like that since the Catastrophe, though, which meant, at some point, someone had been here.

When she looked up at Nelken, though, it wasn't the fields he was staring at as they crawled forward, but the road ahead, which she noticed now was blocked on the shoulders for a couple feet by piles of metal scraps that formed a low wall. A pair of heavy chains completed the obstacle, spanned over the road, suspended from one scrap wall to the next and adorned by a sign that read, simply *Keep Out*.

What caught her eye most of all, though, were the two spots that were heavily patched as if someone had performed amateur road repairs.

Or buried something.

She reached out instinctively, dialing out her cloak's range almost without thought, and—

"Stop!" she cried.

Nelken complied with an immediateness that said he'd been about to do so anyway and turned to face her. "Can you feel what's under that pavement?"

Rachel closed her eyes and focused more thoroughly, taking in the small, light metal casings, the odiferous silicon of integrated circuitry, the rampant potential energy of whatever was stored within.

"Something with electronics and a lot of chemical energy," she finally said. "Maybe mines, but..."

She dialed her cloak out to the max and swept her senses past the pair ten yards ahead of them and farther up to check for more devices.

A voice was rumbling something at the edge of her awareness, too far away for her to catch. She drew back to her physical senses and opened her eyes to a grim-looking Nelken.

"What?"

"He asked if there were more ahead," Lea said.

Rachel shook her head. "Not that I can feel yet, at least. If we clear that scrap and drive around those two, I can keep sweeping..."

Her unspoken *as we go* died off in her throat as she took in the others' looks.

If they still wanted to go, those looks said.

Nelken glanced worriedly back at the convoy drawing up to a halt behind them now, clearly conflicted. He shifted his attention back to Rachel and the others in the rear of the Humvee, looking like he couldn't quite decide if he wanted their input or not.

"I say we go for it," Johnny said. "We've come this far, we've got shit for backup plans, and, for all we know, we could have the Incredible Invisible Insect and his evil pals coming down on us at any minute." He pointed up the shallow mountainside. "Judging from everything else, this place is probably deserted, and even if it's not—"

Nelken held up a hand. "Thank you, Mr. Wingard. You make valid points." He looked around the group. "Do the rest of you have anything to add? Al'Drogan? Lea?"

Lea looked at Johnny and traded a heavy look with Rachel before turning back to Nelken. "We came here for a good reason, and we didn't do it for free. I say there's no way we turn back now."

"If the base should turn out to be held by hostile humans," Drogan said, already looking bored with the discussion, "then Rachel Cross and I will have no trouble dealing with them, especially not with the assistance of Nans Grohl and Sorba. I would welcome the return to such a comfortable fight."

Johnny cleared his throat. "Yep. No one mind the trained alien soldier. I'll just sit over here and watch you guys shake your magic sticks and whatnot."

Rachel, on the other hand, wasn't quite sure whether to feel flattered or disturbed that she was the current top pick for Drogan's bruiser squad.

Pryce shot an uneasy glance at Drogan. "I agree we might as well make the best of it now that we're here, but I think we already have quite enough past and future violence without adding a hostile takeover into the mix. Maybe we can try talking if there's someone in there."

Nelken took this all in silently.

When Rachel looked up, he was watching her expectantly.

"And you, Rachel?"

Rachel raised her eyebrows, having thought it was evident enough by her offer to sweep the path ahead.

"I might have left my brother and my—and Jarek to die by coming here. I'm seeing this thing through. I'll blow the door down if I have to."

Johnny cocked his head. "Ehh, I think you underestimate how solid this door is."

"I dropped a mountain on Kul'Ahgo," Rachel said. "And I can pick locks with my mind."

Johnny thought about that and gave her a conciliatory nod. "Okay. Even odds, then."

Rachel turned back to Nelken. "I'm going in there. I'm making damn sure we have a safe place for our people. And then I'm gonna go find the rest of mine."

Nelken gave her a serious nod, though his mouth might have twitched with the hint of a grin. "Well said." He let out a long breath, thinking. "Very well. Lea, Williams, would you mind staying here to guide our people around the road hazards?"

They both gave affirmatives and hopped out of the vehicle.

"And Al'Drogan," Nelken added, "would you be so kind as to—"

But Drogan had already rolled out of the back and was prowling up to the left side of the ramshackle wall. It only came up to his chest in most places and could have easily been circumvented on foot by way of the steep but scalable hill beside it. Clearly, the wall had mostly been intended to funnel persistent vehicular traffic onto their buried gifts.

Luckily, a pile of heavy scraps wasn't much of an obstacle for a raknoth to relocate. Drogan actually seemed to enjoy the chance to flaunt his strength as he pitched tires, doors, metal sheets, and even a rusted car frame across the road and down the mountainside.

Rachel climbed up to take the passenger seat Williams had vacated while Nelken busied himself speaking commands to the convoy over the comms' short-range bands. Soon enough, Drogan rejoined them, and they were off.

Drogan had cleared enough of a gap for their vehicles to maneuver comfortably around the vicinity of the buried explosives, but Nelken kept their progression to a crawl anyway, giving Rachel plenty of time to quest out with her senses in all directions, waiting vigilantly for the first sign of any impending threat.

Even immersed in her extended senses, Rachel couldn't quite ignore the dead silence that hung over the place.

They made it nearly half a mile before Rachel caught wind of another pair of explosives where the road formed a sharp branch that split north and south. These two were buried far more discreetly. No obvious wall giveaway. Much better road patch jobs. It was almost as if someone had buried the first ones as a kind of confidence booster to lure intruders into a false sense of security.

Nelken waited until the convoy had caught up and asked Pryce and Johnny to stand sentinel in front of the second hazard.

Another slow quarter mile and a wide, looping roundabout later, they were looking at a sprawling parking lot that Rachel assumed meant they were drawing close to the bunker's entrance.

"How are we looking?" Nelken asked beside her.

Rachel shifted her attention back to her extended senses for several seconds. "Still good, I think."

"I wouldn't be upset if you refrained from the 'I thinks' for now," he said as they waited for the rest of the convoy to catch up.

Rachel refrained from pointing out that they were talking about her sniffing out landmines with her mind here and that there was going to be some uncertainty intrinsic to the task. Instead, she busied herself studying the scene ahead.

The lots were roughly half-full, and, at a glance, the vehicles all looked long-abandoned.

That was a good sign, at least.

A few buildings stretched along the mountain-side of the bigger parking lot. Old administrative or utility structures, Rachel guessed from the looks of them. The actual bunker entrance, though, she couldn't spot until Nelken started forward again and they rounded the last bit of bushy hillside foliage.

It was actually kind of anti-climactic. An unimposing, arched tunnel jutting out of the eastern side of the mountain, well behind the line of the buildings and the lots. No giant spiked gates or looming battlements or anything.

Rachel nearly jumped when a low growl rumbled right behind her.

"Drogan," she gasped, trading a wide-eyed look with a slightly startled-looking Nelken. "Jesus. What is it?"

The raknoth just pointed in the direction of the distant tunnel entrance. "Take a closer look."

She traded another look with Nelken, and they both tapped on their comms' zoom displays.

A few two-fingered swipe gestures later, she was looking at—

"Holy shit," she whispered.

"That's… unexpected," Nelken agreed.

The image was grainy, relying on digital zooming rather than optical, but the subject on the display was unmistakable.

There, above the plain arch of the tunnel entrance, hung a raknoth in full, scaly battle mode, badly scorched from head to toe and, from the looks of it, long dead.

The three of them stared in silence until the rest of the convoy was caught up and waiting behind them.

The vehicle shifted with the weight of someone climbing aboard, then Johnny spoke in a quiet voice behind.

"What's going on, guys—Oh…"

Rachel finally turned to see Johnny was leaning forward to see her comm display.

"Holy shit," he said, utterly lacking any of his usual cheer.

"That's what I said," Rachel said numbly.

She couldn't help but think about Alton Parker. Couldn't help but remind herself that, a couple weeks ago, she'd been so pissed at him and the rest of the raknoth for their role in her mom's death that some part of her might've actually felt some kind of sick satisfaction at the grisly display ahead of them.

That thought alone nearly made her feel more ill than the sight itself already had.

She leaned over the passenger-side door, thinking for a moment she might actually lose it and hurl, but the feeling slowly receded, breath by deep breath.

Footsteps behind the vehicle drew her attention, and she saw Lea, Pryce, and Williams returning to take their places in the Humvee. Johnny brought them up to speed with his own zoomed comm while the convoy idled behind, waiting for Nelken to make the next move.

"This doesn't change the plan," Lea said. "Right?"

By way of reply, Drogan hopped out of the Humvee and started trudging in the direction of the entrance tunnel.

"Guess not," Johnny mumbled, hopping out after him.

Rachel looked to Nelken, her brain apparently still too stunned to form its own opinion on what to think about that.

"Al'Drogan," Nelken said quietly, knowing the raknoth would hear him.

Drogan, however, didn't even pause. Not until Nelken spoke again, this time with a less authoritative tone.

"Drogan… Just give us a moment to park the convoy. We'll go in together."

Drogan didn't quite look back, but he gave a faint nod and went to sit on a rock just off the road, Johnny trailing after him with his rifle handy.

Nelken led the convoy to the eastern end of the first parking lot. By his instructions, their people staggered their parking spots among the copious abandoned vehicles enough that the congregation might not be noticed by, say, a passing rakul ship. Not that any of them would be holding their breaths for it to work if that happened.

With impressive efficiency, Nelken picked a dozen men to accompany them into the tunnel and split the remaining ninety or so into teams to either check the surrounding buildings or stick with the vehicles and protect their non-combatants. Their two raknoth, Nan'Grohl and Nan'Sorba, Nelken made sure were posted with the Enochians.

That done, he gestured to Rachel, Lea, and his chosen twelve, and they all started toward the entrance tunnel.

Johnny and Drogan appeared at Rachel's side as they crept across the quiet lot, both looking ready for a fight.

The silence pressed in on them with viscous pressure, convincing Rachel some manner of explosion was not only imminent but inevitable.

With each passing step, she found herself worrying less and less about mines and more and more about someone—or several *someones*, rather—popping out from the mountain rocks above with rifles, rockets, and god knew what else they'd used to leave a raknoth looking like that.

There were a few murmurs and whispers from the group as they drew close enough to get a better look at the charred trophy, but Nelken quickly silenced the chatter with a glare and a sharp chop of his hand.

Fifty feet out from the tunnel, Rachel saw something she hadn't noticed on the comm zoom earlier—a pair of words scrawled across the inner surface of the tunnel wall near the entrance.

Drogan let out a soft growl before Rachel was close enough to finally make out what it said.

Vamps Beware.

"Easy, buddy," Johnny murmured to Drogan. "If these guys are still in there, I'm guessing now's not the time to let out the red eyes."

Easy wasn't the word Rachel would have used to describe the look on Drogan's face after that, but he at least stopped growling as they paused outside the entryway.

The tunnel was more spacious than Rachel had gauged from a distance—probably wide enough to squeeze two of their trucks side by side, and tall enough to leave at least a few feet of clearance. She wondered if they shouldn't have driven into the tunnel. The presence of the landmines outside said probably not. And, when she spotted what looked like tracks for a thick security door near the mouth of the tunnel, that uneasy train of thought only strengthened.

At least until they'd been hoofing it in the dark with comms and flashlights for what felt like half an hour.

To be fair, she might've been letting the claustrophobic pressure of yet another underground tunnel and the looming possibility of unfriendlies ahead warp her estimations. In reality, half an hour had probably been more like eight or nine minutes and no more than half a mile.

"Goddamn tunnels," she muttered under her breath.

Drogan glanced at her but was too preoccupied to take any amusement from her discomfort.

Understandable enough, given the well-done raknoth hanging at the entrance of the tunnel they were currently padding blindly into.

Rachel tried to cling to the hope that they were about to march in to find a perfectly viable mountain bunker with no headaches whatsoever—human or otherwise.

An easy win, for once.

Was that so much to ask for?

The further they progressed, the more she was afraid it might be.

For one thing, Drogan seemed to be sniffing entirely too much for a long-abandoned tunnel. For another, Rachel couldn't quite push away the feeling that the tunnel had been deliberately made to look like it was in a state of disuse.

Maybe it was claustrophobic paranoia, plain and simple.

Or maybe it was the fact that, despite the dusty silence of the tunnel, there was electricity flowing through one of the cables along the top of the ceiling's arch. It was faint, barely a trickle, but it was there in her senses—a veritable lit match in otherwise perfect darkness.

When she told Nelken in a low murmur, he pointed out in an equally quiet voice that it might just be a residual system running on some automated, renewable power supply. Cameras, or something along those lines. But he seemed less than convinced by his own words. His telling her to keep an eye out was more than a little redundant.

Finally, their lights touched on a bend in the tunnel ahead. And there, at the elbow of the curve, was what looked to be Johnny's ridiculously thick door.

"There it is," Johnny whispered.

Gear and weapons rustled and clicked as their already tense group moved into full-on twitchy trigger finger territory.

Rachel honed in on the door as they approached, anticipatory combat adrenaline warring with her rational mind for control of her focus. As she began to take in the immense door with her extended senses, though, tingling apprehension shifted to hesitant hopefulness.

Because, while those faintly trickling power lines did bore into the concrete above the door and disappear to the edge of her cloak, the door itself and its archaic button panel were completely without power, as far as her senses could tell.

Was it possible?

Could this place really be on ice, just waiting for them with a subsystem or two still puttering along?

Nelken looked around at their assembled group, seeming to wonder the same thing.

"I think the door's dead," Rachel said to him, speaking quietly part out of residual fear someone might be watching and part out of some deep hesitance to disrupt the silence of the old concrete and stone.

"Might be a good sign," he said. "Still…"

He stepped forward and pressed each of the three old buttons beside the door, waiting for a healthy ten count between each button.

A long silence stretched.

Slowly, and looking like he was positive it was an exercise in futility, Nelken raised his cane, gave the door three hard raps, and tried the buttons again.

"Right, then…" he finally said after another long wait. He looked back at the group. "Any ideas?" He focused on Rachel. "Think you could poke around and see—"

"Already on it," Rachel said, sliding her eyes closed and sinking deeper into her extended senses.

She drifted through multiple feet of steel door and brushed across a seemingly endless number of mechanical tidbits behind.

"Ahh," came Johnny's voice, sounding distant as focused as she was. "And so we come to it. Mountain-dropping woman versus nuke-stopping door."

Rachel opened her eyes and her mouth to tell him she was about to drop a mountain of boots in his ass if he didn't let her work.

An electronic click sounded somewhere above the door and reverberated down the tunnel before she could.

They all tensed.

Weapons raising. Eyes darting, seeking incoming threats.

A hidden speaker?

If so, what were they waiting fo—

Another series of clicks, these ones mechanical.

Two sections of the flat wall ten feet to either side of the door fell open with a harsh pair of cracks, and suddenly the group was staring down a pair of heavy Gatling guns that looked like they belonged on a giant mech from some old Japanese cartoon.

As one, the guns spun up with a whirring promise of devastation to come.

"Who are you people?" a strong voice crackled from an unseen speaker above the door. "And what the fuck are you doing here?"

CHAPTER TWELVE

To say there'd been dissension in the ranks over the past few days would've been putting it lightly. Hell, even blind ol' Aunty Sally could've seen it'd been there ever since Jarek and his Resistance pals had linked up with the Mosenites. Still, all the naysaying and leers and worse from the past couple weeks paled in comparison to the tension that had fallen over their group after Pittsburgh.

Suffice it to say, Mosen was none too convinced by Jarek's arcane intel. And after Jarek's panic-attack-induced runaway act, he wasn't exactly pulling the punches. Jarek had already lost count of the number of times the incessant a-hole had pointed out to the group that Jarek might well have cracked—that they'd found him on his knees with his arms wrapped around a concrete pillar for Christ's sake.

Jarek had to admit he hadn't done himself any favors falling apart in front of the group like that. Then again, it wasn't like he'd had much say in the matter. He hadn't chosen to lose his shit.

Even Al had been rattled, for the love of god.

Whether or not anyone believed Jarek's story about the arcane voice message, though, at least there'd been plenty of tangible evidence that someone had left town in a hurry.

The scene at the hotel lobby. The tracks of the flight through the rail tunnel. The clear signs of the rumble on the bridge. And, beyond that, the mysteriously collapsed tunnel, which Jarek had a strong gut feeling had been either the handiwork of Nelken's planning or the casualty of Rachel's power.

Mosen, of course, had pointed out that, even if it had been their allies—and he highly doubted Rachel could have pulled such a feat off, by the way—they damn well still could've collapsed the tunnel on themselves, and they might all still be buried down there.

Jarek had returned that Mosen was a miserable twit and that, unless he wanted to set up a work zone and start digging, their only real play was to assume their allies had made it and to hit the road after them. Unless, of course, they wanted to sit around and see if any rakul came back to visit.

Needless to say, the westward drive was not shaping up to be a cheery one. Add in the fact that they'd been forced to travel in plain daylight to vacate the scene of the crime, not to mention to keep an eye out for their allies, and they were all about a match strike away from an explosion.

Assuming the rakul didn't drop down on their heads to finish the job first.

At least their being on the road kept Jarek and Mosen in separate vehicles. Then again, that arrangement came with its own set of downsides, not the least of which being that Jarek wasn't around to defend himself while Mosen no doubt slandered his good name—and, more importantly, his sanity—to his faithful Mosenites.

That was frustrating enough.

What was truly disturbing, though, was that, after an afternoon and evening spent unsuccessfully sweeping the shell of Columbus for any sign of their allies, even some of the Resistance troops seemed to be wondering if Mosen wasn't right about him.

Maybe he *had* cracked, Jarek could all but hear them thinking. Maybe there'd been no message at all. Maybe *he'd* scrawled that symbol on the pillar with his own blood, and now they were all headed west on the word of a man who'd, after all, already been talking to the voice in his head for over a decade now.

That Al corroborated Jarek's story was all but meaningless. He was Jarek's AI, after all, and most of the Resistance troops had never really gotten comfortable with the idea of an actual digital being, capable of its own free thought.

And so Jarek seemed to have found his way to a slippery slope.

One day of this bullshit, and he was already starting to understand how infuriatingly helpless it was when people started pointing the crazy finger. Once that bad boy started flying, it almost became a self-fulfilling prophecy. Crazy or not, you would be soon enough.

"Forget about them," Michael said that night while he bedded down beside Chambers in the musty motel room they'd claimed. "Once we find Rachel and Nelken and everyone else tomorrow, they'll forget all about this. They'll probably be thanking you."

"I wouldn't hold my breath on the thank you bit," Chambers said.

"Took the words right outta my mouth," Jarek said quietly.

He didn't say the other part—that he was worried Michael's *once* should be swapped for a big fat *if.*

If we find them tomorrow.

It was ludicrous to expect to simply bump into Rachel and the others after only a few hours of looking. Especially based on no more detailed directions than a highway and a city.

It didn't help that he had no way of knowing how long ago Rachel had left that message in Pittsburgh. The bodies of the fallen horde members in the parking lot had looked and smelled plenty ripe enough to think they'd missed the action by at least a couple days, but that wasn't exactly a precise indicator.

All things considered, it was unrealistic to expect the search to pay off overnight.

Of course, that didn't really alleviate the worried weight on his chest, no matter how many times he repeated the logic to himself. And it sure as hell hadn't kept the hounds at bay that evening as Mosen had led loud discussions cataloging and highlighting the day's extensive failures.

"Hey, at least we've got a mission, here," Chambers said as she went to work binding Michael's wrists for the night. "Better than scurrying aimlessly from hole to hole every night just to survive."

"Yeah," Michael added, staring pointedly at his wrist bindings and lifting his legs so Jarek could slip another around his ankles. "That'd just be crazy."

Despite everything, that still got a smile out of Jarek.

Chambers chuckled too.

Jarek finished securing the binding and patted Michael's leg. "We wouldn't want that, would we?"

Chambers pulled Michael's blanket up for him, covering their handiwork. Should anyone manage to sneak a peek through the blinders, Michael would by all appearances look to be lying there like a good little boy and definitely not tied up next to Chambers and Jarek for god knew why.

Then again, the way his public perception was faring right now, Jarek probably could've just explained something as trivial as a few bindings away with nothing more than a sultry wink and an assurance that they really didn't want to know.

Given that they'd all spent the past twenty-four hours awake, driving to Pittsburgh, exploring the ruins, and then making their roundabout way to this dismal Columbus motel, most of their people were probably too tired to be snooping around anyway. He wasn't even sure anyone had noticed the three of them sneaking off to their own room.

At this point, he was too tired to care.

And, apparently, too worried to sleep, he soon found out, laying on the floor at Michael's bedside, shifting in a way that had nothing to do with any shortcoming in Fela's supportive interior.

Alone in the darkness but for the breathing of his sleeping roommates, the memory of Rachel's voice whispered in his head, over and over.

West, Jarek. Don't give up. Don't stop. Please.

He had to find her. It was the only thing he knew for sure anymore.

Everything else—seeing these men and women to safety, marshaling their forces, taking on the rakul…

If he could just find Rachel, Jarek was convinced the rest of it would fall into place.

She was already with Nelken and Drogan and a good chunk of the Resistance forces. They had the Enochians. The Enochians who, Maker willing, might yet prove to be the nuclear option they'd been looking for since Kul'Gada had been an ugly twinkle on their horizon.

Finding Rachel meant finding their best hope of surviving this thing. That was what he needed to make the others understand.

The Mosenites certainly didn't care about the rest—that he missed her, needed her. That, without her, he felt like little more than a suit and a sword, hunted, alone, and outclassed.

But survival?

That was the one thing he was sure everyone in this building was interested in.

Together, they were stronger. Together, they'd find the only hope there was to find.

Out here, eventually, they were all going to die.

On and on these thoughts turned, having neither the mercy to abate nor the decency to produce some useful conclusion. When Al wordlessly opted to add a soothing ambient track to the feedback coming through Jarek's earpieces, he resisted the urge to snip at his friend for the coddling.

Al meant well, after all, and if Jarek didn't get some sleep, it was more than his good mood he was putting at risk.

So he sank into the relaxing sounds, focusing on deep breaths as completely as he could manage. It was even in danger of actually working when the sound of Michael's snoring shifted to frustrated grunting and the rustle and bed creaks of subdued struggles.

Jarek opened his eyes and came back to full awareness with a sharp breath.

It figured.

After the day they'd just had, it was probably best to operate under the assumption that Things, as they so stood, had made the collective decision to go on strike where running smoothly was concerned.

He sat up to see that Chambers was already awake and waiting at Michael's side in case he managed to wriggle his way off the bed or out of his bonds.

"You know," Jarek whispered, "you're pretty damn good at all this. Keeping secrets. Flying under the radar. Throwing snark like… frisbies? Rolling with the punches, I guess I'm trying to say."

She propped herself up on one arm to look over at him in the dark. "I'm gonna assume you mean all that as a compliment."

"Sadly, yes."

In the silence, Michael wriggled on.

"Also, snark frisbies?"

Jarek sat up straighter and shrugged in the dark. "I'm tired, okay? I was kinda hoping I might actually get to sleep tonight."

"Yeah, I hear that," Chambers whispered. Then, after another few moments of Michael's zombie-like floundering, she added, "God, this is creepy."

She wasn't wrong, Jarek decided after a silent stretch of staring at Michael's flopping, expressionless features on his in-helmet display.

"Are you really sure this isn't… I don't know, like rakul GPS or something?"

Jarek shook his head. "No. But Rachel and the raknoth never seemed to think it was, and they're the experts."

Not exactly confidence-inspiring, he had to admit.

"Honestly," he added, "if it were, I can't imagine we'd still be breathing right now."

Way more helpful.

"Fair point." She sighed in the dark. "We really need to find them, don't we?"

He gave her a wan smile despite the fact that she couldn't see it in the dark and behind his faceplate.

At least Chambers got it.

"We really do. Just gotta convince the Moseni—"

"Sir! Someone at the door!"

No sooner had Al said it than the door popped open with a splintering crack of old, dry wood. It hit the doorstopper and bounced back only to thud to a halt against a raised hand.

Jarek caught a glint of red eyes, and his stomach sank.

"Well, well," Mosen chided. "Whatever do we have here?"

"You're pissed," Jarek said.

Understatement of the century, clearly.

"I get it, Mosen," he continued, "but this isn't nearly as catastrophic as you think it is."

Mosen paced back and forth, neck muscles tensed and eyes casting glints of red. Finally, he paused and looked around at the audience he'd woken and assembled in the motel lobby by virtue of his racket alone. His gaze settled back on Jarek. "How long have you been covering this up? How many times?"

"Syracuse was the first time," Michael answered before Jarek could. "Tonight was the third."

The onlookers muttered among themselves.

Mosen uncrossed his arms. Flexed and unflexed his fists. "Carver's out. We can't have him with us anymore."

"That's not happening," Jarek said.

Michael swallowed. "Maybe he's right, Jar—"

"It's not happening, Carver," Chambers interrupted at his side.

Michael looked from Chambers to Jarek with an expression that was half-grateful, half-pleading.

Jarek tilted his head at Chambers. "You heard the lady, Mikey. Not happening."

"You two are free to go with him," Mosen said. "If you're going to put the safety of the entire group at risk for one helpless runt, we don't want you, fancy suit"—his cold eyes flicked maliciously to Chambers—"or otherwise."

"This isn't your personal dictatorship," Jarek said. "Michael's an equal part of this group. We all are. An unfortunate accident and a fucked up head don't change that. If anyone should be able to sympathize with that one, it's you, Mosen."

Mosen's lip curled in a soundless snarl that he quickly gained control of and replaced with a frosty glare. "This isn't a charity we're running. We can't help every sad puppy we find."

Jarek gave a humorless laugh. "You do remember they literally call me Soldier of Charity, right?"

"*Called* you, Slater. Past tense. *They* are probably all dead by now, considering what's happening out there. This is survival. You don't have to like it."

"Ah, survival. You know, that's exactly what the guy who gave me the nickname told me, once upon a time."

"Sounds like a smart guy. Maybe you should've listened to him."

"Thought about it," Jarek said. "Cut his head off instead. Took three bullets doing it."

Mosen threw his hands up, his calm expression cracking into a growl. "You think I give a shit? This talking is pointless. Carver goes. End of story."

Jarek shook his head, "We don't toss our own out on the streets for rakul meal time."

"No?" Mosen said. "And what do you call driving around in broad daylight"—he jabbed a finger toward Michael—"with a fucking rakul satellite dish, looking for your girlfriend because the voices in your head say so?"

"That's kind of putting it—"

"And where are they, by the way, Slater?" Mosen snapped, looking around, arms spread wide. "If this hasn't all just been one giant bumblefuck of a goose chase, where the fuck are they?"

Jarek hesitated a second too long, weighing potential answers against the receptions they'd likely find with the not-so-friendly onlookers.

Mosen sneered. "That's what I thought." He looked around at the gathered crowd, which had grown in number since they'd started, and jabbed a finger dramatically in Jarek's direction. "He has no idea what he's doing."

"And you do, Mosen?" Michael asked. "What's your big master plan, here, man?"

"Patching our leaks first, Kul-bait," Mosen said. "After that—"

"Oh, fuck this…" Jarek breathed to himself.

Except apparently not to himself, judging by all the heads that suddenly swiveled his way with surprised expressions.

Fine. That was fine.

He didn't care anymore.

Never mind that the smarmy little shit was relying on straw man sensationalism to make his argument. Never mind that they could have argued back and pointed out quite convincingly that Mosen was even more lost and hopeless than Jarek.

Jarek was done.

Done letting Mosen prance around like he was some big badass who merited fearful respect. Done watching this group cannibalize itself in slow motion.

Done running from what clearly needed to happen if any of them were going to make it through this.

"Okay, Mosen. You're not gonna stop until we see whose is bigger? Fine. Whip it out, big guy. I'll fight you for it."

Mosen eyed him wearily, taken aback. "What are you talking about?"

"Head honcho." Jarek splayed his hands wide. "There can only be one, right? And I know that that there thick skull of yours don't do so good with the words, so fuck it. Let's settle this thing like the damn dirty apes we are. Winner takes the reins."

That sure got the crowd talking.

Mosen gave him a contemptuous sneer through the sea of agitated murmurs and whispers. "Big words coming from a guy in a weaponized exosuit."

Jarek couldn't deny that. So he gave the mental command.

"Are you sure about this, sir?" Al asked.

He looked around at the crowd. To Michael and Chambers. He thought about Rachel and Pryce. The Enochians. The rakul.

Finally, he looked back to Mosen, standing there with arms crossed, barring the way as best he could to the one path Jarek truly believed to be their best hope.

They could do this.

He just had to clear the way, first.

"I'm sure, buddy," he said quietly.

And with the familiar series of clicks, clacks, and whirs, Fela began peeling open for him.

"Please, Mosen," he said more loudly, stepping out of Fela's embrace to face his foe with naught but a thin pair of briefs. "I don't need a fancy suit to kick your ass."

He looked around the room again, conscious of both the cool air and the dozens of eyes currently assaulting his thinly-briefed equipment.

"Just, you know, maybe pants first."

CHAPTER THIRTEEN

If the silence in the mountain tunnel had been tense before, it could have suspended the Golden Gate Bridge now. That was just as well, as far as Rachel was concerned. She needed the empty seconds to will her adrenaline-soaked brain to get its shit together and focus.

She was almost proud of just how damn quickly she'd managed to throw a telekinetic barrier into place. Or would have been, if she weren't so busy splitting her mind to maintain the defense while also reaching out to try to disable the oversized Gatling guns preparing to tear their entire group to bloody ribbons.

It might've been a waste even bothering with the barrier. Judging from the looks of those guns, she'd be on her knees or unconscious in under ten seconds if they decided to open up with her trying to protect the group.

Her own bullet catcher would keep her and those immediately behind her safe. At least until the thing sucked enough heat from the already chilly tunnel air to freeze them to death. Either way, she resisted the urge to shout *Get behind me!* and set off whatever itchy trigger fingers might be watching them.

"Just to be clear," came the voice from the speaker, crackling over the mechanical whir of the ready guns, "this is the part where you answer."

That seemed to unfreeze everyone.

Johnny raised a hand in peace, opening his mouth to say something.

Nelken clamped a hand over Johnny's mouth and faced the speaker that sounded to be somewhere above the door. "We're refugees from the eastern US," he said in his best strong commander voice. "And we're not here for trouble."

"Oh, good," said the voice. "Well, in that case, why don't you go ahead and get the hell out of here? We're not looking for more mouths to feed."

"And what about trained, armed ones looking for secure walls to help defend?"

There was a huff of garbled laughter. "If you didn't notice, we can defend ourselves just fine in here. Now kindly get the f—"

"We've fought the vamps," Nelken said, apparently deciding to shift gears. "And we've won, too. Judging from your decorations outside, I'd think that'd mean something to you. Please, we've come a long way."

With their mysterious trigger man engaged in asking Nelken why it was they were running if they were such prodigious vamp slayers, Rachel felt marginally safer shifting the entirety of her focus to disabling the guns. It was deciding exactly how to accomplish that feat that was giving her pause.

She entertained thoughts of firing pins, bullet-feeding mechanisms, and other moving parts for all of three seconds, but it was too risky, her knowledge too shallow to be sure any of it would work the way she intended.

So instead, she found the cables running to the robotic housings controlling the guns, telekinetically undid the connectors, and yanked them free.

The whirring of the spinning guns began to descend in tone like music to her ears, assuring she'd broken the connection to whoever was in control of the weapons.

She let out a relieved breath.

"—more than just the vamps out here," Nelken was saying. "I know it's hard to believe, but you're not as safe behind this door as you'd like to think. Let us in to talk, and I'll explain everything."

"Look," the speaker said, "I appreciate your struggle, and that all sounds nice and scary, but if you don't quit your babbling and evacuate this tunnel, I will—"

"You'll what?" Rachel called, stepping to Nelken's side. "Gun us all down? Go for it, bunker boy."

Nelken snapped to her with a horrified stare, but she tilted her head at one of the guns, and his horror shifted to uncertainty.

"Don't tempt me, lady," the speaker voice said. "You wouldn't—Hey . . . Hey, what the fuck did you do out there?"

She shot Nelken a quick wink, and his face shifted to an expression that might've been exasperated or pleased. Maybe both.

"I think the door's about to go too," she said. "Wanna let us in before I break your fancy toy? We just wanna talk."

Nelken seemed to give up on trying to be irritated with her bold play and waited quietly beside her.

Silence stretched. Rachel could only hope it meant whoever was on the other side of that speaker was running their request up whatever chain of command might exist in there.

She swept her senses all around them again while they waited, searching for any hidden surprises she might have missed while distracted by the enormous Gatling guns staring them down.

Finally, the speaker voice returned.

"No weapons. No more than three of you. The rest wait at the north portal while we talk."

Rachel traded a look with Nelken.

"Agreed," Nelken said.

After a moment's hesitation, he gestured for Rachel and Drogan to join him then turned to hand off his weapons and address the others.

"You heard him, people. Head back to the entrance. Sit tight. Eyes peeled."

Several looked miffed at being told to sit out while an arcanist and a raknoth accompanied their commander into potential enemy territory, but no one argued.

Johnny looked like a kid who'd just been told he was too short to ride the rides, but he allowed Lea to turn him around by the shoulders and followed obediently after the slowly retreating crowd, head hung low.

Rachel silently wondered at the wisdom of bringing Drogan into the facility that was boasting a dead raknoth as a trophy. It was a risky idea on multiple levels. But, then again, everything about this situation was risky, and if the shit actually hit, it'd take more than a few humans with big guns to take down Drogan.

"What did you do to my guns, lady?" the speaker voice asked as the sounds of their retreating allies faded to distant echoes. "And what's with the staff?"

"Trade secrets," Rachel said. "Explicitly reserved for people who haven't threatened to kill me and my friends in the past five minutes."

The speaker chuckled. "Well shit, at least today's not gonna be another boring day. I think it goes without saying you're gonna need to toss the stick, though."

She shrugged and bent down to slide her staff a good way down the smooth tunnel floor.

"I trust no one's hiding any other weapons?" the speaker asked.

Rachel resisted the urge to make some stupid *I AM the weapon* comment.

No need to put their soon-to-be hosts on edge more than necessary. Better to keep it to themselves that, together, she and Drogan could wreak havoc on their base, weapons or no.

"All clear out here," Nelken said. "Unless you'd like me to leave the cane."

Apparently, that didn't merit a response.

"You see that box by the door?" the speaker asked.

Rachel had noticed the little metal box sitting there, but she hadn't paid it much mind what with the giant guns and everything.

"We see it," Nelken said.

"Open it," the voice said. "And put them on."

Rachel's trap-o-meter started tingling as Drogan started forward to inspect the box. It didn't really look threatening. It was the kind of thing someone might've once kept bread in. She scanned it with her extended senses all the same.

Nothing but a few little pieces of metal. Silver, maybe.

Jewelry?

Drogan stood from the box and confirmed her findings. Three silver pendants hung in his hand—completely ordinary and benign in every way Rachel could sense.

Confused, they each slid one over their heads.

For a long moment, nothing happened.

"Good," the speaker voice said quietly. "Good. Step back, then."

They complied, trading another confused look.

What the hell had that been about?

Before she could wonder about it too much, a series of deep clacks vibrated from the immense bulk of the bunker door, at least ten in total.

With a groan of heavy machinery at work, the enormous door began to swing open. It moved with a ponderous slowness that was agonizing to wait through and yet probably inevitable given how much the door must weigh. The groan of laboring motors grew louder as the door opened to spill out a beam of yellow light that grew steadily wider and wider across the tunnel floor.

Finally, the door swung far enough to grant them line of sight into the space beyond.

Pale, cream-colored walls, spanned by networks of cables and pipes and—

She resisted the urge to flinch as the door swung wider and revealed the gruff, no-nonsense face staring them down from behind the barrel of an assault rifle.

Wider, and there were three more men. All dressed in military fatigues. All pointing weapons at them.

A fifth man stood at the end of the firing line, rifle held ready across his chest but not actively pointing at them. It was this last man who'd been talking to them through the speaker, Rachel was almost sure of it, though she couldn't quite say why.

Maybe it was the look of semi-guarded superiority in his dark eyes as he waited to see their reactions to the surprise firing squad.

Apart from those smug eyes, he wore a beanie cap, sported a dark beard, and generally looked like a guy who might give her reason to punch him at some point down the road.

For now, though, he just watched them until the door came to a jarring halt and the sounds of groaning motors abated.

"Come on in," Beanie Cap called, his voice confirming he had indeed been the speaker. "No sudden movements and so forth."

Rachel traded a look with Nelken and Drogan, and they all walked past the huge door and through the wide doorway, hands held in plain sight.

As soon as they'd crossed the threshold, Beanie reached over to press something on the wall, and the door began its slow, groaning journey to close them in.

Rachel did her best to brush aside the tickle of panic that bubbled up in her chest at the thought of being trapped behind that door. When that failed, she reminded herself that, A, she was an arcanist and perfectly capable of escaping most locked boxes and that, B, she wasn't trapped in here with them so much as they were now trapped in here with her and Drogan.

Or so she hoped.

At any rate, she took heart from Nelken, who strode into the room, head held high, and paused at a non-threatening distance from the firing squad. Drogan, oddly, acted a bit timid.

After a painful wait, the door finally closed behind them with a decisive boom and a series of locking clacks, and Beanie turned from the controls to face them.

"Much as I'd like to trust you good folks," he said, "I'm gonna have to search you before we go any farther."

"We understand," Nelken said, handing his cane to Drogan and spreading his arms wide.

Easy for him to say. He probably wasn't about to get taken to Grope City.

Beanie made quick and efficient work of patting down Nelken, as if the act were routine for him, and moved on to Drogan, who thankfully didn't growl.

The gunmen watched silently—alert, but not overly threatening.

Rachel's stomach wriggled a bit as Beanie finished with Drogan and approached her, but she held his gaze evenly.

To her relief, he was as professional with her pat down as he had been with the men. At least until…

"What's this?"

Rachel mentally braced for the inevitable ass-grab, insisting to herself that she must not punch, no matter where that hand landed. When Beanie tugged on her bullet catcher and battery packs, though, she couldn't keep the heat from spreading to her face at her overly-aggressive assumption about the man's honor.

"Just some old batteries," she said.

He leaned around from behind to show her his skeptical frown. "You just keep batteries on your belt? And what the hell are those etchings supposed to be?"

"It's… personal."

Jesus. She was just on fire today.

"Uh-huh," Beanie said slowly. "Mind if I hold onto this stuff, all the same?"

"I kinda do."

He scrunched his face in an expression that was only mockingly apologetic and went to work trying to pull the gear from her belt.

After a few moments of his awkward fumbling, she sighed, unfastened her belt, and let him take the whole getup.

"Happy?" she asked with a scathing glare as Beanie tucked her things neatly into his vest pockets and returned to his men.

Beanie considered the three of them and shook his head. "Probably as much as I'm gonna be today." He nodded to his men. "Let's head in."

Another impressively thick blast door and an equally impressive wait longer, they were shuttled into a wide, vaguely cavern-esque hallway that, past dozens of crates of supplies, led to yet another door and yet another tunnel.

This tunnel, Rachel was pretty sure, was the beginning of the actual complex. It spanned wide and high, its floors smooth but its walls angling into uneven, rocky features that reminded her they were inside a mountain. Faded white buildings lined the tunnel, each one propped up by dozens of the thickest springs she'd ever seen.

A few unarmed onlookers openly gaped at them, but Rachel didn't get a chance to take in much more before Beanie hustled them up and into the closest of the white buildings. Inside, the building's hallway sort of reminded Rachel of your average hospital or maybe a rather depressing administrative building. Linoleum floor squares. Bland tones.

Beanie and his men funneled them into a plain square room whose contents consisted of nothing more than a metal table with a pair of hard-looking chairs on either side.

It could have been a tiny conference room, but it sure felt like one intended more specifically for interrogations.

Beanie scooted one of the chairs around the table so that it was three on one side and one on the other, then he bade them to sit with their backs facing the door. His men posted up along the wall at his back while he settled into the lone chair opposite Rachel, Nelken, and Drogan.

"So…" Beanie said, propping his rifle up and laying his hands on the tabletop, seemingly more at ease now that they had multiple blast doors between them and the rest of Nelken's men. "We got off to a colorful start." He laid a hand on his chest. "My name's Zach."

Zach watched them expectantly.

"Commander Nelken," Nelken said.

Zach gave a sarcastically impressed head bob. "A commander, huh? So what does that make you two, then?"

Drogan gave an uncharacteristically timid shrug, and when he spoke, his tone was decidedly less regal than usual. "I'm just Derek."

So apparently Drogan could act when the situation called for it.

"And I'm just Rachel," she added. "Nothing special to see here, folks."

Zach considered her. "Nothing special… Hmm. You mind telling me how it is our guns went offline out there, Rachel?"

"You tell me," she said. "I just heard 'em winding down and wanted to pretend I was a badass." She shrugged. "Sue me."

Zach clearly didn't buy it.

"As far as I can tell," he said, "both guns had their cables yanked. Neat trick, unplugging a pair of autocannons that are thirty feet apart behind steel plates"—he spread his hands—"without any of you moving an inch."

Zach watched her like a hawk as he allowed time for his words to sink in, like he was hoping she'd spontaneously crack and spill everything.

She just shrugged, trying to look as helplessly lost as she could. "I don't know what to tell you, man. Did I wanna be a magician when I was a kid? Maybe. But I sure as shit didn't make your big machine gun cables go poof."

"If you don't know what's going on out there," Nelken interjected before Zach could call bullshit, "I think we might have more pressing matters than why your rotary cannons went down."

Zach kept his gaze on Rachel for another long moment before finally sitting back with a sigh and waving a hand in invitation to Nelken.

"Let's have it then, Commander. What is this bright new doomsday you claim to be running from?"

Nelken started and stopped himself a few times before finally settling on a direction. "How much do you know about the raknoth?"

None of the men looked happy.

Zach's grin was violently chilling. "We know how to kill 'em. Don't see what else you'd need to know about a vamp. Get to the point."

"All right, then," Nelken said. "What if I told you the… vamps have bosses they used to answer to. Bosses who are far older and more dangerous than they are. Bosses who aren't too happy that their servants skipped town on them to hide out here on Earth after the Catastrophe."

Zach blew out a humorless laugh, his icy expression taking on a derisive edge. "Ah. So you people come from the alien theory camp..."

Nelken frowned. "I don't kn—"

"Let me save you some breath, commander," Zach said. He gestured to the men behind him. "We here in The Complex don't put much stock in that alien invasion bullshit you people have been bouncing around the Net for the past fifteen years."

Nelken looked uncertain as he pressed on. "The raknoth came here from another planet. We've heard as much from one we captured."

One who just so happened to be sitting right next to them.

"And you might have noticed the Net's down?" Rachel added. "We're pretty sure it's these bosses we have to thank for..."

Normally, Rachel might have ignored the hand Zach raised for silence. But the way he was suddenly trembling with rage gave her pause.

"The vamps," Zach growled, "are servants of hell."

A sick feeling crept into Rachel's gut at the change coming over Zach—the fanatic gleam slipping into his eyes.

"The only master they have is Satan himself," he continued. "You can't trust a single word out of their blood-stained mouths. And if you three hadn't passed the silver test..."

The silver test?

Was that what they thought? That they could spot a raknoth with a goddamn little piece of ordinary silver?

Zach was shaking his head, some of his rage dissipating though he still studied them with narrowed eyes. "You three passed the test, but you sure claim to know a lot about them. I can't help but wonder why that is."

Bogus test or no, Rachel's stomach sank further at the reactions of the men behind Zach.

Distrustful stares. Grips tightening on weapons.

What the hell had they stumbled into here?

Nelken was surveying the men with his neutral commander face.

"How long have you boys been down here? What's the last news you had from outside?"

Zach smiled, and the expression felt several degrees saner than a second ago, as if he'd thrown the blanket back over whatever fanaticism had just fallen momentarily out of hiding.

"You're not a man of faith, are you Commander Nelken?"

Nelken's gaze flicked to Rachel and Drogan before answering. "Maybe not in the conventional sense, but I do have faith."

Zach chewed over Nelken's words for a long handful of seconds, weighing them for god only knew what. Finally, he seemed to come to some conclusion.

"Fine. It's for the Mayor to decide when he gets here anyway."

Something about the way he said it set another batch of the creepies wriggling in Rachel's stomach.

"The Mayor?" Nelken asked, apparently feeling similarly.

Zach waved the question away. "Let's take it from the top for now. You wanna tell us about some fresh slice of hell roaming around out there,"—he raised a hand in invitation—"tell us."

With a hesitant look, Nelken started to recount Kul'Gada's arrival, deliberately avoiding the fact that said arrival had indeed been via alien spaceship. He was just starting to explain the first furor that had hit HQ when Rachel felt it.

A telepathic mind. Just outside the room.

The authoritative clunk of the door handle behind her nearly made her jump.

The door swung open with a mournful creak.

As one, the men all snapped to attention, Zach included, rising from his seat to join the others in planting fist over chest in some manner of salute.

"Mayor Dillard," Zach said, stepping aside to offer up his own seat.

Rachel turned to take in this Mayor.

Tall. Dark hair, slicked back. Strong build. Strong jaw. Everything she would have expected from the magnanimous leader of The Complex.

Except that he was a raknoth.

CHAPTER FOURTEEN

Of all the many, many fights he'd been through in his not-so-long life, Jarek was pretty sure he could count the number of times he'd been truly afraid on his fingers alone.

There'd been his fight with Drogan—the first time he'd ever had the audacity to square off against a raknoth.

There'd been Zar'Golga, whose strength and ferocity—not to mention that ridiculously enormous club—had had Jarek shaking in his suit even after he'd begun acclimating to fighting enemies who could handily outpower Fela.

There'd been taking on Alton Parker with naught but his own squishy meat suit. Squaring off against the monstrosity that was Kul'-Gada. Fleeing that savage, hairless lupine Kul as HQ had fallen.

But, above all else, there'd been Conner.

Facing down his old boss—the leader of the Iron Eagles and arguably the only real role model he'd had in those years—had changed him. But he hadn't had a choice.

Each time he'd been terrified. But each time, it'd been the right thing to do. The only thing to do.

And now, circling warily with Mosen in the poorly-lit motel lobby, he was looking at another one of those times.

It wasn't just that he was afraid for his own life, though that was certainly part of it. He would've been an idiot not to be.

On top of being a generally vicious bastard, and a particularly pissed one at that right now, after years serving his old Overlord, Zar'Golga, and receiving ample doses of the vitamin R for his efforts, Mosen was superhumanly strong and resilient. Not enough so to take a raknoth in an arm-wrestling contest, maybe. But more than enough to take two or three Jareks.

Worse, Mosen didn't look nearly as overconfident as Jarek had been hoping.

They circled one another amid the beams of the onlookers' comm lights and the wider swaths of the camp lights placed around the room. Where Jarek had hoped to see a confident sneer and cocky chest-thumping, he saw only a predatory focus from Mosen as the creepy bastard shook his vitamin-R-infused muscles loose.

An opponent who was not only considerably stronger but also patient, disciplined?

As usual, Jarek probably should've listened to Al. Or at least found a shirt.

"Are we really doing this, people?" Chambers asked the murmuring onlookers. "Big alien monsters hunting us across the country, sweeping up town after town, and we're gonna sit here and watch two grown men whale on each other?"

"This is ridiculous," Michael added. "We should discuss our options. Put it to a vote."

A few of the Resistance folks seemed to agree with the sentiment. Most of the people in the room, though, were ready to see someone bleed.

Much as Jarek had been desiring the chance to give Mosen a good punch or five over the past days, he didn't want this fight. And he sure as hell didn't want it while he was in squishy meat-sack form.

But it was too late.

It was done, and now all that was left was to make sure he won.

Because if he lost, even if Mosen didn't kill him in the process (which was a pretty big if), they could kiss their hopes of finding the others—and, consequently, surviving—goodbye. At least without causing a small civil war.

Despite everything, though—dire stakes and punchable faces and all—Jarek couldn't bring himself to relish the coming violence as he not so long ago might have.

Jesus, was he getting old?

He paused his pacing, cracked his knuckles, and spread his hands wide. "So this is like, to first pin, right?"

Mosen didn't answer—just rushed in like he'd only been waiting for Jarek to say something stupid.

Jarek pivoted clear of the first punch and ducked back from the second.

Mosen stalked warily after him. "Come on, Slater. Where'd all that swagger go?"

"I'm just wondering what happened to the whole *not the face* thing." He frowned from Mosen's hands to his bare feet. "And whether or not you're going to start sprouting claws."

By way of reply, Mosen aimed a sweeping kick at Jarek's head.

Jarek dipped to the outside, planted, and caught Mosen with a hard side-kick in his disturbingly solid ribs.

Mosen's hand snaked down lightning fast and caught Jarek's ankle in a crushing grip before he could pull the kick back.

With little hope of breaking free, and no desire to be bodily wishboned, Jarek launched himself with his planted foot and twisted into an awkward spinning heel kick.

There was a wet smack and the sensation of heel striking what felt more like leather-covered hardwood than a face, then Jarek hit the ground hard on his side.

A growled curse and stomping feet were all the warning he had.

He spun on the ground, kicking semi-blindly, and caught a charging Mosen straight in the hip, halting his momentum dead and nearly causing him to tumble on top of Jarek.

Jarek followed up with his aching heel to Mosen's chest and then rolled to his feet in the moment it bought him.

Squared off again, Jarek saw Mosen's mouth and chin were wet with oddly dark blood, and his eyes were gleaming pale red in the lights.

It was damn creepy.

And the demonically violent grin on his bloody mouth didn't help matters as he lunged for Jarek's throat with both hands.

This time, Jarek didn't shy away.

He went with the grab, sweeping a leg back and twisting at the last moment to deflect Mosen's hands with the armpit of his raised right arm—the same arm whose elbow he drove straight into Mosen's waiting bloody face.

Mosen spat and staggered.

Jarek followed with a knee to the gut and twisted to throw his other elbow into the side of Mosen's head.

They were good strikes. Solid strikes.

Mosen shoved through anyway and nearly knocked Jarek over with a shoulder check that sent him reeling for his balance. He found it just in time to see the fist coming.

No dodging. No blocking. No time.

An idiot. He'd been a damn idiot.

The punch hit like a pneumatic sledgehammer.

Jarek's world exploded in a kaleidoscope of brilliant dancing shapes and spirits.

A distant jostle, and, for a little while, he was alone in his own little universe. The darkness, his addled mind decided, wasn't so bad. At least it was quiet. Except for the ringing. And if it weren't for that damn pain throbbing through everything…

Rhythmic pulses of hot daggers, riding over the deep steady ache of—

A sound.

Something.

"—rek!"

Someone.

Michael.

"JAREK!"

He snapped his eyes open, already moving into a sideways roll out of some deep-seated reflex.

Mosen's bare foot stomped down on the space he'd just vacated with an alarmingly solid thump.

Jarek scrambled to his feet and fell straight back over when the profound spinning in his head failed to settle. He landed on his butt and shuffled a few feet backward in an awkward crabwalk. The room took a few seconds to stop rotating around him, and Mosen's satisfied leer seemed to take too long to resolve into focus.

That wasn't good.

Concussion? Check.

Right along with a broken cheekbone, if the fire on the left side of his face was any indication.

"You don't look so good, Slater," Mosen said, wiping some of the blood from his mouth.

With the utmost effort to avoid letting on just how disoriented he was, Jarek rose to one knee, pointing at Mosen's still-planted stomping foot. "I kinda get the feeling you're not even trying for that pin, man."

Mosen's sneer deepened. "I wonder how many shots like that it'll take to finally shut that goddamn mouth of yours up."

"Eh…" Jarek touched at the point of impact, winced, and took the risk of standing to wobbly feet. "It's a moot point. Al would haunt your ass with the playbacks of my greatest hits until you came to join me in hell."

"Dutifully, sir," Al said through Fela's speakers.

The exosuit was standing at the ready in a way that made Jarek think Al was debating stepping in to end this thing before anyone got seriously hurt. Or more seriously, at least.

Mosen was shaking his head. "Fancy toys and a smart mouth are never going to make you a leader, Slater. I don't give a shit what my father says. You don't deserve their respect. And you're sure as hell not getting mine."

That sneer…

So contemptuous it almost seemed to border on insincere. And speaking of Alaric…

Maybe it was just the concussion talking, but suddenly it all came into focus with a clarity that was ironic, given the current state of his head.

Underneath it all—the anger, the violence, the relentless pursuit of control and dominance…

Mosen was afraid.

Maybe not of him. Maybe not even of dying.

But afraid all the same.

"What are you gonna do, Mosen? When you get what you want and realize it didn't work?"

Mosen started to lean forward as if to attack, then settled his weight back, deciding against it, watching Jarek warily. "What are you talking about?"

It was a reach, but given how sturdily Mosen had handled Jarek's beating so far, it seemed better than dancing around waiting for him to land another good punch.

So Jarek shrugged and started in on Mosen's less resilient half. "You're afraid, man. I get it. I would be to in your situation."

"What the fuck are you babbling about now?" Mosen said, starting to circle Jarek.

"Life's been hard," Jarek said, matching Mosen's footwork. "Enslaved by Golga—"

"I wasn't a slave."

"—forced to fight your friends, hate your own fathe—"

Mosen threw a testing jab, which Jarek dipped woozily back from.

"You don't know what you're talking about," Mosen growled.

"Oh, I know a little bit…"

Jarek deflected a second jab—

"I know what it's like to have no one."

—hopped back to avoid the followup.

"I know what it is to clock out and tell yourself there's nothing but the fight—nothing but survival—until you can't even imagine you deserve a place with the rest of humanity anymore."

"Shut up," Mosen hissed. "You don't know me."

Jarek tensed his jaw, not at all enjoying what came next. "I know that he made you kill your own mother."

Mosen sprang forward with a growl, and Jarek caught him with another momentum-killing hip kick that left him staggering back with a string of curses.

"I did what I had to!" he shouted. "You wouldn't have lasted two days in my place, Slater."

"Maybe not. Maybe so. Maybe I'd have lived to know the fear of years lived under a monster's thumb."

Jarek twisted to the outside of a half-hearted punch from Mosen and continued circling.

"Maybe I'd come to know what it is to be afraid that that monster is the closest fucked up thing to family I'd ever have again. That I'd already killed or alienated everyone else who'd ever care."

"Shut up and fight, you bastard!"

"Maybe I'd do anything just to claim an ounce of control. Over my situation. Over my group. Just to try to convince myself I could ever be good enough to be worth a damn to anyone ever agai—"

A savage cry erupted from Mosen's throat, and he charged Jarek like a wild animal.

Jarek leapt to meet his tackle, catching him around the torso with his legs, locking his feet together behind Mosen's back and pulling him close with his arms.

Mosen drove into him, unperturbed.

They hit the ground hard enough to shock Jarek's diaphragm into sputtering inaction. He held on tight, legs locked above Mosen's hips, controlling his position as he scrambled to pull away from Jarek and into an adequate pummeling position.

Jarek didn't stop him—just kept his legs tight while Mosen planted his left hand by Jarek's side and cocked his right to strike.

As soon as Mosen's support hand touched down, Jarek clamped down on Mosen's wrist and drove it out from under him with a stiff arm. He twisted and rose, slipping his left shoulder to the inside of Mosen's, snaking his arm over and under Mosen's to complete the grip.

Grip secured, he shifted his legs and hips and turned into the floor, leveraging Mosen's arm until it was twisted at an unnatural angle and his only options were to eat the floor or risk violent dislocation.

"Yield," Jarek grunted.

Mosen gave a wordless bellow and began to rise, lifting Jarek bodily along for the ride despite the awkward mechanical disadvantage.

"I said yield!" Jarek barked.

Mosen showed no sign of stopping.

So Jarek twisted until, with a sickening pop, the tension in Mosen's shoulder gave way.

Mosen howled and threw a wild, cross-body punch into Jarek's ribs with his good arm.

The pain was breathtaking.

And, as Mosen tensed and lifted him higher, Jarek was pretty sure it wouldn't be the last of it if he didn't move.

So, at the apex of the Body Slam Express, Jarek dropped his leg lock and threw himself in behind Mosen. He scored a quick kick to the back of Mosen's right knee and hopped into a piggyback position, hooking his feet through the backs of Mosen's knees and his arms around Mosen's throat and head to complete the transition.

"Yield, ass-hat!"

Mosen obliged by throwing their combined bulk into the lobby counter, Jarek-first.

They hit hard. Fresh pain lanced across Jarek's back, blinding in its intensity. Jarek held tight as they tumbled to the floor in a shower of falling items—too pissed to even wonder how he'd managed to not lose his grip on impact, some of that old fire finally burning to the surface now.

When he noticed the knife that had fallen from the counter with Mosen's belt, Jarek didn't think twice. He yanked the blade free from its sheath with one hand and put the blade to his opponent's throat.

"It's over, Mosen," he panted next to Mosen's ear.

"Do it!" Mosen growled, breathing heavily himself now. "If you're not going to do what it takes with Carver, with the rest of it, you might as well just bury that knife in my throat right now."

Jarek almost thought about it.

Then he tossed the knife to the floor and gave Mosen a pat on the cheek.

"Come on, Seth…"

Mosen flinched at his casual use of the name.

"You know I'm too good a sport for that kind of thing," Jarek continued. "Honor. Duty." He released Mosen and stood, taking a few steps away from Mosen and toward Fela. "That stuff's my jam, man."

The room seemed to have released a collective breath when Jarek tossed away his weapon and relinquished his hold on Mosen. But still, no one said a word, all of them waiting for some conclusive end to the episode.

"You're going to get us all killed," Mosen said quietly, the fight seeming to have left him now.

"Does that mean you yield?"

Mosen pulled himself to his feet, dusted himself off, and grabbed his gear from the floor and the countertop. "It means you can go fuck yourself, Slater."

And with that, he left.

Satisfied they'd seen the end of it, the onlookers finally broke their silence. Some talked among themselves, glancing warily at Jarek and in the direction Mosen had disappeared. A few congratulated Jarek on a fight well-won.

One guy—Stevens, Jarek thought it was—even clapped but was quickly silenced by his fellow Resistance buddies, who glanced anxiously at a group of glaring Mosenites.

Jarek realized he'd been standing there in a daze for too long when Michael and Chambers appeared at his sides and pushed him toward the chair Al had apparently carried over with Fela.

He resisted, not overly keen to make his first post-fight act a sad, blubbering collapse.

"Show's over, people," Chambers called, apparently picking up on the source of his hesitation. "Let's all try to get some sleep."

Jarek noticed a few faces turning from her to him.

"You heard her, folks. Big first day tomorrow. Seize the carp and all that."

The crowd began to disperse with a fair share of vaguely concerned looks from some of the Resistance troops and not-so-vaguely disgusted looks from some of the more loyal Mosenites.

"Seize the carp?" Chambers asked quietly.

Jarek frowned then only half-succeeded at suppressing a delirious giggle. "Is that what I said? Not… carpe…? Fuck, my head hurts."

He didn't resist this time when Michael and Chambers guided him to the chair.

"You make it hard sometimes, you know," Michael said easing him down.

"Hear, hear," Al added through Fela's speakers.

Jarek grinned at Chambers. "What, you're not gonna call *them* out on the phrasing issues?"

Chambers masked her own grin beneath a semi-stern frown. "Not when they're making a good point, I won't. You could've died. I kind of thought you might've for a second after that punch."

Jarek tested the cheek with a fingertip and groaned at the fresh pain that flared up from the already considerable aching. "Necessary evil, I think."

"And all that stuff you said to him…" Michael added.

Jarek looked down, all the satisfied amusement bleeding out of him as he reflected on what he'd done—relying on psychological warfare to break Mosen's good reason.

Just like Jarek had done to Alaric back when they'd first met.

Something told him he wasn't getting invited to any Weston family picnics in the future.

"You did what you had to," Chambers said, not a trace of judgment in her voice.

"Yeah," Michael said. "Heck, maybe it's a good thing. Probably all needed to be said."

Jarek didn't look up. "Maybe so."

Michael laid a hand on his shoulder. "Thank you, Jarek."

"Yeah, well"—he forced himself to look up at Michael and grin—"I wouldn't thank me yet. Not before we take care of the important stuff. Like picking a team name, for instance."

"Oh my god," Chambers said, looking as if she'd just come to a sudden realization. "Mosen was right. We're all gonna die."

CHAPTER FIFTEEN

Rachel gaped at the striking man in the doorway, trying to wrap her brain around it.

The Mayor of the reigning anti-raknoth capital of the USA was, in fact, a raknoth.

The irony might have made her laugh. If she'd had the time.

The attack was swift and ruthless, his mind crashing into hers without the slightest warning. Not even a facial tick, outside of the poised frown he'd fixed them with.

As much practice as she'd had with telepathic clashes in the past months, he nearly took her from the start thanks to sheer startlement. But her reflexes bought her a second, and she built on it.

He wasn't weak. None of the raknoth were. But as far as his kind went, he wasn't exceptional either.

Once she managed to pull her defenses into tighter order, the attack quickly shifted to more of a deadlock.

"Mayor Dillard?" Zach said, somewhere far away.

The mental pressure vanished like the flipping of a switch, and Rachel was left staring dumbly at the Mayor. He stared right back, looking as if he'd like nothing more than to lunge forward and tear her head straight from her shoulders.

Beside her, Drogan had gone still. Maybe he'd smelled the arrival of his kind. She could practically feel his hand itching to rip off his cloaking pendant and confirm it for certain.

Luckily, Mayor Dillard seemed a little too preoccupied with her to notice the telepathically disguised raknoth sitting next to her.

"Is everything okay, sir?" Zach asked, looking between her and Dillard in clear confusion.

That probably answered the question of whether or not Dillard's loyal subjects knew what he actually was.

"Apologies," Dillard finally said. He gathered himself and strode around the table to take Zach's offered chair. "It's just been one of those—"

"Who are you, and what are you doing here?" his voice hissed in her mind, cutting through whatever it was he was saying out loud to the rest of the room.

"—don't you fill me in, Zachary?" he finished out loud.

"I might ask you the same questions," Rachel sent as Zach began his report, *"right along with why the fuck you have one of your dead kin hanging over your front door."*

Dillard was still and controlled, but Rachel again had the distinct impression that, in his mind, he was dreaming of committing the most intense of violences to her.

Zach continued on with his assessment, pointedly letting them know just how utterly they'd been in his scopes the entire way in, utterly unaware himself of how laughable his intimidation tactics were while she sat here silently facing down their wolf in sheep's clothing.

Across from her, Dillard took a long but discreet inhale. *"What are you? You smell—"*

"Human? I am. Now your turn. What is this place, why's there a dead raknoth outside, and why the hell are you playing house with—"

"I will ask the questions here," Dillard sent, his mental tone growing irritated. *"Do not test me, human."*

"Something tells me you're not gonna go all red-eyes in front of your frothing vamp-a-phobes here."

Dillard showed her a hint of a cold, predatory smile. *"I have no qualms with killing you all in a most bloody fashion and wiping these men's minds after the fact. It wouldn't be the first time."*

Rachel refrained from pointing out he'd be hard-pressed to take both her and Drogan. Might as well keep their telepathically-cloaked Ace up the sleeve until there was reason to reveal it.

Dillard had other plans.

"—was a... malfunction with the guns," Zach was saying, "but once we'd—"

"Malfunction?" Dillard interjected, his eyes flicking suspiciously to Rachel. "Please explain."

Zach nodded diligently, eager to please. "Yes, Mayor." He was eyeing Rachel dubiously again himself. "We're still not entirely sure what happened, but it seems..."

Rachel lost track of what Zach was saying when Dillard lightly sniffed again, frowned, and looked straight at Drogan with renewed suspicion.

"What is this?" Dillard's lip twitched in a narrowly-contained snarl. *"What is he doing here, and why can't I feel him?"*

Shit.

So much for the element of surprise.

"We're not looking for trouble..." she started, glancing at Drogan.

He seemed to have caught onto the slight shift in Dillard's behavior. He looked questioningly at Rachel, fingering the cloaking pendant at his breast.

No point in hiding it now. Two against one was easier anyway.

So Rachel gave Drogan the faintest of nods, and the raknoth reached to flick the cloak off.

"—and then Commander Nelken here," Zach was saying, "started trying to tell us that it's the vamps' bosses we need to be worried about. The rakul, was it, Commander? Right, and—Mayor?"

At the mention of the rakul, Dillard's composure had slipped, concern and alarm rippling across his expression, his focus on her and Drogan momentarily forgotten.

Rachel wasn't watching Drogan, but the bright flare of his mind winking into existence beside her indicated he'd chosen that distracted moment to uncloak.

Dillard, meanwhile, looked like he was debating whether he could play the reaction off as something casual.

But Zach pushed on. "Do you know something about this, Mayor? Are they really…?"

"Is this true?" Dillard sent as Zach trailed off, watching his Mayor expectantly. *"The rakul…"*

"They have come, brother," came Drogan's mental reply. *"We fled two but yesterday."*

Dillard let out a heavy sigh, gave an equally heavy nod, and leaned forward on the table. Given the news, Rachel doubted the reaction was disingenuous, but, to the non-telepaths, it probably looked like quite the dramatic show in response to Zach's question.

For a second, Rachel thought Dillard might lose it right there—go berserk or, at the very least, telepathically compel his men to leave the room and forget what they'd heard.

Finally, though, he spoke.

"When we'd discovered Rollins' secret, before we…" He stroked the thin stubble on his jaw, either genuinely haunted by whatever distant memory he was seeing or putting on a phenomenal act. "Before we took care of the problem, I went to see him one last time. I wanted to see if there was anything left of our friend beneath the demon's influence."

The demon's influence? Was that Complex speak for saying this Rollins guy had been a raknoth?

Dillard shook his head, lost in the memory. "He cursed my name and told me that his masters would one day come to have their vengeance on us."

"We will have words about this, brother," Drogan sent, his mental tone akin to a warning growl.

It only strengthened Rachel's suspicion that Rollins must've been the barbequed raknoth hanging at the north entrance.

Zach and his men looked stunned for completely different reasons.

"God almighty," Zach muttered. "Why didn't you tell us?"

The bitterness in Dillard's face looked real. "Because I'd hoped it was nothing more than the desperate last words of a demon preparing to return to his maker."

Drogan's presence grew, a threatening mental pressure Rachel had a feeling Dillard felt much more profoundly than her.

Zach's men were shifting uncomfortably and shooting one another worried looks now. Zach himself looked like he'd just noticed a cold, slimy worm wriggling its way down his fatigues.

"You're saying…" He seemed to remember himself, then, and turned a hard look on Rachel, Nelken, and Drogan. "What should we do with these ones, then?"

Dillard studied them, thinking.

"We can help, Mayor," said Nelken, who seemed to have picked up on some of Rachel's tension but no doubt remained unclear on the exact source. "Our people know how to fight. We just need solid walls around us."

"I already explained we can't well take in an extra hundred-plus hungry mouths," Zach said to Dillard.

"Have you led the rakul to my doorstep?" Dillard sent to Rachel and Drogan, still silently debating.

"We detected no sign of pursuit," Drogan sent, *"but, sooner or later, they will find us."*

"Mayor?" Zach asked, watching Dillard with a worried expression.

Dillard pursed his lips, on the cusp of some decision.

"Convince them," he sent. Then he spoke out loud.

"All I ever wanted for us here was to be able to live on peacefully in a world that had gone insane." He raised a hand to Nelken. "If what you say is true, then tell me why I should allow your people in and risk bringing the fury of these… rakul creatures down on my own?"

"If I may, sir?" Drogan asked, again in that timid voice that sounded so bizarre coming from him.

Nelken frowned over at him, looking certain now that some funny business was going on behind the scenes of his perception, but he nodded to Drogan's request without a word.

Drogan turned to Dillard and Zach. "I know it sounds crazy, but to answer your question, Mayor Dillard, I think it'd be more of a risk to turn us away. We've... Well, we've seen some shit out there, sir. Entire cities going mad with rage. Red-eyed monsters straight out of..." He shook his head. "I don't think those rakul will stop until this whole planet's dust and ashes." He fixed Zach with a grave stare. "At the end of the day, whether we like it or not, I think we're all in this together."

"Damn, Drogan," Rachel sent to Drogan only. *"I didn't know you were capable of sounding like a real person."*

"Bah," Drogan replied. *"My tongue requires cleansing. How you and yours speak such gibberish routinely is beyond comprehension."*

Dillard made the appearance of turning Drogan's words over, though a hint of glib amusement tugged at his expression.

"Make light of this charade," Drogan sent to him, *"and I will break you."*

Rachel expected the threat would either only deepen Dillard's amusement or spark an aggressive, territorial response, but Drogan's fire actually seemed to rattle him.

Dillard sat quietly after that. His mind already looked to be made up, but his eyes flicked toward Zach a few times as if he were waiting to make sure his men would absorb the new information without their heads exploding.

"Very well," Dillard finally said.

The words startled the men out of their silent reveries.

Zach gaped down at him. "But Mayor, we can't—We've never... Where are we going to—"

"We'll find a way to manage." Dillard stood and gave Zach a reassuring pat on the shoulder. "Just as we always do."

Zach stared at him like he'd just proposed they all go skydiving without parachutes, but Dillard paid him no mind.

The Mayor moved for the door, waving for them all to join him. "Come. I won't promise anything more than temporary shelter while we discuss this development, but for now, let's find workable quarters for our new guests."

CHAPTER SIXTEEN

When Jarek awoke the next morning, he was surprised roughly in equal parts by three things. First, that he'd managed to sleep at all. Second, that, according to Al's report from the ship scanners, the Mosenites' vehicles were all still there outside. And third, that, despite the first two things, his throat was still miraculously knife-free.

It was shaping up to be an okay day. At least until he sat up from the floor and basked in the landscape of pain last night's brawl with Mosen had painted across his body.

"Ouchie," he groaned.

"How are we feeling this morning, sir?" Al asked.

It was a terrible question.

His back hurt. His elbows and his heel hurt.

His everything hurt.

But the worst of the pains was the warm, sickly ache radiating through his left cheek. Maker help him if it was fractured. Complications aside, his beautiful man-face could only take so much abuse, and he already had three strikes—or raknoth claw scars, rather—going against him.

"It fucking hurts, buddy." He worked his jaw experimentally and winced at the pain in his cheek. "Agh. Whatever happened to *not the face?*"

"I can't say you didn't bring it on yourself, sir, picking a bare-knuckle fight with a raknoth hybrid superhuman."

Despite Al's decided lack of verbal coddling, the inner membrane of Jarek's helmet, already comfortably cool, grew several degrees cooler on the left side. Jarek sighed in relief.

He'd slept with the faceplate closed. Judging by how soothing its presence felt on the aching mess of his face, he had a feeling it was going to be a faceplate-closed kind of day, too.

The pain wasn't anything he wasn't used to dealing with. The bigger concern was whether there'd be any lasting cognitive effects from having his bell so thoroughly rung. His thoughts felt coherent enough. But then again, there was no guarantee he wasn't just too impaired to recognize his own impairment.

"Any chance I can count on you to let me know if I do anything unreasonable, Mr. Robot?"

He started at the sound of Chambers' voice from the bed behind him. "You mean past the usual amount of unreasonable? That's kind of a tricky order, coming from you."

"Agent Chambers raises a valid point, sir," Al said, speaking through Fela's speakers now so Chambers could hear as well.

It was only by the time Jarek had turned to shoot his affronted glare at Chambers that he remembered his faceplate was closed. She seemed to get the gist anyway.

A thin smile pulled at her mouth as she touched two fingers to her forehead in salute and mouthed, "Sir."

Beside her, Michael slept on through it all with the unshakeable resolve of a praying monk.

"I have faith, Mr. Robot," Jarek said. "You'll know it when you see it."

"Right, then," Al said. "Seize the carp, sir."

Chambers laughed, and Michael gave a few sleep snorts but rolled over and continued his slumber.

"Everyone's a critic," Jarek muttered, pulling himself painstakingly to his feet. "Jesus, whose idea was it to get myself beaten to a pulp when we have a bunch of intergalactic conquerors on our tails?" He held up a hand and shook his head. "Don't answer that."

Chambers just gave another salute instead.

"That's gonna have to stop."

"Sir, yes, sir," she replied.

"Can we un-invite her to the team, Al?"

"Al and I are starting our own team anyway," Chambers said before Al could respond. "Team Think Before You Punch."

"Oh, that does sound enticing, sir."

Jarek shook his head. "Et tu, Mr. Robot?"

Michael chose that moment to snap awake and look at them with bleary eyes.

The suddenness of it put a twinge of rakul-related worry in Jarek's gut, but then Michael started shaking the sleep off like a normal disheveled twenty-year-old.

"What's up, guys?" He seemed to remember something, and he looked to Jarek with a grin. "We ready to seize the carp?"

"Oh, har har!" Jarek said. "Let's all make fun of the concussed guy!" He waved a dismissive hand at Michael and, in a tone that suggested it negated the validity of Michael's words, added, "You sleep tied up."

Michael and Chambers just watched him with amused expressions.

Jarek sighed. "We're not letting this go, are we?"

Michael and Chambers traded a look, then turned back to him.

"The carp has been seized," Chambers said.

Michael nodded with a mock-apologetic expression. "You can't just unseize the carp, man."

"You really can't, sir," Al added.

"That's it"—Jarek turned for the door, shaking his head all the way —"I'm gonna go see if anyone wants to put me out of my misery."

Outside, the sunlight hit harshly, snuffing out the light-hearted amusement they'd shared behind the safety of the closed door and replacing it with worry, weight, and the reminder of just how far he might be from finding Rachel, despite how far they'd already come.

But hey, that was life, right?

It just felt a bit more dire now that there was something worthwhile at the end of the tunnel. Though the aforementioned intergalactic conquerors didn't exactly lighten the mood, either.

Their camp had a sad breakfast of cold beans and what other tidbits the troops had scavenged while searching Columbus yesterday, and then they set out to sweep the northern reaches of the city, farther off their highway lifeline than they'd managed to explore before the light had failed them the previous evening.

Mosen, who was bruised as extensively as Jarek but looked suspiciously farther along in the healing process, seemed to be making a point of keeping his distance from Jarek.

Not that Jarek minded the fact.

As long as no one cried, "Mutiny," and started shooting, he'd consider the day a win. And, though the grumbles and dark looks abounded, their happy little family spent the morning sweeping the streets of Columbus without major incident.

By the time the sun hung high overhead, though, Jarek was worrying less about team morale and more about the fact that no one had seen any sign of their wayward allies.

Hope peaked at the far northern reach of town when they came across a small community that had either survived in their little suburban haven since the Catastrophe or, more than likely, settled there since the dust had done likewise.

That hope just as quickly died, though, at the terrified looks of the few villagers who hadn't managed to flee at their approach.

These people hadn't seen new faces in a long while. Or at least not friendly ones, judging by the few old rifles he spotted poking out at the convoy from open windows here and there.

Jarek poked his head and a raised hand out the driver's side window of the SUV. The exosuit probably wasn't going to put anyone at ease, but if their trigger fingers were particularly itchy, he'd rather the first shot be aimed at him and his armor.

"We come in peace, guys," he called, amplifying his voice through

Fela's speakers. "Just passing through looking for our people. We'll leave if you haven't seen them."

Silent faces stared back at him with different flavors of terror—frozen and helpless from those on the street, finicky and uncertain from those behind the rifles.

"Right, we're leaving," he called, looking back to gesture the convoy to turn around.

Rachel and the others must've moved on from Columbus. It was the only explanation he could accept right now. He was just going to have to pray to the Maker that they'd stuck with I-70.

For a few seconds, he wondered if he shouldn't try to get the locals to evacuate—to flee farther from the city, or maybe even to follow their convoy.

But would that really be any better than letting them stay here in peace?

There was no way to know. Not when they had no idea where the rakul were or what to expect them to do next.

Plus, there was the fact that these people seemed to have few weapons, few vehicles from the looks of it, and zero trust for Jarek or anyone else in the group.

The road wouldn't do them any favors, and Jarek's gut told him they wouldn't be improving their safety by joining the human who'd killed Kul'Armin and coming along on his quest to find the friends who'd helped him do it.

If the rakul were coming for any humans in particular after they'd meted out vengeance to the raknoth, it was probably Jarek Slater and his friends.

So he bade the poor people batten down what hatches they had to batten and ordered the convoy back to I-70. Tense stares and poised trigger fingers followed their retreat until they'd rounded out of sight back toward the city.

No one, Jarek included, was excited about hitting the highway west again without any clear plan or destination. Jarek half-expected Mosen to break at that point and either declare mutiny or just drive off on his own.

But no, he followed silently along. For the first hour, at least.

They had just passed Springfield when Mosen finally pulled his truck out from the rear of the convoy and accelerated until he was drawing even with Jarek's SUV.

Leaning over the slightly-uncomfortable looking Mosenite in his passenger seat, Mosen gave Jarek an aggressive tilt of his head. A sign, Jarek took it, for *I'm too stubborn or pissed to break radio silence, but your stupid ass better pull over so we can talk all the same.*

Jarek sighed and guided the SUV gently over to a stop on the side of the road next to a sprawling field of wild grass.

"Sit tight, kids," Jarek said, turning to face his full SUV and glad the faceplate was there to hide the pained wince the movement caused him. "Mommy and Daddy just have to talk for a second."

Michael's frown deepened.

Chambers shot him a look that said *Talk with your words, not your fists.*

Jarek hopped out of the SUV and went to meet Mosen where he'd likewise pulled over.

Personally, he wouldn't so much mind having the chance to pay Mosen back a good shot or two with Fela's strength behind him, but something told him it wouldn't be necessary, or particularly helpful.

"So what," Mosen said when they drew up to one another, "we're just gonna keep truckin' down 70 until we hit California?"

Jarek turned a frown westward. "I don't think 70 actually makes it that far…"

Mosen tensed.

"… but I'm guessing that's not your point."

"My point," Mosen said, gesturing back toward Springfield, "is that we might as well stop and take a quick look if we're going to bother driving across the country blind."

Jarek wasn't so convinced that was what they were in fact doing, but he wasn't eager to explain his reasoning to anyone—least of all to Mosen. Standing under Mosen's expectant stare, though, it seemed there weren't any great alternatives.

"They'll leave us a sign," Jarek said quietly. "All we have to do is stick to 70."

When he looked up, he expected it to be Mosen's signature sneer that met him, but the man only closed his eyes for a long moment, jaw tight.

"You mean *she'll* leave us one, don't you?" he finally asked.

Jarek started to argue, but Mosen pushed on.

"And even if she did, you're willing to bet our convoy on your girl-friend being clever enough to leave some sign that won't be a big flying rakul trap waiting to happen?"

Jesus, why was Mosen making sense all of a sudden?

"You think driving around in tight city streets is better?" Jarek shot back, but it felt like a half-hearted argument. "It's hard to keep track, Mosen, what with the flipping and the flopping and the violent head trauma. You *don't* wanna go west and look for our allies. You *do* wanna go west and stop at every damn town along the way." He spread his hands. "What was the point of getting my face smashed in if we're still gonna bicker about every little decision?"

Mosen rolled his eyes and sighed, and Jarek had the uncomfortable thought that maybe it was him, and not Mosen, who was being the confrontational jackass for once.

Maybe.

But Mosen still looked plenty confrontational—and at least a little jackass-ish—as he shook his head and turned back for his truck. "I'm just saying it wouldn't hurt to poke around for fifteen minutes to make sure."

He probably wasn't wrong about that.

Confrontational or not, it wasn't the worst idea in the world.

Jarek had already considered as much and had simply come to the conclusion that they were best off making up lost ground on their allies. Allies who, in his mind, must either still be westward bound or settled in some new safe hidey-hole. One that they'd have thought to somehow tip off to any following friendlies.

The only downside was that Jarek could be dead wrong.

Fifteen minutes.

It was a small price to pay—and probably a smart one—for a little peace of mind.

He was just opening his mouth to say so to Mosen when Al cried out.

"Sir, here!"

Jarek had to glance around to see that *here* must've been the spot a couple hundred yards up the road where Al was currently drifting along with the ship, waiting to see what they would decide.

"What is it?" Jarek asked.

Mosen paused and looked back, waiting to see what this new development was.

"I do believe I've found your sign, sir, or I'm a circuit-scrambled Arduino."

Jarek's heart jumped. "What? It's… What does it say?"

Mosen spread his hands in question, no doubt wondering what the fuss was about.

"Well, sir," Al said, "I do believe it's addressed to me."

Jarek gestured to the ship, and Mosen broke into a run beside him without further explanation.

"What do you mean, it's to you?" Jarek asked as they ran. "What is it?"

"Best you see it for yourself, sir."

"Drama queen," Jarek snapped.

"What's the robot got?" Mosen asked between breaths, his sprint doing a fair job of keeping level with Jarek's easy run in Fela.

"First off," Jarek said, "I'm the only one who gets to call him a robot. And secondly…"

They were drawing close to the hovering ship now, but Jarek didn't see anything other than the same field of wild grass, a distant old farmhouse, and, closer to the road, a bunch of bushes and trees and—

He frowned, taking in the shape of a fallen log.

No, not fallen. Broken. As if by a giant. Or a raknoth in a hurry.

And not *a* log, he saw, but several of them.

He traded a look with Mosen, both of them too intent on the spectacle ahead to waste words.

They drew up to the logs and Jarek immediately saw what Al had meant.

It would have been easy to miss from the road just driving by, but standing right at the base—or hovering above, as Al was doing with the ship—it was clear enough.

AL.

The logs had been broken at the proper lengths and laid out to form the two uppercase letters, unmistakable.

Jarek whipped his head around, too excited to care about the twinges of pain the movement caused. Outside of that first moment hearing Rachel's voice back in Pittsburgh, he couldn't remember the last time he'd felt so relieved—so light despite the monumental challenges that still lay before them.

Because those challenges and obstacles didn't matter right now.

They had their sign.

CHAPTER SEVENTEEN

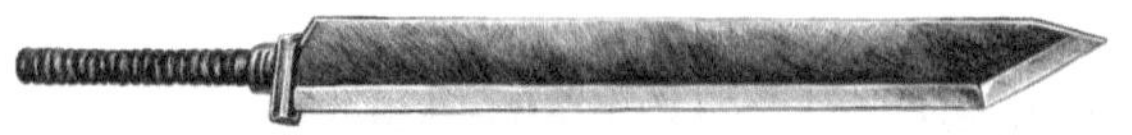

"It's a couple roadside logs, Slater," Mosen said with a dismissive wave of his hand. "I think you might need a little more to go on before you start throwing around the *I told you sos*."

Jarek was tempted to relinquish the cool relief of Fela's faceplate for the first time that day just to show Mosen his incredulous stare. "They spell out Al, for the love of Christ."

Mosen shrugged, looking around in stubborn silence.

"You know," Jarek said, going to inspect the logs more carefully, turning them over and looking for anything of interest, "it's a shame you're not made of wool."

Mosen dubiously began his own inspection of the bottom leg of the L. "What the hell's that supposed to mean?"

Jarek paused to look up from his work and meet Mosen's gaze. "Well, if you're gonna be such a wet blanket all the time and everything…"

Mosen rolled his eyes. "Well aren't you just pleased as fucking punch."

"I am." Jarek stood and swept their surroundings again, looking for a likely spot to leave a message. "I so totally am."

He wasn't even saying it to piss Mosen off. Or not solely for that reason, at least.

Rachel had been here. By some brilliant stroke of luck, they'd found her sign. And, either here or somewhere nearby, Jarek was sure there must be another one waiting for them.

Back on the highway, the convoy was creeping up to join them after their mad dash to Al and the ship, Michael having slipped over to take the wheel of the SUV and one of the Mosenites having done the same in Mosen's truck.

Jarek flagged them to park by the logs, made a gesture he hoped would be understood as *Have a look around,* and turned to head toward the old farmhouse on the other side of a hundred or so yards of dry, tan wild grass.

"Come on," he said.

"Come on what?" Mosen called after him.

"Your ass is coming along to see the message this time," Jarek called, not looking back as he broke into an easy jog through the belly-high tangle.

Quietly, to himself, he added, "No more of this hearing voices crap."

"You tell them, sir," Al said.

"See? That. That—"

"Was only tenuously ironic, sir," Al said. "But I suppose I'll give it to you."

Behind, the steady rustling of displaced grass and the equally steady stream of muttered curses confirmed Mosen was following along.

"It never really stops being creepy, you know," Mosen called from a few yards behind, "you talking to yourself all the time."

Jarek arched his brows expectantly, an amused smile splitting his face but quickly retreating at the fire it sparked in his bruised cheek.

Al sighed. "Very well. We have achieved ironic liftoff, sir."

"Ha!" Jarek reached the edge of the wild grass and pushed out into the slightly shorter, greener stuff that surrounded the house.

Mosen stumbled out of the field shaking his head and muttering something about goddamn weirdoes.

"Yeah," Jarek said, starting for the house's front deck, "coming from you…"

"Where are you going?" Mosen called after him.

He glanced back and spread his hands as if to say *Where the hell do you think?* and almost bit it when the old wood of the first porch step gave out under his weight.

"Gah! We're looking for a glyph, or a note, or some other kind of sign. Obviously."

He was acutely aware of Mosen watching him from below as he inched cautiously up the creaking steps.

"So, what?" Mosen said. "We can't spare fifteen minutes to peek around Springfield, but you want to go over some old farm with a microscope because someone did some coincidental tree art?"

"Pretty much." Jarek paused at the top porch step, his eyes immediately settling on the fresh gouges beside the ruined screen door. "Not sure we're gonna be needing that microscope, though."

The stairs groaned below as Mosen started picking his way carefully after Jarek. "Yeah? Is that what your gut's telling you now?"

"Mostly the eyes," Jarek said as Mosen stepped onto the porch beside him and caught sight of the unmistakable glyph set carved in the dilapidated wall.

"I won't say it…" Jarek said slowly, then reconsidered with a little shrug, "but I fucking told you so."

Mosen kept his eyes straight ahead with a surly expression that would've made Alaric proud.

"Fine," he finally said, waving at the symbol in invitation, "let's see what we're dealing with."

Jarek approached the glyph cautiously, almost scared to touch it now that it was here in front of him, waiting and undeniably real.

Closer up, he saw that the symbol wasn't carved into the wood so much as scratched through the layer of aged discoloration that had set into the surface over the years. The design of the glyph was vaguely similar to the last one, but slightly more intricate and neatly arranged.

But that didn't really matter, did it? He was just stalling.

So he took a breath, reached slowly out... and paused, hand in midair.

"Al?"

"Already recording video, sir," Al said, talking through Fela's speakers so Mosen could hear as well.

"What would I do without you, buddy?"

"Flounder most spectacularly, sir. Or so one might imagine."

"Is that not what this is?" Mosen muttered.

Jarek spared a glance over his shoulder. "Pay attention, wet blanket."

He pressed his palm to the glyph.

As soon as his hand touched, the scratched lines came alive and cast a soft azure glow across his hand and the age-darkened wood.

Warmth touched his hand through Fela's tactile sensors, soft, and smooth, and—

There.

Rachel.

As it had in Pittsburgh, her presence seemed to envelop him—her warmth, the ripe yet sweet scent of her after too long on the road. He closed his eyes and tried to absorb every bit of it.

"Jarek..."

Her voice wasn't tense as it had been last time. Just tired, and maybe a shade mournful.

"I don't know if you'll ever hear this." She blew out a dubious huff, and his heart trilled as the faintest trace of her breath tickled at his cheek. "Hell, we'd probably already be breaking the odds if you even found my message back in Pittsburgh. And I would've at least left a message in Columbus like I said, but..."

A sigh, and he could all but see her pulling her composure together.

"That doesn't matter now. I'm just gonna have to believe you'll find this. And when you do, you need to head to Cheyenne Mountain, in Colorado. I don't know why Johnny knows this, or who the hell thought it was a good idea to—never mind. Point is, there's supposed to be one hell of a bunker there. Nelken's thinking it's our best bet to hole up there while we recoup and wait for our Enochian super soldiers to—what?"

Jarek tensed, expecting gunshots, monstrous shrieks, or worse, but there was just a mumbled voice he couldn't make out.

"Do you wanna say something?" Rachel asked.

Another muffled, distant voice.

When Rachel spoke again, he could hear the smile in her voice.

"Drogan says he hopes you won't die before he has the chance to slay another rakul with you at his side."

Jarek couldn't help but smile. "Me at *his* side?" he mumbled to himself.

Rachel started to say something, but the glyph's glow wavered, along with her voice.

"Shit," she said when it stabilized. "I'm not sure if this is all making it down or not. I'd better wrap up. Get to Cheyenne Mountain, Jarek. Keep Michael safe. Tell him I love him. And…"

He held his breath, part of him suddenly hoping she might fill that pregnant silence with three words, the other part insisting it didn't matter when she took a breath and moved on.

"And I should do a roll count," she said. "Just so you know."

Rachel proceeded to list off names and give a rough group count. It sounded like they hadn't lost anyone since Pittsburgh, aside from Al'Brandt, who'd left to take any pursuing rakul on a decoy chase, but when the glyph sputtered out and died, she hadn't mentioned either Alaric or Commander Daniels.

Jarek stared at the apathetic wall, waiting to see if there'd be any more. When he was sure there wouldn't be, he tried removing his hand and re-activating the glyph, but was unsurprised to find nothing happened.

So, finally, he turned to take in Mosen's reaction.

Alaric's son was still fixed on the glyph with a tight-lipped stare.

"I'll be damned," he finally said.

"Probably," Jarek agreed.

Mosen finally broke his gaze away from the glyph to sneer at Jarek. "No *I love you*, though, huh? That's cold, man."

Jarek sputtered through a few false starts before finally settling with, "Oh, eat a dick, Mosen."

That just got a satisfied smirk out of the bastard, but it didn't last long. Soon enough, his expression sobered.

"Well, congratulations Slater. You were right."

Slowly, emphasizing the movement, Jarek slid a hand up to cup behind one ear, as if trying to hear better.

Mosen shook his head and looked back toward their convoy before replying. "You're an unbearable prick, you know that?"

Jarek shrugged. "Only to people who've broken my face in the past twenty-four hours. Them's the rules."

He hesitated over his next words.

"For what it's worth, though, I'm sorry about all the shit I said last night. If it makes you feel any better, I only turned to psychological warfare because I thought you might actually kill me if I didn't shake things up."

"I would have," Mosen said quietly, his gaze distant, pensive, and maybe just a bit troubled.

The candid detachment in his words made Jarek feel cold inside.

"You don't understand what it's like, Slater—what these men have been through. What it's like to be made a puppet, to serve for over a decade whether you want to or not."

Jarek's mouth was halfway open to say he knew a thing or two about being made to march to the beat of someone else's deranged drum before it really hit him. Everything he'd experienced with Conner. Everything since then. Terrible as it all had been, it really did pale in comparison to what Zar'Golga and his raknoth had done to some of the humans under them. Especially to Mosen.

"I guess I haven't really thought it all through," Jarek finally admitted. "It's always been a little too easy to cast you all as comic book bad guys in my head." He turned his hands palms-up. "Especially when you were all actively trying to kill me and whatnot. But you're right…"

"Christ, Slater. Keep going and I'm almost going to be sorry I tried to kill you"—he looked up as if counting—"four times."

"Well don't go soft on me now, big guy."

Jarek willed his faceplate open with a careful thought.

Mosen seemed suspicious of the dropping of barriers until his gaze fell on what Jarek could only assume was the epically extensive bruising on the left half of his face.

"We have to go to Cheyenne Mountain, Mosen. From there, we can see about sending out search parties for Krogoth and your fath— and Alaric. But right now, we've got exactly one real shot at getting our people someplace safe. Cheyenne's the right call."

Mosen silently worked his jaw in a fashion that reminded Jarek just a little too much of Alaric's habitual leaf-chewing.

"Fine," he finally said, and started to turn back for the convoy.

"Mosen."

Slowly, Mosen looked back over his shoulder.

Jarek fumbled for the words he'd thought he'd wanted to say. He probably shouldn't have opened his mouth without a plan. But now that he had…

"It's not too late, you know."

Mosen said nothing, so he pushed on.

"Once we make it to the bunker, after we hand these rakul bastards their asses on a nice shiny platter… I know it's bad, man, but there's no damage that can't be overcome. Golga's not around anymore and—"

"And what?" Mosen said quietly. "You going to say I can get off the sauce and have another shot at getting my pa back and having a nice, happy life?"

Jarek winced. "See, it sounds silly when you say it like that."

Mosen started down the steps, apparently not seeing fit to dignify that with a response.

"C'mon, guy," Jarek called after him. "I'm just saying maybe if we make it through all this, we can all have another shot at our lives."

Mosen at least told him to shove it after that, but Jarek was pretty sure it was only halfheartedly.

"You should talk to your father, young man!"

Mosen just marched into the field of wild grass, middle finger held high over his head.

"Good talk," Jarek muttered to himself.

"Masterfully done, sir," Al confirmed.

———

WITH A CLEAR TARGET in sight and far too much nervous energy riding in the platoon, Jarek figured they might as well make all haste. Especially since getting further away from Pittsburgh and Columbus seemed prudent.

They drove on through the remainder of the day and most of that night. Michael was ecstatic when Jarek told him the news of Rachel's message. On the whole, the spirits of the convoy seemed to be coming around after last night's breaking point.

Things were good. Almost too good.

There were no issues at all, really, except for the deer one of their trucks hit in the pre-dawn hours. Fortunately, the truck managed to shed enough speed that the damage wasn't too bad and the deer wasn't pulverized. They quickly loaded it into the truck to be used for the day's meal once they were ready to stop.

At least it wouldn't go to waste. The troops actually seemed pretty excited at the thought of eating something that hadn't come from a can or the soil.

When the light of dawn finally began to stretch over the horizon and his sleeping passengers began to rise with complaints of aching legs and empty bellies, Jarek guided the convoy to a halt by a spacious, out of the way farmhouse that looked to be in decent repair. Or standing, at least.

It was in good enough shape that he wondered if it would be occupied. A quick sweep inside, though, revealed it was neither occupied nor in nearly as good a shape as he'd originally thought.

Still, it'd do for a meal and a quick rest.

According to Al, they were only a few hours out from this

Cheyenne Mountain Complex. He'd been sorely tempted to just keep driving until they had their answer—and, universe willing, he had Rachel in his arms. But his men's grumbles, his own rumbling belly, and the tiny voice of caution in the back of his mind had won out.

Every square inch of him wanted to believe they'd be safe when they reached Cheyenne. That their people would be waiting for them with open arms, thick walls, and heavy weapons to cover their asses.

But he didn't know it. Not for sure. And until he did, it just didn't make sense to approach a potentially dangerous situation without a bit of food and rest.

Now wasn't the time to get careless.

With the venison, the last of their canned goods, and the wild onions a couple of their men had had the acumen to identify and pick while Jarek and Mosen had been investigating Rachel's trail, they could have whipped up a lovely little stew. As it was, though, everyone was too damn tired and hungry to wait, so breakfast consisted mostly of cold canned goods, tiny fried onions, and hunks of pan-seared venison the platoon sucked down as fast as their two poor cooks could toss them out.

Once most of them had filled their indignant bellies, they swapped their lookouts so the last hungry mouths could dig in, and everyone else set to the familiar routine of preparing to bed down for the day hours.

Jarek ate with the last shift, ruminating over their next moves. He didn't plan on waiting till nightfall. Approaching in daylight meant they'd be easier to see coming, but he'd rather be able to clearly see the lay of the unfamiliar land than go flying in under the radar but completely blind.

They'd sleep until early afternoon, then be on their way.

He found Michael and Chambers in one of the upstairs rooms, Michael grinning abashedly as Chambers, also slightly flushed in the cheeks, carefully bound his ankles and wrists. After the scene at the motel, it seemed no one else had any desire to be sleeping anywhere near Michael.

"Did you crazy kids want a touch of privacy?" Jarek asked from the doorway.

Chambers shot him a dirty look.

He spread his hands, putting on his best innocent face. "Just don't forget the safe word. That's all I'm saying."

"Grow up, man," Michael said, only blushing all the harder.

"Not if I can help it." Jarek strolled into the room and, seeing that Chambers had already finished up, tossed Michael's blanket over him and handed Chambers' blanket to her before he lay down beside Michael opposite Chambers.

Chambers adjusted Michael's blanket for him before laying down next to him and getting herself comfortable. Jarek resisted the reflexive itch to make light of the affectionate kindness. It was actually kind of nice to see. Two people just doing their thing, surviving, and still managing to stumble onto a tiny bit of the normal human experience in the midst of all this shit.

So Jarek just lay back and tried to relax as Michael drifted off between them and Chambers continued rustling around for a comfortable spot.

Tired as he was, sleep didn't come. Nor did that relaxation.

There were just too many thoughts racing through his mind. Too many hopes and problems and potential complications to even dream of stilling them without a gallon of whiskey or some weapons-grade anxiety meds.

What if he'd been wrong? Made the wrong call?

What if he got them all killed?

He'd never wanted this. The leadership. The responsibility. Part of him wished he could go back to the way things had been when it had just been him and Al and their ship, no deliberate cares and no set compass but their annoyingly persistent morals. No one else to worry about. No one to let down. No danger of becoming everything he'd despised about Conner and the rest of the big wigs he'd had the displeasure of meeting throughout the years.

He missed it.

Then he looked over and saw that Chambers seemed to have

finally drifted off with her back pressed up against Michael's side. For some reason, it made him smile. And with that smile came the first stirrings of peace to his troubled mind.

How long had he been lying there now?

It didn't matter.

Rachel. Rachel mattered.

For the first time, Jarek allowed himself to feel the hope that'd been trying to kindle in his chest since he'd heard Rachel's second message. So close. They were so damn close he could all but feel her skin at his fingertips.

Tomorrow.

Tomorrow they'd find their people. And he'd find Rachel.

The gentle arms of sleep were reaching out for his tired mind now, memories of his and Rachel's too-brief encounter in the ship drifting pleasantly through his head.

Tomorrow.

A languid smile stretched across his face.

Then a gut-wrenching roar shook the air and the lookouts started shouting bloody murder.

CHAPTER EIGHTEEN

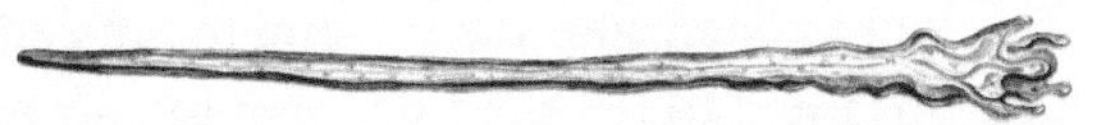

"I'm in," Johnny said before Rachel had even finished her sentence.

She looked around the spartan barracks room that had been an acting supply storage closet before the Enochians claimed it as their temporary home in The Complex. They were all there now, discussing next moves. Except for Nelken and Pryce, who were off seeing the facility's backup generators or some such with Dillard's systems engineers.

Rachel had seen a lot more of The Complex as they'd moved the rest of their people in. She'd even wandered out for part of the official tour and taken a gander at the base's cavernous water reservoirs and the crops they'd cultivated outside, well out of view of the main road.

It was all plenty interesting and impressive. But it was time for her to get back to the plan. It was time to go find Jarek and Michael, and to do it fast.

Which brought her back to the matter at hand.

"First off," she said to a waiting Johnny, "you're not invited—"

Johnny started to make an indignant gesture.

"—for multiple reasons," Rachel pushed on before he could speak.

"Not the least of which being because we need those big guns of yours watching your friends here twenty-four seven until we get back."

"And," Drogan said, "because I cannot run as fast with two should we lose our transportation and need to flee."

"And because this is a crapshoot operation to start off with," Franco added from beside Elise's cot, frowning up at the lot of them as he finished working that morning's rations through her gastric input. "I don't need to be from this planet to know the chances of finding a few men out in open country are slim to nonexistent."

Much as Rachel wanted to tell the Enochian to take his pessimism and shove it, Franco wasn't wrong. And she couldn't really blame him for being short on polite smiles these days, given what was happening to his daughter right before his eyes.

The knowledge alone that she was becoming something alien was probably bad enough. The Enochians' changing appearances couldn't be helping matters either.

Haldin and Elise looked more like extras from an old Star Trek movie than humans at this point. Rachel had expected the change might follow along a similar progression to that of a raknoth shifting to battle mode. Scaly green hide. Slightly elongated snout and angled brows. Fangs and claws.

What was happening to the Enochians, though, was much less outlandish, and somehow all the more disturbing because of it.

True, their skin had taken on a kind of cracked appearance, not unlike a dry clay bed, and a slight greenish tinge had begun to set in. But the oddest part was the host of subtle anatomical changes that seemed to be taking place.

Head, elbows, hands, shins, feet—every surface that could conceivably be used for striking seemed to be shifting to structures more suited for hitting or being hit. The Enochians were being forged into humanoid weapons. And, unlike the way the raknoth could normally switch their adaptations back and forth with their human hosts, Rachel got the impression that these changes wouldn't be so readily reversed.

She sighed and rubbed at her eyes with her palms, searching for anything to say to justify her and Drogan's decision to go back out looking for Jarek, Michael, and whoever else happened to be with them.

No surprise wisdom leapt out at her. Just the desire for a nap.

Between her mind's relentless worrying about Jarek and Michael and the tense toss-and-turn fest that had been trying to actually sleep in The Complex surrounded by Zach, his raknoth-hating zealots, and their secret raknoth leader, Rachel hadn't managed to get much rest last night.

Go figure.

"Franco's probably right," she finally said, "but we have to try anyway." She looked at Johnny. "Just like you have to stay here and make sure none of the crazies come try to set fire to your not-so-earthly best friends.

"Yeah," Johnny said slowly, looking back at the still forms of Haldin and Elise. "When you put it that way . . ."

"When she puts it that way," Franco said, his eyes fixed on Elise's still face, "it almost sounds as if she feels she's no longer bound by her promise."

The words came from a place of anguish rather than reason. She knew that. But it didn't make them cut any less deep.

"Franco..." James said, his tone lightly chiding, or maybe pleading.

"We'll keep her safe," Phineas said, his face impassive, his eyes never leaving Elise.

Johnny looked like he wanted to say something in Rachel's defense but wasn't ready to tread on the grieving father's toes for it.

"I'm doing the best I can," Rachel said quietly.

It was inadequate. Unhelpful. But it was all she could say.

"I will see to it that Nan'Grohl and Nan'Sorba remain here as well," Drogan added. "They will not require sleep, and it would be wise to keep them away from the local population anyway."

Franco shut his eyes as if reciting something to himself and tore his gaze away from Elise to look at Rachel and Drogan. "Of course. I'm sorry, I... Well, I hope you find the others."

Rachel forced a wan smile and gave him a grateful nod. Then she and Drogan left the barracks to go find Nelken.

Slim chances and settling the details with Nelken aside, only one other question remained.

Did they tell Mayor Dillard—or Nan'Dola, as Drogan had since identified him—that the two of them were even thinking about leaving?

Their own people giving them the tenuous go-ahead was one thing. Clearing the air with their odd new host might be another.

Assuming he didn't end up arguing with the venture, as he well might, knowing Dola was on board would be a welcome reassurance. But would the Mayor take advantage of their absence? Could this place really be safe for their people if he knew they were gone?

It was probably a moot point, as they were pretty sure they wouldn't be getting out of The Complex without the cooperation of Zach or whoever else might be manning the doors. Not without some hasty telepathic compulsion, at least, and that didn't seem the wisest of choices.

"What are you thinking?" she asked Drogan, who seemed to be contemplating their relative lack of departure options himself.

"We will talk to Nan'Dola," Drogan finally said, looking none too pleased about it, "and I will see to it that he listens."

That settled that, then.

***

THE COMPLEX'S main command room featured an impressive collection of computers, entire walls of displays whose numbers bordered on overwhelming, and other equipment Rachel couldn't even guess at. A good deal of it even still seemed to be working, though she wasn't sure how much good that could be doing anyone now that the Net was down.

As she'd half-expected, if not hoped, they found Zach there, poring over a group of displays with a couple others. There was, however, no Mayor to be found.

"We were hoping to talk to Dillard," Rachel said when Zach looked up to take in her and Drogan.

Zach eyed them as if it was an unreasonable and highly annoying request. Since his Mayor's decision to accept their forces into The Complex, Zach seemed to have come to the decision that, if there really was some fresh new hell coming for them all, it must've solely been the fault of the pesky newcomers.

"I'll check if the Mayor is available."

He said it as if there were every chance he might check only to find Dillard had stepped out for a coffee or a mid-morning golf appointment. As if the guy could've been anywhere other than locked into this cozy bunker with the rest of them.

Zach sat at a nearby console and proceeded to click around for entirely longer than Rachel thought he actually had to. Finally, though, he stood and beckoned to them with a hint of irritation.

"He'll see you. Just finished touring the facilities with your commander."

That was unexpected.

She hadn't realized his high Mayor-ness had been planning to take the time to accompany Nelken and Pryce around the base.

It made her uneasy.

"Thanks, Zach," she said, keeping her tone as sincere as she could manage.

Whatever else was going on, no reason they couldn't try to play nice. Especially not if they were going to think about trusting these people with precious cargo in their absence.

Zach considered her, and she had the distinct impression his mind traveled out to the big rotary guns, which he'd no doubt discovered by now had indeed been disconnected. Finally, though, he shrugged, mumbled, "No problem," and turned to guide them to Dillard.

The Mayor's office was close to the command room, just down the hallway opposite the one they'd entered through.

Zach knocked and, upon the muffled call to enter, made a point of sticking his head in to have a private word with his beloved raknoth Mayor before allowing the pesky outsiders entry. Not that Drogan couldn't probably hear it all, and Rachel as well if she'd properly focused her senses. But Zach didn't know that.

When Zach pulled back, he looked miffed, and when he swung the door open wider and waved them through, Rachel saw why.

Nelken was already there waiting for them.

From across a small gray coffee table, Dillard waved them wordlessly to join him and Nelken in the pair of empty, no-frills armchairs.

"Thank you, Zachary," he said. "That'll be all for now."

"Mayor," Zach said slowly. "Sir, wouldn't it be better if I—"

"Oh, don't worry about me, Zachary," Dillard said with a convincing smile. "I think we all have bigger concerns on the horizon than a hostile takeover. I'll be safe enough."

Zach looked less than convinced. "Sir, I don't feel comfortable leaving you with—"

Dillard sighed, and Zach quieted.

"You do feel comfortable," Dillard said in a flat voice. "You will return to your duties, knowing that I am safe and that you have done well."

Zach nodded blankly. "Yes, Mayor."

And with that, he stepped out of the room and closed the door behind him.

Nelken looked suspiciously between the closed door and Dillard like he wanted to say something.

Rachel, having felt the tendril of telepathic influence Dillard had just used on Zach, was less than pleased by the display herself, but she swallowed the reservation and reminded herself why they'd come.

Inside, the office was arranged to the textbook definition of minimalism. A standing desk to one side of the room housed a computer, its display, and absolutely zero clutter. A single cabinet beside it must've housed everything else Dola ever required in his day-to-day activities.

Other than those two pieces of furniture, there were the four armchairs, not decadent by any sense of the word, and the small gray coffee table between them. The light blue-gray tone of the walls was uninterrupted throughout the room, except for the single framed photograph of a beach sunset hanging on the wall by the computer desk.

"Don't tell me you're a beach guy," Rachel said as she and Drogan settled down in the empty pair of armchairs, facing each other across the table while Nelken and Nan'Dola did the same.

Apparently, Dola wasn't interested in banter. "I've been expecting you," he said, looking between them. "You must have a lot of questions."

Drogan wasted no time. "Was it you who killed our brother?"

Dola only hesitated a second before giving a curt nod. "Nan'Troga. He and I had ever-deepening disagreements on how things should be run here."

"Explain." There was no question in Drogan's tone.

"He did not wish to conceal his true identity any longer."

"And so you murdered your brother for his failure to embrace your life of cowardice?" Drogan rumbled. "You used his demise to elevate yourself amongst your pathetic flock."

Rachel thought she saw Dola give a nervous swallow, though his expression remained controlled and his hands still rested lightly on the arms of his chair.

"All I ever wanted," he finally said, "was to be left alone. To forget my doomed heritage and simply live my own life away from our people."

"Coward," Drogan said.

Dola stared through the table with a distant gaze, not arguing.

"But why this?" Rachel asked before she could stop herself. "The silver thing, all the holy demon propaganda… Why make a camp of anti-raknoth zealots?"

"Oh, for several reasons," Dola said, not looking up. "For starters" —he plucked the silver pendant hanging at his chest and held it up demonstratively—"controlling the facts of vamp existence allowed me to place myself above the shadow of doubt in their eyes, while simultaneously condemning Nan'Troga. As for the religious zealotry…"

He finally stirred himself from his distant stare to look between

Rachel and Nelken, a humorless smile pulling at his mouth. "Well, I don't have to explain to the two of you how powerful a tool religion has proved in the rapid propagation of unquestioned dogma among your kind. It seemed the easiest of the options before me. And..." He shrugged, lost in thought again. "Perhaps some part of me wished to forget the truth as well."

Across from Rachel, Drogan shook his head, looking at Dola as if he were too disgusted to even bother with putting it into words.

After a length of silence, Dola roused himself. "Alas, it was never to be." He gestured toward Nelken. "If what you have all told me is true, and I have no reason to doubt that it is, my time of pretending has come to an end, whether I choose to admit it or not."

"How awfully accepting of you," Rachel said.

Across from her, Drogan gave an unsympathetic grunt.

"Yes," Dola said slowly. "Well, now that we're here and they are most unfortunately out there,"—he waved at the wall in a distant gesture—"I suppose it's prudent we should begin discussing your plan for the impossible."

"We should," Rachel said, "but we have something else to discuss first."

Dola took in her and Drogan's resolute expressions and Nelken's slightly soured one. "I take it there are plans of which I have yet to be made aware?"

Rachel looked to Nelken, waiting for him to acknowledge their discussing the plan, rough as it was, with their raknoth host.

Reluctantly, he nodded.

"We still have people out there," Rachel said. "Good people. People we're gonna want around when the shit inevitably hits."

"I see," Dola said slowly. "People, I take it, you'd like to bring into The Complex."

"Once we find them," Rachel said.

Dola tapped on the arm of his chair, glancing at Drogan intermittently in the thoughtful silence. "Al'Drogan did not come here to ask my permission for such a mission."

"Decidedly not," Drogan said.

Dola nodded, looking like he wanted nothing more than to look up only to find that he was alone in the room and that they'd never come along and ruined his peace and quiet.

"How, then, might I be of service?"

"We need your word we can trust you with our people while we're gone," Rachel said.

The first hints of anger colored Dola's face. "You sit safely in my home and think to question my intentions, human?"

Rachel didn't flinch away from his stare. "You murdered your own brother and brainwashed these people for fifteen years. Why the hell wouldn't we question every word out of your mouth?"

Dillard showed them a humorless smile. "Because you already know exactly what I'll do to protect this little haven of mine. And because you know as well as I do that I lack any means of hoping to defend against the rakul on my own. If you have allies who stand any hope of offering us some chance, they will be welcome here."

Rachel glanced at Drogan, who met her eyes with a meaningful look.

"Well that's good to hear," Rachel said, "but you'll have to forgive us if we're not ready to take your spoken word for it."

Dola's expression darkened. "I don't suppose I have much choice in the matter."

"None," Drogan said.

Rachel almost felt bad for Dola, so suddenly relegated from master of his domain down to pawing for Drogan's mercy. Then she remembered the little factoids. That said domain had been built from brainwashed humans. That Dola had betrayed and slain one of his own to secure it.

He deserved more than some of Drogan's intimidation for what he'd done.

And he was about to get a little taste of it.

Dola closed his eyes, absorbing what was to come next, and finally gave a nod. "Very well. I suppose it's not worth asking for you to be gentle about—"

Judging from the pained looked wince that took Dola's features,

Drogan was anything but gentle as he punched his way into the other raknoth's mind to assess his trustworthiness in the only way that was above doubt.

Rachel started to reach out to have her own look beside Drogan but paused, thinking.

After everything she'd seen the raknoth do and everything she'd learned…

It wasn't the first time the thought had occurred to her.

To see the things they'd seen—to do all the terrible shit they'd done to Earth and god knew how many planets and species before that…

She still couldn't really see how any raknoth could live with all of that for thousands of years without a good amount of either insanity or cold, hard psychopathy. And even if they could, she wasn't so sure she wanted to go rolling around in a mind that could pull all that off and keep living with itself.

So she withdrew her extended senses and waited as Drogan sat with eyes closed, calmly scanning a less-than-comfortable looking Dola for any hint of dishonesty or treachery.

"He will not harm our people," Drogan finally said a handful of minutes later, sounding almost a touch disappointed with the finding.

"So glad we could sort that out," Dola said, opening his eyes to shoot a dark glare at Drogan.

"We might as well tell him the rest of it," Drogan said, ignoring Dola's displeasure.

Neither Nelken nor Rachel saw fit to argue.

"Pray tell," Dola seethed. "What happy secret am I privy to now that I've joined this most precious circle of trust?"

It was the first time Rachel could ever recall seeing Drogan roll his eyes. He waved at her in invitation, apparently too exasperated to do the honors himself.

"The two we brought in on covered stretchers," Rachel started slowly, "they were… special."

Dola wrinkled his nose. "And you question *my* honesty. Special how?"

"Kind of like me," Rachel said. "But also…"

"They are bound symbiotically with two of our own," Drogan said.

A deep frown creased Dola's brow. "Symbiosis? But who of our brethren would consider such a thing? And why not simply take—"

"Because our brethren require these allies' skills and powers just as much as those allies require the strength our kind can offer them," Drogan said.

"Skills and powers," Dola mumbled, tearing his incredulous stare from Drogan to study Rachel. "Special… You said these humans were like you. Forgive me for having to ask, but what on earth could be so remarkable about a human—even a mentally gifted one—that a raknoth would resign themselves to"—he wrinkled his nose in distaste—"symbiosis?"

Rachel smiled. "Well, remarkable might be a strong word, but…"

Gathering her will, she telekinetically yanked Dola several feet into the air.

He gave a startled grunt, reflexively trying to extending his legs and arms only to find them pinned concretely in place.

". . . I guess I can be useful here and there," Rachel concluded.

With that, she released her hold and watched with some small satisfaction as Dola plunked back down to his chair and proceeded to gape from her to Drogan to the chair and back to her.

"I… see," he finally said. "I'd heard rumors, but never seen any evidence that…" He frowned. "The defenses at the front entrance."

Rachel shrugged. "Just a couple yanked cables. No big deal."

Dola tapped the chair arm. "Most interesting. And the raknoth who have volunteered for this… unusual alliance?"

"Al'Braka," Drogan said, "and one of the Shieth."

Dola turned that over for a stretch, the rest of the resentment fading from his expression. "Well, it seems the fates are clearly determined to deprive me of my boredom."

"You should thank The Void they do not yet deprive you of more," Drogan said, glancing impatiently at the door.

"We don't really know how much longer their, uh, transition is going to take," Rachel said, "which is why we wanna do whatever we can to keep your people from stumbling onto them and busting out the holy water."

Dola nodded. "I will see to it these . . . symbiotes remain undisturbed."

"You might be wise to start thinking on how you're going to break the news to your people, too," Nelken said. "We learned the hard way that fear of a greater evil isn't sufficient motivation to get everyone to join hands and play nice. I can't imagine your people will take it any easier than ours did, but we don't want to leave that moment for if and when the red eyes have to come out."

Dola closed his eyes and rubbed his temples in a very human fashion.

"Commander Nelken speaks truth," Drogan added, to which Dola only rubbed harder. "In the meanwhile, it will likely lessen complications if Rachel Cross and I are able to leave The Complex discretely."

"That, at least," Dola said, glancing up, "I have an easy solution to."

CHAPTER NINETEEN

Out of all the bullshit, psychopathic "sentiment" Conner had tried to fill his head with—especially right at the bitter end—one piece of the deluded bastard's wisdom had always stuck with Jarek.

"The moment you think everything's well and good—the moment you're sure you've got it in the bag… That's exactly when things are most ready to blow up in your face, kid."

Goddamn Conner.

And goddamn his undying "wisdom."

As Jarek descended the stairs, there was an abrupt wrenching sound outside, like the world's largest can being smashed to a crumpled heap, followed by another chest-rumbling roar from the thing that could only be Kul'Gada.

"Gear up, people!" Jarek shouted into the chaotic living room. "We're outta here as soon as we make the trucks."

"It's—it's fucking huge," a wide-eyed Mosenite sputtered from his perch at the corner window.

Definitely sounded like Gada.

"Yep." Jarek picked up the Big Whacker 2.0 and strapped it to the waiting connectors on Fela's back, uncomfortably aware of how many aches the simple motion caused. "You let me worry about that big bastard."

He turned to Mosen and Chambers. "Get them on the road, whatever it takes.

Over on the stairs, Michael was shaking his head. "Jarek, we're—"

"Getting the hell out of here alive," Jarek snapped, turning for the entryway. "No waiting. No heroics."

A second awful metallic screech from outside reminded him he didn't have time to wait for any answers.

By the time he reached the front door, Mosen was barking orders at the stunned platoon.

Jarek clenched his fists and kicked the door clean from its hinges—in part to draw Gada's attention away from what sounded like the ruthless slaughter of their convoy vehicles and in part just to psych himself up.

Drawing Gada's attention, at least, worked just fine.

For one gut-sinking moment, Jarek took in the devastation Gada had already wrought on two of their ground vehicles. Then Gada whirled to face him, eyes blazing crimson, gleaming fangs bared in an eager snarl.

Fucking huge was not a bad place to start in describing Gada. Spiky, steroid-abusing bipedal dinosaur from hell wasn't too shabby either.

The Kul's enormous fingers began lengthening to chitinous claw-blades at the sight of Jarek stepping onto the porch—a creepy but sure sign of Gada's murderous arousal.

Jarek suppressed a shudder. "Guess you're happy to see me, huh, Spike?"

By way of reply, Gada flexed his growing blade fingers and let loose another roar.

It was only on second glance Jarek realized Gada didn't look so good.

Spikes and claws and scaly hide aside, the Kul looked, for lack of a better word, haggard. Like he'd been battered or maybe even tortured in the weeks since Jarek had last seen him.

Even a raknoth, with their inferior abilities, could regrow a lost limb in a matter of days, and yet the bulk of Gada's tail, which Jarek had severed with the Whacker a couple weeks earlier, remained missing—had actually been removed even further than where Jarek had originally hewn it off, he was pretty sure. On top of that, Gada's back and flanks were still lightly charred from the explosion he'd endured and the multiple lightning strikes Rachel had called down on him.

It didn't make sense.

Were these artifacts of fights he'd had with other raknoth and humans since returning to Earth with his kin? Or had it been his kin themselves who'd done this, maybe as punishment for his haste and ultimate failure in attacking ahead of their arrival?

Ahead, Gada reached out to flip another one of their trucks.

Jarek reached for his sword and leapt down the porch steps, reminding himself the rest didn't matter one damn bit right now.

He couldn't let Gada wipe out their transportation, had to draw the big bastard away from—

Movement above threw Jarek's heart into his throat, and then something large slammed to the ground right in his path.

Jarek touched down from his staircase leap and threw himself to the side in the same movement, turning through a sideways roll before coming to his feet to face… something.

Something dark and wriggling.

The thing that could only be another Kul reached for him with a pair of oddly amorphous limbs, its form shifting like the universe's creepiest and most sizeable bag of worms.

"Open fire!" someone—Chambers, he thought—bellowed from one of the farmhouse windows.

And open fire they did.

Gada, who'd just wrapped his claws underneath their SUV, gave an irritated growl and thrust the vehicle toward the house as if he were tossing a stone. The SUV rolled and bounced its way across the yard with frightening speed. It smashed through the deck and halfway through the front wall.

Resistance soldiers and Mosenites alike were pouring out onto the porch, firing at Gada and the newcomer alike.

The Incredible Wriggling Monstrosity recoiled under the storm of incoming lead, its movements more that of a startled or curious animal than those of one in pain or distress. Jarek flipped the switch on the Whacker's pommel and took a swing before it could decide the bullets weren't so interesting.

Azure fire flashed in the wake of the blade's edge, and a smell like ozone and burnt plastic hit Jarek.

The blade passed with less resistance than expected, spattering the ground with… not blood?

"What the fuck?" Jarek snapped, recoiling back.

Wriggles gave a horrendous screech at the new and oddly blood-less gash in his hide and made a wobbly undulation toward the porch.

In his wake, the Kul left a scattering of several dozen inch-long Wriggles Juniors squirming in the dirt.

Jarek turned after Wriggles, torn between heading him off or going to stop Gada before—

"SIR, INCOM—"

The shock of impact blurred the world, crushing everything else from Jarek's awareness until the raw sensation overload poured over into pain and spinning motion.

He was airborne, sailing like a ballistic missile after a hit that would've embarrassed a freight train. The question of who or what had hit him was only becoming a twinkle at the edge of Jarek's mind when his abrupt flight ended.

Hard dirt smacked into his shoulder, bucking against his momentum and sending him flipping end-over-end too fast to get his bearings and stabilize.

The ground seemed to come at him from all sides at once, pummeling his tumbling body until, some unknown time later, he was staring at crisp blue sky with the dull realization that he was no longer moving.

He could barely breathe through the pain.

"Get up, sir," Al's voice crackled in his ear.

Easy for him to say, Jarek decided as the ship floated by overhead, out of easy reach.

"Your sword, sir, he's…"

His sword!

He hadn't even realized he'd dropped it—probably because he'd actually been hit hard enough for Fela's iron grip to even fail him in the first place.

Jarek sat up with a deep wince and saw nothing but bad news.

Gada was approaching from the left with a leisurely swagger, as if he were immensely enjoying the moment.

To the right, Wriggles, having already taken down a few of their men, had reached the front door of the farmhouse and cut off the direct path to the vehicles.

And straight ahead…

The thing that had hit Jarek might have been taken for a gargoyle if you removed about two-hundred pounds of muscle and swapped the gray, leathery hide for stone. Short, stubby horns jutted over long, pointy ears. A demonic face, complete with fiery red eyes. Spindly wings, half-furled over its shoulders. Disproportionately long arms with fingers to match.

And, in those long, clawed fingers, the creature held his sword, turning it over with a kind of casual curiosity.

"Here," Jarek tried to call, though his voice came out more of a croak as he pushed himself to shaky feet, "let me show you how to use that thing, Mr. Satan, sir."

"Insouciant to its last," came the disjointed choir of whispers that was Gada's voice from the left, the words shaped oddly by his alien tongue. "Do you see, brother?"

By way of reply, the Anabolic Gargoyle cast the Whacker aside like a cheap toy. It hit the house and dropped to the porch with a heavy thunk. The gargoyle leapt forward, not bothering to unfurl his wings for the short flight, and slammed down a few yards in front of Jarek, several hundred pounds of dark, muscly monstrosity.

"This is the one?" the gargoyle said in a deep growl of a voice.

Jarek swallowed, cold fear constricting around his insides and freezing his limbs as the meaning of the Kul's words dawned on him and Gada drew up beside them.

"It is, brother," Gada said. "The one who slew Kul'Armin."

The gargoyle looked at Gada, in no apparent state of urgency.

Gunfire and an agonized scream from the house had the opposite effect on Jarek.

"The one who nearly slew you, brother," the gargoyle said. "Pathetic."

Behind the two rakul, some of the troops were spilling out into the yard from around the back of the house now. Wriggles was nowhere in sight, and sounds of fighting were pouring out of the house, whose front wall appeared to have been violently breached by the amorphous Kul.

Move.

Jarek had to move.

Get his sword. Clear the way to the trucks and…

Glass shattered from the direction of the house.

Impossible, his exhausted mind whispered as the gargoyle took his first step forward.

It was impossible.

Hold off three Kul? He'd be lucky to manage one on a good day, and this was the furthest thing from—

"Slater!"

The two rakul followed Jarek's gaze to the porch—just in time to see Mosen cock back and hurl the Whacker straight at Jarek.

Jarek reached for the blade without thought, instinctively calculating arc and rotation until the hilt smacked into his waiting hand, reverse-grip.

"Do it for Blondie!" Mosen called.

Then he turned and dove back through the ruined window toward the sounds of fighting inside.

Jarek gripped the Whacker's hilt tight, letting Mosen's words and the feelings they stirred flow through him like a cleansing fire, burning away his fear, leaving behind nothing but thrumming determination.

It was impossible. He was hopelessly outmatched.

But Jarek would be damned if he was going to let that stop him now.

"Let's go, ass-hats."

The words were barely out of his mouth when the gargoyle lunged forward with a sound like a bellowing bull.

Jarek dipped low, spinning far to the outside and coming around in time to clip the gargoyle's passing left wing with a reverse-grip rising strike.

What little satisfaction the gargoyle's aggravated grunt bought Jarek was snuffed by the sight of Gada rushing in on his brother's flank.

Gada pounced.

Jarek leapt twenty feet straight up into the air, pulling into a horizontal corkscrew. He swept his sword around and carved a smoking line of charred hide across the back of Gada's thick neck from above as the Kul fought to draw up from his fruitless charge.

Gada halted faster than anything his size had business doing. Certainly faster than Jarek had expected as he reached the zenith of his jump and began falling—straight for the Kul's spiky shoulders.

Jarek tucked and spun as fast as he could. Just fast enough to get his feet back under him as he slammed down to the aggressive terrain of Gada's back.

Unthinking, Jarek thrust his sword into the spiky mess for purchase.

It didn't sink far, but it was something to hold onto as Gada roared and whipped around, trying to shake him free.

He was about to take his chances with yanking the sword free to take a shot at Gada's head when Al cried out, "Incoming!"

Below, The Anabolic Gargoyle was already springing from the ground, bound straight for Jarek.

Jarek started to jump then rethought trying to out-elevate the gargoyle's unfurling wings and instead tucked into a low backward roll down Gada's left flank.

The gargoyle's claws narrowly missed him as he tumbled down and landed off-balance.

Gada's backhand didn't.

This time, Jarek managed to hold onto his sword right up to the moment he slammed into the crumpled mess of the truck Gada had trashed.

He groaned, trying to blink his vision clear and rise above the waves of pain rolling through him.

To the left, some of the Resistance troops and Mosenites alike were reaching the other convoy vehicles now. That was good. But there were still too many shouts and gunshots pouring out of the house, and he didn't see Mosen, Chambers, or Michael. That was less good.

And, as he came back to his senses and focused dead ahead, he saw that the gargoyle was gliding straight for him on leathery wings, long arms outstretched.

That was least good.

Jarek dropped like a sack of bricks. The gargoyle crashed into the truck and sent it flying into the adjacent field with a velocity that made Jarek wince.

He rolled to the side, feeling more than seeing the earth-shaking stomp he avoided as he scrambled back to his feet.

The gargoyle didn't give him time to shake it off.

He came after Jarek at a more controlled speed this time, leaving no room to maneuver outside of his charge. Worse, he seemed to have caught on that the Whacker posed some threat—however small—to even a Kul's resilient hide.

The gargoyle twisted and dodged outside of Jarek's first few strikes, closing on him all the while, those damned long arms seeking to wrap him under control.

Rhythmic vibrations in the earth underfoot told him Gada was charging in at the same time Al did.

Jarek stepped between the gargoyle and Gada, feigning ignorance of Gada's approach with his turned back. He cocked his sword back for another strike at the gargoyle…

And threw himself to the side at the last possible second, praying to the gods that an over-eager Gada would plow headlong into his brother as Jarek turned through an aerial and landed ten yards away.

No crash. No aggravated roars.

The sight of the two crimson-eyed rakul calmly stalking after him would have made him blush if it wasn't too busy shriveling his insides.

How had he expected that to work?

And what the hell else was he supposed to try?

Behind him, a window shattered, and he glanced back to see Mosen slam to a rough landing beside the house as if he'd been thrown by something strong and wriggly.

Michael and Chambers came around the back of the house at a sprint and hauled him to his feet just as Wriggles began folding his way through the too-small window.

"Go!" Jarek shouted at them. Above, Al was banking the ship down to offer them entry to the open rear hatch. "Get the hell out of here!"

He didn't wait to see if they'd listen. Didn't have time.

Gada and the gargoyle Kul moved on him as a pair this time, fanning to either side of him.

Jarek took a long jump away from the convoy, determined to draw them away from his friends and, at the same time, trying to avoid entertaining attack from both directions.

The maneuver was half-successful, at least.

The rakul sprang after him, their movements different than before, like a pair of seasoned pack hunters refusing to let their prey slip out from between them.

The fight took on a new quality for Jarek after that, and not for the better.

He dipped and weaved, parrying Gada's blades here, pressing the offensive against the gargoyle's shorter claws and more vulnerable forearms there. He gave himself over to the deadly dance completely —until his mind was blank and there was nothing but action and reaction, attack and counterattack. No space for pain or fear.

He was perfect.

And it wasn't enough.

Alone, against one Kul, he'd have had his hands more than full. Against two, with no Rachel or Drogan to watch his back, it was inevitable.

The blow that hammered him to the dirt had come from the gargoyle, his addled brain reasoned as he lay there, waiting for breath and focus to return with a horrible, creeping sense of acceptance.

It had come from the gargoyle, his brain continued to hash out, because, pulverized shoulder and lung aside, he was still physically in one piece, decidedly not hacked in two by Gada's wicked blades.

But he might as well have been.

Because there was no getting back to his feet this time, he knew, as he rolled over to face the rakul and found his sword hand already trapped beneath the gargoyle's massive foot. No stopping Gada as the leering dinosaur approached, flexing his finger-blades in anticipation.

"Get up, sir," Al pleaded in his earpiece.

Words failed him.

They'd done their best. He'd done his best. And now, just like that, all of it was about to be rendered worthless. All the fighting. All the pain.

Rachel.

He'd been so close. So fucking close.

The moment you think everything's well and good...

Gada paused at Jarek's feet, the violent delight evident even on his alien features as he leaned in to plant an enormous foot on Jarek's torso.

The moment you're sure you've got it in the bag...

"GET UP!" Al bellowed.

That's exactly when things are most ready to blow up in your face, kid.

"I'm sorry, Goldilocks," he whispered, closing his tired eyes as Gada raised his blades.

CHAPTER TWENTY

Lying in the dirt, eyes closed in some futile attempt for a moment of quiet peace with the image of Rachel in his mind's eye, and the last thing that Jarek would ever hear, of course, was the bestial roar of a damn Kul.

The air vibrated with it—a roar that might've come from a lion the size of a truck.

A roar, he realized, that didn't belong to Kul'Gada.

Jarek knew that roar.

Just like he knew the rust-red raknoth who slammed into Gada's shoulder as Jarek snapped his eyes open.

"RUSTYYY!!" Jarek bellowed in an incoherent flood of relief.

He didn't have time to ask how or why.

Zar'Krogoth's rust-red form ducked Gada's counterattack, and two more scaly green raknoth flew in to catch Gada in a tandem kick that took the Kul from his feet and shook the earth with his landing.

Three more raknoth sprang in to tackle the gargoyle away from Jarek before the Kul could pick up Gada's work and stomp him into armor-covered paste.

Krogoth spun around and yanked Jarek bodily to his feet.

"Gather your wits, Jarek Slater," he rumbled. "We must flee and regroup."

"Best idea I've heard all goddamn day," Jarek said, relief and residual swirls of icy terror rendering his mind numb as he looked around in a stupor.

A few more raknoth were sweeping in to help contain the three rakul—roughly ten in total at a glance. Rumbling engines to the right drew his attention to an approaching convoy of trucks similar to their own, but larger in number.

The trucks were all driven by humans, as far as he could see. And behind the wheel of the lead truck—

"Alaric?" Jarek asked to no one in particular.

The sight of the wiry Resistance commander, and the additional recognition of Commander Daniels beside him, sent another wave of warm relief through Jarek. Relief that was quickly tempered by Gada's roar of fury as the enormous Kul rocked back to his feet to engage the raknoth alongside his brother.

Time to move.

He dodged a wild lunge from Gada, hacked his own slash at one of the gargoyle's furled wings, and was rewarded with a pained screech.

The gargoyle Kul spun from the two raknoth he'd been facing to retaliate with a sweeping backhand, but Jarek was already throwing himself out of harm's way. Past the farmhouse porch.

Straight at Wriggles, who looked to be a second away from hurling his leathery form at the ship Mosen, Michael, and Chambers were hurrying toward.

Jarek thought for a few steps about trying to hack the wriggling blob clean in two. But that hadn't worked so well the first time. All they needed right then was space to get out of there.

So when Wriggles turned at his approach, Jarek lowered his shoulder and charged.

The impact was jarring and far from pain-free, but it did the job. Wriggles smashed down amid the thick weeds fifteen yards away. Michael, Chambers, and Mosen hesitated for a second, then clambered up the boarding ramp of the ship Al had hovered in just behind them.

Jarek turned to the soldiers who'd frozen halfway to the convoy to watch the ongoing fight. Behind them, Alaric's trucks were pulling up and throwing open doors and hatches to take on additional passengers.

"Get to the vehicles, people!" he bellowed. "Now! Go!"

Wriggles was gliding back toward him through the thick brush now.

Jarek glanced around to make sure everyone was clear. His stomach fell at the sight of the rakul ship hovering patiently above the battle—the one that must've carried Gada and his pals here. That ship had to go if they had any hope of losing these three. But how?

He turned, painfully aware of Wriggles' proximity at his back, and darted back to Krogoth and the other raknoth, who were still locked in a furious battle with Gada and the gargoyle.

Blow the ship. Clear out.

Simple.

But he had no idea how the hell they'd pull it off.

He caught Gada with a surprise hack to the right flank that left the Kul hobbling for balance. Then Wriggles caught up, and Jarek's focus shifted solely to not dying as the battle resumed at full tilt.

For the first minute, Jarek wondered if they might not just turn the tide and finish the three rakul then and there. But then Gada's leg seemed to begin recovering from Jarek's cut, his movements growing steadier, his attacks more vicious. Wriggles and the gargoyle, while both accruing their fair share of wounds, were dealing out far more damage than they were taking. One raknoth already lay dead, his body mangled and his head caved in.

A wave of relief—tinged with a tiny hint of panic—washed through Jarek when he chanced a glance and saw most of the convoy rolling away down the road.

All that was left, aside from the crumpled heaps Gada had made of two of their vehicles, was a single large truck, looping back around to get closer to them. That, and Jarek's ship, which he realized with a jolt

Al was guiding sneakily from the escaping convoy back toward the rakul ship above.

"What the hell, Al?" he hissed.

The lone truck cut into the adjacent field and kicked up a rolling cloud of dust as it circled around to point its back toward them and its hood toward the retreating convoy. Alaric was hanging out the open rear hatch, shouting and waving them on.

"We have a plan, sir," Al said, his words slightly strained, as they often were when he was running too many tasks and conversations all at once. "Get the raknoth on that truck. We'll take care of the ship."

We?

Jarek didn't have time to question it as another raknoth shrieked and hit the dirt, his left arm dangling by little more than a thread of scaly hide.

Either Al had reached out to Krogoth as well, or the raknoth had already had the same thought himself, because his kin were all shifting formation now, angling around their foes to give themselves better lines of retreat to the waiting truck.

Then it was like a switch had been thrown.

Rakul pounced. Raknoth leapt. For a moment, every single body in the fight seemed to be airborne.

Krogoth, apparently not trusting Jarek to catch on, wrapped a powerful rust-red arm around his chest and hoisted him backward in a mighty jump that ended in an awkward landing right by the waiting truck.

Before Jarek could buck free and ask Krogoth what the hell he was thinking, the raknoth bodily tossed him through the open hatch and into the truck's trailer.

Son of a bitch.

Jarek scrambled to his feet.

"Look out," Alaric snapped.

He turned and just managed to sidestep out of the way as one, two, three raknoth came diving into the trailer. The third overdid his jump and hit the front wall hard enough to dent it.

A frustrated roar from outside. Gada's.

At the rear of the truck, Krogoth was waving like a goddamn air traffic controller while more raknoth continued to pile in.

Jarek reached the hatch just as a raknoth came spinning limply through the air as if he'd been thrown—one arm wobbling bizarrely on a single thread of hide.

Krogoth caught the raknoth, paying no mind when the dangling arm tore free with the force of the impact. He just hopped into the trailer with his raknoth in tow.

"Drive!" he roared.

But Jarek had just looked over and saw that they were still short one. Al'Brandt. He must've been the one who'd thrown that last raknoth. And Gada and the gargoyle were both closing on him.

Jarek started to hop out, but Krogoth caught him in the chest and shoved him back in.

"He will manage himself."

Jarek started to tell him to shove his barbaric sense of leadership up his ass, but it turned out Krogoth's point was well-made.

In a flat out race, any of the Kul might have bested Brandt. None of them, however, were as agile. In fact, Jarek was pretty sure he'd never seen anyone as agile as Brandt—save for maybe Haldin and Elise.

The raknoth moved with preternatural grace and speed, dipping outside of the gargoyle's long-armed grab, ducking Gada's finger blades and actually using the Kul's thick left flank as a springboard as he launched his way over the reaching tendrils of Wriggles' swelling form and toward the accelerating truck.

He turned neatly through the air and hit the ground running, Gada and the gargoyle in hot pursuit. He was fast. Maybe even faster than the two pursuing rakul. But that barely mattered, considering all three of them would be more than fast enough to catch the truck.

Before they'd made it more than a few lumbering steps, though, Gada and the gargoyle pulled up short and spun around at something Jarek neither saw nor heard. His stomach sank when both of their heads snapped straight up at Jarek's ship, which was now hovering with its rear hatch tight against the side of the dark purplish length of the rakul vessel.

"Al, you have to get out of th—"

"I can't, sir."

"What?"

"I can't leave. Mosen's aboard."

"What?!"

We'll take care of the ship, Al had said.

Shit. Shit. Shit.

Jarek's panic only grew when Alaric looked at him then the ships, slow, horrible realization dawning on his wizened face.

This time, it was Alaric who Krogoth had to catch before he could throw himself out of the open hatch in frantic desperation.

"Let me go!" Alaric roared.

"Al," Jarek said, "you have to get him out of—"

"I found your grenades, Slater."

Mosen's voice, smooth and cavalier, but with a small undercurrent of fear Jarek didn't miss. Al must've patched him through.

"Mosen. Whatever you're—"

"I know what I'm doing. It's too late to talk me out of it anyway."

As if in testament, the pop of a distant explosion carried down to the fleeing truck, and the rakul ship wobbled unsteadily in the air.

Alaric's struggles had weakened now. He was riveted on Jarek, sensing he was his only hope, his eyes pleading for him to somehow put a stop to this. To save his son.

Brandt caught up and hopped into the speeding truck, his small victory like an icy slap in the wake of Mosen's predicament.

"Mosen," Jarek growled, "get in the damn ship. Get out of there. Now!"

Mosen just chuckled in Jarek's earpiece, though Jarek could tell the nonchalance was forced. "I don't really see the point of doing that unless you happen to be hiding one hell of a gun under that armor of yours. There's no other way you're getting out of here without them on your tail."

Below, the gargoyle gathered himself and sprang for the point where the two ships met. Al tried to swat him aside with the hull of his ship. It was a good hit, but the Kul managed to clamp onto one of the stubby wings anyway, using his own leathery wings to stabilize himself.

With a hideous squeal of wrenching metal, the gargoyle tore the wing from the ship, which immediately began to spiral drunkenly downward.

"Goddammit, Mosen, we're n—"

"Gonna get to Cheyenne and kill these fuckers, is what you're going to do," Mosen said through gritted teeth, "or I'll see your ass in hell."

Jarek watched, wordless, stupefied, as his ship smashed down beside the farmhouse and Gada joined his brother Kul in violently dismantling the sleek matte box that had been his home for over six years now.

"Seth . . ." Alaric groaned.

"My father..." Mosen said, as if he'd heard through Jarek's comm.

"He's here," Jarek said.

He didn't know what else to say—what else to do.

"Just... just tell him . . ."

Jarek waited, watching hopelessly as the rakul finished with his ship and turned their attention back to their own.

"I will, Seth."

"Seth!" Alaric shouted, resuming his hopeless struggling against Krogoth's iron grip with more ferocity than before. "Don't you—don't —don't..."

"Make it count, Slater," Seth said quietly in his ear over Alaric's broken groans.

Then the rakul ship disappeared in a blossoming ball of teal fire.

It started small, flames licking out from the stern and along the length of the ship until something critical ignited. The flames roared outward with a deafening boom, engulfing everything in a hundred-yard radius—the farmhouse, the rakul, everything—for one furious split-second, so blinding that Fela's filters simply shut down.

Then, as quickly as they came, the flames were gone, leaving nothing but smoke and charred Earth. A few larger hunks of debris thudded into the weeds on either side of the rode.

They drove on.

The farmhouse was a smoking wreck, fading into the distance. There was movement on the scorched lawn—Gada and that damn gargoyle picking themselves up, charred and hurting, but clearly not dead. Wriggles' blackened shape swelled upright from the ground a few seconds later.

The rakul were too far now—and hopefully hurting too much—to try to catch them on foot. Or so Jarek's numb brain told him. The thought didn't bring any sense of victory or relief. He couldn't seem to move.

Alaric had gone nearly catatonic, huddled at the rear of the trailer where he'd collapsed after the explosion.

They drove on, dead silence hanging in the trailer, broken only by the hum of the truck and the faint pitter-patter of the smoky bits of ship debris still raining down, even this far away.

Jarek fell to the bench behind him, head spinning.

They drove on.

CHAPTER TWENTY-ONE

Just a few months ago, had someone told Rachel she was going to be leaving Unity to fight for the fate of the planet, at the very least, she would have called them stupendously imaginative. If they'd told her she'd be fixing up for a road trip with a raknoth, she would have laughed them off-stage.

And yet here she was, staring down from the top of Cheyenne Mountain beside Drogan and Dola and trying to figure out which car it was they were taking.

Life strangeness aside, it was still nice to get outside of the stifling walls of The Complex, even after having only been down there for a day. How some of those people had been living down there for over a decade was beyond her. Actually, it probably explained a few things.

As Dola pointed out from the mountaintop, though, his people didn't spend all of their time within The Complex. Some hunted. Others tended the crop fields they'd replanted north of the lots after they'd deemed the ones by the main road too much of a giveaway to passing marauders. Some even just stepped out for the occasional stroll—during the allowed hours and in the allowed locations, of course.

Semi-daily strolls outside or no, Rachel still shuddered at the thought of years spent as an inhabitant of The Complex. Maybe she was just a hint claustrophobic. Or maybe the place's vibe—the creepily zealous raknoth haters with their disguised raknoth leader—just gave her the heebie-jeebies.

Either way, she'd been grateful for the secret lift Dola had excavated up to the mountain's peak from a hidden room in his office over the long years. Apparently, Dola enjoyed fresh air and sunrises as much as he enjoyed privacy.

Rachel was just relieved to have been spared another mini-interrogation with Zach and his goons, who might've initially been glad to see them go but would just as likely have raised hell when they'd realized they meant to return with more people—and quite possibly with more heat on their tails.

Treading quietly was the name of the game here.

"You might as well take my car," Dola was saying, pointing down from the bushy ridge to the distant stretch of the southern lot. "The blue Subaru Sol down there. I've seen to it the vehicle has been well-kept over the years, though I've rarely had occasion to use it."

Rachel followed his pointing finger. She was still wondering how the hell he could even distinguish one car from another at this distance, much less make or model, when Drogan gave an affirmative grunt and turned to her with outstretched arms.

"You are ready, Rachel Cross?"

"Hardly," Rachel said, deciding for the first time that maybe leaving through the front door wouldn't have been the worst thing in the world.

Still, it was just falling. Nothing she couldn't control. Even if it had to be in Drogan's arms.

"But let's go," she added, shifting her arms and her staff so Drogan could scoop her up with one arm under the crook of her knees and the other wrapped behind her back.

"You are certain you can handle this?" Drogan asked.

Her lip twitched. "Don't tell me you're worried about me, Drogan?"

He only grunted and turned to Dola. "We will return as soon as we can. Do not let anything happen to our people."

If Dola had anything to say to that, Drogan didn't wait around to hear it. Instead, he charged forward and bounded off the mountain ridge.

It was one hell of a jump. And not exactly an insignificant deceleration act on her part seven or eight seconds later.

They landed with a soft thump maybe two-thirds of the way down the mountain, Drogan's arms as sturdy as the walls of The Complex beneath her.

Her head lightly buzzed with the channeling fatigue of catching both herself and a plummeting raknoth, but it wasn't particularly bothersome. One bright side of this whole catastrophic shit-storm— her abilities had grown by leaps and bounds.

Drogan looked down at her thoughtfully. "That was... considerably more pleasant than I am accustomed to."

"Yeah, good times all around." Rachel shook the residual tingles from her head and frowned. "Do those big jumps normally hurt?"

"Hurt is a relative concept, but"—he gave a slight shrug—"they can be less than pleasant. Are you ready?"

She nodded, and they were off again.

Two bounds, a short walk, and fifteen minutes later, they were in Dola's car, past the landmines, and turning north onto CO Route 115. Beyond backtracking east on 70 and seeing what they saw, the plan was sadly lacking. But without Net communications or anything else to guide them, it was all they really had.

Neither of them could pretend like it was the smartest idea, but at least with just the two of them, they were highly mobile. They could tread softly and, should the worst happen, move quickly.

Personally, Rachel wasn't nearly so worried about herself and Drogan as she was about the others, both ahead and behind.

It all felt so uncertain, so unsteady. All this work, all the fighting and hiding and soldiering on. And all of it ready to come crashing down around them with the faintest brush of bad luck.

Looking at the entire picture, it was almost impossible not to despair.

Everything they'd done in the name of preparing to take on the rakul, and yet, whenever she stopped to think about it, she couldn't help but think that maybe it was all just a grand gesture at delaying the inevitable. That maybe, deep down, they all knew they were doomed. That pretending they were fighting it was just their way of deluding themselves that they'd done their best in an impossible situation.

She closed her eyes, let out a long breath, and finally looked over at Drogan, wondering if he was having similar thoughts.

Rachel bit back a laugh at what she saw.

It wasn't like she hadn't expected to find the raknoth driving the car. But something about seeing Al'Drogan—the freaking Red King and second eldest of the raknoth left on Earth—driving with eyes firmly on the road ahead and hands secured at the ten and two o'clock positions on the wheel nearly made her lose it.

Apparently, her amusement wasn't lost on him.

"What is it?" he asked without looking over as he guided the car through a left turn onto what the sign dubbed Route 21.

"Just…" She shook her head. "Nothing."

Drogan drove on silently for another ten minutes or so, until Rachel could no longer stand her mind's dark ruminations.

"Outside of Pittsburgh," she said, not really sure where she was going with this, "when you said the rakul have forgotten what it means to fear death . . ."

Drogan glanced at her, waiting for the conclusion to a question she hadn't quite figured out yet.

"Why do they do it?" she finally said. "The raknoth infiltrating, the rakul invading… What's the point of any of it? What do they want?"

Drogan didn't answer for a long while. She couldn't tell if he was debating what he should and shouldn't tell her about his people or simply deciding where best to start.

"The conventional answer among my people," he finally said, "would be that they do it for what you might call sport."

That was the impression she'd gotten from much of what they'd first learned of the rakul. And yet...

"What about the unconventional answer?"

Drogan looked at her more closely this time, weighing her with his eyes. "I think they do it for the same reason any lifeform does anything. Because they are afraid."

Rachel looked out the passenger-side window, absentmindedly staring at the sprawling plains and crumbling housing developments flying by as she turned that over in her mind, trying to find Drogan's angle.

"They don't look so scared to me," she finally said.

Drogan nodded as if this were something he'd already thought over more than once. "They do not. But that does not mean they are absent fear. Not even if they have forgotten that fear themselves."

Rachel frowned at a particularly gnarly tree in the field they were passing. "Is this one of those immortal things my puny human brain can't hope to adequately comprehend?"

The hint of a smile touched at Drogan's mouth. "It is possible. Though, as it is difficult for you to understand the perspective of one who has lived for thousands of years, so too is it problematic for me to recall my own capacity for understanding such feelings in the first few decades of my own existence. It's been awhile, as you might say."

"I kinda get it." She frowned. "I think. But let's start with the basics, then. What exactly do the rakul even have to be afraid of in the first place?"

"Again—"

"The same things as the rest of us," Rachel said, "I get it. But you're gonna tell me they intended to wipe out humanity because they were afraid we were some kind of threat?"

"Yes," Drogan said. "Not now, clearly, and maybe not for several of your millennia to come, but mankind exhibited every sign of eventually becoming a genuine threat to the galactic dominance of the rakul." He tilted his head. "Provided you did not fall into the not-uncommon pattern of eradicating your own species before it could reach that stage."

"Yeah, someone kinda beat us to the punch there," Rachel muttered. "Fine. So they're committing, what? Preemptive genocide?"

"That is one way to perceive it."

"Well, that's…" Rachel shook her head, uncertain how to adequately capture the sentiment.

Fucked up didn't quite seem to cut it.

"What's the point of even living if that's your legacy?" Rachel asked when she'd given up on expressing her revulsion.

"Your question betrays the belief intrinsic to most young species—that there should be any point to existence at all."

Rachel stared at him, looking for some sign of insincerity. "You're saying you don't believe there is?"

"Why should I? It is a vain belief, and one that grows more tedious with each passing year, each passing planet. We simply choose existence over the alternative. The rest follows, and the cycle perpetuates."

Jesus. Remind her never to let a raknoth try to talk someone off the edge.

She was about to point out that being nihilists only made what they did that much more fucked up when she registered the last thing he'd said.

"Cycle? What cycle?"

Drogan seemed to be amused by the question. "We may seem ancient by virtue of our lifespans, but I will point out that the oldest of the rakul is not so much older than the civilization of mankind. Where the age of the universe itself is concerned, we are still but hatchlings."

"Point being?"

"That we were hardly the first beings to dominate The Void," Drogan said, shooting her a look that might've been condescending.

She was too busy contemplating the implications to care.

"There were others? Before the rakul?" She frowned, considering the entirety of his story. "Were your people…?"

She trailed off, looking around in confusion as Drogan slowed the car and guided them over to a halt at the side of the road.

All she saw were more houses, more fields, and, maybe half a mile ahead, a crappy little saloon that looked like it was two light breezes from crumbling to the ground.

Judging from the way Drogan was staring ahead and sniffing the air through his cracked driver's side window, though, something interesting was afoot.

"What is it?" she asked.

He wrinkled his nose and turned to her with a wary expression.

"We walk from here."

CHAPTER TWENTY-TWO

When Krogoth called the convoy to a halt a mere fifty miles from the rakul they'd too-narrowly left behind, Jarek had been as alarmed as the rest of his people. Then Krogoth had explained himself, and they'd all dropped their arguments and obediently funneled into the old ramshackle saloon they'd stopped at to keep out of sight while Krogoth and his raknoth went over each and every one of them from head to toe.

The problem at this point, as Krogoth explained, was only half in outrunning the three Kul and whichever of their brethren they might've already alerted before their ship had been destroyed. The other half was making sure they weren't leading the rakul straight to Cheyenne.

It seemed that, aside from being physically dangerous and virtually impossible to kill, Wriggles—or Kul'Vermaga, as Krogoth identified him—was capable of controlling and communicating with every little wriggly bit of himself, be they near or far. Worse, Krogoth was worried that each of Vermaga's units might possess enough of his power to be able to exert some telepathic influence over unprotected minds.

And, as if that all wasn't bad enough already, they could also multiply.

Once Krogoth had laid it out, no one had argued with his instructing his raknoth to conduct a full sweep. Turns out, it had been a wise fear to have.

The raknoth had already found several of the wormy little things crawling around in their vehicles and half a dozen more clinging to their people in various bags and pockets. Each one they found, they crushed and tossed into the small garbage-can fire they kindled up.

Which made it twice they all would've been dead if it hadn't been for Krogoth.

No. For Krogoth and Mosen . . .

For the hundredth time in the past half-hour, Jarek's hands curled into painfully tight fists, fruitlessly seeking some purchase to keep him from plummeting into the black hole of guilt—or at least a Kul throat to choke about it.

He'd done his best. Done everything he could to see his people safely through to Cheyenne.

How the rakul had even managed to track them down was still a mystery, but that only made things worse. Because, without knowing where they'd messed up, Jarek couldn't shut out the thoughts whispering that, maybe, if he'd done things differently—traveled at different hours, taken a more roundabout route...

Maybe he could have saved them.

But it was too late now.

Mosen was dead, along with five more of their group who'd died trying to hold against Vermaga while Jarek had been busy getting his ass handed to him by Gada and the gargoyle—or Kul'Ogrin as Krogoth had called the big gray monstrosity.

And here it had only been a few days ago that Jarek had been thinking life would be so much easier if he could simply drop Mosen from his plate of worries. As it already had several times in the past hour, shame burned hot in his cheeks and throat.

Those few short days felt more like a lifetime now.

Worst of all was the fact that Alaric had found them just in time to see his son ripped away. As heavy as Mosen's sacrifice rested on Jarek's shoulders, looking at Alaric now…

Jarek wished the wiry old commander would say something. Anything. Hell, he would've taken Alaric coming at him with fist or bullet over nothing.

But *nothing* was all Alaric seemed capable of right now.

He just sat at the bar, stringy gray hair unkempt, an untouched bottle of whiskey sitting forgotten in his hands as he stared with unseeing eyes into the depths of a personal hell Jarek could only guess at.

Commander Daniels sat beside Alaric with an arm draped over his shoulders, not bothering to try with words.

The only shred of light—paltry as it seemed in the face of everything else—was Al'Brandt, who'd told Jarek, between sweeping the troops for Vermaga's pieces, that he'd been with Rachel and the others less than a week ago.

It wasn't much Jarek didn't already know—that they'd fled the rakul in Pittsburgh and opted to try their luck with Johnny's recommendation of the Cheyenne Mountain bunker. But it was more of a relief than Jarek would have expected to hear the story confirmed from another mouth.

Jarek wasn't the only one for whom Brandt's presence had been a blessing either, from the sound of it. A day after having ditched the ship he'd used to distract any rakul pursuing Rachel and the others out of Pittsburgh, Brandt had found Krogoth's group on foot and informed them of the new objective, Cheyenne Mountain.

Looking at it all from a bird's eye view, it seemed a minor miracle any of them were still alive at this point.

But they *were* alive. Soon they'd be back together with the rest of their allies. And from there…

From there, they had a small army, a dozen pairs of claws, an arcanist, and one Big Whacker that all said the rakul were going to bleed long and deep if they wanted to take this planet.

Jarek held the thought in his mind like a mantra, pushing it over and over again against the thoughts of Mosen and the rakul no doubt closing on them as the raknoth finished sweeping their people for bits of Vermaga.

He'd almost convinced himself he had the guilt and doubt under control for the time being when Brandt tensed next to him and threw a steaming pile of dread over his burgeoning zen.

It couldn't be. Not again. Not so soon.

But across the room, Krogoth was perked up too now, testing the air with his short, rust-red snout.

Give them a fucking break.

Krogoth caught Jarek's and Brandt's stares and nodded toward the front door, opposite the rusty kitchen they'd entered from the back parking lot.

Jarek and Brandt traded a dark look and moved for the door together.

The open space of the saloon, already somber enough in the aftermath of their near escape, dropped to dead silence as everyone caught on that something was up.

The silence only emphasized the pounding of Jarek's heart and the fire in his shoulder and back as he reached back to draw the Whacker.

They were nearly to the door when Jarek heard it. The patter of footsteps in the dirt lot outside, quieter than he would've been able to hear without Fela's sensors. And they were headed their way.

Krogoth appeared at Jarek's left shoulder, listening as well.

It was two people, from the sound of it. One clearly heavier than the other judging from the creak of the wooden deck out front.

Heavier, maybe, but not so heavy as to believe it was two rakul outside.

Jarek exchanged a hopeful look with Brandt and Krogoth, some of the tension bleeding out of their faces.

Not rakul.

And if it wasn't the rakul…

A new hope fluttered in his chest, as cautious as it was unlikely.

He grabbed the door handle. Waited for Krogoth's affirmative nod. Then he threw the door open, shooting through the doorway, sword at the ready.

As hopeful as he'd been, he wasn't ready for the relief that poured through him at the sight of the glyph-etched staff in his face and Rachel's wide eyes behind it.

He gasped, scared to even move for a moment.

Then he pushed her staff aside and wrapped her in a desperate hug.

This was a trick, his mind whispered. He was hallucinating. He'd died back in front of that farmhouse.

But Rachel was still there, solid and real in his arms, and—

"Can't… breathe…" she wheezed, and yet her staff had fallen to the deck, and her arms clung to him just as tightly.

He loosened his hold incrementally and pulled back just enough to take her in, his throat aching with emotion as she looked up at him with wide hazel eyes.

"Michael?" she whispered.

Jarek nodded, struggling to find words at first. "He's inside. He's okay."

Rachel closed her eyes and let out a heavy breath of relief, then she looked back up at him and tapped his faceplate. "And you? I'm not getting Al-swapped right now, am I?"

"Perish the thought, ma'am," Al said through Fela's speakers while Jarek willed his faceplate open.

To his own two eyes, Rachel looked even more beautiful, her eyes and skin somehow more alive with a subtle palette of soft tones no sensor-to-display interface could ever perfectly recreate.

The sight of his face, apparently, wasn't quite so relieving to her.

"Jesus," she said, reaching up to touch lightly at his left cheek. "Did you try to kill a Kul with your cheekbones or something?"

He almost smiled before the reminder of the bruise's source hit him like another of Mosen's punches.

"Something like that," he said, thinking of Alaric sitting mutely at the bar.

The sound of a throat clearing yanked them back to their surroundings, where they had faces staring at them through the windows and three raknoth standing around them, including—

"Stumpy!" Jarek cried.

Drogan furtively extended a fist in invitation for a fist bump.

"Aw, bring it in, you old stumpy bastard," Jarek said, swatting the fist aside and wrapping the stunned raknoth in a back-thumping hug.

When Jarek pulled back, Drogan's entire body was comically rigid. Krogoth, Brandt, and the few other raknoth watching through the windows all looked like they weren't quite sure whether to be disgusted with Drogan or to laugh at him.

"We should move," Krogoth said, looking back at the sea of curious faces in the saloon. "Kul'Vermaga will have felt us disposing of his little spies. They will not tarry in reaching this place."

Drogan stiffened anew at that. "Kul'Vermaga tracks you?"

"Back to the vehicles," Krogoth called into the saloon. Then, in a quieter tone to Drogan, "We have dealt with it as best we presently can, brother. Kul'Gada and Kul'Ogrin come as well, and likely others by now."

"Cursed Void," Drogan growled under his breath, exchanging a dark look with Rachel.

"You tangled with three of them?" Rachel asked. "How'd you get away?"

Jarek's gaze tracked in Alaric's direction by its own accord only to find the saloon wall instead. "Long story."

"One we'd best save until we're behind thicker walls," came Commander Daniels' strong voice from the doorway.

Jarek turned to see that most of their people had already cleared back out to the vehicles. Which meant they should probably cut this off and get moving.

Understandably, though, Daniels had to quietly first ask, after a nervous glance back toward Alaric, "Lea?"

"She's safe," Rachel said. "And worried sick about you."

"Thank God," Daniels breathed.

"Sounds like it's high-time for a reunion," Jarek said.

"Splendid," Krogoth said in a tone that sounded anything but splendiferous. "Let us move out, then."

Rachel shared a knowing look with Drogan, the faintest hint of a satisfied grin tugging at her mouth.

"Zach is gonna be *so* pissed."

CHAPTER TWENTY-THREE

In the race to Cheyenne Mountain, no speed limits were observed, and no accelerator pedals spared. Jarek sat clutching Rachel's hand in the back of the rearmost truck in their convoy, only silently allowing himself to hope they might make it to safety without pursuit. As much as the AI-trained side of his brain insisted the concept of a jinx was utterly ridiculous bullshit, some less logical corner whispered that he'd be a fool to say the words aloud—or to even think them too intently—and risk inviting disaster down on their heads.

It was that stupid superstitious bit that whispered a gleeful little *Told you so!* when Drogan stiffened on the bench opposite them.

"My kin have spotted aerial pursuit."

Everyone else in the back of the truck sat up a little straighter, checking weapons and trading woeful looks. Not that Jarek blamed them on the last part.

If woe was anyone, it was absolutely them right now.

He grasped the release lever on the truck's rear hatch. "Everyone secure?"

After the round of somber affirmatives, he pulled.

The door slid up into the ceiling compartment by its own power, opening their view to a wide square of cloudy blue sky. And there, streaming through those distant clouds like a prowling shark, was their aerial pursuit.

A rakul ship. He didn't want to know how many of the bastards might be on board.

"Shit," Rachel said.

"It will be a close race," Drogan agreed.

A very close race, it turned out, as the truck hung a right and practically begged the pursuing ship to make use of its aerial freedom to take the direct hypotenuse between their silly little human roads. The winding of the current road only worsened matters.

"Tell me we're close," Jarek said.

"Three-point-four miles, sir," Al said through Fela's speakers. "Uphill."

Jarek groaned. "You just had to include that last part, didn't you?"

"It felt pertinent, sir."

"They will likely catch us," Drogan said.

"Well aren't we just a happy bunch of downers today," Jarek muttered.

Rachel stiffened as if she'd just remembered something important. "The landmines."

Drogan waved her concern away. "I have already informed my brothers throughout the convoy."

Rachel partially relaxed and looked at Jarek. "See how much simpler things would be if you were a telepath?"

"Hey, I can do mind stuff." He closed his faceplate with a careful thought and spread his hands as if to say *Ta-da!*

Rachel's response was cut short by Drogan's growl, which drew their attention back to their closing pursuit. Icy panic shot through Jarek's gut at the sight of the thing plummeting from the ship.

It was still a fair distance away, but the shape was unmistakable. It was the same one that had been haunting his nightmares since it had chased him and Michael out of HQ a few weeks prior. A hairless, quadrupedal monstrosity that could only vaguely be compared to some mix between a wolf and a bear.

A giant, jacked one who probably ate real bears for breakfast.

"Kul'Harga," Drogan growled as the cracking thud of the thing's landing carried to them through the green roadside foliage.

A dissonant, alien bellow filled the air, declaring Harga's hunt in session.

The sound made Jarek cringe inwardly. But he took up the Whacker and rose to grab one of the support handles by the open hatch anyway.

Drogan came to stand beside him. Both of them listened with sharpened senses to the steadily approaching series of thuds, crashes, and eager snarling sounds as Harga hounded after his prey.

Closer. Closer.

The thuds of huge, thundering paws abruptly ended.

Then Harga's pale, hairless bulk came flying clear over the roadside greenery to slam down on the pavement behind them.

The beast shook itself, locked burning eyes on Jarek and Drogan, and surged after them with another sonorous bellow.

Jarek braced himself as the truck cornered into a rightward turn on the winding road. He prepared his swing as they leveled out, cocking the Whacker back in the space outside the truck and—

The truck whipped left, skirting off the road and startling his balance. A few jostles and bumps. They cruised by a pile of scraps that looked like the remainder of a ramshackle wall. Then the truck cut back onto the road. Jarek didn't have time to wonder about the maneuver.

Harga was closing.

Jarek leaned back out and raised the Whacker, praying to the gods the support handle would hold when he swung.

Harga picked up his pace, his crimson eyes and flapping jowls radiating eager anticipation at the sight of the challenge.

Twenty-five yards.

Fifteen.

Jarek was cocking his sword for the swing when Rachel's staff jutted out past him.

There was a low thrum of power, and the tree trunks of Harga's front legs tripped back under his charging body as if they'd encountered an invisible barrier right next to the remnants of the scrap wall.

The Kul proceeded to eat a patched section of pavement with ground-shaking force. A patched section of pavement that inexplicably detonated upon his impact.

A relieved sound of victory barked its way from Jarek's throat as he realized they must've just passed the mines Rachel had been worried about.

The relief, though, was short-lived as Harga ambled to his massive feet, clearly not incapacitated. The Kul rose to his hind legs, revealing a bloody mess of scorched underbelly, and gave a furious roar. Then he slammed back to the pavement and lumbered after them.

Harga's pace, at least, seemed to have been reduced by the explosion.

Another cry from above—one Jarek thought he'd already heard that day—announced that their worries weren't even close to over yet, though.

Drogan leaned out to take a look overhead.

Jarek was about to join him when the truck weaved, maneuvering around what must've been a second set of mines.

At whatever he saw, Drogan gripped the top edge of the open hatch without a word and flipped himself out and up to the truck roof with surprising agility.

Jarek poked out to see the distant shape of the gargoyle Kul'Ogrin gliding toward them on leathery wings.

"Well that guy looks like fun," Rachel muttered as she appeared at his side, staff held at the ready in Harga's direction.

"Yeah," Jarek said, "and he's sporting serious murder wood for Armin's killer."

Rachel glanced at him. "Well, aren't you lucky?"

"Would it be cheesy if I said 'now that I found you'?"

"Yes." She leveled her staff, brow furrowed in concentration, and a section of road Harga had slowed to eye suspiciously exploded in a booming flash of fire, shrapnel, and dust. "Yes, it would."

Harga padded a few steps back, sniffed at the air a few times, and cut a wide berth around the exploded road, trotting up the adjacent hill instead of following them into a wide roundabout.

For a few moments, there was nothing but heavy tension and squealing tires. Then they leveled out of the turn, and Harga's lumbering form crested the hill after them, having gained significant ground on his shortcut.

"Sword, Jarek Slater!" Drogan called above.

"Seriously, Stumpy?" Jarek called back. "We're kinda busy down h—"

"Give me the cursed Whacker!" Drogan boomed.

Rachel nodded, hefting her staff to point out they weren't without defenses.

Jarek flipped the blade reverse-grip, slapped the power on, and thrust it up to Drogan.

The raknoth snatched it roughly and tore it straight into a hard rising sweep.

There was a flash of blue light and an ugly screech, then something —presumably Ogrin or Drogan—hit the top of the truck and thudded diagonally across with a series of groaning impacts that left the roof half caved in.

Jarek tightened at what sounded too much like a Drogan-sized object bouncing over the edge of the truck roof, but then the Whacker punched through the ceiling at an awkward angle, and a pair of impacts rocked the side of the truck as if Drogan were using the blade to hold on.

All the troops in the compartment scurried away from the thud, weapons trained that way. And not a second too soon.

A pair of challenging roars shook the trailer. Three claws tore through the wall like tin foil, gray leathery fingers looking for purchase. The strong gray arm got a grip inside, and the section of wall beside it and below the sword crumpled a foot inward, as if Ogrin had body-slammed a dangling Drogan into it.

Ahead, Harga had renewed his charge, emboldened by whatever he'd just seen.

Jarek glanced between the incoming Kul and the top of the truck, debating.

"Go!" Rachel said. "I've got this."

She wasn't just saying it either.

On foot, Rachel might've been hard-pressed to slow Harga down enough to make a difference. From the back of a speeding truck, though, each of her telekinetic trip-ups bought them real breathing room.

So Jarek turned his back to Harga and the open hatch, grabbed the top edge of the truck trailer, and jumped.

The metal of the truck groaned and shifted beneath his fingers, but it held enough for him to flop up to the top with about one-hundredth of Drogan's style.

Behind, Harga growled in frustration.

Ahead, Drogan cried out in pain.

Ogrin had his right shoulder in a vise grip, his long gray thumb driven deep into Drogan's chest.

Somehow, Drogan still managed to throw a few awkward upper-cuts into Ogrin's protruding lower jaw with the hand that wasn't anchoring him to the truck by the Whacker's hilt.

Ogrin paid the feeble blows no mind—just leaned in as if intending to tear Drogan's head from his shoulders with nothing but his misaligned teeth.

Jarek didn't wait around to see how that would work out.

He darted forward, dropped down, and slipped an arm around Ogrin's throat in a choke hold. Ogrin growled and struggled, but his tremendous strength didn't do him nearly as much good while he was dangling from the side of a truck by one hand.

Jarek grabbed Ogrin's wrist and began trying to pry the Kul's enormous hand from Drogan's shoulder.

With a snarl, Drogan grabbed Ogrin's wrist just above Jarek's hand and added his own strength.

They were starting to make some headway when a Resistance soldier poked up from the passenger-side window of the truck cab.

For a second, he gaped at Ogrin, then he turned to Jarek and shouted over the wind, "Get down!" pointing emphatically ahead.

It was only then Jarek realized how close they were to the low entrance tunnel cut in the side of the mountain.

Shit.

And was that a…?

No time.

Jarek jutted his chin forward. "Just keep driving!"

Turning back to the struggle at hand, Jarek caught Drogan's eye and jerked his head left in a sign he hoped the raknoth would understand to mean *Let's toss this a-hole overboard!*

"One," Drogan called, apparently catching on.

Ahead, the tunnel seemed to be approaching faster and faster.

"Two," Jarek added, planting his right foot to Ogrin's shoulder.

Fifty feet. Thirty feet.

"THREE!"

He wrenched and kicked all at once. On the other side, Drogan did the same.

Ogrin's claws tore free from Drogan's shoulder and the truck alike, grasping at Jarek's leg and then thin air as the Kul took involuntary flight, bound straight for the rocky wall at the side of—

The tunnel!

Jarek threw himself flat against the truck as the lip of the semi-circular tunnel whooshed by overhead.

A bellow followed after them. Harga's he thought. Then there was a momentous scraping sound and the daylight disappeared as something heavy boomed at the mouth of the tunnel.

Jarek raised his head and saw a solid-looking door had dropped down like a guillotine blade to bar the tunnel entrance upon their passing.

Something—probably Harga—hit the door with a violent crash and a metallic groan that told Jarek it probably wouldn't hold indefinitely if the Kul was determined.

Despite that, he laid his head back to the truck and allowed himself a few moments of nothing but blissful gulps of air in the dim tunnel lighting, listening to the rumble and hum of the convoy engines.

Ahead, Drogan began to chuckle.

Jarek was surprised at first but soon found himself chuckling too, giddy with the excitement of their narrow survival.

"You guys having fun up there?" Rachel's voice called from the back of the truck.

"The battle was well-fought, Rachel Cross," Drogan called back as if it were all the answer she should need.

"Yeah…" Jarek added. "Total giggle fest up here."

Overhead, the tunnel ceiling and its intermittent lights weren't quite as low-hanging as he'd originally worried they'd be. He was contemplating sitting up when there was a wrenching screech from Drogan's direction.

Jarek looked around in time to see the Whacker thud down beside him.

"Come, Jarek Slater," Drogan said, clawing his way along the side of the truck toward the open rear hatch. "We are not safe yet."

A solid thud and the groan of protesting metal from the direction of the tunnel entrance punctuated the statement quite nicely.

Jarek grabbed his sword, maneuvered it awkwardly in the limited space onto the connectors on his back, and scrambled on all fours to the back of the ruined truck.

The rim of the hatch tore free as he swung himself in through the open rear, but Rachel and one of the Resistance soldiers caught on and dragged him in before he could lose his balance and tumble out.

Drogan crawled in a second later from around the side of the truck.

At the sight of Drogan's dimming red eyes, Jarek remembered what he'd briefly glimpsed above the mouth of the tunnel.

"Was that a dead raknoth back there?"

Rachel and Drogan exchanged an uncomfortable look.

"Any chance our friends ahead can all stow the red eyes?" Rachel asked Drogan.

The raknoth's gaze went distant for several seconds. Then, "It is likely too late for that."

"Shit." Rachel sighed. "Well, hopefully Dola's paying attention in there."

"That's the leader?" Jarek asked. "The raknoth you mentioned?"

Rachel nodded, looking worried. "Yeah. I just didn't get to finish explaining the part where his people don't know what he is"—she grimaced—"and that they kinda have a religious hatred of all things raknoth."

Jarek thought back to the charred form hanging over the tunnel entrance. "Yeah, no kidding."

"Let's just…" Rachel said.

"Behave casually?" Drogan asked with the faintest of smirks, his appearance now fully human.

Rachel rubbed at her forehead in weary exasperation then looked up as the truck began to slow.

Drogan hopped swiftly out and headed for the head of the convoy.

"Casual it is, then," Jarek said, hopping out and turning to offer Rachel a hand down. "What could possibly go wrong?"

Rachel took his hand and hopped down, grumbling something about how they were about to find out.

Ahead, the convoy had arrived at a wide elbow in the tunnel. Commander Daniels and a grim-looking Alaric had climbed out of their vehicles to join Drogan in approaching the wall that Jarek realized at a second glance was actually a door.

Behind them, most of the soldiers were cautiously unloading from the vehicles, murmuring to each other and shooting worried looks back at the pounding sounds echoing after them from the direction of the tunnel entrance.

The raknoth, apparently having gotten the message from Drogan, lingered in the vehicles, keeping a low profile.

"Come on, people!" Rachel cried, waving at the door as she caught up to Drogan. "Open sesame! What are you waiting for? Zach? Dillard?"

Granted, Jarek wasn't a pro at secret handshake protocols, but the hidden compartments that popped open to reveal a pair of nasty-looking rotary autocannons didn't seem like an encouraging sign.

"I knew there was something off about you, lady," said a male voice from a hidden speaker somewhere above the door, "but running around with fucking vamps?"

Drogan held his hands up, suddenly looking meeker than Jarek had ever thought to see in his life. "What are you talking about, man?" he cried in a voice that was decidedly un-Drogan-ly. "Those things are after us and our friends! You have to—"

"Cut the shit!" the speaker-voice cried. "I saw the red eyes on the cams out there, *Derek*. You can't lie to me, demon. I'll be damned if—"

"Open the door, you fool!" Drogan roared, dropping all appearances. "We are your only hope of surviving what's outside."

The autocannons began spinning up.

Jarek started to step protectively ahead of Rachel, then, noting she had her bullet-catcher on, sidled in on her flank instead.

"Zach," Rachel said, hands held open and unthreatening. "You know I can decommission your guns. But we're gonna need 'em. There's good reason for all of this, but for now, you need to let us in. Ask Dillard if you have to, he'll tell you the same."

"Bullshit," Zach snarled. "I'll die before—"

"Zach!" Rachel shouted in a tone that could've shriveled cold stone. "Open the fucking door or I'll tear it down and—"

They all jerked to attention as the steady pounding echoes gave way to a mournful wrenching sound from the distant tunnel entrance.

"The gate has fallen," Drogan growled.

Rachel whipped back to the enormous vault door. "Zach…"

"Open the door, Rachel Cross," Drogan said.

Behind them, the raknoth were piling out of the vehicles now, preparing to meet their coming masters.

Rachel was extending a hand toward the enormous door when a series of thick pops rang out, clearly surprising her, and the door began inching open.

If not Rachel, though…

"It's taken care of," said a new speaker-voice, also male but smoother, "though I cannot say I'm pleased to see you return with the enemy on your heels."

"That makes two of us," Rachel growled under her breath. Then, louder, "Let's go, people! Through the big scary door!"

No one argued. They just hustled their asses off, raknoth and human alike, to squeeze past the maddeningly slow-opening door and into the open room beyond. It was a tight fit, but with at least two bellowing rakul storming down the tunnel after them, they found a way to make it work.

Jarek, Rachel, Drogan, and Krogoth were the last ones in before the huge vault door began its equally slow swing shut.

"Can we hurry this shit up?" Jarek asked.

"Sincerest apologies if my fortress isn't up to your standards, human," someone—this Dola, probably—growled under his breath a little ways back.

Jarek was too distracted by Harga's bulk charging into view to worry about it.

Rachel pointed her staff through the slowly-closing gap, and Harga hit an invisible wall. Jarek slipped an arm around Rachel, recognizing the wobbly knees of channeling fatigue, but she managed to hold long enough for the autocannons to open fire.

The ridiculously large guns didn't tear the Kul to ribbons like every physical law said they should have, but they sure as hell didn't seem to tickle, either.

Harga gave a furious roar and darted back the way he'd come.

Rachel withdrew her staff, and the enormous door slammed shut and locked with a long series of decisive clacks.

Dead silence gripped the room, everyone holding their breaths to see if the rakul would simply leave it at that for now. For a long handful of moments, it actually seemed like they might.

Then someone grunted a curse by the control consoles, and the autocannons roared back to life. Through the thick door, their tandem rapid-fire report sounded more like a muffled choir of chainsaws than a pair of automatic weapons.

Jarek nearly jumped when two somethings—Harga and Ogrin,

probably—slammed into the door, but its multi-foot-thick steel build was more than a little solid. Left to their leisure, the two Kul might have eventually worked their way through it, but for now, it held with little more than a round of low thuds.

One last muffled roar vibrated the floor, and then the cannons ceased their fire.

"They have retreated," Krogoth said. "For now."

Someone let out a relieved cry, and it spread until most of the room was cheering.

Most of the room, that was, except for the raknoth and the commanders and a few of the soldiers who seemed to be realizing what Rachel's tight expression told Jarek as she met his eyes.

They'd made it to safety.

And now they were trapped here.

CHAPTER TWENTY-FOUR

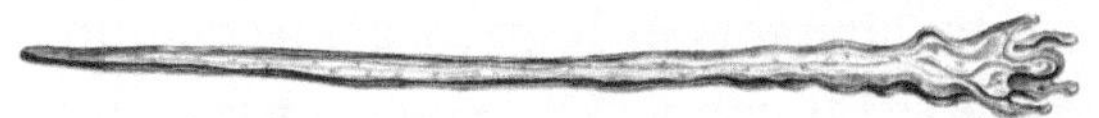

Rachel had never thought to feel an ounce of remorse about scorning the hospitality of a raknoth—and especially not a fratricidal, cult-leader-ish one at that. Yet as they all stood there in The Complex's entrance antechamber under Nan'Dola's bewildered stare, she couldn't help but feel a touch of pity for the raknoth.

It wasn't like she and Drogan had merely tracked a bit of mud into the house, after all. They'd brought another hundred-plus mouths in need of food and shelter they already knew Dola didn't really have.

Infinitely more importantly, they'd brought the rakul. The rakul who were only minutes gone and were no doubt calling for the rest of their brethren outside. And meanwhile, their frazzled group stood here in the antechamber, good and safe and trapped, their momentary celebration fading to dumb stares as those who'd been excited to simply be alive a minute ago turned to wondering what came next.

She wasn't sure anyone in the room had an answer to that one, but looking at Jarek and Michael and the rest of the men and women safe and alive around them, Rachel knew she would've done it all over again anyway.

"I'd rather thought," Dola finally said when silence had crept back over the room and he'd pushed his way over to them, "that you might be gone for longer than a couple hours. And"—a red glow lit in his angry eyes —"that you wouldn't be returning with the cursed Masters themselves breathing down your cursed necks."

A worried glance at Zach and his men told Rachel that Dola had them telepathically on heel for the moment. But a few disillusioned Complex zealots were probably the least of their concerns right now.

Drogan was stepping forward—probably to remind the Nan of his station, judging by the fire in his eyes—when Krogoth cut him off and gave Dola the full, scaly red-eyed stare-down first.

Krogoth hadn't dropped his rust-red raknoth appearance to appease Dola or anyone else. He'd never dropped it at all, as far as Rachel could remember. She didn't even know what his human host looked like. It was hard to think of him as anything other than raknoth.

Even standing to the side as an observer, the raw ferocity of his presence made Rachel want to shudder. Dola held for all of three seconds before taking a step back and bowing his head in begrudging deference.

"Tend to your flock, young Nan," Krogoth rumbled, the calm of his tone seeming all the deadlier for his menacing posture.

Dola shot a bitter look at Drogan and Rachel, and, deflated, quietly keyed the rear door open and marched Zach and the rest of his puppet crew off.

"You had best prepare them for the truth," Drogan called after him. "There will be no hiding from it henceforth."

Dola paused to look back, gave a hesitant nod, and then was gone.

Why did Rachel feel bad for the manipulative bastard?

Maybe because, no matter which way Dola tried to swing it, there was no way explaining away his decade-plus monument of demon-vamp lies was going to be a fun time. Not for him, and not for the inhabitants of The Complex—provided they had an ounce of free will left in there, at least.

But Dola had brought this all on himself.

So maybe it was Zach and the rest of the radicals down here she actually felt bad for.

"Is it just me," Jarek asked quietly beside her as they watched Zach and his men funnel through the door after Dola, "or am I picking up a real creepy-culty vibe, here?"

She shook her head. "It's definitely not just you."

Krogoth and Commander Daniels took charge of moving everyone along into The Complex, with Drogan taking the lead in guiding their forces to the barracks where Nelken and the rest of their people would be.

There was little talk of touching the vehicles that were still in the tunnel outside. There was nowhere to run now, and they'd already grabbed what little supplies they had on their way in.

No one pointed out just how scant those supplies were. Just like no one spoke the thought that was probably on most of their minds.

If the rakul were converging on The Complex, which seemed all too likely, they might not all be living long enough for a food shortage to become a serious problem in there.

Still, when the flow of foot traffic started jamming up in the wide, open tunnel around the corner from the building where Nelken's people and the Enochians were staying, it quickly became apparent that—food or no—Zach and Dola hadn't been wrong about the space issues.

"—pick their spot and clear out for now," Nelken was calling up ahead. "We'll see what we can rustle up for extra padding and blankets in the meanwhile."

There was no doubt about it. A lot of troops were going to be bunking in the tunnels tonight, no matter how they played it. Luckily, the tunnels were wide, and vertically more spacious than any of the rooms she'd seen so far in The Complex.

Maybe they could build themselves a nice network of bunks if they lived long enough to need them.

For the time being, though, no one seemed particularly upset at the thought of camping out in the tunnels. At least they were relatively safe. And, after weeks of roughing it out on the road, a bed of stone and bundled clothes and blankets probably didn't sound so bad to most of their people anyway.

Even so, it was impossible to miss the dark cloud creeping over their forces as they went about getting settled and finally turning their attention to the problems they hadn't had the bandwidth to take care of for the past hours—minor injuries, empty bellies, and other nuisances.

Pryce rounded the corner with several Resistance soldiers on his heels, though he appeared to be talking more to himself than to them.

"—should've started working on bunks the minute we got here." He shook his head. "Stupid. Stup—"

The words caught in Pryce's throat when he looked up and caught sight of Jarek.

Rachel couldn't help but smile at the excited whoop that escaped the older man. Then Pryce took closer stock of Jarek's battered face and armor, which Rachel saw was even more battle-scarred than she'd had time to realize earlier.

Finally, Pryce's eyes returned to Jarek's bruised face.

"You look like hell, old man," Jarek said.

Pryce's shocked gape broke into a grateful smile. "Yeah, well, it's been a tough few weeks." He glanced away from Jarek and took in Michael's ragged appearance. "Clearly not something you two would know much about."

Jarek's smile mirrored Pryce's, and Rachel was reminded of the first time she'd met the older man—when they'd just busted out of Drogan's Red Fortress and Jarek had brought her and Michael to Pryce's shop and had a good giggle about all of it.

Christ, it seemed like a lifetime ago now.

How had shit fallen apart so fast?

Thinking back on it, it felt like she'd been a different person then, consumed with nothing but pulling Michael out of his mess and getting the hell away from it. Away from Jarek and the Resistance, and back to Unity to stick her head in the sand, right where it belonged.

And now?

Now, she would've given pretty much anything just to not feel hunted for a little while, just to—

"—right, Rache?"

Rachel snapped out of her reverie to find Jarek, Pryce, and Michael all staring at her expectantly.

"Uh…"

"Yeesh," Jarek said, shaking his head. "I'm the one with the head injury here, Goldilocks."

"We should take a look at that, by the way," Pryce said, wrinkling his nose as he leaned in to inspect the scarred, bruised mess of Jarek's face. "How's that poor brain looking in there, Al? Scrambled?"

"You have no idea," Michael said with a small smile.

"Only marginally more scrambled than usual, sir," Al added from Fela's speakers. "I haven't monitored any particularly troubling developments… Though I would recommend avoiding any traumatic head injuries in the near future, if anyone were so inclined to listen."

"Yeah, tell that to Mos—"

Rachel had never seen one of Jarek's smiles die so fast.

"—to the rakul, buddy," Jarek tried and failed to cover up the slip. "Tell it to the rakul."

"Right you are, sir," Al chirped, just a bit too brightly for it not to sound like an act.

Silence stretched a few moments too long between them.

"Maybe you three can help me out," Pryce said, clearly picking up that a new topic was prudent, if unclear as to exactly why. "If you're not busy, I mean."

"I think our schedules are wide open," Michael said.

"Right." Pryce bobbed his head, licking his lips nervously. "Well I'm just going to see about finding anything that might be used as bedding. I could use the extra hands."

"We've got those," Rachel said, waving for him to take the lead.

"You guys go ahead," Jarek said. "I'm just gonna—I need to check in with Nelken."

"Yeah," Rachel said, searching his face for… she wasn't quite sure what. "Yeah, sure. We'll be right back."

He held her eyes for another moment, and she thought he might say something, but then he turned and strode away through the crowd.

She watched him go with an odd, churning feeling in her stomach and turned back to find Pryce watching Jarek's retreating back as well, worriedly nibbling at his lip all the while.

He noticed her looking and met her eyes with an unhappy shrug. "He'll tell you, I imagine. When he's ready."

"Yeah…" Rachel tilted her head down the hallway, suddenly wanting nothing more than to move on from the subject. "Let's just go find pillows or whatever."

They'd been walking for a couple minutes and Pryce was leading the way back into the narrower beige hallways of one of the underground buildings when Rachel's legs stopped seemingly by their own accord.

She had to go check on him.

"Rache?" Michael asked, watching her from the stairs to the building's entrance.

It was stupid. They'd only be a few minutes here. She knew that. But suddenly she couldn't stand the thought of letting Jarek wallow alone a second longer. Not after everything they'd been through to make it here. Not when the rakul were out there, probably circling the mountain like hungry sharks.

What good was waiting for "ready" when they might not live long enough to make it there?

Not much good. That was what.

So she swallowed and hooked a thumb back down the tunnel. "I gotta go…"

"Check in with Nelken?" Michael asked with the faintest arch of an eyebrow.

"That's the one," she said, trying to stifle the embarrassed smile.

For a second, Michael didn't seem to be quite sure how he felt about that, but then he shrugged and gave her a nod. "We'll see you in a few, then."

Rachel started back the way they'd come, her pace quickened by some half-formed worry she couldn't quite put a finger on. She pushed into the bustling crowd of troops, searching, searching.

Jarek was nowhere to be seen.

She spotted Nelken through the throng and started pushing her way over.

"Haven't seen him yet," Nelken said when she asked. "But let him know I'd like to whenever you find him."

The first touch of panic flickered in her gut.

It was irrational. Crazy.

Jarek was fine. She was sure of it. He'd probably just stepped away from the crowd to have a moment's quiet peace.

So why was her heart pounding like she was staring down a Kul?

She nearly jumped at Drogan's voice by her ear.

"Jarek Slater retreated to the southern tunnel."

There was thoughtfulness—concern, even?—on the raknoth's face when she turned.

"Never does a weight feel so heavy," Drogan added slowly, "than the moment one realizes they have born it just as far as was required. No more. No less."

She wasn't sure what to say to that.

Drogan just tilted his head in the direction of the southern tunnel, not seeming to expect anything more.

Unsure what else to do, she mumbled a thank you and set off through the crowd.

Voices echoed readily after her well after she'd left the heart of the throng, though their intensity dropped precipitously when she turned the corner into the next tunnel.

Finding Jarek didn't take long.

The southern corner of The Complex wasn't busy, save for the few resident engineers she passed going about their routine upkeep operations. She paid little attention to their wary stares.

When she heard the trickle of running water from the showers that ran right off the adjacent reservoirs, she cast out her senses, and there was Fela, curled in standby in the otherwise empty room. She couldn't feel Jarek's cloaked mind, of course, but when she pushed the door gently open and padded into the room, he was there.

She nearly gasped at the evidence of the beating he'd taken on the road. Bruised skin might've actually covered more territory than the unbruised across the surface of his scarred back. The sight left her knees wobbly.

He stood with his hands planted against the tiled wall, his head fully immersed in a steaming downpour. Probably why he hadn't heard her yet.

She watched him, scared to interrupt now that she was here, unsure what she'd even come here to say.

He turned before she could figure it out.

Her breath stopped. She waited for the wave of embarrassment at having been caught staring. Waited for Jarek to make some half-hearted jab about eyeing an innocent man's goods while he tried to clean up. But the embarrassment didn't come, and Jarek only held her gaze, searching her eyes for she didn't know what.

There was something there in his dark eyes. Something she was certain now he'd been holding in since she'd found him at that saloon —maybe since well before that. Something that made her heart ache.

He'd lost a part of himself out there.

She wasn't sure how she knew it. Only that she did.

And the way he was staring at her now, like he was standing on the precipice and she was the only thing on the planet that could hope to keep him from tumbling over...

The weight of hot tears settled against the backs of her eyes, as sudden as it was unexpected.

This wasn't how it was supposed to be. Not after how hard they'd fought to make it here, together.

They were supposed to fall into each other's arms and joke and laugh and pick right back up where they'd left off in Jarek's ship a few weeks ago, before Gada had had to go and start his war and tear them apart.

They were supposed to be happy—if only for a moment.

But looking at him now, Rachel's lips threatened to tremble. The full weight of just how close she'd come to losing him crashed down on her—somehow so much heavier than when they'd been apart.

Losing him…

It was a terrible emptiness, that thought.

She couldn't—wouldn't—let it happen. Not again.

Just like she couldn't let him stand there alone, drowning in steaming water and self-doubt. She needed to go to him. To hold him to her—tell him that she had him and that it was going to be okay. She needed to hear him tell her the same.

So she let her hands move. Ignored the voice of doubt in the back of her head. Pulled her jacket free and tossed it to the tiled floor beside Fela.

Jarek watched her, his somber gloom not quite concealing the flicker of hunger in his eyes.

Her shirt followed the jacket as she kicked her boots off. Then went the jeans, their eyes locked all the while.

Her breath was coming faster now, apprehensive trills tingling up and down her body.

No more waiting.

She'd waited long enough. Too long.

If the rakul were going to tear this mountain down and stomp the Earth until they were all dead and gone, so be it. Let them come.

She and Jarek would fight them till the last—would die together if they had to.

But the bastards weren't keeping them apart any longer.

She didn't need telepathy to know Jarek felt the same.

He stood tall, all but trembling with need, hands clenched at his sides as if he were fighting to restrain himself from tearing across the short distance between them and consuming her.

Instead, he waited, open and bare before her, silently pleading that she come—and that she come to stay.

So she reached back to fuse the door lock shut.

And she went to him.

CHAPTER TWENTY-FIVE

When Jarek blearily woke, naked and ungodly sore in a nest of damp clothes and towels, his first impulse was to roll over and go straight back to sleep. He'd barely had more than a few winks in damn near going on two days now, after all.

But then he registered the soft, equally-naked warmth stretched across his left side. And that seemed to warrant proper attention, sleep deprivation or no.

Growing up in an apocalyptic wasteland, Jarek had never really had occasion to understand the phrase, *heart-melting.*

He'd come close, maybe, with Rose. Back before Conner and everything else had driven them apart. He'd quietly felt the stirring hints of it again on a dozen different nights, cooped up in the ship watching cheesy old movies he'd verbally scoffed at in some obstinate attempt to convince both Al and himself that such things were beyond the scope of any potential future for him.

Yet the warm, syrupy melting sensation right in the pit of his chest indicated that *heart-melting* was precisely the right choice of words when he beheld the sight of Rachel's oh-so-lovely nakedness pressed against his side. Then she nestled more cozily against his chest with a grumble and an adorable little sleep frown, and his heart went full gravy.

It was as alarming a sensation as it was an undeniably good one, and, for a few seconds, he thought he'd simply burst with it.

She was beautiful. Beautiful in ways that had little to do with the lean athleticism of her bare back and the intriguing curves along the rest of her posterior chain (though he didn't exactly mind those, either).

Looking at the sleeping arcanist, it was as if someone had flipped a switch and revealed the hidden *aha* feature of every lovey-dovey cliché he'd ever had the bad fortune to suffer.

Some stubborn part of him tried to point out that he was getting carried away—that this was all probably just his mildly-concussed brain reeling from what had undeniably been a pretty enormous hit of the feel-goods. But even the undying cynic in him couldn't quell the truth.

This was irrefutably different.

He'd known his feelings for Rachel were strong—had even been pretty sure he'd stumbled onto that big L word people, well, *loved* to toss around.

But now he was damn-near loopy with it.

Watching her shoulders rise and fall with each gentle breath, he was nearly consumed with the desire to pull her tighter until they could be no closer. Until he was inside her and they were locked together in every conceivable way.

Thinking of the enemies converging outside The Complex, intending to take her away from him, Jarek was gripped by an insane urge to run outside, beating his naked chest, and rip them apart with his bare hands.

Whether it was his tensing at the thought or some subtle shift in his breathing, Rachel woke then. Maybe it was a good thing she did, the way his crazy thoughts were headed.

She lifted her tousled head, glancing around in disorientation for a second before her eyes fell on Jarek's nakedness and, slowly, up to his smiling face.

"Oh god," she groaned, plopping her head back down to his chest in a defeated manner. "Please don't be cheesy."

He put on his best indignant face. "Hey, who do you think I am?"

She shifted to shoot him a dubious look.

Seized by the motion of her bare breasts against his abdomen and another surge of mad, overwhelming emotion, he hooked a hand behind her neck and pulled her mouth to his.

The kiss lingered, deep and tantalizing, with none of the reservation he'd felt the first time (and the second) he'd ever kissed her.

"That's better," she whispered when they came apart for breath, her lips tickling his as they moved. "No cheese required. No need to—"

He couldn't help himself.

"Yay and though we lie here on the bathroom floor," he declared in a crummy approximation of Shakespearean lyric, "amid soiled rags and the drying stains of our own copious and passionate squalor, I doth admit, my lady, that never such a beauty have I dreamed to lay eyes on."

She tried to glare at him but ended up snorting into a breathy chuckle before she managed to get there.

"You done?" she finally asked.

"Only if you're done—"

She rolled her eyes. "Don't."

"—being such an adorable—"

"You're the worst."

"—little energy-bending cutie p—"

"Oh, it's just like the nightmares," she groaned, laying her head back down on his chest.

"There, there," he said, patting the soft, lovely curve of her backside. "It could be worse."

She didn't say anything when she looked up at him, but she didn't really need to. The worry in her eyes brought them both back to reality.

It was worse. About as worse as worse could get.

But for a comfortable little while, they simply allowed themselves to lie there, wrapped in their own thoughts, Jarek tracing the lines of her smooth back over and over again with idle fingertips.

He wanted to tell her… something. Everything. Yet the words hung in his chest.

It was almost laughable, the thought that they could lie here, on the post end of what he was reasonably certain had been mutually world-rocking sex, having waded through death to be here—and with plenty more circling around—and yet he could still be hesitant to open his mouth and let the words out.

"I thought I'd lost you," he finally said, his voice barely above a whisper. "Back in Pittsburgh, when we found the hotel, and again in Columbus. Before that, even. I…"

She found his free hand with hers and planted a warm kiss on his knuckles before pressing his hand to her cheek.

Straight-up heart gravy.

With her touch melting away the consternation in his gut, the words came more readily.

"The thought of finding you… it was the only thing that kept me going out there, through the Net going down, and the hordes and the fights and…" He closed his eyes, took a breath, and forced the words out. "And everything with Mosen."

He felt her shifting, felt her desire to ask about Mosen, but she remained silent, waiting for him to speak his mind.

"If you hadn't told me to keep going… If I hadn't had those words to hold onto…" He shook his head. "I think I would've given up out there."

She looked up at him then, weighing his words with a worried expression. "But you didn't." She squeezed his hand. "And now we're here. Together."

He dropped her gaze. "Not all of us."

"Jarek…"

"I know," he murmured, pointedly staring at the tiled wall.

He shouldn't blame himself for the men who'd died today. Not when he'd fought to what should have been his death trying to defend them. Not when following Rachel and the others west had clearly been the best of their crappy bunch of decisions.

And Mosen…

Mosen had been a grown-ass man. He'd known exactly what he'd been doing when he'd decided to run off and go rogue martyr.

But at the end of the day, no matter how many times he repeated these logical mantras internally…

How couldn't he blame himself?

Best move or no, the decisions that had led them to that farmhouse had been his, and—

"Do you wanna talk about it?" Rachel asked quietly.

He honestly didn't know.

"Alaric should be the one to hear it," he finally said.

Rachel didn't argue—just laid quietly on his chest, running her fingers along his scars and bruises.

Jarek was caught in his ruminations, floating midway between the feeling that they should vacate the showers and the desire to drift back off to sleep, when Rachel spoke.

"I was afraid too, you know."

He looked down at the top of her tousled golden head.

"Just for the record," she added with a small shrug, too pointedly absorbed in her study of his torso to look up.

"Right," Jarek said. "Well, let the record show that I'm not letting your ass out of my sight again"—he glanced down along the curve of her back—"so to speak."

She looked up in time to catch him staring and gave him a grin that set his pulse to pounding.

"No?" she asked softly, inching her way up his torso. She slid her left leg across his lap, hovering just above him. "Not even if you can see my front?"

"Front's, uh—"

She descended on him, pulling his mouth to hers.

"Front's good," he breathed when they broke apart, sliding his hands over her bare hips. "Front's definitely—Agh!"

He whipped his gaze around to the sharp sound of something

slamming into the door, body tensed, combat reflexes kicking into gear.

It came again. Three pounds this time.

Definitely a human fist.

"Dammit," Jarek muttered, some of the tension bleeding out of him.

Just someone in need of the facilities they'd admittedly been hogging, though Rachel had been convinced no one would wander over this way.

"These facilities are currently in use for, uh, important debriefing operations," Jarek cried.

"What?" came a male voice, muffled through the door but clearly disgruntled.

"What?" Jarek called back. "It's a shower debrief. You've never heard of a sh—"

Rachel clamped a hand over his mouth. "Could you just use another—"

"They're all full!" the guy cried, pounding on the door again. "Please!"

"Well," Jarek murmured, "you know what they say about all good things . . ."

Rachel arched a brow. "You call that good?"

"Aww c'mon now. Don't do that. Don't do that to a guy."

She just kissed his cheek and rose from their nest of clothes in a most alluring fashion to start getting dressed. "I doth admit that you were perfectly satisfactory, my shining knight, but I think the time has come to don thine pan—"

"Guys, please!" the voice groaned outside the door. "I think I'm gonna hurl!"

Rachel winced. "Oh, shit."

She yanked her jeans the rest of the way up, waving for Jarek to hurry up himself, then extended a hand toward the door to undo whatever she'd done to jam up the lock.

"Satisfactory," Jarek grumbled under his breath, rolling one of their towels around his waist and tucking it snug.

Rachel must've either telekinetically opened the door or unlocked it at the exact right moment, because the guy burst through so aggressively he nearly fell over.

He looked like hell—pale, sweaty, and trembling—and he barely had time to moan half an apology before diving for the showers and letting loose.

"Oh, shit," Rachel said again, clutching at her stomach with one hand, her face contorted in squeamish discomfort as she snagged her boots and scrambled for the door.

Jarek watched it all unfold before picking himself up from the floor, towel wrapped firmly at his waist. "Man, I didn't think we were that nauseating."

"Ugh," the Resistance soldier groaned between wretches. "Goddamn expired canned goods."

"Oh, yeah." Jarek nodded. "We've all been there, man."

He was pretty sure the guy was one of the soldiers who'd come in with Alaric and Krogoth's group. Whatever else they'd been through in the past weeks, it clearly went without saying that the guy was having a rough day.

So Jarek padded over and gave the heaving man a supportive pat on the back. "There, there, buddy. That's it. Get it all out."

He half-expected the guy to tell him to F off, but instead, the guy just bobbed his head appreciatively.

"Hey," he said weakly when he finally had a chance to glance back between heaves, "you're Jarek Slater."

Jarek nodded. "It's not as impressive as it sounds, trust me."

"But you're the one who—who—"

The rest of the thought was lost to a violent wretch and the wet smack of vomit striking tile.

"I might—hrnghh—be a few minutes," the guy grunted, wiping at his mouth with the back of one hand. "Thanks. And, uh, sorry I interrupted..."

That made two of them. But Jarek just patted the guy's back.

"You got this under control?"

He bobbed his head. "I got this."

"Hell yeah you do, man," Jarek said with one last pat before turning for Fela's waiting form. "You're on Team Earth. Those canned goods aren't gonna know what hit 'em."

ONCE THE SOLDIER had finished and gone to find something with which to clean his mess, the showers were quiet but for the faint pitter-patter of dripping water slowly carrying his pile of sick down the gunky drain.

Drip. Drip. Drip.

Then something else. The wet slurp of something shifting near the drain, right in the middle of the watery mess.

A swollen, wriggling shape emerged from the watery puddle and began slithering its way across the tiles, inch by inch. It was already several feet from the drain when the tremors began. Shakes and convulsions, as if the thing had been gripped by some manner of seizure.

A faint line began to form along the length of the bulging organism, pale and growing in opacity and depth until it almost looked to bisect the creature. Until, finally, with a jerky shudder and a wet ripping sound, the wriggling thing split in two and ceased its trembling.

For a long handful of seconds, there was nothing but the dripping of water and vomit in the shower drain.

Then the two little bits of Kul'Vermaga roused wearily from their exertions and began scaling their slimy way up the wall to the ventilation shaft.

CHAPTER TWENTY-SIX

"What happened to a month?" Jarek asked, staring at Rachel with just enough surprise to tell her that he, like her, had been letting hope ride on their Enochian saviors, even if he hadn't quite admitted it to himself. "I thought that was the ETA on the wonder twins saving our asses," he added quietly, his gaze shifting worriedly to the bustle of activity ahead where the wide tunnel was quickly morphing to a functioning barracks. "Shouldn't we be about set?"

"Yeah…" Rachel said. "Well, that was the original estimation. It's been kinda hard to get straight answers out of the comatose merging alien lifeforms, if I'm gonna be honest with you."

"Huh," Jarek said. "Go figure."

Rachel wasn't particularly looking forward to another round of trying to touch base with their transitioning friends. Not after the last psychedelic trip she'd made into raknoth-human-hybrid dreamland.

But that had been back on the Enochians' ship, before Pittsburgh. She needed to get back in there and do everything she could to kick their merging asses into gear. Time was short, and they needed all the allies they could get. Especially those of the arcane-alien-super-soldier variety.

234

"I probably should've gone straight to them when we got back," Rachel said, speaking quietly now as they reached the edge of the tunnel barracks crowd, "instead of slumming it in the showers with unsavory sorts."

"Unsavory, I'll give you," Jarek said, sliding into the throng beside her. "But I submit that the shower debriefing was crucial to our success. Very important for morale."

"Uh-huh."

"Plus, we don't have to die with blue balls now."

She frowned. "Are you referring to yourself collectively, or...?"

"What? You're telling me you don't believe in lady blue balls?"

She shook her head. "You really know how to make a girl feel special, you know that?"

He stopped to help a few soldiers scoot a big storage crate over to the wall, then return to her palms held up. "What? Guy doesn't get any credit for watching you sleep and writing you some touching bathroom-floor poetry?"

A smile pulled across her mouth. "Okay. Maybe a few points."

Jarek made a victorious gesture with an upheld fist.

"Like two points," she added. "Maybe. Slumdog Romeo."

Jarek shrugged off the clarification as they pushed their way back into the crowd, bound for the Enochians' barracks.

His good mood was a welcome sight, even if she could still feel the weight of Mosen and everything else ghosting along not so far behind him.

That good mood was also a bit contagious, it seemed. Or maybe it was just that her own good mood had decided to make a rare appearance. Either way, it was probably more than just a transient shot of the smilies riding through her.

No matter what superficial shenanigans Jarek might play at with his mouth, his eyes seemed to have abandoned any attempt at downplaying how he really felt about her. And the things he'd told her back there, before they'd been so abruptly interrupted...

She wasn't used to this. And she certainly wasn't sure what to do with the feelings roiling through her own head and heart.

Part of her, and not a small part, was reticent to even acknowledge it—to believe that anyone could ever feel so strongly about her. But she'd seen it right there in his eyes.

For some reason that was frankly beyond easy comprehension, Jarek loved her.

It wasn't such a bad realization to come to.

The smile pulling at her lips only widened when she noticed Pryce ahead, talking some poor Resistance soldier's ear off about the functions of the thick springs visible under the adjacent building and the flexible connectors on some of the nearby pipes.

Jarek, seeing the same, shot her a knowing grin that only stirred the odd swirl of excited emotions in her chest.

If only for a moment, Rachel actually felt happy. Truly happy, despite the doom hanging over their heads. Felt for the first time, in fact, like they might even have half a shot at pulling through this thing.

But maybe that was the endorphins talking. God knew it had been long enough since she'd had any kind of sexual release. And never one so deeply meaningful and satisfying, despite what teasing jabs she might make at Jarek.

Or maybe it was simply her mind pulling magic tricks to keep her from collapsing under the weight of despair.

Either way, she was glad to roll with it for the time being.

Pryce caught sight of them and hurried over with an excited wave. He drew up just short of them, his excitement shifting to thoughtful observation as he looked back and forth between them.

"Ah," he finally said.

"Ah, what, you old kook?" Jarek asked, though the meaning of the single syllable had somehow been as transparent as Jarek's uncharacteristically shifty expression currently was.

"Ah, nothing." Pryce shook his head, looking sheepish. "Nothing at all."

"Ah, Jesus," Rachel sighed. "I'm going to check on the Enochians. You children can stay here and fist bump if you want."

"But mooomm," Jarek said, hurrying after her, "I wanna see the Enochians too!"

"And I despise fist bumps," Pryce added indignantly, falling in on their heels.

"Ugh." Rachel shook her head and frowned at Jarek. "Please never call me that again, by the way."

Jarek nodded thoughtfully, looking less than pleased with his own choice of words. "Yeah, that's fair enough."

When they reached their destination, the Enochians were glad to see them.

A little too glad.

With the exceptions of Franco, who sat at Elise's cot, Phineas, who lounged in the nearby corner, and a few of Krogoth's raknoth, who conversed quietly in their own corner, most of the eyes in the room seemed to be shifting back and forth between her and Jarek in a way that made her want to hit them all with a cold blast of air, just to change the topic.

"Hey, mazel tov!" Johnny finally cried, breaking the silence.

"'Bout time," Phineas rumbled from his corner without looking up.

Rachel swore she heard a muttered, "Hear, hear," from Pryce behind them.

She didn't dignify them all with an eye roll.

Jarek looked around the room. "Christ, what are you all, sex hounds?"

"Fiends, maybe," Johnny said, shrugging when Lea, who sat beside him on a supply crate, shot him a dubious look.

"Mostly, they just have eyes," Franco said.

"We've had a little bet going on for a while now," Johnny said, pointing back and forth between himself and Lea. "Pretty much since I first met you guys and a certain shining angel tended to my raknoth-pummeled ribs," he added, patting Lea's thigh. "Looks like someone owes me a hundred fortune cookies."

Lea nodded her apologetic admission of Johnny's claim.

"Yeah?" Jarek jabbed a finger to where Johnny's hand lingered on Lea's leg. "And who's betting on you two, fire-crotch?"

Johnny's hand slipped from Lea's leg as if he'd only just realized he'd rested it on a stove top, and both of them blushed and looked away.

"Delightful as this is," Rachel said, "we should probably move on to the fact that there are still at least two rakul on our doorstep, and probably a shitload more by now. Just in case anyone forgot."

"An astute point, I think," Franco said, finally looking up from Elise's peaceful face. "Welcome back, by the way, Jarek. Glad to see you kept your wits about you out there."

"That might be putting it strongly," Jarek said, "but thanks. It's good to see you guys again."

Rachel took a few tentative steps toward Haldin's and Elise's cots, assessing Franco's demeanor.

"Holy crap," Jarek murmured behind her, no doubt as he took in the two's changed appearances.

She expected the decidedly indelicate reaction might darken Franco's mood, but he just looked subdued, exhausted.

"I wanted to try to talk with them," Rachel said, directing the words at Franco.

He nodded, his dark olive eyes worried. "I expected you would. Al'Drogan came earlier, but he said they were too far gone at the time."

Rachel nodded her understanding, and Franco stood to offer his chair.

"You don't have to—" she started, but he cut her off with a raised hand.

"Quiet would help, yes?"

"Yeah, but you don't have to go."

"I think our legs could all use stretching," Franco said with a meaningful look around the room.

"Yep," Johnny agreed, hopping to his feet. "Rigid as duracrete, here."

"That's not something we tend to brag about in public around here, alien boy," Jarek said. "Just for the record."

Johnny snapped his fingers and pointed at Jarek as if he'd just offered genuinely helpful advice.

Everyone else picked themselves up—Lea with a, "Good luck," Phineas with a stoic grunt—and headed out of the barracks.

"Unless I can help here?" Jarek asked, lingering on the threshold when everyone but Franco and the raknoth had gone.

"Not this time." Rachel cocked her head. "Unless you happen to have some LSD on your person."

"No"—Jarek shot a thoughtful look toward the hallway crowd and back—"but I wouldn't be remotely surprised if Pryce knew how to cook some up."

Rachel couldn't help but smile at that. Namely because it was probably true.

Jarek took one long last look at the comatose Enochians and stepped reluctantly out of the room.

Rachel was about to turn and see what Franco was up to when the Enochian surprised her with a firm squeeze on the shoulder.

"I know she hears me sometimes," he said quietly, staring down at Elise. "Tell her I love her anyway? If you can."

Rachel looked up to meet his eyes. "Of course."

Franco nodded to himself and gave her shoulder another squeeze.

Then he was gone, and it was just Rachel, her hybrid friends, and a few of Krogoth's raknoth. She thought about asking if they wouldn't mind stepping out too, but they saw what was happening, and they knew how to be quiet.

Plus, if it ended up being anything like her past experience reaching out to the Enochian-raknoth dream team, she didn't hate the idea of having someone paying attention while she sunk into la-la-land.

So she plopped Franco's chair down between the two cots, took each of the Enochians by a hand, and closed her eyes, settling deep into her extended senses.

It was a curious feeling, brushing against such powerful beings in her senses only to find no one consciously behind the wheel, so to speak. She'd never felt anything like it, and she still hadn't gotten used to it.

She started with Haldin and Alton, both of whom were largely unresponsive to her queries. It was like tickling a hibernating bear with a feather.

At first, Elise and Lietha were no different. But then there was a stirring. A tendril of thought, tentative and curious at first.

"Did I not hear Al'Drogan's call?" came Lietha's thought, murky and somewhat disoriented, as if she'd just woken from a deep sleep—which, as far as Rachel had previously understood, wasn't really something raknoth normally did. Clearly, the finer points of this transition process escaped her.

"He did," Rachel sent back, *"but that was at least an hour ago, I think."*

"I see." Lietha's thoughts were as guarded as usual, but Rachel thought she detected just a hint of disappointment in the Shieth's mental tone. *"Is there news, then?"*

"There is. The worst news there could be, really."

Lietha let her weary consternation brush at Rachel's mind like a soft sigh.

"Very well. Then perhaps we should attempt to commune with the others below. Will you come with me?"

It was more than a little weird, hearing the alien inside Elise's abdomen ask Rachel to come to some meeting place "below," but it wasn't like that was going to stop her.

"Lead the way," Rachel sent, doing her abstract best to assume a mental state akin to reaching out a hand for guidance.

Lietha's presence formed more fully around her, gently tugging her along in… not a direction, exactly. It was more like being pulled toward a specific thought, or a state of mind, even. A head space.

"Relax your mind, Rachel Cross," Lietha sent. *"You are far too aroused to hope to meld with our internal environment.*

Rachel bit back a retort and instead let out a few deep breaths, shifted to get comfortable in her chair, and then sank down into her senses once more, trying to forget the ultimate goal for a minute and instead simply clear her mind.

Deeper, deeper she sank, guided along by Lietha's light—if not exactly gentle—mental pressure. She sank until she floated in the wispy, delirious darkness between sleeping and waking. Until she barely knew whether she was still conscious or not.

How long passed in that place, she couldn't have said. All she knew was that, when she rightly became aware of her surroundings again, she was standing in a different room.

A room she didn't recognize.

HAD SHE FALLEN ASLEEP?

The place she found herself in looked like some kind of war room. Only...

Rachel looked at her surroundings again and decided her initial impression had been accurate. Wherever she was, she was pretty sure it wasn't of Earth, at least not of Earth in this century.

"We thought you'd come eventually."

Rachel spun at the sound of Haldin's voice and found the Enochian frowning at Alton and Lietha, both in the scaly raknoth battle forms of their old bodies. Though maybe that was just how Rachel's tranced mind was choosing to see them.

Elise was there too, the four of them gathered around a flat command table whose surface was alight with various lists and projected holograms of what appeared to be a few of the rakul.

"How long has it been, by the way?" Haldin asked the raknoth.

When they appeared less than certain themselves, he turned the question to Rachel.

"Since we reached this mountain fortress, I mean."

"Not much more than a day," Rachel said, approaching the command table.

The Enochians and the raknoth shared a look that told her the answer was surprising to them. And not in a good way.

"Drogan and I left to look for Jarek and the others earlier this morning," she added, "but we found them a hell of a lot faster than we'd hoped to. We just got back a few hours ago."

"Suppose that's good news," Haldin mumbled, his grim expression not wavering.

"But what's the bad?" Alton said, his words flowing smoothly after Haldin's, more like he was finishing the Enochian's sentence than speaking his own individual thought.

"How long will this Complex hold before we must fight?" Lietha added, flat, to-the-point, and decidedly not of the same thought stream as Haldin and Alton.

Elise frowned from Lietha to the men, and finally to Rachel. "You see what I'm stuck with in here? Buncha gloomy pessi—Wait..." Elise looked at Lietha. "What do you mean, how long will this Complex hold? Does that mean...?"

By way of reply, Lietha only jutted her mint-green chin toward Rachel.

"They've found us," Alton said, more statement than question.

Rachel tilted her head in acknowledgment. "We didn't make it back to The Complex alone. The ones they call Ogrin and Harga are probably still out there somewhere, and Vermaga and Gada couldn't have been far behind."

"Gada," Lietha hissed through clenched teeth.

Elise laid a hand on Lietha's shoulder. "We will have justice for Zar'Kole," she said softly. "Don't let rage and vengeance blind our path."

Rachel tensed, ready for Lietha to shove off Elise's touch and tell her to keep her pathetic human hands and thoughts to herself, but the raknoth only took a long breath and nodded.

Maybe it was more than just the Enochians' bodies that were changing through all of this.

"Is this...?" Rachel started, looking around the room again.

"Enochia," Haldin confirmed. "Or one of our memories of a place there, at least."

"Right, then." Rachel said.

She shouldn't have been surprised. It wasn't even the first alien planet she'd seen. Not after the secondhand memory Haldin had shown her of The World Ender, Kul'Naga, decimating a tribe of what could only rightly be called frost giants.

But that didn't really make any of this less mind-boggling.

"What plans exist for repelling the rakul from this facility?" Alton asked, his stern tone centering her firmly back in the root of their problem.

"At the moment," Rachel said, "that's a damn good question. We brought back allies. Krogoth, Brandt, and I think ten other raknoth, plus Alaric and Daniels and about a hundred more human fighters. And we have Jarek back. Other than that"—she shook her head—"The Complex has some defenses in place, and one resident raknoth—long story—but I don't think these walls will hold long if we don't do something."

"So… no plan, then," Haldin said, looking more glum than actively accusatory.

"I won't lie," Rachel said, "I was kinda hoping you four might have a bright spot of sunshine to offer."

Haldin met Elise's eyes, something of meaning passing between them, and suddenly they were no longer in the Enochian command room but on a gentle hill crest in the middle of a wide, sweeping plain of lush grass.

Ahead, a crystal-clear lake stretched its shimmering way to the base of an enormous mountain that stretched impossibly high into the crisp blue sky. Above, a bright sun shone down on all of it.

"Sunshine, yes," Elise said.

"Hope, though…" Haldin added.

"Hope…" Alton said, looking to the sky, which began to darken as if in response to his crimson gaze. "Hope is more tenuous than a fickle dream, considering what we face."

"I see what you're saying about the pessimism," Rachel said to Elise. Then, to all of them, "How soon could you realistically be ready to fight?"

Haldin met Alton's eyes while Elise did the same with Lietha. For a long moment, the two pairs seemed to be not so much looking at one another as peering deeper into some intangible whole between them. Finally, the spell broke, and Alton and Lietha engaged in their own silent exchange.

"We must begin our final preparations immediately, it seems," Lietha said when they'd finished.

"But even then," Alton added, "it is somewhat uncertain how soon we can be ready. Perhaps within a few days."

Shit.

Days?

Rachel wasn't sure what she'd been expecting, but somehow the thought of hunkering down for several days with multiple rakul circling outside didn't exactly fill her with confidence.

"And that's assuming," Haldin said, "that we're even able to function with our new, uh…" He waved a hand at Rachel. "Well you've seen what we're dealing with out there, body-wise. It's not like we're just waking up from a nap. This is gonna take serious calibrating."

"How bad is it, by the way?" Elise asked, her hand tracking absent-mindedly to one elegant cheekbone.

Rachel started to open her mouth, searching for something posi-tive to say about the Enochians' significant makeovers.

"Never mind." Elise shook her head as if chiding herself. "It's not important."

"It really isn't," Haldin said.

Alone, the words might've seemed callous. But there was nothing callous about the way he cupped Elise's face and gently stroked her cheeks with his thumbs before planting a warm kiss on her forehead.

She smiled up at him—a tired smile. The look that passed between them was that of a pair of kindred old souls. Somehow, it only reminded Rachel that much more of just how young the two still were, and how much they'd already sacrificed.

"We'll do everything we can out there," Rachel said.

"And we'll do what we can in here," Alton said.

Haldin looked like he was about to say something, but the scene around them grew fuzzy for a few moments.

"We will likely be hard to reach again for the next few days," Alton added, as if in explanation for the interruption. "But we'd best return to the work now, seeing as time is of the essence."

"Right. I'll just see myself out then," Rachel said, though she wasn't entirely sure how it was she was supposed to go about doing that.

She started to think about withdrawing her extended senses, sinking back to her physical body, but something nagged at her. A doubt. Or maybe just guilt.

She looked around at the four of them, Earth's hopeful saviors.

It felt like it wasn't enough. Like she was failing them somehow. But what else was there to do?

"We'll hold them off," she said quietly. "Until you're ready. I promise."

"And if we're not ready?" Elise asked.

Rachel shrugged, and she realized she was now clutching the staff she could've sworn she hadn't had only moments ago. "Then we'll fight anyway. Maybe even leave a few scraps behind for you."

Alton, Haldin, and Elise gave her grim nods of acknowledgment. And for the first time in the entire conversation, Lietha smiled.

CHAPTER TWENTY-SEVEN

Tempted as he'd been to wait and see how Rachel fared trying to pull news from their sleeping beauties—or to use that excuse to avoid talking to Alaric, at least—Jarek hadn't been able to convince his damned conscience that doing either was acceptable. Just like he couldn't run off now to go see Pryce's and James' new toy, much as Pryce wanted him to.

"You're sure you don't want to see?" Pryce asked, clearly deflated at Jarek's lack of wall-bouncing giddiness. "It's right up your alley."

"It's got nothing to do with want, old man, I just need to…"

Pryce's expectant expression softened to one of understanding as he realized what this must be about—or probably guessed close enough to the truth, at least.

Normally, Jarek would've expected James' excited energy to rival Pryce's, but the Enochian was grim, subdued. From what Rachel had told him, the mood had apparently settled over all of the Enochians to some extent since Haldin and Elise had gone under their change.

"You guys can show me your BFG later," Jarek finished.

"BFG?" James asked, perking up just a little.

Pryce's worried expression broke into a smile. "I'll explain later."

Jarek was about to bid them farewell and happy tinkering when a thought occurred to him. "Why was the thing even here in the first place? I thought rail guns were more of a navy thing."

"They were," Pryce said, "but I'm guessing someone was looking to outfit this facility to take out unfriendly warheads." His expression soured. "You know…"

"Before all those other unfriendly warheads made it a moot point?" Jarek asked.

"Precisely."

James shook his head. "I still can't believe things fell apart so quickly here once, well…" He gestured toward the barracks where they'd left Rachel and Krogoth's raknoth.

"To tell the truth," Pryce said, "I think we were already headed that way anyway. You know, even before the raknoth and the arcane blood curse and all that."

"Guess that's why we outlawed nuclear weapons on Enochia." James tilted his head. "Though I guess that kind of thing's probably a bit easier to pull off when your whole planet is pretty much united under one deity and his divine authority."

"Easier, I'm sure," Pryce said slowly. "Better, though…"

He trailed off, drifting to that distant thoughtful place of his until Jarek decided he'd best be on his way.

"You fellas have fun philosophizing," he said, backing away with a wave.

Pryce snapped back to them with a little jerk. "Right." He turned a bemused grin on James. "Well, if we're going to discuss the merits and downfalls of religion and global disarmament, we might as well do it over that enormous gun of ours."

The two of them headed off in the opposite direction as Jarek turned for the tunnels that were now serving as the barracks and commons for their combined forces.

It was time to find Alaric.

He couldn't avoid it any longer. Not when they might be counting on fingers and toes the hours he had left to set things right with the surly old commander.

Jarek wasn't even sure *setting things right* was the right way to feel about it, but it seemed to be what the heaviness in his gut had decided for him. At the very least, he needed to tell Alaric what Mosen—shit, what *Seth*—had wanted his father to hear.

Not that Jarek really knew what that was, exactly.

Sure, he'd gleaned enough insight into Seth's mind to strike a few deep nerves during their fight, but that didn't mean he knew everything that'd been going through the man's head when he'd said those final words, *Just tell him...*

Jarek would just have to do his best.

First, though, he needed to get Alaric alone—a task that seemed as if it should be easy enough once Jarek spotted him over in what was rapidly shifting into a shabby armory.

Alaric barely seemed to be hearing what the two soldiers in front of him were saying. His inattention wasn't going without notice, either. The two men were glancing uncertainly at one another, clearly wondering if they should continue droning at their absentee commander.

Jarek started forward to save all three of them the trouble.

Before he'd made it three steps, though, Drogan stepped in front of him and shoved an old green Gatorade squeeze bottle against his chest.

"You must drink this, Jarek Slater."

Jarek frowned down at the drink in question and back to Drogan before slowly taking the bottle. "I take it this isn't lemon-lime?"

"It did possess a greenish hue, if that pleases you."

"Ick." Jarek made a face at the ominous bottle. "Not really, no."

"You must heal."

"Yeah..." Jarek looked around, searching for some excuse.

Drogan did have a point. He couldn't remember the last time he'd been this beaten up, and Maker knew how long they had before he'd be needing to rumble again.

"Is everyone else getting a dose of the Stumpy Special?"

A faint look of amusement crossed Drogan's face. "Everyone else does not get beaten so frequently and thoroughly as you."

"Uh, thanks?"

"Drink, Jarek Slater. Prepare your body."

"Man, I know you don't mean that sexually, but…"

Drogan was already stalking off.

"Wait," Jarek called. "Is this, like, safe?"

Drogan just kept walking.

"I'm very particular about my complexion!" Jarek called after him. "If this stuff gives me scales, Stumpy, I swear to—yep, he's gone. Great." He eyed the bottle suspiciously. "Well…"

He braced himself and took a pull.

It didn't please him. It didn't please him one damn bit, and the squeeze bottle didn't really help with the whole chugging thing, either. But he'd probably had worse.

He downed about half the bottle, then braced himself again and walked over to Alaric as the two soldiers wrapped up their business—without much success, it seemed—and hurried off.

Alaric didn't turn to face Jarek immediately. At first, he thought the commander was bracing himself. Then he started to wonder if Alaric even realized he was standing there, or if he'd simply checked out for good somewhere in the middle of listening to his men prattling on.

Finally, though, Alaric turned his head, showing Jarek the left side of his face and one downcast, bloodshot eye.

"Spit it out," he said quietly.

Jarek pointedly looked around at the crowd. "Not here."

Alaric gave a neutral grunt, like he'd been expecting Jarek's answer but didn't quite care enough to make a move.

Jarek waited quietly.

Finally, Alaric heaved a heavy sigh and turned in full. "Fine." He waved Jarek on. "Lead the way."

Jarek picked his way through the crowd, rehearsing unsatisfactory lines in his head and doing his best to ignore the curious looks that followed them through the tunnel. More out of familiarity than anything else, he steered them in the direction of the showers where he and Rachel had spent the early afternoon. Where he was headed, he didn't precisely know. Just away from the crowd.

He was thinking about trying the reservoirs he'd seen marked past the showers earlier when Alaric caught him by the shoulder and spun him around with a dark frown.

"Where the hell are we going? I've got more important things to be doing than taking a stroll with you."

Jarek let the words roll off him like the emotional overflow he knew they were. "You're allowed to be hurting, you know."

The words took Alaric by surprise, enough so that he recoiled slightly. "My son hated everything there was to hate about me. And now he's dead. You're seriously stupid enough to think I'm not hurting?"

"Oh, I know you're hurting," Jarek said with a surreptitious glance back down the tunnel.

Several soldiers were watching them from the outskirts of the crowd twenty yards away. Jarek ignored them and turned back to Alaric.

"Which is why I thought I'd better point out that you're not doing anyone any favors trying to put on the Brave Commander face right now."

Alaric started to say something, but Jarek held up a firm hand for silence.

"And it's not true, what you just said about him."

"The hell it isn't," Alaric growled. His face worked, twitching somewhere between a snarl and a grimace.

He looked like he wanted to hit someone. Anyone. Didn't matter who as long as he could transfer an ounce of his pain off his plate.

Jarek found himself wishing for the second time that the commander *would* take a swing at him. That somehow Alaric's angry fists could validate the guilt that'd been sitting in Jarek's gut since they'd drove away from that farmhouse and left Mosen to die for them. Since before then, even.

But that was the self-pity talking. He knew that. Just like he knew there was nothing to be gained and no one to be helped by indulging it.

For both of their sakes, he needed to get his shit together and hold it there.

"He asked me to tell you something," Jarek said.

Alaric watched him with the silent look of a broken man, caught somewhere between desperate anger and bone-deep sorrow.

Just tell him...

"He wanted me to tell you that he was sorry," Jarek started slowly. "That he was . . . afraid. Angry too. Angry at you, at the raknoth, at everything. But mostly just afraid. I think he always wanted to tell you, but..." He glanced back at the curious onlookers, who all scurried hurriedly back to their business. "We should talk about this somewhere else."

Alaric didn't seem to hear the last part. He was dead still, and when he spoke, his voice was barely a creaky murmur.

"Seth said all this?"

For a second, Jarek thought about telling him the truth—that he was only extrapolating what Mosen had wanted Alaric to hear. Looking at Alaric's hunched shoulders, though, he couldn't bring himself to sink one more dagger into the man's ribs.

"He did," Jarek said quietly.

It was what Mosen had wanted to say. He was sure of it.

Wasn't he?

Some part of Alaric saw through his white lie—Jarek was almost certain of it—but the rest of him must've been so desperately overcome with grief that it was willing to overlook the detail for now.

So Jarek took a dry swallow and pushed on. "I tried to talk him down, Alaric. Tried to tell him we'd find another way, but..."

Alaric finally unfroze and crossed into the next tunnel to sink onto a shipping crate and bury his scraggly face in his hands. "But there was no other way," he finally murmured into his palms after a long silence.

"No." Jarek followed and cautiously sat beside Alaric. "I don't think there was."

Alaric's eyes were bloodshot and utterly defeated as they searched Jarek's face, weighing his words and his intent.

"He still loved you, Alaric," Jarek said quietly. "Somewhere in there."

Alaric couldn't quite seem to figure out how to react to that, so, for a while, they sat in silence.

"That's one hell of a shiner you picked up, there," Alaric said after some time.

Jarek shot a questioning look at him, trying to ignore the sinking feeling in his gut.

Alaric watched right back, his bloodshot eyes unreadable. Finally, he tilted his head back the way they'd come from. "Heard a few of the boys talking about their adventures on the road."

Jarek held Alaric's gaze, searching for some hint of what he was driving at. "There were disagreements. And a few good punches."

Alaric bobbed his head, his gaze distant as he turned that tidbit over.

"What did Seth wanna do?" he finally asked. "What was his plan if he wrestled the group from you?"

It was unnerving, how clearly Alaric seemed to see the events unfolding from what few details he'd gathered. But, Jarek reminded himself, he was here to support the man and to help him understand how his son had felt at the end. Not to stand trial for Seth's death.

"I'm not so sure he really had a plan," Jarek said. "Short of making sure the cheeky asshole in the exosuit didn't get his men killed."

For a second, the lines of Alaric's frown lightened marginally, and his lips moved in the ghost of a humorless smile.

It didn't spread to his eyes.

"I think," he said slowly, rising from the crate and turning to face Jarek from a standing position, "that the two of you might've been more alike than you'd like to realize."

Jarek dropped his gaze to the floor, unable to meet Alaric's eyes. "Yeah… The thought occurred to me once or twice out there. Among others."

Conner's bloody, grinning face flashed through his mind unbidden.

All of them pushed to violent action. All of them so damn certain they were the one seeing things clearly…

"You wouldn't have been at that farmhouse," Alaric said quietly. "Not if he'd been the one calling the shots."

His words cut through Jarek like a scalpel, so fine and swift that he couldn't fully appreciate the damage they'd done until the blood began to well along the wound.

He clenched his jaw, fighting the words on the edge of his tongue.

He wouldn't apologize, no matter how loudly his guilty heart screamed for him to do so. No matter how urgently his emotions insisted that he throw himself at Alaric's feet and beg for his forgiveness.

Because that was the point, wasn't it?

It didn't matter that he was sorry. Seth was still dead either way. Just like the other five they'd lost back at the farmhouse were still dead too. And just like the rest of them were still alive.

Jarek had made his decisions. He'd done his best. And now he'd live with the consequences of those actions. The good and the bad.

So he forced himself to meet Alaric's eyes, and he told him what they both needed to hear.

"It was the right call."

The rest of the words couldn't seem to unstick themselves from his throat. That, right call or not, every part of him would always go on wishing everyone could've survived. That, faced with the situation again, he would've made the same call, even now. That, above all else, he'd do everything in his power to never let anyone down again, knowing damn well that he was aiming for the impossible.

Alaric watched him silently for a long time, looking more than anything like he was trying to rekindle the anger that seemed to be burning out of him with each passing second, leaving nothing but profound weariness in its tracks. After what felt like half an eternity, he gave up and turned to leave.

He didn't make it more than half a step, though, before he paused and slowly turned back to Jarek.

"You remember what I told you? Back at HQ, right after those boys were fixing to jump you in medical?"

Jarek forced himself to hold Alaric's gaze. "I remember."

Alaric nodded to himself, his eyes far away. "You're learning," he said quietly.

Then he left.

Jarek watched him go, silently cogitating on what Alaric meant by that. He couldn't quite decide whether he really wanted to know or not.

"You *are* right, sir," Al said quietly in his earpiece. "From a logical standpoint, following the leads to Columbus and then to Cheyenne were the best of the available choices for maximizing our chances for long term surviv—"

"You don't have to tell me, Al," Jarek said. Then, less aggressively, "I appreciate it, buddy, but... I don't know. Surviving and being right aren't exactly synonymous."

"Rightness is hardly guaranteed in any action when we are discussing anything so subjective as human morality, sir," Al said. "Within those tenuous guidelines, I believe the best one can do is to simply strive to act as one they deem a *good* person would."

"Hmm. Most interesting. I think you might have me confused with Pryce, Mr. Robot. Objectively."

Al ignored the comment.

"You are a good person, sir. As far as I understand the premise."

Jarek smiled. "Well if my robot says I'm a good little boy, it has to be true, right? Just like when Mommy and Daddy said they liked my finger paintings."

"I'm sure they did, sir."

Jarek chuckled and shook his head,

"What will you do about Alaric, sir?" Al asked after some time.

"I don't know. Stay out of his way, I guess. And let him have his shot at the rakul when it's time."

"Something tells me that that time is not far off, sir."

Jarek chewed his lip, absentmindedly watching the soldiers ahead —some eating, some maintenancing their equipment, many preparing to bed down for their first full, proper night of sleep in far too long.

It was too good to last.

"Something tells me you're right, Mr. Robot."

CHAPTER TWENTY-EIGHT

It was a pleasant enough planet, Vermaga decided. As much as anything was pleasant anymore, through the stale lens of far too many cycles. The inhabitants of said planet, though…

The World Ender had been wise to target Earth all those cycles ago. These humans. These nefarious little bipeds who pranced about with their feeble weapons.

For now, they were nothing. Held firmly in their helplessness by indignation and willful ignorance. Not yet intelligent enough to understand what they could one day become. Not yet.

But one day they would be. Or would have been, rather. That was entirely the point of the harvest, after all.

Vermaga had watched from the mountaintop for a day and a night now. He hadn't twitched a single unit, save for the ones below—those pieces of himself with which he'd been busy at work, dividing, spreading, commandeering.

He could still feel the odd bubbles there, the ones the craftiest of the humans had somehow constructed to bar the way to his extended senses. A curiosity, to be sure, but it hadn't stopped him from communicating with the pieces of himself below. There was nothing sensory about that.

It was simply what the humans had once spoke in hopeful whispers of as quantum entanglement, and to Vermaga, it occurred as naturally as their breathing.

At least whoever had constructed the barrier—he suspected the female that that wretch, Gada, had warned them about—had attempted some form of resistance. And then there was the armored one and his pathetic band of fighters.

True, the clan of the one who slew Kul'Armin had been utterly inept in allowing Vermaga to slip a few spies among their group and track them all the way from the land of Pittsburgh. But, to their credit, they'd put up a noble struggle back at that crude country house once Vermaga had learned of their allies' location here at Cheyenne and given Ogrin and Gada permission to destroy the convoy.

At least they'd fought.

The same could not be said of the rest of the humans below, who even now danced like sad little puppets to his every thought.

Yes, in a few more of their millennia, these humans might have become troublesome. But for now, it was regrettably easy.

Perhaps he and his brothers should have taken their time in coming to Earth.

Once they'd realized the extent of their confounded underlings' treachery, though, allowing the traitorous raknoth of Earth to escape punishment any longer had been out of the question. It simply would not do, allowing the other factions to believe such wayward disobedience could ever be met by anything other than the full might of their Masters.

So, Vermaga had set each tiny bit of himself in position to destroy the sad final bastion of these humans and his younger kin, and then he had waited for his brothers.

They came as Earth's sun approached the horizon and painted the dark sky a mournful streak of red.

Kul'Fraga and Kul'Vaish. The Dagger and The Wraith.

Vermaga had no great love for either of the cutthroats. Then again, few of the Kul had any great love for much of anything anymore. No strong feelings at all, truly, with the possible exception of their current shared disdain for that meddling sapling, Gada.

It mattered not.

They were simply here to complete the work and restore order. Which meant Fraga and Vaish were exactly the Kuls for the job.

"You are ready inside, brother?" came Fraga's silent question.

No matter how many times he heard it, the sound of Fraga's voice, mental or spoken, never ceased to strike Vermaga as unexpected.

It was simply too thick for a creature so small.

The little gremlin fingered his dark blades, silently reminding Vermaga to move on with it.

"Wait," Vermaga sent.

"The others will be here soon," Fraga said.

Vermaga ignored his brother's reminder and concentrated. Nearly half a mile below, the piece of himself he'd set to wait in the vent dropped down into the isolated storage room he'd picked out hours ago.

The rest of him stirred below, the pitiful servants he had infected throughout the base glancing up in confused anticipation, sensing their moment was fast approaching but not yet comprehending how or why.

"The way is clear," Vermaga thought toward his brothers.

Fraga grabbed onto Vermaga's proffered appendage and glanced back at Vaish. *"You are prepared, wall-walker?"*

Vaish only continued to watch, swirling with nebulous wisps of apathy, as he always did.

Vermaga had always suspected the prolonged quantum uncertainty involved in Vaish's shifting would inevitably touch his mind. He had not been wrong.

"Splendid," Fraga sent.

And with that, Fraga was gone. Or not gone, really, so much as no longer there.

Vermaga felt him below already, standing over his smaller self in the storage room, waiting.

"Tell the wraith to hurry it up," Fraga sent.

Vermaga turned his senses back to the mountainside only to find Vaish had already gone, shifting down through earth and stone as readily as if it were thin air.

"*Tell him yourself,*" Vermaga thought back.

"*As if he'd give a damn. Yes, I'm talking about you, wraith,*" Fraga added as Vermaga felt Vaish shift from one side of the humans' mysterious telepathic bubble to the other.

Vaish, unsurprisingly, did not reply—merely ghosted his way to Fraga's location and glanced around as if he could see through the base's walls, drinking in the numbers and locations of his imminent victims with his senses.

"*Right, then,*" Fraga thought, "*let us begin, brother shade, mine.*"

CHAPTER TWENTY-NINE

Rachel woke to near-complete darkness and a moment of profound disorientation. There were shouts and sounds of booted feet storming by outside.

Outside where?

Her own nakedness and the feel of soft blankets around her, hard floor beneath her, and a chilled, exposed back guided her discombobulated mind back to the tiny little broom closet of a room she'd been nestled up in with—

Where was Jarek?

She rolled groggily over and felt more than saw him already scrambling into Fela in the dark corner of their miniature abode.

"What's happening?" she asked, trying to rub the sleep from her eyes even as the first hints of adrenaline tickled at her chest.

"Three guesses," Jarek said as Fela closed around him with a series of clicks and clacks.

Rachel felt around for her clothes, casting her senses out to search for new, unfriendly minds or anything else out of the ordinary. At first, there was nothing close by, aside from a few small groups of people making their hurried ways past, clearly upset about something.

Then the alarms started.

"That's never good," Jarek murmured. "Are you decent?" he added, a second before she heard the familiar sound of his faceplate sliding shut. Then, "Ooh. I don't think decent does that justice."

Rachel finished yanking on her jeans and reached for her sports bra, too worried about what might be happening out there to even bother rolling her eyes at him.

The sound of gunfire didn't ease her concerns.

"Shit," Jarek hissed, clicking on a light for her as she finished dressing and gathered up her staff and other gear. "Did they get inside?"

He checked to make sure she was ready, then pulled the door open and stepped into the stale yellow light of the hallway outside, one hand on his sword hilt.

For a second, the gunfire lulled. Then it redoubled, along with a choir of alarmed cries that seemed to answer Jarek's question clearly enough. Somehow, the enemy had found a way in as they slept.

Something blurred around the corner ahead.

Jarek whipped his sword free from his back, but at second glance, they realized it was one of Krogoth's younger raknoth. He came bolting toward them, crimson eyes wide with alarm, skin shifting to light green scales in splotches.

"Where are they?" Jarek called.

The raknoth skidded to a halt and jerked his finger down the hallway he'd come from, toward the larger tunnels that ran between buildings.

"How many?" Rachel asked.

"At least two," the raknoth said, waving for them to hurry. "Zar'Krogoth sent me to rouse you as soon as he felt them, Rachel Cross."

That caught her by surprise just as much as it clearly caught Jarek. She couldn't help but smile a tad at the confused tilt of his head as he glanced over at her.

"I'm special," she said.

"Yeah, yeah," Jarek said, returning his sword to his back as he started into a run beside her. "Let's just get there before any more raknoth decide to try to steal my girlfriend."

"Your what?" she gasped, already breathing heavy from the running as they kicked through the door into the larger tunnel.

Jarek, apparently noticing the exertion, scooped her up into his arms and ignored her cry of protest as he put on a burst of speed to catch them up to their raknoth guide.

"Face it, Goldilocks," he said as the cavernous ceiling blurred by overhead. "We're basically stuck with each other at this poi—holy shit!"

Jarek went rigid, digging his sharp heels in to skid them to a stop as something small streaked into the intersection ahead with a light popping sound, almost like a miniature thunderclap.

"Is that a leprechaun?" Jarek murmured.

The thing hit the wall and hung there for longer than seemed to make physical sense until Rachel noticed the many small claws on its foot-like appendages and the dark, glassy dagger it had driven into the wall as if the structure were made of flimsy cardboard.

Leprechaun may have been a fair word to describe the thing in stature, but that was most certainly where the similarities ended. Sickly orange plates covered its body like some kind of organic armor, teeming with burrs and sharp edges. Its face was that of a hellish goblin.

And the way their raknoth guide slid to a halt beside them and threw a warning arm out to block their way could only mean it was a Kul they were looking at.

It turned startlingly crimson eyes on them, its lips pulling into an eager snarl. Then it vanished.

There was a ferocious roar, and Krogoth's rust-red form came flying into the wall the Kul had just vacated. He hit hard enough that the metal crumpled in around the hand and foot he extended to catch himself.

"Move!" he roared.

Too late.

There was another popping sound beside them. Their raknoth

guide shrieked in pain and hit the ground with a long gash across his hamstrings.

Jarek adapted to the impossible faster than Rachel, dishing her to her feet behind him as he spun into a low, sweeping kick.

The Kul effortlessly jumped the kick with a high, twisting aerial maneuver. Jarek kept spinning and whipped his sword free and into a horizontal slice.

The speedy little bastard tucked over again and actually hopped off of the flat of Jarek's blade as it swished through the air he'd just occupied, using the touch point to lunge for Jarek with his gleaming black daggers.

Rachel reached out and caught him with telekinesis, more out of reflex than conscious thought.

The Kul's fiery eyes widened for an instant. Then he hurled one of his daggers at her.

The blade whistled toward her almost faster than her eyes could track. Too fast for her to raise her defenses. Too fast—

The blade jolted to a halt in midair and clattered to the stone floor. It took her stunned brain a moment to realize the Kul had thrown the knife fast enough that her bullet-catcher had picked up on the threat.

Krogoth and his raknoth were coming now.

Rachel clenched her fist and telekinetically slammed the Kul to the ground. Or tried to.

The instant before the little gremlin hit, he disappeared with a pop. A pained roar to the right announced his re-arrival down the tunnel.

By the time Rachel turned, the Kul was already yanking his glassy dagger from a raknoth's chest and aiming another stab at his victim's head.

Krogoth lunged in and forced the Kul off before he could land his killing blow. The creature vanished and popped into existence behind Krogoth, dagger plummeting for the side of his rust-red skull. But Krogoth was already rolling clear of the strike.

Al'Brandt darted in and caught the Kul with a punch that sent him flying toward Jarek and his sword like a lovely gremlin fastball.

Jarek cocked back. Swung.

The Kul vanished just before the blade hit and popped back into existence by Rachel, where he scooped up his thrown dagger and promptly vanished again. He paused further down the tunnel to give them a snarl and a creepy little wave of his daggers, then he scampered away in the direction of the front entrance.

"Son of a bitch," Jarek murmured. "That was one of them?"

"Kul'Fraga," Krogoth confirmed. "We will deal with him." He turned an uncertain look at Rachel. "You should find Al'Drogan. He may need your help with—"

Gunfire from one of the buildings further down the tunnel in the other direction announced that the Kul's partner was still busy at work.

"Kul'Vaish has come," Drogan's voice growled at the edge of Rachel's senses.

"Go," Krogoth said, apparently having heard as well. "We will deal with Kul'Fraga."

He must've been issuing telepathic orders in the meantime, because three of his raknoth stepped to join her and Jarek while Brandt and the rest followed him without a word.

The pack set off after Fraga at an unnaturally fast sprint.

"Be wary, Rachel Cross," Krogoth's voice came to her as he reached the next intersection and rounded out of sight. *"Kul'Vaish is not to be trifled with."*

Were any of the Kul?

Between her near-dagger experience and Krogoth's apparent concern, she was too surprised to make any reply before he was gone.

"C'mon." Jarek started for the sounds of fighting and paused to wave her on. "Let's not leave Stumpy hanging. You okay?"

She nodded dumbly and set off with him and the rest of the raknoth at a run.

WHEN THEY REACHED the big white building the shots were coming from, the dark green raknoth who'd taken the lead ignored the stairs leading up to the doorway. Instead, he threw himself straight up and through the door with a rumbling battle cry. The door gave way with a sharp snap, and the other raknoth rushed into the building, Jarek on their heels and Rachel on his.

At the top of the stairs, Rachel's first sight was of soldiers fleeing toward them, wild-eyed and frantic at whatever they'd just escaped.

Not the best sign.

She hurried after Jarek and the raknoth anyway. When they rounded the corner and caught sight of the thing the troops had fled, she couldn't say she blamed them.

Her first impression was of the Grim Reaper made flesh and blood. Only, at second glance, she wasn't so sure about the flesh, or the blood. Dark swirling cloud of death, was more like it.

Kul'Vaish glided through armed men like flowing smoke—his cruel, spindly appendages incorporeal one moment, then dripping blood the next as they solidified in the center of one man's chest, then another's head.

Drogan faced the wraith with only one other raknoth in the narrow hallway, both of them doing their best to corral the soldiers away from Vaish while keeping their distance themselves.

Drogan turned at their entrance, looking grim.

The wraith turned as well. There were no crimson orbs, no eyes at all that Rachel could see in the swirling darkness. But somehow she was still certain the thing followed Drogan's gaze straight to her.

Her step faltered.

"Rachel Cross," Drogan sent rapidly, *"you must Kul—"*

"Look out!" Jarek barked as, behind Drogan, the wraith surged forward with surprising speed.

Drogan hit the deck just as Vaish's wickedly sharp arm solidified and whistled through the air where his head had been.

Vaish continued on, straight toward them.

Rachel extended her hand and cast out with telekinesis to slow him down. It was like trying to catch sand with a net. Vaish slowed but continued sliding forward.

She raised her staff, thinking to try fire or a strong gale.

The wraith came faster. Too fast.

Armored arms grabbed her and yanked her from her feet, back into the hallway they'd come from. Their raknoth allies scattered in the other direction. Jarek deftly deposited her back to the floor—just as Vaish ghosted through the wall after them.

"Behind you," Rachel snapped.

Jarek was already whirling around with the Whacker.

The hallway flashed azure. The wraith's dark form billowed out in wispy streaks around Jarek's sizzling blade but quickly pulled back into its original shape.

Then something dark and pointy emerged from Jarek's left hamstring, and he cried out in pain.

Desperation gripped Rachel's chest. She reached out, pulling the energy to lash out. To do anything.

Jarek's left leg buckled, taking him to the knee. Above him, Vaish aimed another spiky tendril of darkness. But Jarek wasn't done.

He flipped his sword reverse-grip with an angry snarl and aimed a sweeping cut at the first dark appendage where it protruded from his thigh. Vaish's body still looked incorporeal.

The appendage wasn't.

The air flashed azure again, and Jarek fell back from Vaish with the narrow spear of the Kul's dark, severed appendage still buried in his leg.

Erratic spasms rushed through Vaish's swirling body, and from his dark depths came a sound like the wind itself screaming in agony. The Kul rocked back and bumped into the wall with part of his body, while the rest passed halfway through. It was as if the pain had dulled Vaish's control.

Drogan didn't wait around for him to get it back. He appeared at Vaish's side, sank his claws into the Kul's flickering torso, and yanked Vaish around the corner and away from them. The other raknoth followed with a round of eager roars.

Rachel waited a moment to be sure they were clear, then dropped to the floor beside Jarek, cupping the back of his neck in one hand as she leaned over to inspect the damage.

Jarek dropped his sword and grabbed the severed end of Vaish's appendage with both hands.

"Jarek, wait," she gasped, "are you sure that's—"

He yanked the alien limb free with a heavy groan and a wet sucking sound that made Rachel's stomach squirm.

"It's fine," he grunted. "Missed the bone. Al's compressing it." He looked up at the sound of a pained roar from around the corner. "Got any tricks to keep that shifty bastard solid?"

Several soldiers watched them nearby, weapons clutched tightly, their stares like silent prayers for her to confirm that she did indeed have some master plan to stop that thing.

What had Drogan tried to say?

She must… had he said Kul?

No. Not Kul. That made no sense.

Cool.

"Cold," she muttered as the logic fell into place and she started considering the logistics of how the hell she was going to do it. "I think we need to freeze him."

Jarek's faceplate swung to face her as he considered that, then he shrugged. "Yeah, sure. Why not?" His breathing sounded labored as he looked around this way and that for some kind of inspiration. "Cold things don't move so good, right? You got any ide—"

His attention snapped back to her like he'd found that inspiration.

She was opening her mouth to ask what he was thinking when he snaked a hand around the small of her back and yanked her bullet-catcher from her belt. He held it up and cocked his head in question.

Her eyes widened, and she nodded in astonishment.

It was so simple.

Jarek pulled himself to his feet with a few grunts and gestured to the troops with the disc-shaped bullet-catcher. "Time to shoot some skeet, boys and girls!"

"Get ready to clear the way," Rachel sent at Drogan, who returned a strained affirmative.

Then Jarek rounded the corner and tossed the catcher at

Vaish. It landed just below the swirling darkness of the Kul's lower body.

One of the raknoth already lay dead in the hallway. Drogan and the rest dove clear.

"Open fire!" Jarek bellowed. "Everyone!"

Most of them probably didn't have half a clue what the hell he was up to, but they were past asking questions.

Gunfire erupted from eight or nine weapons beside Rachel and Jarek. At a Fela-amplified shout from Jarek, the troops on the other end of the hallway opened up too, catching Vaish in a cross fire. There was little risk of them hitting each other, as Vaish was finding out.

The Kul shifted confusedly back and forth, observing the hundreds of bullets slamming into thin air just short of his swirling form and falling harmlessly to the floor. A ring of spent lead quickly formed around him, an unnatural breeze sweeping through the hallway as her catcher absorbed the heat from the air to counteract the kinetic energy of each and every one of those bullets, cooling the air rapidly enough to leave a nice, big pressure differential.

That's when Vaish realized what they were up to.

"Do not let him shift out of this hallway, Rachel Cross!" Drogan's voice cried in her mind as Vaish began drifting for the nearest wall.

She reached for the Kul, all too happy to oblige.

It still wasn't easy, latching onto Vaish with telekinesis. But with every bullet that struck the catcher's field, and every degree the hallway dropped, the Kul grew incrementally less slippery to her grip.

Rachel held stubbornly on, channeling even more heat from the hallway to fuel the effort.

Even ten yards away from the center of it, her breath was condensing into beautiful white mist. It was well below freezing, now, by the feel of it.

The soldiers were all still shooting, eyes wide but senses sharp enough to stagger their reloads and keep the pressure on. Jarek had both of his pistols out too.

Vaish let out another airy scream, his nebulous swirling weakening now, slowing until he nearly looked solid throughout. Solid enough that Drogan and another raknoth lunged in to attack.

"Keep shooting the disc!" Jarek cried, holstering his pistols. Then he drew his sword and rushed after them with a pronounced limp.

Drogan must've sensed him coming. The raknoth dodged around Vaish, drawing the Kul's attention just as Jarek closed and brought his sword down.

The blade raked across Vaish's turned back in a bizarre fashion, almost as if it were only cutting at points and passing through others entirely without resistance. So he wasn't as solid as he looked yet. But something still seared, and Vaish didn't look happy about it.

The gunfire had faltered as Jarek and the raknoth charged. Now that the soldiers understood the plan, though, it picked back up quickly enough as they adapted to the development and took more careful aim to hit the catcher and not their allies, who danced in and out of the catcher's field, keeping the disgruntled Kul busy.

With Vaish distracted, Rachel shifted her focus from preventing his escape to cranking their makeshift freezer into overdrive.

Channeling more heat out of the area was the first and most obvious thought, but not the most useful. Their allies' bullets were already sapping plenty of heat from the area, though many of them seemed to be running low on ammo at this point. What she needed to do was make their shots count.

Thermodynamics was the enemy here.

The thought was murky from conception as she reached out to the area around the combatants. If she could somehow bubble off that short section of hallway—somehow stymie the natural flow of heat along its gradient from high to low...

The microscopic picture of what that might look like made her head spin, so she closed her eyes, holding the macroscopic idea firmly in mind, willing it to be true. Then she opened herself to the energy.

It wasn't perfect. She wasn't even sure it was good.

The gentle breeze in her hair and the growing bitter cold on her face and hands attested that her thermal seal was far from leak-proof. And every one of the considerable number of bullets punching into the area poked at her mental construct like tiny holes in a large balloon she was trying to inflate.

But it was working.

The cold around Vaish, Jarek, and the raknoth was profound in her extended senses. So much so that she worried about her allies freezing. But they'd have to manage.

She had her own problems.

Whatever she was doing was burning through energy at an alarming rate. And the drain seemed to be worsening by the second.

She was marginally aware of hard floor hitting her knees as she dropped. But that was okay. It was working.

The last two raknoth had darted in to join the attack on Vaish. Gunfire still barked from both ends of the hallway, but it was dwindling, several soldiers having spent the entirety of their munitions.

Ahead, Vaish's airy protests had gone silent, though the sounds of fighting persisted.

Rachel cracked her eyes open for a disoriented glance. Jarek and the raknoth circled Vaish, their clothes and armor coated by frost that must've condensed and froze over as the temperature had plummeted. They fought well together, the raknoth ripping with tooth and claw, Jarek striking with the Whacker.

Rachel winced at the brilliant flare of azure heat that exploded from the heart of the cold in her extended senses as he took a hard swing, but it was well worth it.

Vaish staggered to the floor, clutching at his front with slender, misshapen arms that looked like they'd solidified into their current forms before the Kul had intended them to.

Something primal awoke in her at the sight of the Kul falling to his knees, or whatever he had beneath those dark folds. Previously, Vaish had seemed to be made of pure, swirling darkness, but now it fell around his hunched form more like a cloak.

Some ludicrous part of her almost felt bad for the creature as it tilted back to regard the eagerly circling raknoth with an air of macabre recognition. The rest just wanted the bastard to pay for everything he'd done—to Earth and to countless planets before that.

Something else was poking at her strained attention now, though.

A voice, crackling from the hallway speakers. Dola's.

"—advised, an additional rakul ship has been spotted approaching."

Her stomach fell.

"Repeat, we are at full emergency alert," Dola continued. "All hands to your stations immediately. This is—"

The speaker cut off with a rustle and a sharp click. The kind that made it sound like something in the system had failed.

That boded about as well as the news that more rakul were about to touch down.

Her focus on the thermal bubble was slipping, but it barely seemed to matter now. Only three or four soldiers still had the ammo to be firing. And together, the raknoth were wrestling Vaish under control, descending on the Kul with remorseless fury.

Since her disheveled awakening, she hadn't had time to properly think about what was happening. Mostly, she'd been hoping this was simply the rakul probing their defenses. Or maybe even two over-eager Kuls making like Gada and moving ahead before their brethren were prepared. But no.

This was it. The rakul were converging.

The full assault was here.

"The Enochians!" she cried, not really sure who the words were even intended for.

"Go!" Jarek and Drogan both shouted at the same time, neither looking back as they helped secure Vaish's struggling form.

"We'll be right behind you," Jarek added over the diminishing gunfire as he raised his sword for a swing.

She hesitated for a second, then clambered to her shaky feet and set off at a wobbly run. Azure light flashed after her. Down the hall-way. Through the smashed-in door to the tunnels.

She ran as hard as she could.

Perhaps within a few days, Alton had said.

A few days. Perhaps.

And that had barely been twelve hours ago.

It didn't matter now. This was either going to work or it wasn't.

Rachel shouldn't have been surprised to find an armory's-worth of Enochian artillery shoved in her face the moment she crossed the threshold of their barracks, but it startled her plenty anyway.

"It's me!" she cried, holding her hands up. "Jesus."

"Sorry," Johnny mumbled, lowering his rifle as Phineas wordlessly pushed past her to check the hallway outside.

"What's happening out there?" Franco asked, lowering his own rifle and looking back at Elise with pained worry carved into his face.

"Two of them got inside somehow," Rachel said, hurrying between Haldin's and Elise's cots and plopping to the floor. "A teleporter and a... wraith-thingy."

"Shit," Johnny said. Then, with a little shrug, "Hey, at least it's not Dola's puppets uprising, though, right? I thought for sure... Uh, I think I'll go watch the hallway with Phineas. Yep. That's, uh..."

Rachel turned to find Johnny sweeping out of the room, Franco staring at his retreating back with a level of intensity she'd never seen from the man. And that was saying something.

"I have to try to pull them out," Rachel said when Franco turned back to her. "I don't think they're ready, but it might be now or never."

Franco watched her for a long second, radiating that grim intensity. Then he gave a curt nod and posted himself at the door with his rifle.

Rachel said a silent prayer to no one in particular and grabbed the Enochians' hard, blocky hands.

"Guys? Knock-knock. We've got a serious problem here."

There was nothing, not even a faint stir of a conscious presence beneath the deep, heavy vastness of the two things that only barely felt alive to her senses. They were down deep. Deeper than they had been yesterday when she'd come to contact them.

"Alton? Lietha? Anyone? Come on guys. If anyone can hear me in there, now's the fucking time!"

Nothing.

Growing anxious, she shifted gears and threw her mind like a javelin into the seemingly bottomless void that was Haldin and Alton's shared space. There was some resistance, but not much.

It didn't matter. Whatever it was she pressed her mind into, there didn't seem to be anyone home, like she'd broken into a small house only to somehow find a vast, empty desert inside. Haldin and Alton had to be in there somewhere, but even if she'd had ample time to root around—which she most certainly did not—she had no idea how long it would've taken to find them.

"Please," she sent out, letting her anxious urgency and some vague mental pictures of what was happening in The Complex drift out into the empty space with her words. *"We're out of time. The rakul are here. You have to wake up."*

For a long while, there was nothing. She repeated her pleas, calling their names until she was sure it was all futile.

Then, the faintest stir of a distant presence.

Alton.

It was barely more than a hint, but she was sure she'd felt it.

"Alton! Fraga and Vaish made it inside. The others are coming. It's time to fight."

Something. Like a distant call, too far out to hear.

Then, clearer but still somehow distant despite the fact that she was holding Haldin and Alton's hand, *"—can't hope..."*

Alton's voice sounded weak.

"Alton? You can't hope what? What do you need me to do?"

"—st tell... others... sync—synchronize before..."

She was reaching for the flicker of Alton's presence, trying to stabilize their bond, when he simply winked out of her senses. Not gone, she thought, but once again too deeply immersed in whatever they were doing in there for her to reach him.

Rachel cursed and withdrew back to her own body, turning her options over.

It wouldn't have hurt if Alton could've made one damn bit of sense with the precious few words he'd managed. *Tell others.* Which others?

And tell them what? Had he meant that he needed to tell the others about the rakul? Or that she should?

And what had he meant by synchronize?

Did that mean he and Haldin were almost ready to wake up and try this dangerous new body of theirs together?

Yep. One damn bit of sense would've been real nice.

Still, the fact that she'd gotten anything out of Alton at all was a decent sign. She was just going to have to operate on the assumption that he'd heard her warning and was doing everything he could in there to get them ready.

"Come on," she whispered to no one in particular. "We can do this."

As far as she knew, two of the twelve rakul were already dead. Assuming nothing had gone critically wrong out there, they were in the process of driving two more out of The Complex. If the Enochians and their raknoth partners could just pull out of this thing…

Maybe—just maybe—there could be hope after all.

Even so, they didn't have time for this.

"Anything?" Franco asked from his post at the door.

"Maybe," she said, turning to face him. "I'm not positive. I think Alton at least knows that the—"

Haldin's hand jerked in hers an instant before Franco's eyes went wide. Elise jerked a second later.

"What's happening?" Franco asked, rushing over to set his rifle against the wall and sink down beside Elise.

"I don't know." Rachel reached out with her senses and felt a confused jumble of activity raging just beneath the surface of each hybrid pair.

"Guys?" she tried. *"What's happening?*

If there was a deliberate answer, it was too convoluted and distorted for her to make sense of. They felt frantic and… was that fear?

"I don't know," she said to Franco's pleading gaze. "I can't tell what's happening in there."

Elise jerked again, a full body affair, and Haldin kicked the way people sometimes did when falling asleep.

"Are they…?" Franco muttered, seemingly to himself.

Rachel wasn't sure how she would've answered anyway. She couldn't tell if they were waking up or seizing or—

Together, Haldin and Elise both gave their most violent jerk yet and then fell limply back to their cots, unmoving.

"What?" Franco hissed.

Rachel looked back and forth between the two. Reached out with her senses.

They weren't breathing.

"No," Franco murmured. "No, no, no…"

Rachel scrambled to Haldin's side and pressed a hand to his chest. Felt the hard alien skin of his neck for any sign.

Nothing.

"No," she breathed.

"Elise?" Franco's voice was thick, wavering. "Sweetie? Please, please… Rachel!"

His desperate cry only ratcheted the building panic in her chest that much higher. They couldn't. They couldn't have just blinked out like that. Not after everything.

"Wake up," she sent. She pounded on Haldin's chest before she knew what she was doing. *"Wake UP, damn you! Wake up!"*

"Rachel." Franco's voice cracked like a whip.

Had she yelled that out loud? She'd definitely been cocking back to hit his chest harder.

She lowered her fist and turned.

"What do we do?" Franco asked, his eyes desperate but his tone level, demanding she get her shit together and help him figure this out.

She looked down at Haldin. Utterly still. No heartbeat. No breathing.

"Call for help," she started weakly, "or… the raknoth… maybe Drogan could—"

Something cracked overhead, and the room was plunged into

darkness. Electric panic seized her. She reached down to feel Haldin's still body. Reached blindly back in Franco's direction. Remembered her comm light and reached for it with a curse.

"Shit!" Johnny's voice called from just outside the doorway. "What the—"

Alarms yipped and red lights flicked to life on either side of the room, revealing Franco fumbling for his own comm and Johnny's armed form in the doorway, gaping in horror at Haldin and Elise.

"—peat," crackled a speaker in the corner, "The Complex's defenses have been de—"

The lights and the speaker all cut out with another sharp click

"What's happening?" Johnny whispered, sounding more afraid than she'd ever thought to hear him sound.

Rachel couldn't find the words. Couldn't breathe.

For a long moment, there was nothing but darkness, the sound of Johnny's panting at the doorway, and the hide of Haldin's neck against her fingertips, cool and lifeless.

A distant roar in the tunnels outside, bestial and terrifying.

"Prepare yourself, Rachel Cross," came Drogan's voice from somewhere toward the front entrance.

"The rakul come."

CHAPTER THIRTY

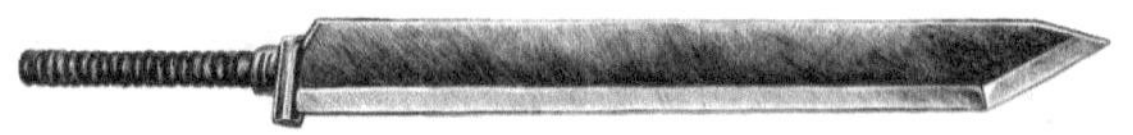

Jarek looked up at Drogan's puffed cheeks and the expectant angle of his reptilian brows and sighed. Then he shifted on his knees, and the sharp lance of pain in his thigh smacked him with an equally sharp reminder as to why he had to go through with this in the first place.

So he tilted his head back, started to open his mouth wide... and paused.

"No one ever hears about this, Stumpy. Ever."

"Rrr eehhnng rrra hhggh," Drogan growled through what sounded like an entire mouthful of spit.

"Yeah, I love you too, buddy. But still."

Drogan waved impatiently. And for good reason, too.

They needed to move.

Kul'Vaish lay in dismantled—and thankfully corporeal—pieces behind them, but there wasn't time to celebrate. Not when Fraga was still at large, apparently along with an unknown number of Vermaga's unwilling puppets.

It was only in the silent moments following Vaish's death that Drogan had sniffed out the presence of one of the Kul's little wormies nearby. When the raknoth had all focused together, they'd realized it

276

was more than just the one.

The rest of the raknoth and humans had already moved out to sweep The Complex for the intruders. Jarek and Drogan needed to go help secure the front entrance and deal with Fraga. It was just that moving wasn't so pleasant right now after having taken a spindly Kul arm straight through the thigh.

So Jarek tilted back, opened wide like a baby bird waiting for its worms, and accepted a disturbingly large globule of saliva from Drogan's mouth.

He might've preferred regurgitated worms. The fluid was warm and viscous, with an overpowering wave of bitterness and a light, sickly twinge of acidity. He tried to pretend it was just another shot of the good stuff and downed it as such.

It didn't go down nearly as well.

He wiped furiously at his mouth, coughing and sputtering.

Drogan wiped his own mouth, looking slightly amused by Jarek's reaction. "I said you are behaving like a child."

"Yeah, thanks for the clarification." Jarek spat on the floor. "Jesus Christ, I need some mouth wash. Or some whiskey. Or…"

Something trilled through him, starting in his head and rushing down through his chest and limbs. A tidal wave of pure, tingling weapons-grade energy.

"Holy fuck, Stumpy." He hopped to his feet with barely more than a twinge from his leg. "What did you give me, raknoth crack?"

He was talking too fast. Couldn't stop fidgeting. Had to move.

"Something akin to it, yes," Drogan said. "Along with a strong dose of heal—"

"Healing stuff! Shit yeah! Got it! I feel like a fucking—gah!" In a surge of relentless energy, Jarek turned and punched a hole through the adjacent wall.

He looked back at Drogan, momentarily sobered by his own rash display of poor self-control. "Well, that was unnecessary."

Drogan cocked his head. "Perhaps I overestimated with the stimulants. Regardless, we should get moving."

Overestimated? That didn't seem cool, but hey, who cared?

Jarek was bouncing on his feet, and Drogan had just used the word moving. Moving was good.

Jesus. Was this how dogs felt before walks?

Whatever. At least Drogan was in a hurry too.

They bounded down the hallways, out of the building, and through the tall tunnels outside.

By the time they were drawing close to the front entrance, the initial high was resolving back down from the level of *tweaking balls* to that of being merely hyper-caffeinated. The ache was creeping back into his leg, but it wasn't terrible. Not yet, at least.

"How are we looking down there, Mr. Robot?" Jarek asked as the compression provided by Fela's internal membrane reoriented around the wound site—presumably by Al's doing.

"Surprisingly well, sir. Blood loss is minimal, considering, and whatever Drogan gave you is already pulling some of the superficial tissues back together."

"Probably explains why I could go for a steak right now."

They rounded the corner to find Krogoth standing alone over the body of a man who'd died with an expression of clear agony frozen on his face. His front was a bloody mess, his abdominal cavity grotesquely opened as if it had somehow imploded. A dead raknoth lay beside him.

"What happened?" Jarek asked.

"Kul'Fraga reclaimed a segment of Kul'Vermaga from this host and used it as a link to teleport to safety," Drogan said. Apparently he'd already had the telepathic briefing on their way.

"I will kill the coward for this," Krogoth growled, staring down at his dead raknoth.

It took Jarek a second to follow the logic and connect it to the man's gruesome abdominal wound. Fraga must've ripped into the man's insides to extract Vermaga's little intruder.

So apparently they hadn't found all of Vermaga's pieces back at that ratty saloon.

"If Vermaga still has people on the inside…" Jarek started.

"We are tracking them." Krogoth said it as if he were actively participating in the effort even as he stood there—which maybe he was, for all Jarek knew. "Most were smart enough to find cloaked bodies to hide within, but Al'Brandt has already found and secured two others." He glanced in the direction of the entrance. "As soon as we confirm the door is once again secure, we will—"

A series of sharp, electronic cracking sounds echoed down the tunnel. Then the power died, casting the entire tunnel into pitch-black darkness so deep that even the extended spectrum of Fela's optical sensors couldn't offer much illumination.

"—let them knock all our defenses offline?" Jarek finished for the raknoth in a low mutter.

Al switched on Fela's external lights before the light trill of panic crept too far up Jarek's spine.

The raknoth were silent for a long second, listening.

Jarek did the same, and his heart quickened at what he heard. Heavy, loping steps. Quadruped.

Very large quadruped.

"The door," Krogoth hissed.

They all set off at a sprint.

Krogoth was shouldering through the door to the entrance tunnel when soft red light flooded the space. Emergency lights.

They kept running.

Speakers snapped on along the tunnel and someone—that Mayor character, Jarek thought—managed a few words that sounded a whole hell of a lot like bad news. The speakers and the emergency lights cut out before the voice could finish telling them just how screwed they were.

They kept running, the raknoth flipping on what lights they had to add to the pool of illumination Fela cast out around them.

Ahead, the first of the two heavy vault doors stood half-open, leaving them plenty of room to slip into the front antechamber. And also plenty of room for the first nard-shriveling roar to reach their ears as they approached.

"Back!" someone was shouting up ahead. "Fall back!"

It didn't sound like such a bad idea. Jarek charged through the breach alongside Drogan and Krogoth anyway.

Just as the giant hairless wolf-beast, Kul'Harga, plowed in straight through the men and raknoth who'd been trying to pull the main door shut on the other side of the antechamber.

Harga roared and snatched up one of the men with his powerful jaws. Krogoth snapped orders, and he, Drogan, and the other two raknoth fanned out around Harga as the big hairless beast padded into the room, holding the lifeless body in his jaws like a chew toy.

On Krogoth's orders, the human soldiers fell back to get ready to close the huge secondary door. They just needed to keep Harga from shouldering into The Complex with them.

Jarek drew his sword and was stepping to join the raknoth when Al spoke in his ear.

"Sir, there's something else in here."

Al had barely finished the sentence when two of the men working beside Zach at the door controls were yanked violently and inexplicably into the air, bloody wounds appearing out of nowhere as if they'd been snagged by a pair of invisible meat hooks.

Al tweaked the spectrum on Jarek's display, and the faint red shape of what looked something like an enormous praying mantis appeared behind the two men—it's shape oily and uncertain even in the infrared, as if light simply didn't behave as it should around the thing.

Was this the Kul'Shimo Rachel had told him about?

It hardly mattered. Chaos was taking the room.

Flashlight beams danced through the darkness as their allies scrambled to action. The raknoth harried Harga as a pack. Zach's and Krogoth's men frantically rushed for the entrance tunnel or to the futile aid of the two men dangling from the sharp, spiny forelegs of the invisible insectoid.

Shimo tossed the two men aside and impaled another for his efforts. Jarek stepped around a fleeing soldier and darted in to make the Kul pay for it.

He swung for the closest of Shimo's stalky legs, which numbered four, not counting the front two which were only half-regrown after having allegedly been ripped off by Drogan. The Kul was fast. He scuttled clear of the strike and responded with a jab of his own, which scraped the armor of Jarek's left shoulder as he barely twisted clear.

Whether it was a problem of duration or multitasking—or maybe just a point of pride or intimidation—Shimo dropped his camouflage as they moved into a rapid-fire exchange blows. It was difficult, trying to fight something that wasn't even marginally humanoid. Jarek had no idea what to expect—how Shimo might move and attack, when his best chances were to catch the Kul off balance. It was all alien.

Jarek nearly paid for his unfamiliarity several times in the first few exchanges alone. And the throaty bellow of another Kul approaching the main door from outside reminded him that their situation was only about to get worse.

They needed to get out of the antechamber.

He was opening his mouth to suggest they do so with gusto when Shimo sprang forward unexpectedly.

Jarek staggered back, raising his sword to deflect the incoming stab. But Shimo jerked to a violent halt a few feet short.

"Now, Jarek Slater!" Drogan roared from somewhere behind the Kul.

Jarek was already stepping into a heavy diagonal cut, aiming to cleave Shimo's buggy little face clean through between his big, bulbous eyes.

Shimo pivoted and swiped a hopeless foreleg up to slap the blow aside. Azure light flashed, and the Kul's foreleg hit the ground, smoke rising from its severed end.

Jarek aimed another swing at Shimo's head to silence the grating shriek for good, but the Kul bucked free of Drogan's grip and scuttled clear.

Drogan planted a kick on Shimo's thorax that sent the Kul sailing into the wall with a thud, and they whirled to evaluate the battle raging to their left. And not in their favor, it turned out.

Kul'Harga had Krogoth pinned on his back, eager jaws and

gleaming fangs a mere foot from the raknoth's head, held at bay only by Krogoth's strong hands on the Kul's throat.

"Go!" Krogoth roared at the two raknoth preparing to rush to his side.

Krogoth was strong, but Harga was stronger. The Kul's gaping jaws were slipping closer and closer to engulfing Krogoth's head.

Jarek and Drogan exchanged a single glance, painfully aware of the sounds of Shimo recovering behind them and yet another heavy Kul nearing the main door. Then they rushed for Krogoth and Harga, side by side.

Krogoth, seeing them coming, gave a great, roaring heave and managed to get his feet up and planted under Harga's thick chest like the world's most terrifying leg press.

Harga growled and snapped his jaws, crimson eyes burning brighter as he redoubled his efforts.

Then Krogoth kicked.

At a rough estimate, Harga must've weighed at least three or four tons. That didn't keep him from nearly hitting the high ceiling of the antechamber at the end of his flight.

Krogoth was already rolling to his feet. Drogan grabbed his arm, Jarek grabbed the other, and they pulled Krogoth along against his growling protests, hurrying back for the second security door.

The ground shook with the force of Harga's landing behind them. The patter of Shimo's scuttling legs drew closer. A bellow erupted from the main door, where their reinforcement—Ogrin, from the sound of it—had arrived.

Krogoth wasn't resisting now. Together, the three of them darted through the crack of the security doorway. Krogoth's raknoth were waiting on the other side to pull the enormous door shut as soon as they cleared it.

Something that sounded Harga-sized slammed into the door, followed a second later by another angry Kul. The door wavered with each hit—not exactly loose on its hinges, given the sheer mass of the thing, but definitely not locked either. And without power...

Another floor-shaking thud hit the door.

With the threat of death relegated from immediate to just uncomfortably close, Jarek's adrenaline and Drogan's waning stimulant cocktail dipped enough for the throbbing ache in his leg to reclaim its spot as profoundly unpleasant.

They needed to get the damn door locked.

"This is where we could use an arcanist," Jarek muttered.

"But we do not have one here," Drogan said.

"Yeah, thanks for that, Stumpy." He looked around. "Anybody else got a bright idea?"

"We should be able to get some of the systems back online in utilities," Zach said. "Enough to lock the door at least. Depending on the damage back there. Until then, though, we're sitting—"

Krogoth lunged forward with a deep roar and punched straight through the multi-inch thick acrylic that paneled the back of the enormous door. That done, he jammed himself arm-deep into the door's internal cavity and started manually shoving the thick steel tumblers in place, one by one.

"Yeah…" Jarek said slowly. "That works too."

"Rally the others," Krogoth said to Jarek and Drogan, deadly calm. "And you," he added to Zach, "You restore your systems. I will see to it the door holds until then."

Zach bristled at being ordered around by one of the creatures whose kind he'd apparently taken to be actual demons up until only a day ago. But apparently he was pragmatic enough to recognize this wasn't the time to argue. Or maybe he'd just been whipped unnaturally hard into shape by "Mayor Dillard" in the past twenty-four hours. Either way, Zach took his men and hurried back to the main body of The Complex.

Jarek and Drogan followed and quickly passed them.

He was about to ask Al to try to get Rachel on a short range comm channel when he remembered he had a much more direct method running right beside him.

"Can you radio ahead to Rachel, Stumpy?" Jarek asked.

"I have already informed her of recent developments," Drogan said.

"Great. What'd she say?"

"That the Enochians have perished."

Jarek nearly fell over as he whipped around to face Drogan. "What?! What do you mean, perished?"

"I do not yet know," he said, frowning. "She is… quite distraught."

"You think?" Jarek cried.

If the Enochians were really gone…

"We would be wise to get over there promptly."

"No shit," Jarek muttered, shaking his head as they reached the next door.

Whatever happened, he'd meant what he'd said the other day.

Nothing was going to tear him away from Rachel again.

Whatever happened, they'd face it together.

So Jarek pushed through the doorway, ignoring the periodic jolts of pain in his leg, and kept running.

CHAPTER THIRTY-ONE

Jarek's mind was a screaming torrent of long shots and hopeless prayers as he loped painfully along beside Drogan. He'd been more than a little skeptical about Operation Enochian Super Soldier since Rachel had first explained it to him by comm a few weeks ago. But he'd trusted Rachel when she'd told him she believed it was their best hope at gaining a surprise advantage. He'd even started to believe himself once he'd seen the changes Haldin and Elise had gone through.

And now the rakul were here in force, literally pounding down their front door, and the Enochians simply *perished*?

"Teach me to ever get my hopes up again," Jarek muttered.

"As I tried to explain to Rachel Cross," Drogan said, not breaking stride, "it is possible that this is a part of the process."

"Possible or likely?"

Drogan hesitated. "Possible."

"Great. Real helpful."

"There is hardly adequate precedent by which to judge," Drogan growled as they barreled into the tunnel Jarek was pretty sure was the right one.

Snippy. Apparently Jarek wasn't the only one who'd been starting to hope. And he certainly wasn't the only one who was on the verge of losing it.

The feel inside the Enochians' barracks was one of rampant panic. Jarek had heard the thuds before they reached the door. As he stepped in, he saw that Rachel was pounding on Haldin's chest, and Franco was similarly applying rhythmic compressions to Elise's.

At the sound of their entrance, Johnny and Phineas whipped around and trained weapons on them, their eyes shocked and frantic behind the sights of their rifles.

Jarek spread his hands, and they lowered the weapons, looking no less panicked. It wasn't the threat of intruders they feared right now.

Rachel and Franco hadn't looked up—hadn't noticed them at all, occupied as they were.

"Rache," Jarek said softly, sliding in behind her.

She kept at it. Rolled her shoulder out from under his hand when he touched her.

Jarek looked back at Drogan, who was leaned over Elise, inspecting her closely. Franco broke away from his compressions to shoot a desperate look at Drogan.

"Will compressions help?" Jarek asked the raknoth.

"I do not know."

Jarek stared dumbly at Drogan for a moment, then turned and gently shouldered in past Rachel. "Here, let me."

She fought for a second, then scooted aside and leaned against the wall with a heavy sigh. Behind him, Jarek heard Drogan similarly take over for Franco, though Franco didn't collapse to rest—just hovered there, frozen in shock and horror.

For a long stretch, no one said anything, and there was nothing but the rhythmic groans of protest from the pair of cots and the sounds of distant tumult out in the tunnels.

Haldin's chest gave about as readily as steel plating. It was a wonder Rachel hadn't broken her fists pounding on it like she had been. Maybe she had.

"What's our next step?" Jarek forced himself to ask as he worked, trying to keep his voice level, confident. "We've got three at the front entrance, already past the first door. We've got at least two more outside, probably more than that."

He paused to see if anyone would add their input.

They didn't.

Not until Drogan spoke up.

"I am in communication with my kin. They believe they are converging on the last of Kul'Vermaga's insurgents. Our allies have restrained the others afflicted. And the people of The Complex are busy at work restoring the essential systems."

"We've gotta do something," Jarek said. "I have a feeling that door's not gonna hold for long." He looked at Rachel, trying to catch her eye.

She was too busy staring at the floor, dejected.

"You said there's a back door, right?" he asked. "A private lift?"

Rachel closed her eyes, seemed to pull herself back from somewhere far away, then met his gaze, somber but resolute, and nodded.

"You wanna go out there?" Johnny asked.

"That is madness," Drogan agreed.

"Madder than waiting to face down a giant wolf, a 'roid-raging gargoyle, and the praying mantis from hell in an enclosed tunnel?" Jarek shot back. "God knows who else is about to join the party. Gada can't be far behind."

"Perhaps you have a point," Drogan said.

"It's not like we're gonna be able to work the funnel angle in here. Not against them. But we've got the agility."

"You have a hole in your leg," Drogan said.

"You've got the agility, then. And the rest of your kin, too. At least out there you can use it. We go up. We get to open ground, lead them south. Maybe we even give our bystanders a chance to slip out the north portal."

"And what about my daughter?" Franco asked, his tone so flat and lifeless Jarek couldn't help but wince.

Drogan gave Elise another three compressions before answering, slowly. "If this state is an intended part of the process..." He seemed to rethink his words with uncharacteristic restraint. "Al'Braka and Shieth'Lietha would not have deliberately ended the process without a plan. And if it was unintentional… Even if Haldin Raish, Elise Fields, and my kin yet live in some capacity, I do not believe there is anything in our power left to do for them."

Jarek glanced back and immediately wanted to turn away from the raw, shocked pain radiating from Franco's pale face. He looked like he couldn't remember how to breathe. Like a father who'd just realized he'd lost his daughter—for good this time.

Drogan had stopped applying compressions.

Jarek realized with a tinge of guilt that he'd stopped compressing Haldin's chest as well, almost without thinking about it. Rachel looked for a second like she wanted to argue, but she couldn't.

The two Enochians were cold, pale. Utterly still.

Whatever had happened, if there was still any flicker of life in there, it was up to them now. But every moment they sat here was one less moment to do something before a squadron of rakul burst into The Complex and annihilated what few of them were left to resist.

So Jarek forced himself to stand, suppressing a wince of pain, and offered Rachel a hand. She took it and rose nearly as stiffly as he had.

"What… What do we do with them?" Johnny asked softly. He stumbled back and dropped heavily onto a storage crate, looking as dejected as Franco, his empty gaze locked on Haldin. "We can't leave them here."

"No," whispered Franco quickly, desperately. Then, more loudly, "No. We take them with us."

Drogan wordlessly began to scoop Elise up, but Phineas stepped in and bade him move with a stoic stare. Drogan stepped respectfully back to allow him room.

Judging from what he'd felt of Haldin's build and what he knew of the density of the average raknoth, Jarek was guessing Elise, who'd already been tall and built like a warrior, must weigh nearly three hundred pounds now, if not more. Phineas didn't complain, though. Just hefted her laboriously up across his beefy shoulders with a little help from Franco, stumbled once, then stood waiting, resolute and ready to move.

Right, then.

Jarek glanced at Johnny, seeing if the Enochian had any ambition to try to do the same with Haldin. He probably would've liked to, but he seemed to understand it wasn't physically feasible, especially loaded with weapons and gear as he was. So Jarek scooped Haldin up over his armored shoulder and turned for the door.

His guess about Elise had probably been close enough. At a rough estimate, Haldin weighed a good three-hundred and fifty pounds. It should have been bizarre, but Jarek was getting used enough to dealing with raknoth by now. The much more important question was where they were headed and exactly what they were going to do when they got there.

Everyone in the room seemed to be waiting for something. Probably a miracle.

If only.

Being about two-and-a-half decades out of practice in garnering divine intervention credits, Jarek resigned himself to giving them a verbal prod instead.

"To the lift, then," he said, trying to sound confident about it. "You wanna lead the way?" he added to Drogan.

No one argued.

They set off quietly, dark stone tunnels dancing beneath the bouncing streams of their lights as they went. Rachel stayed at Jarek's side, though they didn't speak. The tunnels echoed with shouts and the sounds of soldiers and Complex civilians rushing about the underground network, but there were no sounds of fighting for now.

They passed a group who was on their way to help restart the generators. At the next intersection, they found Al'Brandt waiting for them. And not just Brandt, Jarek realized as he approached the intersection. Alaric was there too, along with a small squad of troops that included Michael, Chambers, and Lea.

Eyes fell on the limp forms draped over Jarek's and Phineas' shoulders. Michael and Rachel shared a quick hug, and Lea moved to Johnny's side, but no one saw fit to break the grim silence. They fell in together and continued on. Brandt and Alaric seemed to know where they were headed, probably having already had the news from Drogan.

When they reached the command center a few minutes later, it wasn't the flurry of activity Jarek had been expecting.

Sure, the few Complex personnel darting around trying to get their equipment back online seethed plenty of frantic energy to go around. But the rest of the crowd, the few dozen armed men and women gathered in the room and throughout the surrounding hallways, were simply waiting. Some in terror. Some with hard determination in their eyes. Plenty in clear shock.

There was a rustle of weapons being aimed at them as they came into view and then lowered again as they drew close enough to the assembled forces to be recognized. There were a few hopeful murmurs from the command center crowd at the sight of the reinforcements. Panicked whispers joined the mix as they got a better look at the dead weights Jarek and Phineas carried.

Jarek wasn't even sure whether the majority of their forces had known about the hopeful plan to grow themselves a pair of Enochian secret weapons. Either way, the cloud hanging over their group must've made it clear enough that shit had gone awry, to say the least.

"This way," Drogan said, pushing on through the corridor of armed soldiers.

No one gave half a thought to stopping them, though several looked like they wanted to ask what the hell was happening, and what they were going to do about it.

They pushed on into the command room, following Drogan as he began to angle them toward the next hallway over, where Dola's private office and backdoor lift must've been situated. Commander Nelken hobbled his way over to them, his already grim expression falling as he took in the sight of Haldin and Elise.

His eyes burned a question at Jarek.

Jarek gave a slight shake of his head, not wanting to say anything that would call attention to the significant setback. The crowd's silent tension broke anyway.

"What's happening out there?" someone shouted.

"What happened to those two?" another voice added.

Jarek turned in the speakers' general direction, though it was hard to tell exactly who'd spoken in the patchwork light of the command room. He looked to Nelken, whose face was drawn tight, his eyes distant. He looked to Alaric, who was watching Jarek silently, his eyes not so much expectant as just clocked out. Detached.

Neither one of them was going to say a thing.

"What are we gonna do?" someone shouted.

The question and several more like it were spreading through the ranks with growing restlessness.

They had to move. That door wasn't going to last forever.

Jarek looked at Rachel.

She gave a subtle nod and tilted her head toward the discontented crowd.

Jarek drew a deep breath.

The door wasn't going to last forever. But they also couldn't just parade off to fight and expect their people to be ready to move, either.

"Listen up, folks," Jarek called.

They quieted, waiting. He didn't even need to amplify his voice with Fela's speakers.

"You know what's out there, what's coming for us." He shook his head. "I'm not gonna sugar coat it. We're in a tight spot here. But we're not dead yet."

Jarek hardly needed the uneasy sounds rippling through the crowd to know it wasn't his best work.

"We're all gonna die," someone whimpered nearby—a bigger guy, hunkered down against one of the consoles, rocking back and forth with knees to chest, head buried.

Yep. Definitely not his best work.

Shit.

Jarek started to unload Haldin from his shoulder, intending to set the Enochian down for a second. Instead, Drogan stepped in and smoothly accepted Haldin's weight without a word.

Several hundred pounds lighter, Jarek turned and crouched down in front of the big, cowering soldier.

The crowd watched with bated breath as if waiting for another one of those miracles. Jarek still didn't have one.

"C'mon, guy," he said "Are you dead yet?"

"No, but the, the—"

Jarek was louder this time. "Are you dead yet, soldier?"

He felt ridiculous saying it, but at least the big guy lifted his head.

"N—No!"

Jarek grabbed him by the utility vest, yanked him smoothly to his feet, and proceeded to make a point of smoothing out the guy's shirt and gear.

"Goddamn right, you're not." He clapped him on the shoulder. "You down for holding your shit together until we get through this?"

The guy just stared at him for a second, then he bobbed his head emphatically. "Yes. Yes, sir."

Again with the *sir* thing.

He was just wondering how to react and keep the good momentum rolling when the lights snapped on throughout the room and nearby hallways and a round of cheers spread through the crowd.

Back in business.

"See?" Jarek called, looking around. "All peaches from here. Isn't that right, folks?"

There were tentative sounds of agreement.

Then Rachel cried, "Hell yeah, sir!" and the crowd latched onto the call with an excited energy.

"Carpe diem!" Michael cried.

"Seize that goddamn carp!" Chambers added.

Rachel shot Jarek a wink, a hint of amusement creeping past the grimness that had hung over her since the barracks. Despite everything, Jarek couldn't help but smile.

"Good." He bobbed his head appreciatively, looking around the room. "Good. Now who here can organize an evacuation?"

No one said anything right away, but several fingers pointed to a short brunette woman. The sleeves of her overalls were rolled up, and she was busy tapping and clicking away at one of the room's computer stations. Busy enough that she didn't notice all the pointing fingers. Not until she felt the entire room's attention on her and turned to take it in with wide eyes.

She looked mortified. "I can't—How are we—" She gathered herself and dropped her abashed look for a highly skeptical one. "An evacuation to where, exactly? Last I checked, we're kinda stuck here."

"We're workin' on it," Jarek said. "You just make sure every non-combatant we have is ready to bail posthaste once the entrance tunnel is clear. Escorts. Vehicles. The whole deal. You got it?"

She hesitated, glancing from her console to the hallway he was pretty sure led to Dola's office.

"Do it, Mel," someone called from the hallway.

A second later, Dola appeared in the entranceway to a round of uncertain murmurs among his people.

"And whatever your plan is," Dola added to Jarek, "I'm told we should hurry."

Drogan gave Jarek a meaningful nod as if he'd received similar word. Word from Krogoth? Either way, they needed to move before the rakul managed to bust that door down.

"Right." Jarek pointed up and in what he was pretty sure was the direction of the south portal. "We're gonna go out there, and we're gonna give those giant bastards something a lot more interesting than a big door to play with."

"How?" someone called.

"I have a way," Dola provided.

"And you'll all have a way too, once we get out there," Jarek pushed on before Dola's people could dwell on what else their esteemed leader had been hiding from them. "We'll draw them to the south portal and keep them there long enough for you to slip out."

"And what are you going to do after that?" asked the elected coordinator, Mel.

Jarek looked to Rachel and Drogan.

They nodded, resolute.

"Well," he said back to Mel, "I was kinda thinking we'd just see if we can't kill the whole damn lot of them while we're at it."

Heavy silence fell on the room as everyone considered what that would almost certainly mean. He couldn't let it settle.

"Let's move, people!" he barked, starting for Dola's hallway with an authority that felt a little too easy. Arrogant, even.

But they didn't have time for him to worry about playing nice. All that mattered was that neither Dola, the commanders, nor any of the other raknoth who'd trickled in took verbal issue with his authority. Not until their small group had packed into Dola's office, at least.

"*That's* your plan?" Dola hissed. "Sacrifice yourselves on the off chance you might buy a hundred people the chance to run for a few more days—a few weeks, at best?"

"You got a better plan?" Jarek asked.

Dola said nothing.

"I'm not sacrificing shit, Mr. Mayor," he pushed on. "I meant what I said back there."

Dola sneered. "Oh yes? That you're all just going to turn around and smite down the rakul you've been fleeing for the past month?"

Jarek held his gaze, refusing to let the uncertainty creep onto his face.

He was just about to tell Dola that, yes, that was indeed the plan when the door swung open and Krogoth strode in, followed shortly by a few more raknoth, Zach, and a few of his men.

"Rid yourself of that smirk, Nan," Krogoth growled. "It wreaks of your pathetic fear. We are beyond the point of talking. Jarek Slater has chosen the only honorable option left to us. Now reveal this lift of yours."

"Yeah, Nan," Jarek said, trying and failing to suppress a morbidly amused grin. "What Krogoth said."

In truth, honor had been just about the last thing on Jarek's mind since the attack began—or pretty much any time before that. It was more just that, in his eyes, this was the only real choice left to them at all, honorable or no.

Running wasn't happening. Not for all of them, at least. The rakul would never let them escape now. And fighting the ferocious creatures in the confines of The Complex didn't feel particularly advantageous.

They might as well face the rakul on their own terms, kill as many of the bastards as they could, and give the others a chance at slipping out while they were at it.

And hell, he thought, looking at Haldin's limp body in Drogan's arms, maybe by some minor miracle they'd even manage to win without their super weapons.

Three Kul were already dead, as far as he knew. And judging by the thankful lack of giant space dragons thus far, he was pretty sure not all of the remaining nine were actually here yet. Definitely not here at The Complex, and maybe not even here on Earth, for all they knew.

It was a start.

Dola tapped at his comm, looking none too happy about it, and a section of the wall in the corner of the room glid smoothly open.

"So, we all going up?" Johnny asked. His eyes were hard, his tone lacking his usual humor.

"Yeah," Michael said,

"Hell yeah," Chambers added.

Beside them, Lea nodded with a determined fire in her eyes.

"No," Alaric said, lowering his finger from his earpiece. He pointed at Lea. "Commander Daniels needs your help interfacing our forces with our hosts'." His finger drifted toward Michael and Chambers. "And you two are with me."

Everyone made to protest, but Alaric silenced them all with a look. "We all have jobs to do. We'll be more useful down here."

"Doing what, though?" Michael asked.

"Pryce needs our help with something."

A feral grin pulled at Jarek's mouth. "BFG related?"

Alaric nodded and turned for the door without ceremony. "Good luck out there."

"Got it!" One of Zach's men called out of the blue, triumphantly lofting a small tablet.

Alaric paused.

Zach snatched the tablet and waved them all in. "We've got eyes outside."

They crowded around the tablet for a look.

Harga, Shimo, and Ogrin were still in the entrance antechamber, taking turns on the second security door, which didn't look long for this world.

Zach swiped through the camera feeds, and they spotted Vermaga undulating down the mountainside near the north portal. Zach flicked to an east-facing camera that looked out over the expansive parking lot by the north portal. He zoomed to the dark blip of an approaching ship.

The vessel might've been three miles out or thirty, depending on its size. The shape that fell from the craft a second later, though, somehow left little doubt that it leaned toward the enormous side.

The falling creature was a Kul. No doubt about that.

At a brief glance, it reminded Jarek somewhat of a woolly mammoth. A woolly mammoth that must've stood nearly ten stories tall, that was, with glowing red eyes and a horned snout that might've looked more at home on an island-sized rhinoceros.

On the tablet display, the Kul hit the Earth in an explosion of rock and soil and moved seamlessly into a loping charge for the mountain.

"I swear I just felt that," Johnny muttered.

Jarek knew what he meant, though he was sure he must've imagined the soft shudder in the Earth.

"What the fuck is that thing?" Zach asked.

Jarek blew out a delirious laugh. "What, you've never seen a goddamn space mammoth before?"

"It is Kul'Mada," Drogan supplied.

Zach stared between them, mouth ajar. "And you still want to go out there?"

Hell no.

Jarek wanted to go find a bigger, more secure mountain to hide under.

But instead, he just shrugged. "All the more reason now. Do you wanna wait and see whether that big fella can knock a mountain down on our heads?"

"Fuck," Zach said after a long moment's consideration.

It was time. No more avoiding it.

Himself, Rachel, nine raknoth, the Enochians, and Dola and his men if they so chose to come along.

Jarek looked over at Alaric. "I think we're gonna be needing that BFG, cowboy."

Alaric almost looked amused for a second. "Looks that way." He started to turn. Hesitated. Looked back to meet Jarek's eyes. "Don't go gettin' stupid out there, son."

The words hit him harder than he rightly understood at first. Maybe it was just nice to know Alaric still cared. Or maybe it was that Alaric had used the word Jarek only then realized he'd avoided in their last talk. Son.

Guilt filled him, an image of Mosen flashing to mind. Guilt, and the determination to make sure Alaric's true son's sacrifice hadn't been in vain. To do better than he had last time, back at the farmhouse.

He couldn't find the right words. So he just nodded.

Alaric turned for the door, looking satisfied.

"Alright, folks," Jarek said, clapping his hands together with anxious determination. "Plans is plans. Let's go kill us some rakul."

Dola watched him approach from the corner by the lift, his expression incredulous, pleading.

"We cannot win," he said quietly, though every raknoth in the room would hear anyway.

The humorless smile that split Jarek's face must've been packing a fair touch of craziness to boot, judging by Dola's reaction.

"Welcome to Team Earth, buddy," Jarek said, clapping Dola on the shoulder as he passed to head for the lift. "We've been winning fights we couldn't since before my balls dropped."

CHAPTER THIRTY-TWO

"Okay," Jarek admitted with a begrudging nod. "That is one fucking gigantic space mammoth."

"I have seen bigger," Drogan murmured behind him.

Jarek turned to Rachel beside him and shared a moment's amusement before turning back to the inevitability thundering toward them.

It had been a quiet lift ride up. The kind that desperately could've used an injection of well-timed elevator music. Instead, they'd had thick, doomed silence.

Rachel had held his hand tightly the whole way up.

Their half of the party had hoofed it over to the ridge near the south portal while the lift had returned below for the rest of their little last stand army. It was there they stood now, watching.

Below, maybe two miles away still, Kul'Mada charged on, each enormous step seeming a physical impossibility, thundering against the earth and spewing explosions of dust and soil into the air.

Closer to the mountain, at the southern edge of the wide parking lot, Jarek spotted that shifty little bastard Fraga watching them with an alien smirk. The Kul must've seen Jarek looking, because he gave a creepy wave with one dagger and vanished.

"So was there a plan?" Rachel asked, extracting her hand from his and shifting her staff. "Sir?" she added, her lip quirking upward.

Jarek looked to the approaching ships—three of them now—and couldn't help but grin that she was still ribbing him here and now, at what was quite possibly the end. It was no wonder she'd managed to weasel her way so thoroughly past every defense he thought the past fifteen years had hardwired into him.

"Do not stop until they are dead," Krogoth rumbled behind them before Jarek could think of anything better.

No one pointed out the glaringly obvious addendum.

Do not stop until they are dead... or we are.

Drogan stepped up to the ridge beside Jarek, craning for a look down the bushy mountainside. "The three from the main entrance have taken note of our challenge. They will be at the south portal soon."

"Lovely," Jarek said quietly.

Mada was closing now, the faint vibrations of his steps growing to actual, unmissable tremors. Jarek realized with a huff of bemused exasperation that Fraga had teleported up to ride into battle on his brother's enormous furry back.

A glance back told him their second lift-load of fighters would be at their side within the minute. Which, as far as he could tell, was also right about when Mada the mammoth would be plowing straight into the mountainside with that enormous horn-like protrusion of his, provided he stayed the course.

The big hairy bastard didn't look like he was planning on stopping anytime soon.

Jarek drew the Whacker, an odd calm filling him, easing the tension from his shoulders. Like they'd already left the hard part behind. Like they'd made their decision, and now all that was left to do was fight the best they knew how.

People were depending on them below. He was probably going to die out here today. They all might.

And somehow he felt completely at home.

"Who's up for a giant mammoth ride?" he asked, not looking back.

"I am with you, Jarek Slater," Drogan said.

"Guess I'd better stick close too if you're still planning on keeping my ass in sight," Rachel added.

"Till the sweet, sweet end," Jarek acknowledged. "Pun absolutely intended."

"We will meet Kul'Harga and his ilk as they ascend from the south portal," Krogoth declared as the rest of the raknoth wordlessly fell in with him. "I yet have business with that lupine brute."

Jarek nodded. "Kick his hairless ass, Rusty."

Krogoth showed his fangs in what might've been a smile—a murderous one, but a smile nonetheless.

Off to the left, the Enochians were approaching at a moderate run along with Zach, several soldiers, and Dola and Brandt, who'd had to wait for the second lift up.

"Ready to roll, people?" Jarek called.

The ground was shaking beneath their feet now.

Johnny looked skeptically past him to the rapidly closing behemoth causing the minor earthquake. "Yeah, you guys—you handle that." He looked doubtfully at his big rifle, which was still laughably small in the context of Mada's bulk, and back up to Jarek. "We'll... cover you?"

Thud-thud. Thud-thud.

Jarek smiled. "That'll do, fire-crotch."

Johnny gave him a kind of casual *nice knowing you* salute, and Jarek turned to face the oncoming titan.

Mada looked up at them with crimson eyes that looked beady in his enormous head despite the fact that they were probably each the circumference of a family dinner table. Then the beast let loose a colossal bellow and lowered his horned snout to charge.

The Kul's battle cry sounded something like a foghorn, and it hit like a windy slap in the face, hard enough that Rachel actually staggered back half a step.

Forty seconds. Maybe less.

Jarek swallowed. "You guys ever wonder what happens when an unstoppable mammoth meets an immovable—"

"We're not exactly immovable here," Rachel said.

"And we shall prove presently that Kul'Mada is far from unstoppable," Drogan added, eyes blazing violent crimson.

"Man," Jarek muttered, "you guys ruin all the fun."

"So we're, uh, jumping?" Rachel asked, the first notes of real panic slipping into her voice.

"Oh yeah," Jarek said, half to her, half to himself. "We're talking tunes blaring, epic slow motion leap of faith shit right here."

Three hundred yards.

"Uh, before or after?" Rachel asked.

Two hundred yards.

"Wait, what?"

"Before or after he hits?!" Rachel snapped.

"Uh…"

Shit.

"Stumpy?"

A hundred yards.

Jesus Christ, that thing was enormous.

"Stumpy?! Why didn't we—"

"Brace!" Drogan roared.

Jarek slapped the Whacker onto his back, scooped Rachel into his arms, and dropped into a stable stance.

He'd been in multiple crashes throughout his life. He'd felt the turbulence when Golga's men had shot his ship down with an RPG back in New York. Somehow, even those experiences didn't quite prepare him for the feeling when Mada hit Cheyenne Mountain with a deep boom.

Some part of his brain screamed that it didn't make physical sense for hard, rocky ground to move like that. The rest just worked to keep his ass from falling over.

The air was full of dust and debris. The sound of crumbling rock seemed to be everywhere, steady as a waterfall.

"Holy fuck," Rachel whispered, coughing in his arms as, behind them, Johnny and the others chimed in with their own colorful additions.

For a second, the world felt still, silence pressing in on them from the thick, dusty air. It was almost peaceful in an *end of the world* kind of way.

Then the stony ridge shuddered beneath their feet with a profoundly deep cracking sound, like a mountain-sized bone snapping. Something roared off to the left. Harga, Jarek thought. And the enormous shape that could've been mistaken for part of the mountain in the debris-laden air began to shift below them, sending ripples of aftershock through the ground.

Mada. Backing up.

The aftershock intensified, and the ground lurched beneath them with another crack and a low rumble of stone shifting on heavy stone.

"Now, Jarek Slater!" Drogan cried, pointing emphatically to the edge of the ridge.

Jarek willed his legs to move.

This might be the stupidest thing he'd ever do. But they couldn't let that thing have free run of the mountain and their vehicles.

And, if the shifting ground underfoot was any indication, he didn't exactly have time to second guess the decision now anyway. It felt like the entire ridge was about to come down.

Drogan was already plunging forward with a wordless bellow.

"Shit," Jarek whispered.

If Rachel had encouraging words, she kept them to herself.

Al didn't.

"Tunes blaring, sir."

Then Al broke their long-standing rule of minimizing distractions during battle and started blasting Led Zeppelin's *Immigrant Song* through Fela's speakers loud enough that half the mountain could probably hear.

Jarek barked a laugh, the hesitation melting from his limbs.

The ridge was most certainly teetering underfoot now.

He didn't care. He let the electric energy of that guitar riff flow through him, filling his head with all sorts of ridiculous delusions of grandeur. He kissed Rachel's forehead, securing her in his arms, and slid his face plate closed with a thought.

"Epic slow motion jump time, then."

And with that, he darted forward, pumping Fela's powerful legs after Drogan.

Ahead, Drogan reached the edge and leapt into the dusty sky with a mighty roar. Jarek wasn't far behind.

His brain screamed at him to stop. He centered himself in the music, the pulsing beat, the shrill battle cry. They reached the edge.

He jumped. And then they were flying, and he was yelling—a mad, wordless battle cry of his own.

Behind, a series of cracks and rumbling crashes announced the crumbling downfall of the ridge they'd jumped from.

Below, the dark shape of Mada's bulk rose up through the dusty air to greet them. Jarek spotted Drogan, peering up with crimson eyes from behind Mada's massive front shoulders.

Something wasn't right. That was all Jarek had time to register before he braced for impact, preparing to spring into a wide, looping roll so as not to crush Rachel.

There was no need.

In the last twenty feet, their fall inexplicably slowed as if they were reaching the end of an invisible bungee cord's stretch.

And that was why it was nice to have an arcanist around.

They touched easily down between Mada's front shoulders, which probably spanned about fifty feet in width, if not more.

Massive didn't even begin to describe this thing.

Jarek looked around, testing the furry terrain with an armored boot that disappeared like they were standing in a field of overgrown grass. "Kind of anticlimactic, don'tcha—Shit!"

He nearly face-planted with Rachel as the ground—or Mada's back, rather—lurched backward with one of Mada's great steps away from the crumbling ridge.

Fraga.

It hit him like a punch as he staggered upright. That's what had been wrong.

The little gremlin had been riding Mada's back. Where had the shifty bastard gone?

No sooner did Jarek have the thought than the air popped just behind him and Rachel drew a sharp breath. She jabbed her hand past Jarek's head, and there was a low thrum and the irritated snarl of something rocketing away from them.

Jarek was about to spin to face the threat when Fraga popped into existence straight ahead, flying toward them, daggers at the ready.

"Agh!" Jarek threw a reflexive high kick before he could think about it.

It was an awkward affair, kicking that high with Rachel still in his arms, but his armored foot connected, and Fraga's flight took a violent course correction.

Drogan stepped to their side as Jarek set Rachel down. Fraga twisted around and watched them with fiery eyes as he sailed calmly through the air. Then he vanished.

Jarek tensed, but Drogan touched his shoulder and pointed to the south portal where Fraga had reappeared beside his emerging brethren.

Harga's size didn't seem nearly so intimidating looking down from the back of the colossal mammoth.

"Can you turn the damn music off, Al?" Rachel said.

Jarek almost laughed. He'd nearly forgotten it was even playing, absorbed as he was in the jump and the fight that had abruptly followed. Now, it did seem like a silly juxtaposition to the collapsing wreckage of Mada's impact and the sight of the rakul leaping their way up the mountainside toward Krogoth and his raknoth.

Al killed the music. A deadly silence seemed to press in around them in its absence, despite the roars and gunfire beginning to erupt from the mountain.

"I thought it was quite cinematic, sir."

"You done good, buddy. We'll tell them all about it when they decide to make a movie about—Shit!"

Jarek staggered forward as Mada took another aggressive step back. He reached over and caught onto Rachel, steadying both of them. Mada lurched again.

Was the Kul trying to throw them off?

It was hard to tell from their turbulent vantage point as the beast backed out of the mess he'd just made of the mountainside, but Mada's movements seemed unsteady, slightly drunken. As if maybe running headlong into a freaking mountain had actually fazed him. As if maybe he wasn't so unstoppable.

Fazed or not, they needed to take Mada down before he could wreak any more havoc or destroy the escape route from The Complex.

"Where are we aiming, Stumpy?" he called.

Drogan started toward Mada's head and made quick sign language for *eyes* and then for *shush*, reminding Jarek that this wasn't some dumb brute they were riding. Mada was probably listening, and Jarek doubted the Kul would be pleased with their plan to come gouge his eyes out.

So he drew the Whacker quietly and started forward to join Drogan, figuring speed was their best friend right now. Rachel padded along right beside him.

When Mada lurched backward another step, they were ready for it. But when the Kul actually tried to throw them off…

Jarek had been wondering whether Mada was simply too stunned or too large to notice—or care—about the little pests on his back. But no. He'd just been waiting for them to get closer to his head for maximum whiplash effect.

Jarek fell to his left knee on the first sweep of Mada's gigantic head. He jammed his sword blade down into the thick scruff of the Kul's neck hide and reached for Rachel, who teetered dangerously. The sword sank deep enough to give him some semblance of an anchor, but Rachel was too far to reach—at least until she jabbed her staff his way.

He grabbed the staff and yanked her to him just as Mada finished the first half of his enormous head shake and flung them back the other way.

It was like a demented amusement ride.

Jarek held on, squeezing Rachel to him, planting his knee against the buried blade for support. They reached the apex of the swing. Stilled for one peaceful moment. Jarek's stomach fell as Mada tilted his head to an angle that rendered his sword useless as an anchor.

Then the Kul whipped his head high right.

"No!" Jarek growled, gripping Rachel close, trying in futility to hold on.

The sword slid free, and they left Mada's head, flying into open sky.

For an instant, Jarek was frozen—time seeming to dilate just long enough to make him painfully aware of just how completely helpless he was.

Then something clamped around his wrist, and Drogan was there, belly down in Mada's fur, limbs spread wide, every claw that wasn't gripping Jarek's wrist buried firmly in the Kul's hide.

Mada's enormous head braked at the end of the swing, dropping them back to the furry terrain. They all took copious handfuls of the thick fur just before the Kul tilted his head up to loose a frustrated bellow that made Jarek's insides vibrate oddly.

They scrambled to their feet and pushed on as best they could on the shaky terrain, determined to reach their target before Mada tried to uproot them again.

Up on the mountain ridge, Jarek caught a glimpse of Harga streaking around with a rust-red Krogoth clinging to his thick back. The rest of Krogoth's raknoth were busy with Shimo and a vaguely robotic-looking Kul Jarek had never seen. Ogrin circled on leathery wings above, preparing to dive.

Jarek was just beginning to wonder where the new Kul-bot had come from when a low rushing sound overhead announced the passing of the most likely answer. A rakul ship.

Something landed on Mada's back behind them with a thud that almost made Jarek feel bad for the Kul. Almost.

Mada made a mournful sound like the universe's most enormous cow as Jarek spun to face the newcomer.

Kul'Gada.

Wonderful.

Gada didn't seem to notice or care about the pain his landing had caused his enormous brother. He just stalked toward them across Mada's back, finger blades elongating.

"Jarek Slater." He hissed the name with a kind of fanatic hunger that made Jarek's insides crawl.

Jarek waved anyway. "Hey Gada."

Beneath them, Mada gave a rumbling groan that sounded decidedly indignant.

Jarek looked down at the furry landmass and back to Gada. "Why is it I keep getting the feeling no one really likes you?"

Gada's only answer was a deep roar as he broke into a charge.

Jarek glanced back to tell Drogan and Rachel to get on with the mammoth problem while he held Gada off. He froze at what he saw.

"Down!" he barked.

They dropped without question—just in time to avoid Ogrin's flyby tackle. Jarek tucked into a sideways roll as the big gargoyle banked around to try to catch him instead. Long gray fingers missed him by a few inches, and Ogrin slammed down to a hard landing beside Gada, empty-handed.

In response, Mada discharged a monstrous snort.

Jarek picked himself up, and a wave of fearful déjà vu swept through him at the sight of the two Kul stalking toward him. With it came the painful reminder of Mosen's final moments, and he clutched his sword tighter.

"Just the two a-holes I wanted to kill," he muttered.

Gada gave a vicious snarl.

Ogrin just seemed to sneer.

Then the two Kul rushed in eagerly to finish what they'd started at the farmhouse.

Only Jarek wasn't alone this time.

When he dipped back from Ogrin's lunging grab, Drogan was there to catch the muscly gargoyle with a cold clock to the side of the head. When Gada sprang in to catch Jarek at the end of his dodge, Rachel was there with a telekinetic blast that nearly sent the Kul tumbling off of Mada's wide back.

After that, Gada and Ogrin grew more disciplined, and the fighting quickly grew in ferocity.

As well as they fought together, Jarek had little doubt he and Drogan would've been in trouble had it just been the two of them. But for every advantage the two Kuls held over them in strength and durability, Rachel was there, telekinetically tipping balances and deflecting blows, conjuring flashes of fire and light to harry and distract.

The furry plane of Mada's back shifted below them as they fought, tilting steeper, steeper, until they nearly had to find handholds to avoid falling.

Mada was mounting the mountain, Jarek realized. Perhaps intending to go squish Krogoth and his raknoth underfoot. Or maybe just to stomp until The Complex collapsed below.

Whether that was physically possible or not, Jarek couldn't really fathom. He didn't want to find out. But before they could stop Mada, they had to get Ogrin and Gada off their backs—or off Mada's, at least.

Jarek was drawing back to hack at Ogrin's exposed flank when a sonorous crack from below startled all of them.

With a sound like a watermelon hitting pavement from a ten story drop, a section of Mada's enormous head exploded outward in a shower of dark blood, shattered skull, and god knew what else.

Jarek's brain had only begun to register that something had shot the Kul—something big—when Mada pitched sideways with a mournful bellow.

Jarek wasn't ready for it. He had nothing to grab. Nothing to stabilize with. He caught a glimpse of Drogan holding Rachel in one arm and clinging to Mada's fur with the other. Then gravity took him past the tipping point, and he was tumbling for open sky.

"Jarek!"

Rachel's shout. Too distant.

He tucked and spun as fast as he could, free hand flailing wildly for something—anything—as he tried to reorient his feet downward. The world spun. His stomach quailed in protest.

Something brushed his hand.

He grabbed and squeezed. Held on for dear life. A handful of Mada's thick hairs yanked his descent to a halt—or nearly to a halt, at least, before they tore free with a dry ripping sound.

The next handful held. Then Mada hit the mountainside, and for a second, Jarek was thrown against the furry wall of the Kul's bulk so hard that he couldn't have fallen even if he'd let go. He only barely managed to hold onto the Whacker through the impact. Then Mada moved through a series of colossal shifts, and he nearly had to ditch the blade anyway in favor of a second handful of furry lifeline.

When the madness stopped, he strapped the sword to his back and grabbed another furry handhold. He was suspended maybe a third of the way down Mada's front right leg, which still put him probably a good eighty feet off the ground. The enormous Kul seemed to have stabilized itself, despite the small hole that'd just been blown through his head.

And as for who'd blown said hole through said head...

Jarek saw them below now—several men in a frenzy of activity by a few trucks at the mouth of the south portal, working around a car-sized heap of metal, coils, and cables that had to be Pryce's railgun. They must've moved it out with one of the trucks.

And there, right beside the thing, snapping commands and tapping away at a tablet, was Pryce. James was there too, and Michael and Chambers, helping the Enochian load something into the rear end of the big weapon.

No sooner had Jarek recognized his friends than Ogrin swooped down overhead, bound straight for them.

"No!" he shouted.

There was nothing he could do—nothing but to watch helplessly.

The gargoyle slammed to a hard landing and slapped Pryce across the asphalt like a cheap toy.

Jarek felt sick. "Pryce!"

He wasn't moving.

James was down too, clipped by the same blow that had taken Pryce—a blow that probably could've overturned a car.

Michael and Chambers were scrambling for their weapons.

Ogrin approached James with predatory confidence, paying them no mind. The Enochian scuttled backward in an awkward crab walk, one arm hanging loosely at his side.

A gunshot cracked below, and another—each one coinciding with tiny jerks that might've been bullets striking Ogrin's head. The Kul paused, glancing around to the spot ten yards in front of the rail gun. The spot where Jarek only now noticed Alaric.

The commander stood with a single smoking revolver raised, every bone in his body screaming defiance in the face of Ogrin's clear superiority.

Ogrin sneered and leapt for Alaric, wings unfurling to shift his jump into a glide.

Jarek half-expected Alaric to hold his ground till the bitter end. Instead, the wiry old commander turned and dove over the edge of a small rocky crag behind him. Not that the cover would do him much good.

Jarek had to get down there.

He was preparing to drop into a fur-ripping leapfrog down Mada's leg when he noticed James tapping furiously at the tablet he'd crawled to after Ogrin had left him.

Michael shouted something from the rear of the rail gun. Chambers yanked him aside. Ogrin landed over Alaric. Turned.

James jabbed his finger to the tablet.

There was another loud cracking sound, and Ogrin's head disappeared in an explosion of black ichor.

Served the fucker right.

"Make a broadcast, Al," Jarek growled, beginning the hand-over-hand climb up Mada's furry leg. "Tell them to get their asses out here with whatever medical they have."

"Already on it, sir."

Jarek climbed in silence for the next several seconds, too flustered to make much sense out of the commotion carrying to his ears from multiple battles above.

A heavy thud off to the left drew his attention, and he saw Gada lying belly up in a small crater over a hundred feet below, having apparently fallen from Mada's back.

Drogan lay face down a few yards away from Gada, unmoving.

Jarek gritted his teeth and kept climbing, part of him hoping Gada was dead and Drogan was fine, and the other part hoping they were both fine—just so he and Drogan could finish kicking Gada's ass to pieces together. First, though, he needed to find Rachel, and end Mada's lumbering stampede.

He reached for the next handful of fur.

Something landed on his back and wrapped an arm around his throat. He had a split-second to register the orange appendage as Fraga's before a dark, glassy dagger plunged for his chest.

His breath caught.

Nothing. There was nothing he could d—

The dagger hit a wall of thin air and careened wildly off.

Jarek stared dumbly for a moment, then grabbed the short leg dangling by his right side in a crushing grip and hurled Fraga as hard as he could. The little bastard nearly managed to keep his hold on Jarek's throat but finally lost his grip and shot away with a snarl. His second dagger left a shallow gash across Jarek's chest plates.

Jarek didn't bother trying to figure out where Fraga was headed when he vanished. He just grabbed another handful of Mada's fur and kept climbing toward his golden-haired savior.

Invisible hands lightened the last few feet of his climb, and then Rachel was there, helping him up the rest of the way. She looked pale and exhausted, like she'd already channeled more than enough energy for the rest of the decade.

"This ride sucks," she groaned between heavy breaths.

"You said it."

Jarek drew his sword and scanned the mountain ridge Mada

appeared to be preparing to make another push for. He wasn't sure it was worth the Kul's effort.

Only three raknoth still stood, as far as he could see, and none of them looked as if they had great chances of remaining that way much longer with Shimo, Harga, and the mysterious mechanized Kul-bot pressing in on them.

The human forces had scattered. The Enochians, Zach, and a few others were beating a retreat down the mountainside. James and the others at the south portal were scrambling to retreat into the tunnel and away from Fraga, who'd already left three soldiers dead and the rail gun in a smoking heap.

They were losing.

Ogrin might be dead, and Gada and this unholy mammoth at least injured, but they were still losing. No doubt about it.

Jarek looked to the northeast and felt a small flutter of hope at the sight of tiny figures piling into vans and trucks in the distant lot. The Complex evacuees, fleeing the base.

There was that, at least.

"Rachel Cross!"

The roar tore Jarek's gaze back to the mountain in time to see Krogoth hurl a man-sized boulder off a nearby ridge in an arcing trajectory toward Mada's head. The stone must've broken loose in one of Mada's impacts. It was long and more flat than round, vaguely resembling a giant arrowhead.

Which was exactly what Krogoth intended it to be, he realized.

Rachel extended her hand, eyes drifting closed.

On the ridge above, Fraga popped into existence right beside Krogoth.

"Krogoth!" Jarek shouted, starting helplessly forward.

Too late.

Fraga's dagger plunged into Krogoth's ribs before the word finished leaving his mouth.

Krogoth roared and grabbed Fraga by the throat.

Jarek froze, unsure what to do, how to help anyone in time. Apparently, Rachel didn't share his dilemma, focused as she was.

Her wordless cry erupted from behind, and the boulder, already tumbling rapidly toward Mada's raised head, accelerated downward as if fired from its own invisible rail gun. Jarek couldn't imagine how much energy it took to shoot something that big that fast.

It punched straight through Mada's eye like an enormous bullet, a resounding wet thud smacking through the air.

Mada jerked—the kind of sickly jerk Jarek had come to associate with someone being brained. And given the way the furry back under Jarek's feet began to sway, he was guessing that interpretation might apply to giant mammoths as well.

Time to bail.

He turned to tell Rachel—just in time to see her unconscious body tumbling limply over Mada's side as the giant beast swayed.

"Rachel!"

He lunged desperately forward.

No time. No chance of catching her before it was too late.

So he dove for her without another thought.

No time for thought. Not until he caught her in his arms and found himself in free fall with her.

He wasted a precious second staring dumbly at the rapidly rising ground.

"The Whacker, sir!" Al cried.

"Wha—"

"Swing the Whacker!"

Jarek didn't have time to question. He swung the damn Whacker—and immediately realized what Al was driving at when the weapon flashed weak blue light and resisted his hand as if it were fixed to something more than thin air.

He swung again.

Sixty feet.

It was like trying to do a one-armed pullup on a bar suspended by wobbly bands. It wasn't going to be enough.

He swung again anyway.

Twenty feet.

He cocked his arm back for another swing, thinking about how he'd try to roll when they hit.

Then Drogan appeared directly below them, arms outstretched.

Jarek tucked and spun as best he could, offering his back to Drogan and two bodies' worth of buffer to Rachel.

They hit.

It wasn't pretty.

The world became a jumbled blur of colors, motion, and jarring impacts—no coherent thoughts in his mind aside from sympathy for Drogan, who was crushed beneath them on impact, and the overwhelming need to keep Rachel safe as they bounced and skipped through a few rough revolutions down the mountainside.

He managed to plant his feet and pull them out of the tumble sitting in an upright position with Rachel's limp body cradled in his arms. Shaken, he turned to see how Drogan had fared.

A hard shove hit him in the back and sent them sailing before he could.

Uncomprehending, desperate, he twisted through the air and landed so his back was to the ground and Rachel was on his chest. They hit and kept sliding down the rocky grade, Jarek reaching out to stop them—until he saw the enormous furry wall collapsing down on top of them.

Mada. Falling.

He caught a flash of Drogan's red eyes.

Then Mada's bulk slammed down with a thunderous boom, burying his friend and missing him and Rachel by mere yards.

"Stumpy!" Jarek shouted. Then again, louder.

The air was filled with dust and the sound of crumbling rock. So much of it coming down.

A roar and a shriek in the distance.

Then nothing.

"Stumpy," Jarek groaned, pulling himself up, careful not to jostle Rachel in the process. "Shit."

Was there any way the raknoth had survived that?

He didn't know. But there was probably nothing Jarek could do for him right now. Not before he checked on Rachel, at least.

She was still alive. He was confident about that as he carted her further down the mountain, away from the dust and shifting rocks. Or maybe it was just that he wasn't ready to even think about the alternative.

But no. As he settled to the ground with her, she shifted uneasily and murmured a few disoriented words.

Thank god.

He nestled her carefully against himself, keeping her shoulders and head supported against his leg and arm. He looked back at the devastation, trying to take stock and gauge their current predicament.

Everything hurt, head to toe. The worst was his pierced leg, radiating a profound sickly ache with pulsing overcurrents of sharper pain.

Drogan was still smashed under Mada's bulk—alive or dead, he didn't know.

To the right, the south portal had collapsed—or was at least obscured—under the rivers of rubble Mada's collapse had brought down. Jarek could only hope to god Pryce, Alaric, the Enochians, and all the other soldiers had managed to retreat far enough down the tunnel in time to avoid being crushed.

On the mountainside above, Krogoth lay bloody and torn beside Harga, whose enormous jaws had been torn apart, his entire head nearly split in two. Neither of them were moving. Nor were the rest of the raknoth above.

The rakul, on the other hand…

They picked their way through the dust and crumbling rock, making their unhurried ways down the mountainside—Shimo, Fraga, and the oddly robotic Kul that scuttled over the uneven terrain on four mechanical appendages. Too many crimson eyes still burning. All of them fixed on Jarek and Rachel.

Jarek's mouth was entirely too dry to swallow, but his throat tried all the same.

The only spot of sunshine was the line of vehicles rolling down the road to the northeast, ferrying dozens of evacuees steadily away from Cheyenne.

At least there was that.

But that didn't change the fact that he and Rachel were the last two standing—or huddling, as it were—against at least three rakul. The sight of Gada stomping out from around Mada's enormous fallen form and making it an even four didn't make matters any better.

Rachel stirred in his arms with a heavy groan. He slid open his faceplate and bent over her, too worried about her and too tired and beaten to care for the moment about the rakul picking their leisurely way down to them.

She blinked up at him.

"Did we win?" she croaked.

He stroked a few hairs from her forehead. "Not yet, Goldilocks. But I think we have 'em on the ropes."

She looked around woozily, silently taking in the gravity of their situation. Then she met his eyes and, of all things, smiled—the most beautiful, sad smile he'd ever seen. "Got 'em right where we want 'em?"

He smiled back, trying to convey every bit of the love he felt for her in that moment, fighting the tears that suddenly wanted to come. "Exactly."

She touched his face with a pale, cold hand, then tried to sit up with a groan. He was shifting to help her when a shadow sped over them.

Jarek looked up, stomach sinking, expecting to see a rakul ship descending on them.

There was a ship. A big one. Bigger than he could even wrap his head around. But it was the thing plummeting from the enormous hatch in the ship's underbelly that held Jarek's attention.

It dropped like a colossal bird of prey and pulled up maybe a quarter-mile from the ground, unfurling wings that would've put the most massive of sails to shame.

They beat with a sound like crashing thunder. Once. Twice. Three times.

Then the gargantuan beast that Jarek could only describe as an honest-to-Christ dragon dropped to the earth with a resounding boom that jolted straight through Jarek's spine and into his racing heart.

"Kul'Naga," Rachel whispered.

"Yeah," Jarek said slowly. "On second thought, that might put a little wrinkle in things."

CHAPTER THIRTY-THREE

For a long few moments, all Rachel could do was stare. The mountain-sized mothership above was impressive enough, defying her brain's feeble attempts at comprehension. Her attention, though, was more rooted to the monstrosity that had just fallen from said ship. The one that had hit the earth like a force of nature, crushing the last faint inkling of hope they'd had of making it through this thing alive.

Kul'Naga. The World Ender.

It was a bit rich, wasn't it?

Then again, considering the way the beast had seemed to shake the entire planet when he'd landed, maybe not.

Fortunately, Naga didn't appear to be in any great hurry to come stomp their petty little lives back to The Void. And why would he be?

Naga was easily as big as Mada, and ten times as ferocious-looking. Twenty times, actually, once she recalled the memories Haldin had shown her of the beastly dragon tearing his way through that clan of frost giants. And that had been a couple thousand years ago.

How in the hell did she even begin to fathom hurting something so colossally powerful?

She reminded herself that she'd had that exact thought about

Mada before Krogoth had come through with his stony solution. But, as far as she could tell, it was only her and Jarek now. And neither one of them was in any condition to be hurling boulders.

She thought of Haldin and Elise, lying cold and still in Dola's office below, and felt the need both to punch something and to be ill. So much power. Such young, good lives. All gone.

And now it was up to them to… what? Kill this thing? Save the day?

"Suppose it would've been too much to ask for a few storm clouds," she muttered.

Not that striking Naga down with lightning would have been likely to work in that case anyway.

Jarek shifted to look at her. "You know what I wish?"

"What's that?"

He shook his head, looking wistful. "A good month or two. You and me. None of this bullshit. No one trying to destroy the goddamn planet. Definitely no clothes. Would that've been too much to ask?"

She smiled and started pulling her painstaking way to her feet. "You'd have gotten sick of it. Two weeks, tops."

He was watching her from the ground when she turned, utter exhaustion in his eyes. But something else too. Something that made her insides flutter—never mind the galaxy-class killers nearby.

"I could never get sick of you, Goldilocks."

She looked around at the circling rakul and swallowed, fighting the frantic desperation that tried to grab ahold of her good senses. "It's a bet, then?"

He nodded and started crawling to his feet. "As soon as we finish slapping these a-holes silly, you're on. Two months."

It was only then she realized he was missing his sword.

She scanned their surroundings and spotted it near the fallen mass of Mada, closer to where they must've originally landed. She wasn't really sure how they'd even pulled that off without dying, but that might just have to go on the suddenly too-long list of things she probably wasn't going to be getting any closure on.

The rakul were watching them silently, the "small" ones having formed a rough semi-circle about thirty yards away, walling them in toward Naga, who hadn't moved a twitch since he'd landed about two-hundred yards away.

None of them gave one iota of concern to the convoy of vehicles disappearing down the distant road. That was something. If nothing else, at least they'd accomplished that today.

Rachel focused back on the sword and telekinetically yanked it over.

Jarek caught it shakily and gave her a grim nod of thanks. "So how do you wanna do this thing?"

She tried to put on a brave face and ignore how beaten to shit he looked and she felt. "You're telling me you never dreamed of charging into battle with a dragon?"

He gave an amused huff that turned into a dusty cough. "Of course. Totally. So like, on three, then?"

Something broke in her, looking at him. She didn't see it coming— couldn't even say what it was at first. Just something about the look in his eye. Something that went beyond the fear she'd seen in those dark eyes a few times in the past. Something that understood the current situation with morbid certainty.

They were going to die here.

She turned toward Naga, unable to face that horrible realization in Jarek's eyes.

Ahead, Naga started forward with calm detachment, his first steps sending light tremors through the mountainside.

"Rachel?"

Jarek's tone was soft. She looked back at him, trying to keep the tears in, trying to force a smile, if only so it could be the last way he saw her.

He licked his cracked lips, his gaze unwavering from hers despite the enormous alien dragon stomping up the mountain behind her. He swallowed and shook his head, smiling at his own hesitance. Then, with a small shrug, as if he were simply stating the obvious.

"I love you."

Longing and regret and furious frustration all swirled through her underneath the persistent dread at what was coming.

It wasn't fair. Not a single damn part of any of this was fair. That this should happen now, here of all places. But it was happening. All of it was happening. There was nothing left to it.

All she could do was say the words back. Just this once.

But they wouldn't come out. Why wouldn't they come out?

She wanted to cry. *Was* crying, she realized. A bittersweet smile pulling at her lips.

She wanted to say the words. But the smile widened, taking on a life of its own in a way that made her wonder if she hadn't just cracked.

"I know," she whispered, still smiling.

Then she turned and charged straight at the oncoming dragon.

"You—Hey!" Jarek cried after her. "You can't just pull a Solo on me, lady!"

She kept running, heart racing, her smile twisting into something frantic, desperate. He caught up to her, clearly limping, and just as clearly determined to stick with her until he couldn't.

Maybe they were going to die. Whatever they were going to do, it'd be together. And she'd be damned if she was going to give either of them a reason to think they'd found their closure and could give in. Not while they could still draw breath.

"Going for the eyes," Jarek grunted between breaths. His faceplate slid closed. "Might have to climb."

An idea struck her. Not a good one, but she wasn't sure there were any of those left at this point.

"Need a boost?"

He didn't answer right away, and she didn't blame him.

The dread was growing in her chest, heavier and heavier with each step they took, and with every perspective inch of scaly height Naga seemed to gain. He loomed over them, regal and terrible and utterly unthreatened.

When she glanced over, she realized Jarek was slowing down. Or was it her that had started it?

He glanced over his shoulder. She followed his gaze and realized the rest of the rakul were following them, closing slowly, ready to pounce when easy opportunity arose.

Just like that, all the momentum of their combined determination hit a wall, trickling away down the shallow grade of the mountainside.

Her stomach fell, and despair crept in.

What had possessed her to think the others would politely wait their turns? Some feeble hope their honor would mandate that they allow a proper contest, she supposed. But it was probably too late for that.

As far as she knew, it had been well over a thousand years since a Kul had died. Now, since arriving on Earth, the rakul had lost five of their number. They had no intention of making this anything but a slaughter.

Her step faltered. They weren't running anymore—just tensing together, sword and staff at the ready, trying to look every direction at once. They turned back-to-back, Jarek facing Naga, Rachel facing Gada and Shimo and the mountain beyond.

And that was when she noticed the pair of figures standing tall on the mountain ridge high above.

"Jarek!" she whispered, not turning away.

"Is that…?" Jarek started to ask behind her.

Then one of the figures on the ridge reached for something at their chest, and Jarek's voice was washed out by the powerful presence that rolled over her senses, vast and alien, yet familiar in an odd way.

It felt like Haldin. And it felt like Alton.

Somehow, it was both, and it frightened her. But fright spilled over to hope as the thing that was both Haldin Raish and Alton Parker gathered itself and sprang from the mountain.

It was an impossible leap—well beyond what even a raknoth could've managed. He sailed through the air like a humanoid missile, barreling straight for Naga's head, which had raised to inspect the new arrival, cocked with curiosity.

"Is he…" Jarek said slowly. "He's not seriously…"

Neither they nor the rakul below could seem to do anything but gape as the hybrid flew on as if propelled by more than his initial jump.

Naga, on the other hand, growled an earth-shaking growl and swept an enormous hand back, preparing to swat the Haldin-Alton hybrid out of the air like the gnat he comparatively was.

Before he drew within Naga's striking range, though, Haldin threw his arms wide, cocking his own fist back, and pulled to a dead halt in midair. Then, suspended fifty feet above their heads, he thrust an open palm forward with an inhuman cry.

To Rachel's extended senses, the flare of channeled power was like staring straight at the sun. To Naga, though, it must've been a whole lot worse.

It was like the Kul had been struck by a speeding glacier.

It was impossible.

And yet Rachel watched in slack-jawed astonishment as the dragon that was the size of a small mountain toppled backward with a haunting vibration somewhere between a keen and a groan. He slammed onto his back hard enough to cause a minor earthquake beneath their feet.

Haldin dropped the last fifty feet straight down and landed between them and Naga with his own soft thud, radiating confident power despite the fact that the size mismatch should've been laughable. A second later, Elise slammed down beside him, fists clenched and dark hair pulled into a tight ponytail.

For a long moment, no one moved.

Then Jarek thrust his sword to the sky and shouted, "Fuck yes!"

Behind them, Gada growled and took a step forward.

The rest of the rakul only watched on uncertainly as Naga labored to roll back to his gargantuan haunches with a difficulty that suggested it had been millennia since he'd had cause to recover from such a blow.

When he did, though, the roar he let loose was unlike anything Rachel had ever experienced. It hit her entire body, so loud she could barely process what was happening at first. She nearly fell to her knees under the raw telepathic pressure. Jarek held on to her, apparently sensing her instability and at least somewhat protected by Fela.

Haldin and Elise stood steady through the entire thing, wary but strong.

"You picked the wrong species to fuck with," Haldin said when it was over, his voice oddly muffled to her ears in the wake of Naga's roar.

"And now you'll end no more worlds, Kul'Naga," Elise added.

"Yeah, what they said!" Jarek called. "You big scaly a-hole."

If Naga had any thoughts on the matter, he didn't see fit to communicate them.

He just charged.

And, with a hair-raising chorus of shrieks and growls, so did the rest of the rakul.

CHAPTER THIRTY-FOUR

The ground shook with Naga's first attack.

Rachel didn't have time to see if Elise and Haldin had evaded it. She was already whirling around to face the other incoming threats beside Jarek.

Gada was first to lunge in, eager to finally claim their heads.

She felt more than saw Jarek stepping in to catch the Kul with a low sword sweep. She added her own telekinetic battering ram to the side of Gada's head, and their low-high combo took the Kul off his feet and tumbling past them.

Rachel stuck close to Jarek's back as he stepped in to engage Shimo and the robotic-looking Kul with its four mechanical legs and long, snaking arms. She risked a quick glance back and saw Elise darting up one of Naga's forearms while Haldin leapt straight for the Kul's head.

They were powerful, there was no doubt about that. But powerful enough to kill something so gargantuan, so ferocious? That was hard to believe. Almost as hard to believe as the thought that her and Jarek could hope to keep four rakul off their backs while they did it.

Thud.

Make that five rakul, she grimly amended as Vermaga's leathery, amorphous form slammed down from one of the ships above.

Her step faltered at the surprise entrance.

Jarek, on the other hand, opened up with an unexpected burst of speed and claimed Shimo's remaining foreleg with a flash of azure light and a shriek like rusty iron.

Rachel could have cheered if not for the telltale *pop* of Fraga's sudden appearance and the dark obsidian dagger he promptly hurled at Jarek.

She caught the dagger with telekinesis and flung it deep into Vermaga instead. When her extended senses rippled to her exposed right, she didn't think—just swung her staff as hard as she could.

The blow caught Fraga in the torso just as he popped into existence with a dagger cocked back to strike. It wasn't much, her puny human swing, but Fraga was small, and it was enough to knock him away. It was also enough to send her tumbling over when her exhausted legs failed to catch up on her balance.

She hit the dusty rock with a heavy *oomph*. Off to the left, she heard Jarek fighting on. And, to the right, Fraga was already darting in, unperturbed by her staff strike.

She caught him with telekinesis and conjured a flare that left her head buzzing and Fraga's eyes temporarily fried, judging by the way he clutched at them. She hurled him fifty feet straight backward before he could do anything about it then moved to pull herself back to her feet.

The shaking ground informed her there wasn't time for that.

Gada. Charging in from behind to crush her where she lay.

She couldn't move—didn't even have time to try to call for help.

Gada stomped in, raising a thick foot with violent intent.

Rachel drew what energy she could, and—

A dark shape blurred in and hit Gada with a side kick that sent him sailing like a huge, spiky cannonball.

Elise.

Rachel blew out a relieved breath and hurried to her feet, turning back for Jarek.

Elise was already sweeping past her.

Jarek had managed to clamber up onto Shimo's back and was

clinging tightly to his unwilling mount with one arm, throwing wild sword swings at the other Kuls as they tried to close in.

The mechanical Kul had just snared one of its jointed tentacles around Jarek's ankle when Elise slammed into the thing with a shoulder tackle that looked like it should have broken something inside her. Instead, the Kul took flight.

Elise whirled on Shimo, looking ready to tear off his legs.

Fraga appeared with a sneak attack, but Elise was ready. She dodged his out-of-nowhere stab with inhuman speed and slammed a fist down on top of his head so hard that he didn't manage to blink off to safety. He just hit the ground with a low cracking sound.

Elise rounded on Vermaga. Too late.

The Kul caught her with a solid smack that sent her flying for the wreckage of the south portal.

Rachel reached out, thinking to telekinetically catch her. A cry from Jarek drew her attention before she could.

In the chaos, Shimo had somehow bucked Jarek to the ground, and now the big mantis was rounding on him with the sharp stalks of his remaining legs. Shimo reared, and Jarek rolled. The Kul's stomp cracked through hard rock like plastic, missing Jarek by inches.

Desperate, Rachel thrust out with both hands, pulling for power, and hit Shimo with everything she had left.

It wasn't as impressive as the hits Super Elise was throwing, but considering everything Rachel had already been through in the past hour, it wasn't half-bad. Shimo flew far enough that he struck Mada's enormous body before hitting the ground.

Rachel took a more direct route to the stony earth, falling to her knees as the fresh wave of channeling fatigue crashed down on her. She forced herself to look up and reassess their threats.

Shimo was picking himself up from his awkward landing. Vermaga was gliding that way as well, and, looking further back, Rachel realized why.

The smallest of the rakul ships was descending to the right of Mada's fallen bulk, seemingly at the behest of the mechanical Kul, who hadn't bothered rejoining the fight after getting a taste of Elise's linebacker special. But why were they all—

A roar to the left shook her focus. Gada. But he was fixed on the ship as well, roaring at his own kin. Rachel felt the telepathic traffic passing between them but couldn't hear the message—probably wouldn't have understood it even if she could.

Whatever it was, Gada didn't look happy. Especially not as the mechanical Kul gathered itself and sprang up to the open ship hatch a good twenty yards above. Vermaga glided after his kin, looking intent on doing the same, and Shimo seemed to be debating himself.

It was almost like…

Could it be?

Were they *retreating*?

The first flicker of hope touched at her exhausted brain.

Then Gada stomped the ground like a wild animal and turned to charge Jarek.

Rachel lumbered forward, head spinning and stomach churning with the cumulative exhaustion. Jarek rolled to his feet and nearly fell back over.

Why would the rakul retreat now, when they were down to four defenders—two of whom were clearly on their last legs, and one of whom was currently tangling with a goddamn space dragon?

It didn't matter.

All that mattered was that she and Jarek took advantage of the improved odds before the bastards changed their minds.

But Elise darted past before they could.

"Sword!" she cried.

Jarek hesitated for a second, then hurled the Whacker after her. The long, spinning arc of its flight stabilized in mid-air, and the sword snapped to Elise's waiting hand.

She didn't break stride—just charged straight in to meet Gada.

Before the change, Elise, like Haldin, had been astoundingly quick and agile—both of them nearly preternaturally so. Now, though…

It was like watching a choreographed dance. Each of Gada's devastating swipes rushed through nothing but thin air. Elise danced over or under every blow. Outside or inside. She moved like she knew what would happen two steps in advance and was merely shuffling through the requisite counter-steps.

She caught Gada's flank with a sword strike that dropped him to a knee. She twisted under a grab and removed the offending hand at the thick wrist, bladed fingers and all. A deep cut to his chest. Another to the opposite leg. Elise dismantled Gada with disturbing efficiency until he collapsed at her feet, heaving with too much pain and bodily damage to do anything but stare in disbelief.

On his knees, Gada's eyes were only a foot above Elise's. Close enough to level.

She stood facing him, eyes brimming with the faint beginnings of a soft red glow.

"For our master, Zar'Kole," she growled, in a voice that reminded Rachel that Elise was not alone in there.

Gada bared his fangs in a snarl.

Then, with a tremendously fast swipe and a brilliant flash of azure, Elise cut his head off.

Rachel and Jarek watched in stunned silence, leaning heavily on one another.

Elise stood over her kill for a long breath, as if taking the moment to document the memory, then she spun and darted off toward Haldin and Kul'Naga, still clutching Jarek's sword.

A glance down the mountainside showed why.

In the chaos, Rachel hadn't had time to check how Haldin was faring—wasn't even sure she'd wanted to know, considering. The answer was about as well as could be expected.

The colossal dragon towered over Haldin, long neck lowered to their struggle. Haldin was braced on the ground, hands planted against two of Naga's huge fangs. Rachel couldn't quite tell if it was Naga trying to snap his prey up or Haldin trying to force his way in. Either way, neither one of them looked too happy about it.

"Rache," Jarek said behind her.

She followed his gaze and saw Fraga picking himself up from the ground nearby. The small Kul shook himself off and considered the two of them for a long second.

Rachel tensed, reaching for power she wasn't sure she had any hope of finding. But then Fraga looked up to his brothers' ship and vanished with a small pop.

A sound of deep pain rumbled off to the right, and Rachel looked in time to see Jarek's sword tearing free from one of Naga's enormous red eyes to fly back to Elise's hand as if on an invisible mag rail.

Above, the ship drifted higher, easing forward to pass over Naga's battle with the Enochians. A quick scan of the area around Mada told her Shimo and Vermaga must've boarded while Elise had been busy taking Gada to pieces.

So, reasonably sure their backs were safe for the moment, Rachel and Jarek turned and began to limp their way toward Naga and the Enochians. They held onto one another for support, neither of them pointing out that both of their tanks were clearly too far past empty for them to expect to be much help in the fight.

They plodded on anyway.

Haldin was at least a hundred feet in the air now, taken along for the ride when Naga had recoiled from Elise's attack.

Elise called something, and Haldin sprang away from Naga's fangs. Or tried to, at least.

The instant Haldin gave him the room, Naga struck like an oversized viper, catching the Enochian by the left arm with fangs the size of Haldin's body.

Elise's scream joined Haldin's cry of pain and Naga's satisfied rumble.

"No!" Rachel heard herself shout.

Elise cocked Jarek's sword back, preparing to throw.

Naga whipped his huge head before she could, and Haldin tore free like a speeding bullet, minus his left arm.

The Enochian hit the mountainside in an explosion of rock and dirt, faster than Rachel's mind could process until he'd skipped a couple dozen yards toward them.

Ahead, Elise threw the sword. Naga jerked his head to the right, taking the blade on the snout to protect his remaining eye.

Jarek hurried forward to where Haldin was already picking himself up.

"We're fine," Haldin growled as Jarek reached to help him.

We're?

It seemed to take Jarek aback too, but they hardly had time to worry about that—or about the fact that Haldin was apparently going to pretend like he hadn't just lost an arm.

Elise touched down beside them with a heavy thud, Jarek's sword in hand.

"You're okay, my love?" she asked with a quick look at Haldin's arm—or lack thereof.

Haldin stood to his full height by Elise, his gaze never leaving Naga. "It'll take a lot more than that to stop us."

Ahead, Naga shifted, seeming to consider Haldin's words as he watched them with his single crimson eye. His left eye only sputtered with a feeble glow, spilling clear fluids down the side of his enormous head.

Rachel and Jarek drew up beside the Enochians. Elise offered Jarek his sword. He waved for her to keep it, which seemed like a good call, seeing as she could probably swing it about ten times harder than he could right now.

Together, the four of them faced Kul'Naga, who'd grown silent and still.

The huge dragon tilted his snout skyward, considering his allies' ship, now hovering far overhead. For a second, Rachel could've sworn the ship wavered under Naga's gaze.

Then it surged forward, quickly fading into the distance as it ascended to the clouds and beyond.

Naga's enormous head tipped back down, and he swept his gaze around the wreckage of Cheyenne, taking in the extensive damage and casualties before finally settling back on them.

He was going to charge. She was sure of it.

But then he raised a massive forepaw to the ruined mess of his eye.

Slowly. Almost absentmindedly.

Tense silence stretched. Then Naga slammed his forepaws to the earth, gave a gale-force snort and a shake of his head, and leapt into the air on tremendously powerful haunches. His wings shot out, catching the air in a series of quick, sonorous beats, and then he was rising.

"We should stop him," came Haldin's voice in her mind. Or maybe it was Alton's. She could barely tell.

And given that it looked an awful lot like Naga was fixing to leave, she wasn't even sure whether to agree or argue with the sentiment. But she also couldn't fathom what the hell they were supposed to do about it either way.

Each beat of Naga's wings hit them like a small tornado. Rachel would've fallen if Jarek hadn't been holding her. And given how damned beaten he was, Jarek might've fallen too if Elise hadn't been holding him. Even Haldin staggered, finally starting to show hints of looking like a guy who'd just lost an arm.

When Naga was nearly two hundred yards above, he angled around to face them and hung there, bobbing a good twenty yards up and down with each humongous beat of his wings.

"You think yourselves heroes?" came a voice like the stone of an ancient mountain. *"You are but dust, waiting only to be swept back to The Void from whence you came. When this world has moved on, when your distant descendants have forgotten... That is when we will return to see it done."*

And with that, Kul'Naga turned with a few mighty beats of his wings and began climbing for his waiting ship, each thunderous beat drawing him higher and higher.

Haldin looked like he was considering trying to take telekinetic flight after the Kul. *"If he escapes now—"*

"Peace," came Elise's thought. Or maybe it was Lietha's. *"We are not yet ready to see it through to the end."*

Haldin radiated frustration and displeasure, but he didn't argue.

Above, Naga reached his ship and climbed up through the open hatch. Rachel thought she caught a glimpse of his crimson eye staring down at them. Then the enormous hatch drew shut, and the ship began to rise.

They watched in silence until it was a distant speck in the clear blue sky.

Then Jarek collapsed to the ground with a monumental groan that sounded equal parts pained, exhausted, and relieved. Rachel went with him, not even bothering to try for balance with her support pillar gone.

She lay beside him on the dusty, sun-kissed stone, enjoying every grateful breath of air she took in. Much as they'd earned it, she was still a bit surprised when Haldin and Elise likewise hit the dirt, both of them shaking from their exertions—or maybe from something else entirely, something to do with their new bodies.

"You guys okay?" she asked, having to work to even find the energy for the simple act of speaking.

"We are..." Elise started, looking a little uncertain as to how to finish.

"Tired," Haldin provided.

Elise nodded. "But we will survive."

"Amen," Jarek croaked. "I'm never moving again."

He could say that again.

Rachel couldn't remember the last time she'd felt so utterly drained. Probably because she never had been.

There was work to be done. Maybe more now than ever before. She couldn't buy that it was over. Not just like that. But, for the moment, it seemed they were safe and relatively stable.

So Rachel lay her head back, closed her eyes, and, for a while, allowed herself to enjoy the simple pleasure of being alive to feel the sun on her face.

Then a voice broke the silence at the edge of her senses.

"Rachel Cross."

She perked up. *"Drogan?"*

A moment's pause.

Then, *"I believe I require your aid in escaping this confounded furry prison."*

CHAPTER THIRTY-FIVE

"Hang in there, buddy," Jarek called, dubiously eyeing the gigantic furry leg they needed to move—or at least budge—to give Drogan a shot at crawling out of what Jarek figured was best referred to as Mada's furry armpit.

Until we get the world's largest crane in here, he wanted to add.

Somehow, it didn't seem like the most productive comment.

He shifted his gaze to the mammoth's building-sized torso, looking for alternative options, and sighed. No strokes of brilliance. And much as he wanted to get Drogan out of there, the thought of trying to lift any part of the dead Kul was just making him feel even more exhausted than he already was.

Elise, though, was having none of the idle waiting, which struck Jarek as curious until he remembered that it wasn't just Elise in there. It was also Lietha, who seemed to have something of a special bond with Drogan, as far as those things went (or didn't) with raknoth.

It was going to take a little getting used to, this Enochian-raknoth hybrid thing. For now, though, he was just glad he wasn't the one having to do all the heavy lifting. Or any of it, hardly.

Elise put her back into the effort with frightening strength. Haldin raised his remaining hand, presumably to lend his own telekinetic aid. Jarek limped forward to add Fela's strength to the mix.

Mada's leg felt like the kind of thing creatures their size simply had no business lifting. The Enochians lifted it all the same with a bit of help from Jarek. Or shifted it, at least. Not far, but far enough.

When Drogan was finally able to claw his way out from the furry prison between Mada's leg and body, they gratefully let the leg shift back to its original position. Drogan rose to his feet with the utmost dignity, straightening out his clothes and trying for all the world to look as if nothing of note had just happened. Almost as if he was… embarrassed? Something like it, at least.

One of his arms was hanging oddly. Drogan frowned at it and was reaching for the shoulder with his good hand when Elise—or, probably more accurately, Lietha—reached out and touched his cheek.

It was a small touch, gentle and quickly over, but Drogan's eyes pulsed brighter for it, and his embarrassment only seemed to grow. Then Elise gripped his shoulder and popped it back into place with a smooth, confident movement.

Drogan just nodded his thanks, no sign of appreciable pain.

Haldin said nothing but watched the interaction with a slight frown. That was probably fair enough. Raknoth pain-killing techniques or no, Jarek couldn't imagine losing an arm would make anyone less irritable.

Then again, Haldin didn't seem too upset about the loss. He and Alton were pretty certain they could simply grow another.

In the meanwhile, though, Haldin's irritability and Drogan and Lietha's proximity colored the silence a tinge of awkward.

"Thanks for the catch back there, Stumpy," Jarek said, trying to break it up. "Sorry we left you sniffing mammoth pit. I was worried you were, well…" He looked around at the destruction that littered the mountainside.

The lack of survivors seemed to speak for itself.

"It will take more than one falling colossus to end me," Drogan said, though he looked a shade less confident than he sounded. "I only regret I was unable to finish the fight alongside the six of you."

Six? Once again, it took Jarek a second thought to remember the raknoth riding in Haldin's and Elise's bellies.

Definitely going to take a little getting used to.

"It appears the merger was successful," Drogan continued, looking between Haldin and Elise.

"Short-term heart attacks aside," Rachel added.

That might've been putting it mildly on both accounts, but especially on the former. Granted, before their little scare below, Jarek had expected the two—or four, rather—would be impressively strong upon waking.

Powerful arcanists with the strength of raknoth at their disposal? How could they not be?

But the two beings who stood before them now...

Suffice it to say, the new Haldin and Elise were more than a little bit intimidating.

"Sorry for the scare back there," Haldin said, "but the... reboot was necessary for us to properly function together." He spoke slowly, as if he had to search deep within himself for the answers. "We're going to need time to fully understand the extent of our abilities."

"Fortunately," Elise added, "it appears that time is exactly what we have won today."

"Yeah..." Jarek said. "Call me crazy, but are we really so sure it's time to breathe easy and go back to our happy little lives?"

He knew Naga had telepathically said something to the effect that he wouldn't be coming back anytime soon. Rachel had hurriedly explained that much to him, but they'd been in too much of a hurry to come free Drogan to delve into it more. Still, it didn't exactly sound like irrefutable proof of their safety.

"To go back to your lives?" Haldin said. "Yes. To breathe easy? No. We don't believe Naga will return within the millennium. Certainly not within the century. But preparations must begin. This world must be rebuilt."

There was something subtly unnerving about the way Haldin kept using that word, *we*. At first, Jarek had thought he was simply referring to himself and Elise. Now, though... Jarek kind of wanted to ask about what exactly was going on in there, existentially. But then, he also kind of didn't.

"Remind me again how we can be sure he wasn't lying," Jarek said. "Or that you're not just misinterpreting."

Not for the first time, Jarek wished he could've been privy to telepathic radio. It wasn't that he didn't trust Rachel and the Enochians. It was just frustrating, always flying blind in these situations.

"He did say they wouldn't return until our distant descendants had forgotten about all of this," Rachel said.

Jarek looked around the group. "What else did I miss?"

Rachel shrugged. "Not too much. Mostly just a few lines about how we're nothing but star dust that'll imminently be returning to The Void."

"So dude basically ripped off *Dust in the Wind* and then ran off like an angsty little nihilist?"

Rachel considered that, then tipped her head with an expression that said *more or less, pretty much.*

Jarek tried to laugh, but it came out uneasy. "Shit. Maybe that scaly a-hole knew what he was doing. Skip forward two generations and everyone's gonna start saying we probably just sat out here smoking peyote and made all this up. Give it fifty years, and we'll be ripe for invasion."

"We cannot let that happen," Elise growled with an intensity that made Jarek tense and almost take a step back.

"Yeah, all right, all right," Jarek said, patting the air with his hands.

Something told him Elise and Lietha were still working out who got the bigger half of the driver's seat.

Off in the distance, several trucks were approaching now from the direction of the lot and the north portal, probably coming to look for survivors—and, Jarek sincerely hoped, to give him a goddamn drink. Maybe a cookie too.

"I must tend to Zar'Krogoth," Drogan said, staring up at the mountain ridge, where a few soldiers had already arrived by lift to start looking for people to help.

Judging by the way Krogoth's broken body was half-strewn across the mountain beside Harga's mangled head, Jarek wasn't so sure Krogoth was one of those people anymore, but Drogan didn't seem to pay that fact much mind. He set off with Haldin and Elise, bounding up the mountain in a series of long leaps.

As the trucks pulled up by the wreckage near the south portal and the troops began to unload, several of them heading their way, all the shit Jarek had barely realized he was holding at bay started falling on him in earnest.

All the aches and pains. The fear and the fried nerves. All of their wounded and dead.

Pryce.

Jesus, Pryce. And everyone else who'd been out there with him. Alaric. Michael. Chambers. Johnny and the other Enochians.

He needed to know they were all okay. Or that they weren't. Needed to know right now. But somehow, more by the say of gravity and his exhausted body rather than his own free will, Jarek found himself sinking to the ground instead.

"Al?" he groaned. "Can you work your magic? Find out if—"

"Pryce is alive, sir," Al said, speaking through Fela so Rachel could hear too.

Relief spread through him, light and warm until it was somewhat marred by Al's next words.

"It sounds as though he may be in quite poor shape, however. Fortunately, the others appear to have made it safely out of the south portal collapse as well."

"Michael?" Rachel asked.

"Alive and well," Al said. "I believe he and Agent Chambers are currently joining the relief effort."

Rachel nodded her thanks.

Jarek tried to move—wanted to go see Pryce, to be useful—but he couldn't seem to convince his legs it was worth the trouble. Then Rachel sat beside him, and that was that.

She leaned her head against his shoulder. Wrapped her arm around his waist.

It felt good.

Tired and battered and emotionally drained as he was, it felt better in that moment than anything he could seem to recall right just then.

Could it really be over?

He wasn't sure. Probably never would be.

But for a little while, at least, he simply leaned into Rachel's warm side and allowed himself to hope.

THERE WERE no cheers or jubilant dances that day. For the rest of the long afternoon, there was little but wary silence and weary wound-licking, both literal and metaphorical. Once he managed to get back to his feet, Jarek did what he could to help what remained of The Complex do the same.

It wasn't all bad news.

Within the first hour, those who'd evacuated during the fight—and had apparently gotten the all clear sign since—returned to help triage the wounded, tidy up The Complex, and get to work on the considerable task of excavating the south portal. Scattered friends reunited. Order began to restore.

Still, there were no cheers. Not with the gravity of their losses and the not-so-distant threat still looming heavy in the air.

There were, however, firm pats on the back—and a hell of a lot of them throughout the day.

Much as he appreciated the sentiment, Jarek couldn't help but wish they'd stop. For one because he couldn't remember the last time he'd been this battered and bruised. It had to be some kind of record. It hurt to move. To breathe. Hell, it hurt to even think about breathing.

But then there was the other reason. The not-so-tiny voice in the back of his mind that had been insisting since Naga flew off that, gratifying as it had been to watch the giant space dragon turn tail after his posse had abandoned him, it was too good to be true.

For now, though, all he could do was try to offer help where it was needed.

Jarek was surprised to discover Krogoth and Brandt were both still alive. They barely looked it. Both seemed a bit delirious, which was understandable enough, given the number of puncture wounds Brandt had sustained and the fact that Krogoth was missing a leg and had nearly had his torso torn in two above the waist.

The rest of Krogoth's raknoth hadn't made it. Nor had Nan'Dola, which everyone seemed to loosely agree put Zach in charge of things within The Complex.

Thankfully, the bodies of the rakul appeared to remain quite dead as well. They decided to burn them anyway, just to be sure.

A large area was quickly cleared on one of the flatter sections near Mada's enormous body, and a healthy fire soon crackled through the piled brush and foliage, breathing plumes of dark smoke into the clear blue sky.

Haldin, Elise, and Drogan set to the task of hauling Ogrin, Harga, and Gada onto the fire. It wasn't pretty, and Jarek—having been denied another small hit of the Vitamin R from Drogan and thus woefully unequipped to deal with heavy lifting—was more than happy to be left out of it.

Those soldiers and civilians who were around to witness Haldin and Elise floating the hairless lupine alien down the mountainside with telekinesis looked more than a little unsettled by the display. Which was understandable, given that Harga probably weighed a good seven-or-eight-thousand pounds.

Jarek could practically hear their thoughts, especially those of The Complex folk, no doubt wondering what fresh manner of monsters they had to thank for their continued existence.

He wanted to sigh. But he was too tired.

Even with the rakul out of the picture—which he still wasn't totally convinced about—it would be a long, long journey back to anything resembling normal. And, while he was pretty sure there weren't even ten total raknoth left alive on Earth at this point, he was also certain the world wasn't just about to start accepting them with open arms.

Hell, even he was a bit afraid of Haldin and Elise. He had no idea what they were capable of—what they'd even want to do next now that the rakul were on the retreat. He'd be crazy for that not to make him slightly uneasy.

But that was most certainly a problem for the future.

"Why run?" Jarek asked Drogan quietly as they stood with Rachel, watching the flames lick their way across Harga's pale, slowly charring hide. "Fraga. Shimo. Vermaga. That other Kul-bot."

"Kul'Prongar," Drogan provided.

"Prongar. Sure. The four of them and their big, bad dragon." He looked over at Drogan, but the raknoth kept his eyes to the fire. "They could have finished us. Rache and I were about to collapse at the end there."

Rachel bobbed her head in tired agreement.

"And no discredit to you guys," he added toward Haldin and Elise, who were back up on the mountain ridge with Krogoth but might well still be hearing him anyway, "but I'm pretty sure the five of them could've had you too after that."

He actually wasn't entirely sure about that, but the thought still bothered him.

All he really knew right then was that his legs were shaky, his body heavy. The rakul—aside from Mada, who was far too large to move and would have to be handled afterward—were all loaded to burn, with a couple men alternately stoking the fire.

They were done. Weren't they?

Mind and body alike cried for rest, and Jarek was beyond ready to give it to them. Or would be, at least, if he could just set aside the doubts that refused to quiet in his mind.

Drogan was silent for a long while, watching his once-master's thick hide give slow way to the fire.

"Were you afraid the first time we fought one another?" he finally asked.

"No," Jarek said, a touch too quickly.

Drogan finally peeled his eyes away from the flames to shoot him a knowing look. "No? And what about when you faced Zar'Golga in one-on-one combat?"

Jarek swallowed, resisting the urge to touch the three long scars Golga had left on his face as a souvenir. "What's your point?"

"I imagine it was a forgotten novelty to you, feeling true fear in the midst of combat. Such had always been your supremacy with this." He tapped meaningfully on Fela's gouged chest plate.

Jarek shrugged, unsure what to say.

"Imagine it had not been ten years of such supremacy," Drogan continued, "but ten-thousand. With the exception of Gada's ascension to Kul three millennia past, this is what the rakul have known. Even longer for Naga and a few others. Can you imagine what it might feel like to watch not one, but seven, of those indestructible kin meet their ends? To come to the realization that you might shortly share their fate?" Drogan dropped his intense gaze and turned back to the fire. "Do you honestly believe you would not have thought to flee, were you in their position?"

Jarek let Drogan's words soak in. He glanced at Rachel, who appeared lost in her own thoughts.

Finally he shook his head in surrender. "I don't know."

It was too big a question. He was too tired to think it through, and maybe not quite arrogant enough anyway to presume to actually know how he might feel about such things after several thousand years of life and toil.

Drogan seemed to appreciate his uncertainty. "Nor do I, truly. But I do believe we gave the rakul a strong taste of something they'd forgotten existed. Mortality. And they will not return until they are certain they may do so without risking another taste. That much, I believe."

Maybe it was Drogan's conviction, or maybe Jarek was just tired and desperate to believe too, but somehow, Drogan's words brought a quantum of peace to his thoughts.

Finally, when Al's pleas for Jarek to take care of himself were on the verge of growing violent, Jarek gave in and turned away from the burning rakul. Rachel, as she had since Naga had taken to the whirlwind engines he called wings, stayed with him, her staff plunking along on the dusty rocks.

Zach and a few of his men pulled up with Alaric, Michael, and Chambers just as they reached the battered road that wrapped around the mountain to the lot and the north portal.

"You look like you could use a ride," Alaric said.

"And a nap," Michael added, coming forward to wrap Rachel in a hug and pat Jarek on the shoulder.

Chambers took in their dirty faces with a light grimace. "And some medical attention, maybe."

"Hear, hear," Al chimed from Fela's speakers.

Zach surveyed the operations with a deep frown before finally looking at Jarek and Rachel. "I don't know whether to curse you for bringing those things here, or to thank you for sending them away."

Alaric spit in the dirt, and Jarek was actually happy to realize the older man was chewing—if only because it was some sign of Alaric's old self emerging.

"They'd've come here on their own eventually," Alaric said.

"And I'd say the raknoth and our two newest super heroes over there deserve the brunt of the thanks," Rachel added with a pointed look at Zach, like she knew she was telling a vegan to eat a bloody steak and she was too damn tired to care about it.

Zach gave a noncommittal grunt, started to shuffle off, and paused. "Thank you. Both of you." He looked up to where Johnny and Haldin were standing together on the mountain ridge and shook his head. "Them too, I guess."

Jarek didn't bother pointing out that Zach should probably tell them himself. He was too tired, and the nearby truck looked too inviting.

"Why don't I take you guys back inside to get some food and rest?" Michael said.

"Let me," Alaric said, already moving around toward the driver's seat.

Michael shrugged, and he and Chambers bade them happy napping and went to go see how they could help.

Alaric didn't speak until they were halfway back around the mountain.

"I'm not one to call a pony a horse, but it's possible you two might've saved the planet today."

"Hardly," Rachel said. "We were just—"

"Just doing our civic duty, really," Jarek said with a sleepy smile.

She gave him a gentle jab in the ribs. "I was gonna say dangling a big juicy target to keep them busy until everyone else could do the important stuff. Like bring out the big gun. Or rise from the dead with superpowers."

"Ah. Yeah, that too."

Alaric shook his head. "If you two split your egos and shared the average, I think you'd both be about right."

They were apparently both too tired to come up with any response to that.

Jarek must've nodded off, because it seemed like next he knew, they were pulling up outside the massive open door at the entrance to The Complex.

Rachel murmured a bleary thanks to Alaric and hopped out of the truck. Jarek did the same and was sliding his armored bulk through the slightly cramped space to follow her when Alaric twisted around and caught him by the forearm.

Something heavy passed between them, though neither of them spoke for a long moment, and Jarek couldn't have said exactly what it was.

"You did good, son." Alaric finally said. He tilted his head after Rachel. "Both of you. But the job's not done."

Jarek gave a silent nod, his heart racing for some reason he couldn't quite put a finger on. Maybe it was the intensity in Alaric's eyes. Maybe it was simply the exhaustion.

"You rest up. God knows you've earned it. But when the dust starts to clear, we're still gonna need you. Both of you. We're gonna need leaders. And whether you like it or not, you and Rachel just pinned your pretty faces front and center on the banner of Team Earth."

Jarek opened his mouth to argue—wanted to point out that he was about as qualified as a sack of frozen turds when it came to being any manner of leader. But he couldn't. The words wouldn't seem to come.

For one, they wouldn't have been true. A shining example of commendable leadership he was not—and probably never would be—but after everything that had happened, he couldn't pretend he was incapable. Not to Alaric. Not when Jarek's taking the reins was exactly what had set them on the course to losing Seth.

And then there was the other part of the equation. That tiny, naïve fragment that still clung on from his teenage years. The one who'd wanted to save the world from itself. The one who'd been so audacious as to think he actually could.

He'd learned his lessons. He'd spent a good decade trying to drown that nonsense in a steady stream of booze and blood and night after night spent alone with Al in his self-inflicted exile. And now here he was, feeling those same audacious aspirations creeping in again.

Was it really different this time?

He was older—that was a given. But wiser?

He shook his head. "Man, I just wanted to get my damn suit back…"

Alaric tipped his head, the ghost of a smile on his lips. "And I just wanted to put a stop to the raknoth taking our people and crops for their own all those years ago. But here we are."

"Yeah, well, if it's all the same to you, I think I'd rather 'here' be swaddled in soft blankets on the other side of a solid meal right now."

Alaric's smile grew by a fraction, and he gestured for Jarek to have on with it.

Jarek paused halfway out of the truck door. "I'm sorry you lost Seth," he said quietly. "I'm sorry I couldn't stop it."

Alaric nodded, his gaze falling. "I know. Me too."

Silence hung between them, mournful and weighty, but also companionable.

"Get some rest," Alaric said. "Then get back on your feet. Plenty left that needs doin'."

Jarek gave a lazy salute and slid out of the truck. "Yes, sir."

Alaric only fixed him on the end of a surly stare for a few seconds before turning the truck around and heading back out.

Inside, The Complex was a bustle of activity. Men and women

hurried to and fro with toolboxes and bundles of wire and such, attempting to repair the extensive damage wrought by Vermaga's inside men. Others were doing what they could to treat the wounded, or transporting those who were beyond their abilities toward the medical wing. Still more just nervously hopped from one group to the next, swapping news with wide eyes.

Several of those wide eyes fixed on Jarek and Rachel as they made their way to medical. Two Resistance soldiers stepped aside to clear the way for them. Then a small group of Complex residents. Then, before Jarek knew it, the entire busy tunnel was parting before them.

When Jarek's emphatic *carry on* gestures failed, he and Rachel instead hurried through the proffered pathway posthaste.

"This is kinda freaking me out," Rachel murmured quietly, knowing he'd hear her anyway.

He couldn't say he completely disagreed. Having been walking around in a one-of-a-kind exosuit for half his life, Jarek had gotten fairly used to being stared at. Rachel, who routinely walked around with what was basically a wizard's staff—and was far from being hard on the eyes, to boot—had probably done the same. But this was different.

They weren't just stealing glances at the freaky weirdos. They looked… He didn't know what. Grateful, maybe? In awe?

Whatever it was, it felt weird, and he was glad when they reached the medical ward. Glad, at least, until one of the medics led them to Pryce.

Even at his best, the old man had never exactly looked sturdy, but now…

He looked so fragile, lying there on the cot. His face was scraped and bruised, and while he appeared to be asleep or unconscious, something about his resting pallor and pained expression gave Jarek the feeling that the damage extended well below the surface. How could it not, after having been hammered in the torso by a Kul?

"How bad is it?" Jarek asked the medic who'd led them in, keeping his voice low.

The slight wince on her face gave him half his answer before she spoke. "We're optimistic he'll pull through, but it's not good. Most of the ribs on his right side are broken, one of them punctured the lung, and his heart nearly gave out." Her wince deepened. "We're also concerned there may be some spinal cord damage, but it's too early to tell. We're not equipped for that kind of thing, but we'll do our best."

Jarek couldn't seem to do anything but stare. Rachel took his hand and squeezed.

"He's one tough old guy," the medic added. "It'll be okay. Best to let him rest for now, though."

At Rachel's light pressure, Jarek finally started to turn away.

But then Pryce groaned and cracked an eye open.

"J—Jare..."

Jarek dropped to a knee beside the cot and gently pressed the hand Pryce was trying to raise back to his side. "It's okay, Pryce. I'm right here."

Pryce rattled a few breaths, face scrunched in pain, clearly trying to say something.

"Win?" he rasped out.

"You bet your wrinkly ass, we did," Jarek said, trying to hold a smile. "Thanks to our resident tinkerer blowing a few Kul heads off, I might add. You did good out there, you old goat."

Pryce just closed his eye, looking a touch more at peace, and nodded back to sleep.

After that, things were blurry. They found some food. Forced it down. Jarek couldn't have said two minutes later what he'd just eaten. He was too busy limping through the tunnels for his and Rachel's little broom closet bedroom and the blissful promise of cool, quiet peace.

He collapsed into their meager pile of blankets with Rachel.

The floor was hard. The blankets musty.

He pulled Rachel to him.

The Complex safe. Pryce alive.

The rakul gone.

In the darkness, Rachel began to laugh—the kind of laugh that started out almost sounding as if she were crying. But the laugh grew, and soon her body was shaking with it.

There was a moment of concern, a moment of wondering what the hell was so funny and whether or not she might have cracked, but then he was laughing too, not really understanding why, not particularly caring that each laugh set half his body to aching pains, some sharp, others lingering.

He just pulled her closer—their bodies silently shaking together now—and decided it was the most content he'd ever been.

After that, sleep came swiftly.

———

Some indeterminate time later, Jarek woke with a start, expecting blaring alarms and gleaming fangs and roaring dragons.

All he saw was the dim shape of Rachel, her chin resting on his chest, gazing up at him. He groaned at the pain his waking body greeted him with and reached to find her cheek with his hand.

The single light flicked on above them—Rachel's telekinetic doing, he assumed—and he gladly took in the sight of her lovely hazel eyes.

There was something in them. A kind of softness he wasn't accustomed to seeing. It halted the flippant greeting working its way to the edge of his sleepy tongue.

"I do, you know," she said softly.

He didn't immediately grasp what she was talking about. When it hit him, though, he couldn't keep his face from pulling into a big stupid smile—a *really* big one, judging by the pain it drew from his bruised face and cracked lips.

"Okay, okay," she said. "Let's not get carried away. It looks like your face is gonna split in half."

"You love me."

She watched him levelly, her mouth seeming to war between trying to deny it and breaking into a smile.

"You're totally in love with a grown-ass man-child."

"I *will* kill you," she muttered, but the threat somehow lost steam when she crawled up and planted a warm kiss on his lips.

"So what's next?" Jarek asked when she pulled back. "Gonna try to whisk me away from this wild life? Make an honest wife of me?"

"I feel like we might be mixing our lines here." She laid her head down on his shoulder. "And forgetting about certain realities out there."

"Hey, a bet's a bet, Goldilocks. Two whole months. Them's the rules. The rest of the world can wait. Probably gonna take me that long to be able to walk straight anyway."

"Is this the part where I'm supposed to say it'll be three months after I'm through with you?"

He chuckled. "Only if you wanna exacerbate the current lack of blood in my vital organs."

Her lips tickled his shoulder as she smiled.

"Al?" he asked.

"Yes, sir?" came Al's response from Fela's speakers in the corner.

"Be a dear and find us a nice cabin somewhere." He thought about it. "Maybe by a lake."

Not that Al had a mouth, but Jarek could've sworn he heard the pleased smile in his friend's voice. "Of course, sir. I'll do my best."

"Two whole months," Rachel murmured into his shoulder. "They're just gonna love that."

Somehow, after everything he and Rachel had laid down for the planet since first joining the Resistance, Jarek didn't think anyone would begrudge it of them too much now that the sky wasn't actively falling.

They had a lot of work to do in the coming years. An entire world to rebuild.

One day, the rakul would return. And one day far sooner than that, Jarek and Rachel would probably both be called upon to help their planet prepare.

But for now, it kind of felt like they had all the time in the world.

EPILOGUE

"We're gonna be late," Rachel said, glancing down at her comm. "Again."

Jarek straightened from checking the oven window and made a point of straightening out the ridiculous *Kiss the Cook* apron he was wearing. "You can't rush art, Goldilocks. And I'm still not sure what this 'late' thing is that you speak of. Back in my day…"

She couldn't help but smile a little as Jarek launched into yet another tirade about his long years living by the sword and the absurdity of a life so luxurious and cozy that you could actually be expected to arrive at a place on time without being set upon by savage marauders or red-eyed aliens.

Back in his day. Like they hadn't been through it all together. Like it hadn't only been six months ago.

It was a familiar monologue, though he always varied the flavor, just for kicks. And despite the fact that everyone would already be at Pryce's by now, she had a hard time getting too irritated by his lack of punctuality when he was clearly in such high spirits.

Plus, in his defense, it *did* still feel kind of weird, casually planning a party night without a care in the world barely more than ten miles from the spot the rakul invasion had officially kicked off in force just over seven months ago.

Al, as he often did, picked an opportune moment and dove into the rant alongside Jarek, seeming to feel similarly about seeing Jarek enthused about something other than sex, whiskey, and scrappy violence. Not that she minded all of the above. And not that he'd left them behind, either.

Just last week, they'd lost half of their back deck and a good chunk of the northeastern corner of their house when Jarek and Drogan's weekly sparring match had gotten a bit out of hand.

Drogan had given awkward but courteous apologies.

Jarek, still lying in the pile of rubble, had just panted something or another about the importance of staying sharp.

Thinking about the incident, she started tapping her fingernails impatiently on the countertop. "And how long until said art is complete, Picasso?"

She actually felt bad when he absentmindedly traced the lines of the scars on his face, forming a connection she hadn't meant to imply. They could laugh and joke all they wanted—and for the most part, they did—but the reminders of everything they'd been through, and the toll it had all taken, continued to pop up in the little details here and there, often when they least expected it.

Before she could go to him and assure him that she wouldn't have his face any other way, Jarek's thoughtful expression passed and his smile returned. "Couple minutes. So probably just enough time for a…"

She skewered him with her best *we're not having a quickie while we keep our friends waiting for your baked goods* look.

"… kitchen dance party?" he concluded, gauging her reaction.

In the corner of the kitchen, Al's speaker began pumping a bass-heavy rhythm without missing a beat.

"Why?" Jarek asked, wagging his eyebrows. "What'd you think I was talking about?"

She resisted the urge to roll her eyes.

She still wasn't sure what it was with him and this sudden obsession with baking. Something about his having lived without an oven and mostly off of canned goods, wild vegetables, and the odd bit of game here and there for nearly a decade. Guy went nuts for a loaf of fresh-baked bread.

But the baking seemed to be therapeutic for him, and the regular stream of baked goods was definitely therapeutic for her as well, so there wasn't really any reason to complain.

Still, she couldn't just let him off the hook that easily.

So she walked closer, adding an unnecessary sway to her hips. She always felt silly, walking like that, but she never got tired of his reaction. The excited intake of breath. The tight grip on the counter, like he was straining to keep himself from tackling her to the floor and attacking her clothes.

She drew in close. Up on her tip toes, until her lips brushed lightly against his ear. She felt the tension in his body, every fiber of him threatening to rebel against his control and pounce on her.

Gently, as sultrily as she could, she whispered, "I thought you were talking about fucking me until I forget we're late."

She couldn't help but grin as he gave a little gasp and his hand slipped from the countertop.

He swallowed audibly, forced a shrug, and tilted his head at the batter-smeared mixing bowl. "Yeah, well, I've got, you know, very important baking stuff to do, so uh…"

She leaned closer, selling it until she felt her own genuine tingles of excitement building. He started to slide his arms around her waist, slowly, like he was hoping she somehow might not notice. She reminded herself that this was supposed to be the part where she left him hanging and got him back for his little dance party joke.

They really shouldn't right now. She should back away. But…

He pulled her tight and kissed her hungrily. The tingles intensified. She gasped for breath. Cupped a hand on the back of his neck and—

Ding.

The chime of the oven timer hit her like a splash of cold water.

Jarek groaned and jabbed the button to kill the oven's coils. He turned back to her, clearly intending to pick up where they'd left off.

She caught his advance with a hand to his aproned chest and gave him a measuring look. "Don't you have important baking stuff to do?"

He just grinned and pounced on her. Or tried to.

She caught him with telekinesis this time, pecked a quick kiss on his nose, and backed away until the kitchen island was safely between them. "Pack the goodies and let's go. Maybe later, if you're real good…"

Jarek tilted his head questioningly. "Is this about the corner of the house still? Because that was totally Stumpy's fault."

"Uh-huh. Explains why I found you both in the rubble."

"Well, yeah," Jarek said, slipping on a big red crab claw oven mitt and pulling the oven door open. "I mean, he broke it with my face, but it was still him doing the breaking."

Rachel took an appreciative whiff of the thick scent of chocolate filling the kitchen. "Seems kinda like a matter of perspective."

"Yeah," he said, setting the sizable cake pan on the stove top to cool. "Tell that to my face."

She smiled and ran her fingers over the cool granite of the island countertop while Jarek busied himself covering the cake with some manner of dark frosting. She glanced at her comm and was unsurprised to see it free of messages. No one checking where they were.

Likely, everyone already had a fair idea.

It was kind of funny, the ways people could change from one set of circumstances to the next.

When the heat was on, no one else got shit done like Jarek Slater. Remove said heat and plop him down in new-world suburbia, and he became perpetually late and started baking cakes and talking about *back in his day* like a rambling old man.

Somehow, it only made her love him more.

There were still times, and plenty of them, when she couldn't quite believe she'd stumbled so completely into this—whatever this was. Times where she felt almost as if she'd somehow betrayed some quintessential part of the person she was. Or the person she'd been, at least.

Sure, after she'd lost her parents, she'd had Michael and John. She'd had familial love. But, somewhere deep down, she'd never really been able to stop thinking of herself as anything but a lone wolf. She'd never expected to be anything but the cold survivor who'd never be able to give herself to another person completely enough to risk being hurt again.

Sometimes, she still felt like she could never truly be anything but that person.

But then Jarek would pull her to him with this resolute certainty—like she belonged there, like he'd left a piece of himself inside her and needed to touch base with it—and those thoughts would grow quiet, overruled by tender emotions she'd never really expected to have yet somehow couldn't imagine being without now.

Apparently, all it had ever taken to soften those walls of hers had been fighting the raknoth, uniting the planet, and surviving the rakul —all side-by-side with a certain special someone. Simple. Nothing to it, really.

And even now, it wasn't like this thing between them was some kind of storybook happily ever after. They fought. Though said fights ended with both of them laughing at themselves as often as not.

So maybe it *was* happily ever after. Their version of it, at least. She couldn't say for sure. All she knew was that their fires burned well together. That was the best way she could think to put it.

Most days, she was happier than she'd ever really expected she would be. It was more than she'd ever bothered to ask for.

"Frosting for your thoughts, m'lady?"

Rachel came back from her musings and found Jarek holding out a chocolate-glaze-laden spatula for her to lick.

"Double chocolate, huh?" she said, teetering between telling him to forget the spatula and hurry it up and tearing said spatula from his hand and devouring that glistening chocolate delight.

"Oh-ho-ho no, my sexy little concubine. I went full-on *triple* chocolate up in this bitch."

Before she could formulate a reply, something shimmered at the far reaches of her senses, drawing her focus.

"Not really sure where we get off calling it triple chocolate," Jarek continued, waving the spatula in front of her face.

She was too busy pulling up her mental defenses and warily inspecting the group of blazing mental presences that were quickly approaching outside.

"I mean I guess it sounds more snazzy than *shit ton of chocolate in your chocolate*," Jarek was saying somewhere far away. "You sure you don't want a—"

"Jarek."

He froze at her tone, all playfulness forgotten. "What is it?"

"Haldin and Elise. They're here."

A glob of chocolate dripped to the countertop from the extended spatula. Jarek's serious expression slowly shifted to one of surprised thoughtfulness. "Oh… Do you think they want a lick?"

Rachel snorted. "Nothing against your goods, but I'm guessing they're not here for triple chocolate cake."

What they actually were here for, she had no idea. As far as she knew, no one had seen the pair for months now. The last she'd seen them had been when they'd swung by her and Jarek's cabin retreat after Cheyenne.

That had been toward the end of the third week of their proposed two whole months of cabin recovery time. And, as deeply enjoyable as those three weeks of complete privacy had been, the Enochians' visit had also broken the spell and marked the day when both her and Jarek had ceased being able to justify weighing their own blissful recovery against their growing concerns for the fledgling new world order.

So they'd headed back out to rejoin the rest of the world right after Haldin and Elise had departed to do the polar opposite.

The rest of the Enochians had visited the pair somewhere in the Himalayas a few times since then, but all Rachel really knew was that Haldin and Elise—and, of course, Alton and Lietha too—had felt they had some serious shit to sort out with their new existences, and that they'd thought it best they do it in relative isolation.

Jarek tossed the spatula in the sink and wiped his hands with a towel. "What if they want us to do stuff?"

"We could probably stand to do some stuff."

Jarek wagged his eyebrows and started to open his mouth.

"Other stuff," she said with a grin before he could go for the low-hanging fruit.

"Gah. Seems like a whole big thing."

"Don't act like you're not dying for some action. Plus, they can probably hear us right now."

"We can," came Haldin's, Alton's, and Lietha's voices all at once.

"Just a bit," Elise added. *"And I actually wouldn't mind that lick."*

"What is it?" Jarek asked, studying Rachel's face. A grin broke across his mouth. "They want cake, don't they?"

Rachel just gave an exasperated sigh.

"Come on in, boys and girls!" Jarek called.

Haldin and Elise weren't long in reaching the front door. Surprised as she'd been to feel Haldin and Elise, Rachel hadn't noticed Drogan was with them until he walked in and closed the door behind them. But her attention was more focused on the two beings in front of him.

The Enochians had changed. Again. It was far more subtle than their initial transformation, but they looked harder. Stronger. Haldin had finished regrowing his left arm. But there was something else too. Something about their expressions and the way they moved. Somehow, they looked both more alien and yet more themselves than they had before. It was odd.

Apparently, Jarek was less flabbergasted than her. Or at least better at hiding it.

"Well I'll be," he said. "The mountain hermits return, in search of epic triple chocolate cake. Nice arm, by the way."

They smiled, and it only highlighted the change in them. Where before it had seemed like they'd merged both body and mind with Alton and Lietha, now it seemed more like they were their old selves, merely walking around in vastly more powerful bodies with a pair of raknoth comrades in tow.

"Thanks," Haldin said, waving his regrown arm demonstratively. "But I'm afraid it's a happy coincidence on the cake thing."

"A happy coincidence we'll gladly embrace, though," Elise added after deeply inhaling the rich sweetness in the air.

Jarek turned to grab plates and paused. "You guys wanna come to Pryce's? We were just about to head over. Whole gang's gonna be there."

"We actually just came from there," Elise said

"We were hoping to catch everyone together," Haldin said, a small grin pulling across his mouth, "but apparently some have more trouble with punctuality than others."

"Yeah, yeah, military boy," Jarek said, starting to slide plates from a cupboard. "Cake now, then?"

No one argued.

Rachel finally got over her surprise and found her tongue as she gestured for their guests to join her on the island stools. "So what have you guys been up to?"

"Not that much, honestly," Haldin said, sliding onto the stool across from her. He frowned as it groaned a little under his deceptively heavy frame, but it held.

"An aggressive amount of not that much," Elise agreed, seating herself beside Rachel. "Lots of thinking and talking. It's pretty weird, having to discover your own body again."

As she talked, Drogan walked over to join Jarek in the kitchen and reached a finger out to skim a taste off the top of the waiting cake. Jarek slapped his hand. They traded stares that were playful but still dangerously challenging.

Rachel cleared her throat and pointedly turned her eyes in the direction of the damage they'd caused last week.

This time, the look they traded was one of two kids who'd just been caught playing after bed time.

Jarek went back to doling out cake for their guests. Drogan grabbed forks and carried the loaded plates over.

"What about you guys?" Elise asked, smiling at the little display. "The Senate keeping you busy?"

Jarek barked a laugh. "They'd have to make their minds up about something before they could do that."

Much as she wanted to point out for the millionth time that the slow-going was understandable given the circumstances, Rachel couldn't completely disagree with the heart of the sentiment.

It hadn't taken long after leaving their little cabin retreat months ago to realize that their services, as it turned out, weren't so readily helpful. But, then again, no one else's seemed to be right now, either.

It was a question of application.

The world was in an odd kind of pre-golden age flux right now, with everyone ready and willing to dive in, but no one really seeming to know how or where to start. Like a bunch of kids, let loose in the world's largest candy store.

Mostly, their efforts so far had fallen by default to rebuilding infrastructure and trying to get a proper assessment of just how badly the planet had fared through the rakul invasion—not to mention the fifteen years preceding it.

Even before the rakul, when they'd still had passable Net coverage, the presence of the raknoth and the harsh pressures of the Catastrophe's aftermath had thoroughly discouraged the formation of anything beyond the scope of homesteads and tiny villages. Maybe they'd trade here and there. Maybe not.

Places like Newark had basically been death traps, and places like Unity had been few and far between.

All in all, it had been pretty hard to accurately gauge how Earth was doing. And after the Net came down, hard became impossible.

To that end, restoring the Net as globally as they could had been one of the only truly clear focuses off the bat. They needed to know how much devastation the rakul had wrought during their month-long occupation, and they needed to communicate with the rest of the world.

Once that had started coming together, The Senate had seemed like the natural next step. A world-wide coalition of all sorts from all places, all onboard for a better tomorrow. One where they—or their descendants, at least—were strong enough to handle whatever intergalactic threats might come their way.

Just because everyone was onboard, however, didn't necessarily mean the ship was going to magically start moving.

It had been like pulling teeth. Especially when they'd brought in Krogoth, Brandt, and Drogan, and proposed to officially declare the few remaining raknoth of Earth as friends and allies of the planet.

Neither Rachel nor Jarek relished their time spent in Senate conferences. But it was important, she would remind them both. It was arduous and irritating, and sometimes it made her want to blast a hole through the wall, but getting the planet on one page, even a slightly jumbled one, was crucial to their long-term survival as a species.

With the infrastructure steadily strengthening and the threats to life and crop land severely reduced, they'd at least managed to agree on a few things already. Everyone, for instance, was being encouraged to begin repopulating.

On a planet full of people who'd spent fifteen years mostly in fear and more recently escaped from the jaws of certain death by rakul, feverish doses of getting busy wasn't such a hard sell. It seemed plenty of folks got started on their own with that one—several of their friends included. Johnny and Lea, for one, were now publicly shacking up together. Michael and Chambers, to Rachel's decidedly satisfied approval, had recently done the same.

No, enjoying their survival to the fullest came naturally enough. It was convincing everyone it was actually safe to bring children into the world that was taking a bit more doing.

"There's a lot of work to do," Rachel said, coming back to the conversation.

A woeful understatement.

Jarek came up behind her and Drogan and clapped a hand to each of their shoulders. "But we'll just keep on beating up marauders and keeping the peace while the world crawls back together. At least until Rache gets her new Jedi academy up and running."

Haldin and Elise both turned to her with newfound interest.

"An academy?" Elise asked.

"That's very much in the air right now," she said, frowning at Jarek. "They put the call out for anyone with arcane talents. We've had a few step forward. I'm not really holding my breath for many more. Still not sure how it's all gonna play out, but The Senate wants me to teach them to fight and enchant weapons and so forth."

For some reason, that made Haldin and Elise exchange a knowing smile.

"You'll do an amazing job, Rachel," Haldin said.

Elise nodded her confident agreement.

"And what will you two do, exactly?" Jarek asked.

Something in his tone had changed, like he'd just confirmed something sad to be true.

Haldin frowned down at the dark crumbs on his plate. "We're growing stronger."

He didn't sound excited about it.

"We're... worried," Elise added. "About a lot of things." Her hand drifted to her abdomen, presumably where Lietha had taken up residence. "All four of us."

"You want me and Drogan to suit up and smack you around a bit?" Jarek asked. "Remind you what it feels like?"

Haldin smiled. "Guess there'd be a certain poetry in that, considering how we first met back in the woods of Unity."

A soft sadness drifted over Rachel as it dawned on her what Jarek had realized. "I think the poetry would be if you'd come here to say goodbye."

They said nothing.

"You came here to say goodbye, didn't you?"

They both looked... not quite guilty. Just regretful, their smiles wan.

"Why?" Rachel asked.

"In short"—Haldin held up his and Elise's interlocked hands from underneath the cover of the island—"because these hands, lovely as they are," he added with a sidelong glance to Elise, "were made for fighting, not for peace."

Rachel frowned at said hands, not really sure what to say. Finally, she went with, "That's a bit melodramatic, don't you think?"

"Yeah," Jarek added. "Seriously. You could probably plow the shit out of a field with those bad boys."

For a moment, the Enochians' smiles turned to true amusement. Haldin even chuckled. But then that sadness crept back in.

They'd already made their minds up. That much was clear.

"What will you do?" Rachel asked.

"Well…" Haldin started, looking at Elise.

"We were thinking we might go dragon hunting," Elise said.

"Ah," Jarek murmured.

Silence hung in the kitchen for a stretch before he continued.

"Shit. Yep. That's a big one."

Rachel didn't know what to say. She didn't want to see the Enochians just up and leave. For one, the two were by far their strongest defense should Naga and the rest of the Kul decide to get brave and return sooner than later. But, more than that, they were their friends.

"What about the others?" Rachel asked "Johnny and Franco? Phineas? James?"

Real pain crept over both the Enochians' faces.

"We've all decided it's best if they stay here," Haldin said. "For now, at least."

"They can help this planet," Elise said, wiping at what might've been an itch but Rachel suspected was the beginning of a tear. "Teach you lessons from Enochia. And we're not really sure what we're getting into out there anyway. Might not be any place for mortal humans to go flying blindly into."

"Shit," Jarek repeated.

"Shit," Rachel agreed. "When?"

Haldin looked back down at his empty plate. "Guess our last meal was cake."

"We could do worse," Elise said, nudging him in the ribs.

They stood with a heavy finality.

"Stumpy?" Jarek said as Drogan turned to follow them.

"I will remain on Earth," Drogan said, though his eyes didn't leave Elise. "For now."

"Oh, thank god," Jarek sighed, patting at his chest. "No one wants to see a grown man cry right now."

Rachel was a little surprised to find how much the news relieved her as well.

A somber silence seemed to follow them like a living thing as they padded out of the house with the Enochians. They said their last farewells on the front porch, in the fading light of the setting sun.

As sad as it was to be saying goodbye, Rachel had a feeling it was nothing compared to what was going on in Drogan's head.

The raknoth stood close to Elise, looking like he wanted to touch her but was too stubborn to do so. Rachel could feel the telepathic flow between him and Lietha inside of Elise. Then Elise's eyes went distant for a moment, and when she returned, Rachel got the impression Elise had ceded the driver's seat over to her internal companion.

Elise—or Lietha—leaned forward and pressed her forehead to Drogan's.

Drogan didn't hug her—was probably convincing himself at that very moment that such gestures were too foolishly human for him to indulge in. But he did close his eyes and take a long, deep breath, as if absorbing every detail of her presence.

Behind them, Haldin was pointedly looking out at the open sky, clearly trying to give them their moment.

"We'll meet again, Al'Drogan," Elise said when they parted, laying a hand on his shoulder in a way that made Rachel think it was indeed Elise in control once more.

Goddammit, it was sad to watch.

"You know," Jarek said when they were all set to leave, "I don't think I ever actually thanked you two—you four, I mean—for saving our asses."

Haldin waved off his thanks. "I doubt we did anything you wouldn't have. Besides, in the grand scheme of things, this has always been one long effort to keep our own planet safe. The path's just turning out to be… a bit longer than expected."

"And maybe you'll have your chance to repay us someday anyway," Elise added with a wan smile.

"You'll know where to find us," Jarek said.

The Enochians nodded and turned to leave.

They watched them go from the top of the porch steps, not speaking, each wrapped up in their own thoughts. Rachel could only assume there was at least a part of Drogan wishing he'd been the one to merge with Haldin in place of Alton Parker. It would have been perfect. Two lovers playing host to two raknoth who clearly shared some strong affinity for one another, whatever they wanted to call it.

But life was a real bitch sometimes.

She reached over and gave Drogan a comforting pat on the back—a gesture that would've been inconceivable less than a year ago.

"So what do we do now?" She finally asked once the Enochians had boarded their ship and long since disappeared in the distance.

"Drinks at Pryce's," Jarek said. "Many, many drinks at Pryce's."

For once, that plan didn't sound half bad.

As she turned to go grab their stuff with Jarek, though, Drogan caught her wrist.

He cocked his head. Sniffed the air.

She watched him uncertainly, an odd feeling swirling in her stomach. Drogan almost never touched her.

But now he was leaning in closer, sniffing again. He looked meaningfully down at her belly before meeting her eyes.

Her stomach turned a loop through her chest.

"Alcohol may be unwise."

Drogan's words hit her like a throat punch.

She tried to swallow—to breathe. Her mouth suddenly seemed too dry for either.

"What?" Jarek asked the question screaming through her mind on repeat.

He was watching them from the doorway with a confused expression.

She couldn't worry about that now, though. She was too busy plunging her senses inward, searching with frantic desperation for the flicker she was suddenly sure she'd find.

She'd been due in a few days. Was it possible?

"I must have missed it under the cover of all the chocolate inside, but…" Drogan sniffed the air again, checking to be certain.

He needn't have checked.

There.

She felt it there, right at the center of her. The tiniest flicker of life that was both part of her but also somehow distinct of its own.

"Oh my god," she heard herself murmur.

The world spun around her. Drogan caught her before she even processed her knees had buckled.

Her vision reoriented. Jarek was hovering above them, mouth agape, more stunned than she'd ever seen him.

"It's—She's…" he stammered. "Is she—are you…?"

She nodded weakly up at him, waiting for the realization to strike him. For his eyes to widen in horror as he turned tail and ran for it.

He just stood there, mouth agape.

Then he dropped to his knees and pulled her too him, taking her weight from Drogan's arms. He was gasping—with laughs or sobs, she couldn't really tell. He was squeezing her too hard.

She squeezed back, too shocked to do anything else.

Drogan, deciding his job was done, began to pull away to leave them to it. Jarek caught him by the front of his long coat and tugged him back down.

"No way, Stumpy," Jarek said, his voice thick. "This here's a family group hug moment."

Drogan looked mildly alarmed. "I would prefer to let—"

"Oh just hug us, you scaly a-hole," Jarek said, pulling him in.

With painstaking awkwardness, Drogan looped his arms around the two of them, somehow managing to barely touch either of them in the process until he gave them each a pair of uncertain pats on their backs.

"There we go," Jarek said. "One big happy family. I mean, kid's gonna need a godfather, right?"

Rachel and Drogan both recoiled at that.

"Kidding, kidding."

Drogan retreated to the house with a grumpy huff after that.

Rachel and Jarek remained wrapped in each other's arms for some time. Her head was still reeling with the implications, which seemed to mushroom more and more extensively the more she thought about it. Jarek held her all the while, his arms firm and wonderfully warm.

"You're not scared?" Rachel finally asked.

"Are you kidding me?" he asked through a chuckle. "I think I'm having a heart attack right now. But, I dunno. This feels… right, I guess." A playful note crept into his tone. "I mean, if I have to be chained down to one person for the rest of my life…"

She wiped away brimming tears and leaned back to take in his warm smile.

"Such a way with words," she muttered, though she couldn't help but meet his smile. Her mood soon sobered, though. "And this doesn't mean… I mean, you're not…"

What?

Stuck? Obligated?

Was that really how she thought of herself? As an obligation?

"And what if I wanna be?" he whispered before she could decide, his eyes radiating tender care. "I don't want anything else, Rachel. I just want—"

She kissed him, and for a long while, they stayed there like that, tucked into each other against the growing chill of the evening.

Finally, when darkness had fallen and the buzzing of both their comms was becoming too frequent to ignore, they gathered themselves and stood. Drogan joined them on the porch, triple chocolate cake in tow, and together, they set off for Pryce's in the gathering darkness, ready to share their own little light with their new family.

THE END

A LETTER FROM THE AUTHOR

Oh boy, Dear Reader.

Where do I even start?

Well, I guess with the fact that the book—and The Harvesters Series—has indeed reached its intended end.

And if that realization conjures in you a sudden and urgent need to reach for a tissue, rest assured, you're not alone. It probably won't surprise you to hear I've grown quite fond of this series, myself.

Go figure, right?

But hey, it's my first, and holy hoppin' mountain goats, did I have a fun time writing it! The world I've fumbled through building... The delightfully strong and cheeky characters I've discovered along the way...

It's been a hell of a ride.

And I don't want to say goodbye.

... So I might not. Not yet at least. And you don't have to either!

For one thing, I still have two fresh Harvesters short stories to share with you, just to tickle your nostalgia buttons. But I'll get to those in a minute. (After we finish softly weeping together.)

Exactly how I may (or may not) revisit Rachel, Jarek, and Team

Earth in the future remains to be seen. I've got ideas. Big ones. But nothing's quite set in stone yet. Or, like, even in Jello.

What I *can* tell you is that this universe is not closed for business. In fact, there's already another entire trilogy waiting for you.

It's called the Enochian War Trilogy, and if you enjoyed Harvesters, I'm pretty sure you're gonna love it.

… So sure, in fact, that I'd like to give you the first book free today —just to get you started.

You in?

Just go to *lukermitchell.com/retribution-signup* to join my mailing list and grab your free copy of *Shadows of Divinity*!

In addition to your first Enochian War adventure, you'll also get access to Rachel's and Jarek's prequel novellas, *Cursed Blood* and *Soldier of Charity*, as well as those two short stories I mentioned a minute ago: *Scorched Earth* and a little number called *Jarek Slater & the Ballad of the Broken Glass Kids*.

And that's kind of just the beginning.

Suffice it to say, if you've enjoyed this series and are ready for the full Luke Mitchell Experience—complete with behind-the-scenes shenanigans, list-exclusive discounts, and frankly obscene amounts of Freebie Showers—there's really no reason to dilly dally on this one. Go ahead and navigate to that there signup link above for…

• Book One of Haldin's Enochian War Trilogy

• *Both* Harvesters prequels,

• *Both* Harvesters short stories

• List-exclusive discounts and short stories

• PLUS an arm, a leg, *and* Luke's firstborn!

And if newsletters and email shenanigans REALLY aren't your bag, that's cool too.

You can always visit *lukermitchell.com/books* to find the full list of my published work—and to grab *Shadows of Divinity* the old-fashioned way, and prepare for Haldin Raish's epic fight to save his planet from raknoth invasion!

Whichever way you go, I sure hope you enjoy your next adventure.

And lastly, if you're still needing a minute to reflect on Jarek and Rachel's journey and feel all the feels, I totally get it.

In that case—or, really, in *any* case—allow me to simply offer you one last sopping wet *thank you*.

Thank you, Dear Reader, for reading this book and all the others before it. However you found my work, I'm so glad that you did. I hope it's brought you hours of entertainment, and smiles as bright as they were numerous.

Without you, Dear Reader... well, this would all be kind of silly, wouldn't it?

So thank you. Truly.

Peace and Love,
Luke Mitchell

ACKNOWLEDGMENTS

If you've taken a gander at the back matter of each book throughout this series, you'll know I've typically been a man of many acknowledgments. So much so that, quite frankly, if I'm to be honest with you, I'm running out of ways to express my gratitude to my team. Or maybe I'm just getting lazy.

Okay, it's totally the lazy thing.

Even so. Let's hit this thing cliff notes style.

I love my wife. Wait no, my fiancé. Wait no, my wife. Look, I'm not sure exactly what date it is that you're reading this. Suffice it to say, it's pretty serious, and she's been phenomenally supportive about me deciding to forgo a more traditional career path in favor of making things up, writing them down, and trying to convince perfectly random strangers to give me money for it.

What was she thinking?

And speaking of what the women in my life were thinking, I guess I'd better mention I love my mom, too. I'm still not sure why she decided not to let my dad snuff me out in the Spartan-esque agoge of my childhood (I kid. But only a little bit.), but my hat most certainly goes off to the both of them for giving me this life. Or would, if I ever wore a hat. You should ask my mom about that. Drives her bonkers.

As for the rest of my friends and family, I hope it's safe to say you all know I love you, even if I am hard to ferret out of the writing hole for more than the occasional brief spotting.

To my ever-evolving and increasingly-well-oiled book machine team, I offer mad high-fives and copious thanks. Lisa continues to be the stalwart lighthouse to my oft-canting little story-ship. Clarissa and Prokopy continue to dazzle me with amazing book covers. I owe many thanks to my elite little ninja squad of beta readers, who gave me some great street-level insight that helped me tweak, sharpen, and otherwise massage this bad boy into fighting shape. And, as always, my beloved ARC crew once again came through with the amazing support that makes these books (and my feeble little author soul) sing.

Thank you all so much for your work in helping me make this the best damn book I could!

Lastly, I'd obviously be remiss (which I do believe is Latin for "a giant dick" ... right?) if I didn't give a twenty-one thank-you salute to my amazing readers at large. You people rock. (I told you I was running out of ways to say these things.) Seriously, though. It's not an exaggeration to say you are what makes this all worth it. You know, both fiscally and otherwise... :-)

I can't thank you enough for supporting my work. And that goes double for those of you who are constantly bringing me much-needed laughs about flossing dragons and impromptu cookbooks. You know who you are. And if I haven't made it clear—which, let's be honest, I can be pretty sporadic with my correspondence at times—I really do appreciate you.

So thank you so much for reading! The Harvesters Series may be over (for now), but I'm sure as hell not finished telling you stories.

Happy reading, my friends. And may your favorite characters always live, and your most fantastical adventures never tarnish.

Love,
Luke Mitchell

ABOUT THE AUTHOR

Not a llama. Mostly human.

Luke is a storyteller whose dreams include learning the ways of the Force, becoming a sentient robot, and maybe even one day growing up. Also, lots of zombies… Don't ask.

Oh, and that "growing up" bit? That was a lie.

After studying engineering science at Penn State and neuroengineering at Drexel, Luke finally decided to throw in the towel on building a working Iron Man suit and opted instead to simply make things up and write them down. Boy, is he having more fun now.

When he's not holed up in his writing cave trying to string words together, he can often be found powerlifting, video-gaming, reading, and/or drinking the darkest, most roasty beers he can get his mitts on. Sometimes all at once.

But you know what? That's enough about Luke. He's really not that interesting. Still, if you'd like to say hi to him for whatever reason, he'd probably be glad to hear from you!

Go to **lukermitchell.com/retribution-signup** to join the mailing list and grab your free copies of *Soldier of Charity* and the list-exclusive *Cursed Blood*!

<hr>

Additionally (as you wish)…

Follow me on BookBub for new release alerts
bookbub.com/authors/luke-r-mitchell

Browse the rest of my published titles
lukermitchell.com/books

Join the Patreon team for digital copies of ALL of my work (past, present, and future) — and much more!
patreon.com/lukermitchell

Thank you for reading!

9 798885 490030